American Fiction

VOLUME SEVEN

The Best Unpublished Stories
by Emerging Writers

GUEST JUDGE
Tim O'Brien

EDITORS
Alan Davis &
Michael White

NEW RIVERS PRESS

1995

Copyright © 1995 by New Rivers Press
Library of Congress Catalog Card Number 95-069348
ISBN 0-89823-164-7
All Rights Reserved
Edited by Alan Davis and Michael White
Editorial Assistance by Carol Rutz and Mary Roen
Book Production by Peregrine Graphics Services

New Rivers Press is a non-profit literary press dedicated to publishing the very best emerging writers in our region, nation, and world.

The publication of *American Fiction* has been made possible by generous grants from the Elmer L. and Eleanor J. Andersen Foundation, the Bush Foundation, the General Mills Foundation, Liberty State Bank, the McKnight Foundation, the Minnesota State Arts Board (from an appropriation by the Minnesota Legislature), the Star Tribune/Cowles Media Company, the Tennant Company Foundation, and contributing members of New Rivers Press. New Rivers Press is a member agency of United Arts.

American Fiction has been manufactured in the United States of America for New Rivers Press, 420 North 5th Street, Suite 910, Minneapolis, MN 55401 in a first edition.

CONTENTS

EDITOR'S NOTE

THE FICTIONAL VOICE is what all of us here are for, as Tim O'Brien, this year's guest judge, points out in his powerful introduction. In this day of information glut, we are still starved for the truth of the story; story is where wilderness resides, absolutely pure and distinct from the babble around it. Two years ago, guest judge Tobias Wolff wrote that "*American Fiction* is the one anthology that deliberately and exclusively sets out to find the best unpublished stories by 'emerging' writers–a loose category meant to encourage submissions by everyone not yet famous enough to enjoy the certainty of publication elsewhere."

Our method of operation for this latest edition, our seventh, is still much the same as it was when Michael C. White and I first called for stories in 1987. (Though I am now editor and Michael White, associate editor, a reversal of our previous titles, we're still effectively co-editors, as we have been from the beginning.) At that time, we were trying to fill a niche; we had noticed that most annual anthologies of stories chose selections from previously published work which had first appeared in general circulation magazines or literary quarterlies. We wanted to give the best new work by emerging writers a chance to appear first in book form and to compete for prizes and the increase in literary reputation which sometimes follows.

That inaugural year, Ann Beatie was our guest judge and we received over 600 manuscripts; she chose "The Tape Recorder" by Timothy Kelley for First Prize. By the following year, when Ray

1

Carver served as a judge and chose Antonya Nelson's "The Expendables" for First Prize, we had initiated a Second and Third Prize as well. By the sixth edition, when Wallace Stegner was judge (following upon the heels of Tyler, Erdrich, and Wolff), we received over a thousand manuscripts, which meant that Michael White and I read more than 500 stories apiece. It was, we wrote, "both an anguish and a delight. Our anguish is not knowing whether fatigue or mood might have caused us to pass over a gem. Our delight is what you have before you."

The same holds true this year, with one significant exception: we are fortunate to have a staff of five able Assistant Editors, all practicing writers themselves, to screen submissions for us. (Information about each appears in the back of the book.) Without their help, this edition would not have been possible, for I can still remember the ache of lugging huge boxes of manuscripts from the post office to my office, where I would sit surrounded by stories, each a gift or a promise or a hope. I logged in each one, a slow process which required even more time than I had planned because I couldn't resist digging in, taking some for myself before sharing with the other editors. Each story was a voice, a fictional voice longing to speak, to enchant, to have its way with me until *it* chose to let go. A sabbatical bought me some time to lug, log in, read—but I would have read them all, regardless of time, if that had been what was required. It is bad luck to refuse any fiction so long as it repays our attention with interest.

As Tim O'Brien says in his introduction, "In one way or another—by implication, by suggestion, by association—a piece of truly beautiful fiction contains anything that might be said about it." So here they are, without further ado, twenty stories to celebrate. Congratulations to Lisa Gill for "Holding Zeno's Suitcase in Kansas, Flowering," our First Prize winner; to A. Manette Ansay for "July," Second Prize; and to the two writers who share Third Prize: Lon Otto for "A Man in Trouble" and Rosa Shand for "Sophie Was the King." Many thanks to Tim O'Brien, Moorhead State University (especially Gloria Anderson, Lorna Kennedy, and Cindy Sogn), and Springfield College (especially Irene Graves) for their assistance and support. Special thanks for a Creative Activity Grant at Moorhead State and for sabbaticals or release time at both institutions. Thanks as well to everyone who sent their stories to read; we appreciate the chance to see so much good work. Most of all, our thanks and gratitude to New Rivers Press; this is our first issue with them, and we feel it is where we belong, with a press devoted to emerging writers and to the place of literature in a world as various as the one made up twenty times between these covers.

–Alan Davis
EDITOR

INTRODUCTION

WHEN I WAS ASKED, many months ago, to serve as the judge for this year's edition of *American Fiction*, I felt the ruse of some very powerful and contradictory emotions. One impulse was to say, "Sure, of course, anything for the cause." Simultaneously, however, there was a fiercely competing desire to beg off, to decline by muttering something like this: "I don't judge, I *read*." To rank works of art–assigning numbers, declaring victors–strikes me as almost sinfully subversive of art itself, its essence, its soul and purpose, the whole of which in one way or another involves bringing beauty into the world. And beauty, of course, is subject to the uncertainty principle. It is idiosyncratic, purely singular, therefore beyond comparison. Not only does beauty take meaning in the eyes and heart of the beholder, it is also flamboyantly original, flamboyantly *itself*, defiant of any universal standards of measurement. How do we choose between James Joyce's "The Dead" and Flannery O'Connor's "The Artificial Nigger?" How do we proclaim one more shapely, more harmonious, more radiantly sublime than the other? There is no such arithmetic. No best, no better–only the heart's quiet sigh.

Beyond these issues, after it was explained that my responsibilities were to include the composition of an introduction, I felt a secondary jolt of dread mixed with something vaguely rebellious. What could I possibly add to a volume of well-made short stories? Why *should* I add? Every piece of art speaks for itself, figuratively in numerous ways, but also in a nearly literal sense. The authors of these stories must surely

5

have taken great care to say all that could artfully be said, not a word less, not a word more. In one way or another—by implication, by suggestion, by association—a piece of truly beautiful fiction contains anything that might be said about it. We are left speechless. We stand mute—agape.

For this reason, I think, introductory essays almost always indulge in either paraphrase or textual analysis, both of which seem futile at best, corruptive at worst. Why paraphrase a story that will soon unfold in all its detail, completely, lushly, in sentences hard won over many weeks and months by the writer? Why rob a story of its own language? Why undermine a story's magic, its glowing dramatic immanence, by a cold little summary or any other form of critical reduction? Why issue advertisements when the art itself lies in wait only a page or two away? Similarly, the temptation to analyze or explicate inevitably ends in a sort of bleak abstraction, everything neatly shelved, systematically tidied up, the scholar's firm clarity replacing all those messy mysteries and ambiguities and possibilities that the artist worked so long and hard to create. Beauty *is* mystery. Beauty *is* ambiguity. Beauty *is* possibility. To analyze a piece of fiction is to perform a kind of autopsy, severing a character from its setting, ripping out a bloody theme, prying apart the narrative ribs so as to lift out a pound of description or six ounces of dialogue. Problem is, of course, autopsies are performed on the dead. The various organs, no matter how fascinating, neither resemble nor illuminate the living whole—the smile of a story, its love, its spirit. Stories are animate. Stories sit up, stuff in their organs, and walk away. Stories live.

In this introduction, therefore, all I wish to do is celebrate. Dance and cheer. Give you a gentle nudge and point at the horizon and whisper, "Look! What a stunning sunset!"

Here are twenty such sunsets.

Some violet, some pink, some melancholy, some eerie, some wistful, some gray, some angry, some clouded and dark and threatening.

Just look.

Just witness.

Feel your heart seize up as you pass through the final pages of Lisa Gill's "Holding Zeno's Suitcase in Kansas, Flowering." Feel your lungs tighten, your breath quicken as you take pleasure in the subtle artistry

of A. Manette Ansay's "July." (Don't ask why, don't ask how, just be-
hold.) Feel the suspense and mystery–the terror of betrayal, the crav-
ing for trust–that so gently caresses every page of Lon Otto's "A Man
in Trouble." Feel the bizarre, scary, funny-scary charms of Rosa Shand's
"Sophie Was the King." Yes, and then join me in celebration.

–Tim O'Brien

LISA GILL

Holding Zeno's Suitcase in Kansas, Flowering

EMMA IS STANDING on the side of the highway holding a postcard in one hand and one of her mother's old flowered suitcases in the other. The postcard is from her sister, shows a picture of the Grand Canyon, and is signed *Love, Carolyn*. Emma would have put the postcard in the suitcase, binding it with all the others except that she almost forgot it, almost left the orange canyon decorating the white lace doily on her nightstand. She only remembered the card after she had already packed and sealed her bag. The zipper on the case is broken and so when she closes it, she uses duct tape. It isn't the ideal form of luggage and Emma tires sometimes of scrubbing sticky gray glue from the blue and yellow flowered vinyl. Emma is sure that her sister would not use such makeshift traveling gear. Carolyn has been many places across the country; she must pack and unpack frequently, in many hotels, in many states. Emma has in her bag some fifty odd picture postcards Carolyn has sent, all postmarked from different cities and towns.

Each time Emma receives a postcard from her sister she puts it in her suitcase with the others, binding them with a length of yellow ribbon she wore in her hair to be confirmed. All afternoon, as she works the dough, hangs wash to dry, cleans the three bedroom house until there is nothing left to be cleaned, Emma thinks of what she will tell her sister in her letter:

Here, in Kansas, it has been the kind of wind that puts rats in your hair as soon as you walk outside—no matter how well you brushed it. . . . And mother's canary, squawking up such a storm, that I covered

9

the cage today just so I could hear myself read your postcard . . . And one of the slats on the barn door fell off and I almost got another rusty nail in my foot like when I was ten . . . Garden is real pretty, have all these extra tomatoes . . .

Thinking of what she will tell her sister when she sits down to write her, Emma's chores get done as if by somebody else. Postcard days always seem so much fuller than the other days.

Standing next to the highway now, Emma likes having postcards in her bag, the Grand Canyon in her hand. She can almost imagine the time her sister spends standing in front of a wire rack, looking amongst all those different pictures, some horizontal, some vertical, some with words over the photos, some just pretty pictures. And Carolyn turning and turning the rack, saying, "Which one for my sister?" Emma wants to tell her sister: "Thank you for bringing me these places."

Sometimes, the postcards seem like an itinerary. After receiving a postcard, Emma used to pour over the pull-out maps inside *National Geographic*'s. The magazines were stacked on the coffee table until her mother decided to put them in a box in her closet. Emma would interrupt her darning to spread the map over the coffee table, to look for her sister, look for the lines that really go places, especially lines which lead right off the edge of the map.

Sometimes Emma would mark a point on one of the lines to show where she was. Even though the map wasn't labeled Kansas, she would pretend that she was at point A. Then she would put her sister some distance across the map at point B. Emma would take some of her thread, unwind it and place it on the line that leads from A to B. She would diligently make that thread follow every curve until she reached her sister and she would snip there. Holding the thread up, letting it hang down in a straight line, it inevitably seemed like such a long map distance; so Emma would hold the two ends of the measured thread together and cut where the fold indicated half. She would take that half, lay it on the map to see how far half would get her, what the nearest town to the middle point would be. She would lift the thread again, fold and cut. Fold and cut. When the thread could no longer be folded, she would just cut. And, if her mother didn't interrupt and tell her to go back to her darning, Emma would cut that thread in half until there was nothing left but a stub of cotton—no bigger than point A on the map. And then, her mother would say, "Clean up and do your darning."

When her mother had taken the maps away, Emma didn't really get angry because although she had liked gaining a sense of distance and direction from the lines on the maps, she considered the places in the magazines far too exotic; most of the maps didn't even show Kansas. The places on the postcards, however, Emma knows that her sister has seen, and so she knows that they exist and can therefore be reached.

Emma can practically see herself standing in the photographs, although at this point she is just standing on the gravely shoulder which marks the transition between corn and highway. Emma knows where she is and she knows that she should start walking because standing on the side of a two-lane highway in the middle of Kansas in the middle of the night isn't going to get her anywhere; no one will pick her up until the morning. She remains standing partly because she hasn't decided which direction on the road to follow, partly because she is leaving. She is leaving for good, leaving as Carolyn did so many years ago, as her sister left without telling anyone she was leaving, not even telling Emma good-bye. Carolyn wrote, of course, right away–sending letters to her parents and postcards to her sister.

Every time Emma receives a postcard from her sister, she reads it. She reads it over and over all day long until she knows it by heart, words and picture, then she binds it with the others. Sometimes, reading her sister's postcards, she feels older, has to sit in the rocker, drape a shawl over her legs. Those days, her mother ends up calling out for her tea, asks why the dinner is late, asks where the butter is that should have been placed on the table.

In the evenings of the days Emma has received postcards from her sister, she pulls out the fading cardboard box with her old school supplies. When Emma got pulled out of eighth grade, the box had been relegated to the cellar where it remained dormant for more than a decade. Only a few years ago did she remember they had ever existed: paper and pencils, her fountain pen and readers. The day she rediscovered these belongings, the accumulation of dust and sallow discoloration of the paper seemed frightening–almost inaccurate–yet loving in the remembering. These days, Emma sits down with this paper at the kitchen table to write to her sister:

Dear Carolyn,
Thank you for the picture postcard. I have never been there.

And that is as far as Emma gets. She sits at the table and looks at the space beneath that one ink line, and she doesn't know what to say to her sister. Fountain pen in hand, the beginning of a letter in front of her, Emma wonders why she can't put the pen on paper, put one word in front of the other, and get from the top of the page to the bottom. Carolyn fills many a postcard to Emma. Emma remembers how all day she thought of what she wanted to say to her sister, how she so much wanted to write a letter to her sister. She takes a new piece of paper, starts over:

> Dear Carolyn,
> Thank you for the picture postcard. I have never been there.

Emma manages only one line, the same line. The paper is even ruled, not like the stationery of her mother's which is pastel colored and doesn't have any lines. This paper, this old manila school paper should make it easier for Emma to write to her sister, as if the green lines were obligated to show her where to go in her letter. Emma's handwriting is fair, and she should be able to stay on the line.

The line on the highway is yellow and leaves Kansas, just as Carolyn left, as Emma is leaving, streaking out through the middle of the night. Emma feels that she is leaving more than her sister left if only because more time has passed, fourteen years. Only yesterday, her mother said, "You are not like Carolyn."

For a moment Emma tries to give herself the memory of place, in hopes of being able to leave it. Of making a good-bye, of creating partings like creating gaps in memory. And she tries to think of the good things, to let them go, so she will not remain snagged as on the tree, the willow by the stream where she carved her initials, E.R.M. That tree caught her up while she was playing tag with her sister. Calling out to Carolyn to wait up, she had pulled herself free of the tree's limbs and the brambles beneath it and had not realized how ensnared she was until she had already torn her blouse and cut her shoulder. How it had hurt as her sister came running, Emma sitting on the ground, tears streaking her dirty cheeks, and her sister laughing, taunting, "Catch me," and then, "What's wrong?"

Standing on the shoulder of the road, Emma knows that tree as well as if it were there between the yellow lines on the highway, as if she could split it open, count and measure the rings, demarcate each drought and flood, the good years, the rough ones. This night she thinks of the tree, the one at the edge of the property and she knows that the tree refuses the darkness and maintains a pale shade of lime gray at night.

Emma purses her lips and readjusts the suitcase in her hand. She looks down the highway as far as the darkness will allow her but is pulled back to images of the house as if by gravity.

Earlier this evening, at the dinner table with its four place settings, her mother had looked at the empty chair, turned to Emma exasperated and said, "Emma, where is that sister of yours? She ought to know by now . . ."

Emma stopped her mother mid-sentence, "The Grand Canyon."

Her mother turned to stare at her plate and after a moment shook her head, "I was just saying, your sister ought to know by now to keep in better touch." Emma watched her mother butter a slice of bread; her mother's lips tightened into two thin lines. She put her knife down and said, "The Grand Canyon? Did you receive a card from that sister of yours today? Emma Rae, don't you think your father and I might enjoy hearing how Carolyn is doing?"

Emma lifted herself from the table, placed the stenciled cloth napkin next to her plate and went to get the card.

She showed her parents the picture of the Grand Canyon, but she didn't tell them that she was leaving, or where she was going.

Emma is leaving her father to his diminishing land and the back wall of the barn pasted with pin-ups. She is leaving her mother to her family's silver set, all the medication, the chipped bone china and her aging canary. Because she is leaving, moving so drastically and finally, she has the right, Emma might even say, an obligation, to stand still–only yesterday her mother said, "You are not like Carolyn–ungrateful." Emma consciously stands still with her suitcase in her hand, offering a little of her time as one might offer a moment of silence for the dead.

For this moment she thinks she should survey the whole land, the scattered houses: her own with the paint peeling, the crooked porch swing, the wilting garden. Maybe she will tell her sister of all the changes, all the lack of changes. So these things she surveys in great detail and Emma absorbs everything despite the darkness which prevents her from seeing anything except silhouettes and shadowy outlines. For thirty years she has lived in this place. She has taken care of her mother and the house since her mother's first breakdown when Emma was eleven. She has darned her father's socks, made lunches for him to carry out of the house, stuffed him with potatoes and cornbread. She has avoided his drunken stupors, avoided the barn. She has made tea and baked sweet breads for occasions when she covers the bird cage with a dark towel to hush the canary while the parson, or doctor, visits.

After all of this, Emma does not need to see anything in order to see everything. The images are embossed so heavily on her mind's eye that sometimes she doubts whether any other place would be different. But she has the postcards with pictures of all those places that do not look like Kansas, and the postcards are signed *Love, Carolyn,* and the typewritten text on the back of the cards proves that she is not in Kansas. She wants to tell her sister: "Thank you for bringing me places to look at."

Time has a way of getting by Emma, of slipping around her as she sits with her sister's postcards. Her mother asks, "Where is the butter?" Her mother asks this question knowing full well that in the fridge, sitting on the bottom shelf, is an oblong square of butter on a saucer which could have been picked up by anyone on their way to the dinner table.

Even the yellow dashes on the highway begin to look like butter to a person who is thinking about butter. Emma would like to tell her mother that all the butter a family can eat in a lifetime is lining the highway. She might even like to tell her mother that the forgotten butter is being eaten by Carolyn on the back of the postcard with the picture of the Statue of Liberty. All sorts of things are eaten or visited or seen and done on the backs of Carolyn's postcards. If Emma were just to read the words on the backs of her sister's postcards, especially the cards from the East, if just anyone were to look at the backs of the cards like the one with the picture of the Statue of Liberty–

> *Dearest Emma,*
> *Today I saw the Statue of Liberty,*
> *Went to an art museum,*
> *Ate crayfish with butter sauce,*
> *Saw Les Miserables on stage,*
> *Bought you this postcard*
> *From an old woman sitting*

On the pavement outside
Of my hotel.
Love, Carolyn

–the letters would resemble nothing greater than Emma's own list of things to do in Lawrence–

Things to do in town:
Buy butter,
Pick up black thread,
Fill mother's prescription
At the pharmacy on Main,
Choose a better chamomile tea
Than the last
Which turned mother's
Stomach.

   Emma knows that her sister's letters would not really help her with her errands in Lawrence. But sometimes, as she stands next to the highway which leads to Lawrence, she likes to imagine carrying a postcard instead of a shopping list to town, going to the art museum to buy butter, unweaving lengths of black thread from the table cloth under the plate of crayfish, filling her mother's prescription at the theater, gathering leaves of chamomile from an old woman's hair. If Emma wasn't so pressed for time, if she didn't know how much she needed to get moving, she might laugh out loud. She might smile so wide that no one passing by on the highway could misunderstand the wealth of communication between Emma and her sister.

   With the Grand Canyon in her hand, Emma would like to be able to tell someone that her sister writes less impersonal letters when she is not writing from those places on the right side of the map where there are practically as many dots and lines as stars in the sky. If there was someone walking down the highway just now, Emma would hold out the card as proof:

Dearest Emma,
I went to the Grand Canyon,
Walked all the way down
Bright Angel Trail.

Mules carried my bags
Kind of like that boy with
Freckles used to do
When I was in fifth grade and
You were in seventh.
Love, Carolyn

Emma knows that Carolyn, with the writing on the back of each post-card, is telling her more than what the words say, is giving her more than a list of what she is doing and where she is doing it. Reading is not a matter of simply deciphering the meaning of inky shapes on card stock. Because Carolyn is her sister, Emma reads into and beyond the letters and tries to hear her sister's voice as it must sound in the place that is shown on the postcard. When Emma read today's post-card from the Grand Canyon, she imagined her sister standing, bare feet spread slightly for balance, standing at the very spot where the crack in the earth opens wide as a great mouth–her sister there, with her blond hair loose on the wind, her hands outstretched, her voice thick and rusty as the color of the canyons, etching in the rock walls a message to Emma, like letters written in dirt with a stick when they were girls, beginning when the sun rises with *Dearest Emma*, and not closing the letter until the sun sets with *Love, Carolyn*.

Every time Emma receives a postcard from her sister, her mother says, "Emma, don't you think your father and I might also enjoy hear-ing how Carolyn is doing?" Next to the highway, Emma thinks of all the times she has been asked to share her sister but doesn't feel she should have to. If Carolyn had wanted Emma to share the card, she would have written something between the *a* of Emma and the comma, like "Dear Emma and your parents," or "Dear Emma and Miranda and Bill." Emma could hug those commas.

The frame around Emma's window is shaped like a big postcard flipped on end. Sometimes in the winter Emma writes pretend letters in the frost on the window panes:

C a r o l y n,
My finger
I s
As cold
A s

I miss
You.
Luv, Emma

Paint is peeling from the yellow frame of the window, peeling fastest in the places where Emma has crawled out at night, night after night, the places where she has crawled back in. Those bare patches on her window are hers; they belong to Emma. No one else, not even Carolyn, could look at the weathered window ledge and say: "That must be where Emma's fingers were, where she slid out on her butt, spreading the curtains carefully so her suitcase will slide free of this house."

Now, standing a mile from the house, Emma knows those patches where the paint is especially barren. She thinks perhaps she could leave, leave her presence–or her absence–marked until the house should burn down or be repainted. Sometimes Emma thinks she will never be able to really leave until all the paint has finished peeling, so that the rectangular frame of the window is worn smooth as the glossy side of a postcard. Then, Emma might be able to slide out and go away for good–if the window was all slicked up, as if the frame had been greased with butter like Emma had to grease those guard rails on the footbridge to get Carolyn's head unstuck. And then her mother had asked, "Emma, why are your sister's ears so red and why is she all greasy? Give her a bath." Then her mother had asked, "Emma, where is the butter?"

Emma rests her suitcase on the gravel. This is a spot she knows as well as the window frame. With her back to the house, the two ends of the road stretch in opposite directions like mirror images, the hills rolling flatly like sine curves. In order to move, Emma will have to choose a direction, a destination. The Grand Canyon, maybe. Or maybe somewhere else, somewhere she has never seen–not even on a postcard. Then she thinks that it doesn't matter where she goes, just get away from this spot in Kansas. Still, she must choose. West or east. Here to somewhere. Measure her progress in halves, and halfway to the half. Emma knows that you must get halfway to any destination before you can get any farther. She wonders if Topeka is halfway to somewhere.

Even when Emma can imagine getting somewhere, she doubts if she could stand on a street in Texas or next to the Statue of Liberty and see anything without images of Kansas superimposed on top of everything. Images of home, of her mother's hair in a steel knot at the base of her neck, the pin-up on the barn of the girl who looks like Carolyn. All those socks, the house, the mailbox. Emma figures that Kansas will follow her anywhere she might go, as certainly as *here* is contained in *there*.

She also knows that many places which could have been *there*, somewhere else, have come *here* to this house. All those postcards have trapped outside places in Kansas. Like her mother said, "If you can see it in a photo, why do you need to go there?" Emma thinks of all the cards which she has received in the mailbox.

If Emma were to go somewhere like the Grand Canyon and stand where her sister must have stood, then the Grand Canyon–that great orange crack in the earth–would look like nothing more than a flattened cardboard image resting on an oversized white doily. And the Statue of Liberty would have next to it, in the sky, a great wedge of butter because on the kitchen table the Statue of Liberty and the butter had the same dimensions that night her mother wanted to see the card. Like her mother has always said, "A picture is worth a thousand words and not so expensive as taking the train. " Emma wants to tell her sister, "Stop sending all those places here."

Emma looks up, away from the highway as she often does such nights as these. She looks at the stars in the sky. She knows all those pinpricks of light have names, are supposed to form pictures; but to her, this night more than any other, each and every star looks like a hole. A hole in fabric. Small pinpricked patches where the cloth is wearing thin. Like the cloth over the bird cage. Daylight is seeping in, cloaked in another name–*star*. Emma thinks that the cloth–blue, rich and deep–thrown over Kansas is wearing thin. More holes seem to arrive each time she does. She imagines the way the fabric drapes over hills, nestles on the points of trees, slopes down to graze the fields, rises with her house and the electric poles; the sky has taken its shape from the land in the same way as the cloth gains structure over the bird cage.

Carolyn,
Mother's latest canary is getting old. Would be getting gray and hunched if that was how birds age. Even the cloth that I throw over the bird cage is fraying, making holes that must look like stars, new constellations to the bird. And mother, she thinks it's the same canary you gave her all those years ago.

It was Carolyn's idea to cover the cage, make the bird think it was time to sleep so it would be quiet. Emma has been doing what Carolyn suggested and her mother approved for years. She would like to tell the bird:

> *Canary,*
> *I lie to you. I make you think it is night time, make you think you can't fly or sing, just so mother and the visitor can make the house dark and solemn with their words, their sermons and prescriptions.*

Emma knows that canaries can't comprehend such things. So she doesn't talk to the bird, just lets the cloth covering wear thin, thin as the fabric of her housecoat. The dress that she wears to clean and do chores needs patching, but the holes blend right in with the dark areas of the paisley pattern. Emma's mother hasn't even noticed them yet. She hasn't said: "Emma, little holes always get bigger. Nip this in the bud like a good girl." A good thirty-year-old girl.

> *Carolyn,*
> *Mother says that if you have any mending you should send it here, to me. You never learned to sew, never mentioned stitchwork in your postcards. Some things you shouldn't pay strangers to do.*

Emma looks at her hands, all rut and ridge. Even in the semi-light of the highway, Emma's hands show bronze, but not the same kind of darkness that her sister writes of when she says:

> *I got a tan in Mexico,*
> *Am all golden now.*

Emma wouldn't want to tell Carolyn about her own darkness. Looking at her palms, she can see where the hoe fits, where she holds the clothespins, how her knuckles must have been designed just to knead bread. Looking at her hands in the kind of darkness that makes an old black and white photo of everything, Emma sees that her fingers are meant to pick a single pill from a bottle and offer it like a seed to her mother's mouth, make flowers grow.

If Emma could get somewhere to see her sister, if she met her sister at the Golden Gate Bridge in San Francisco, if she offered her sister a bouquet of wild flowers and her sister were to ask, "How's mother?" Emma would smile and say:

> *Mother is beautiful when she is hearing voices. Beautiful when she sleeps and the lines on her face relax, become smooth as sheets on the line, as her hair. When I talk to mother, I can see in her eyes that she is listening to something else. Something wonderful that flutters about my head like the wings of many birds.*

Emma thinks that to talk of birds to her sister she will need to be more specific, say something like *the wings of many small sparrows and robins,* or she might be misunderstood. Once, Carolyn sent a postcard with a picture of an ostrich:

> *Dearest Emma,*
> *Look at this bird.*
> *Wings like dirty angels.*
> *It can't even fly but runs*
> *All gangly like you did.*
> *In Kansas now I hear*
> *There are farms of these birds.*
> *Love, Carolyn*

And her mother asked, "Did you receive a postcard from that sister of yours?" Carolyn became Emma's sister the day she left the state. Mother said, "*Your sister* has run off." Before that it was, "*My daughter Carolyn* is going to sing a duet at church on Sunday," "*My daughter* has the highest marks in her class," or "*My daughter* has been invited to go to a public speaking tournament in Topeka." Emma would like to say to her mother: "You made Carolyn my sister with fewer words than are required to fill the back of a postcard picturing an ostrich."

Emma looks up, does not expect or find any birds flying. Just lots of holes, bright holes. She calculates the number of patches, the hours of stitchwork that it would take to patch the places where fabric is worn. She can already hear her needle, clink, clink, as it passes into the fabric tapping the light bulb she has stretched the sock over in order to do her darning. The rhythm of dusk. Each night, light fades as quietly and unobtrusively as her father's socks regain heels and toes. All those socks. Socks enough for many more feet, it seems, than just her father's. But for Emma, the evening is always, "Emma, your father has some socks that need darning, be a dear." Her mother brings Emma the stack without waiting for a response. *Certainly mother* has come out of her mouth so many times over the years that speech has become gratuitous; echoes and memories replace language.

Emma's mother does rest an awful lot these days. Now, as Emma is standing on the highway, her mother can be nothing but asleep.

> *Carolyn,*
> *Mother is resting now. I will show her your postcard with the picture of the Peace Gardens later. Later when you have stopped bleeding and crying, after you have washed your face, I will tell Mommy that you fell and scraped your knee on the highway, but that it didn't really hurt much, that everything is okay now, and that I have already told you not to roller-skate on the highway again.*

Emma drops her suitcase on the gravel and drops the postcard with the picture of the Grand Canyon. Emma is not eleven or twelve and Carolyn cannot be a child any longer. She must have aged, could be in any number of places across the country.

There is so much that Emma would like to say to her sister, but she also knows how much must remain unspoken, unwritten. If they met in Hershey's Chocolate Factories, Emma might admit:

> *Carolyn, I hate to cook.*

If Emma found her sister riding a mule in the Grand Canyon, she would be awfully tempted to tell Carolyn:

> *The boy who carried your bags, instead of mine, was called Jerry Davenport. And freckles were not his most distinguishing feature.*

If Emma were to run across Carolyn in Graceland, she probably wouldn't say to her sister:

> *We don't go to church anymore. It has been so long that I can't even remember what the chapel you and I were supposed to get married in looks like. The pastor comes to us.*

Emma knows that if she were to meet her sister at Yellowstone and her sister were to ask, "How's mother?" she would not be able to say:

Carolyn, you did not know mother like this. You have not put the pills on her tongue which make her hands shake, make her tired, her stomach queasy. You have not put the pills on her tongue so that she can remember the day of the week, how to fix a cup of tea, who I am.

And if Carolyn were to ask, "How's daddy?" while looking at Mount Rushmore, Emma knows she could not tell her sister:

Our father drinks more than before you left, less of his property remains. He leaves the house each day in overalls with a sack lunch and a bottle of JD. He says he is going to work the land. He doesn't tell her what he sells to pay the doctors bills, to handle the recession. He doesn't tell her that there's not enough work to keep him busy, to keep him from sitting in the back of the barn, drinking and pasting pin-ups on the wall.

Emma knows that standing next to the Statue of Liberty, she would not say:

There is a pin-up of a woman who looks like you did when you were fifteen. She was ripped out of the J.C.Penny catalogue, wears a blue bikini with flowers like that green one of yours that mother made you give to Good Will. She has been there since you left, pasted against the back wall of the barn behind the tractor, next to naked women, in a dark corner where mother never goes. The girl never stops smiling, swinging her blond ponytail in the breeze. Never ages. Wrinkles only as paper does, blush fading, gaining a hint of yellow.

Emma knows that some things could not be said; Emma knows that she would be unable to lie to her sister. Emma feels lightheaded now and a wave of nausea passes through her body. The hills which stretch evenly out from the point where Emma is standing begin to roll under her feet. The land seems to undulate as if the highway and the fields, even the house that stands behind Emma on its squared plot, as if these coverings constitute some great carpet which is being pulled out from beneath her feet. A carpet that is going to fly away without Emma, leaving her in exactly the same spot except that she will have fallen.

Emma sits down on her suitcase and tries to collect herself. This has happened before. On other nights she has had to go back to the house, take a spoonful of Emetrol to calm her stomach, unpack the suitcase, replacing the vinyl bag under the bed, trying to sleep.

Carolyn,
Do you remember how I always won when we used to race, walking backwards between rows of corn?

Sitting on her suitcase next to the highway, Emma doesn't want this night to be another one of those nights when she goes in early, swallowing a spoonful of Emetrol, telling herself as she has told her mother so many times before, "You shouldn't travel when you aren't feeling well." She doesn't want to lie in bed, in her own bed with its brass headboard; she doesn't want to lie in that bed wrapped round in the quilt her mother made for her when she was eight, the quilt with single lavender flowers in each square. She doesn't want to lie wrapped in that quilt and try to sleep. She doesn't want to count like sheep the number of times she has used illness as an excuse to go back to the house, to leave the highway, to abandon the dotted yellow line which leads like a fraying rope away from the house.

Carolyn,
Lavender looks better on you. Even mother knows that, giving you the purple dress to wear to the dance and making mine from navy knit. That dress I matched the table cloth in.

Emma wishes she felt better; in the middle of the night, she is beginning to sweat. She wishes a car would come by right now to pick her up. Or a bull would come charging towards her from the barn. Or the ghost of the woman in the pin-up that looks like her sister would shriek through the corn wearing an old sheet. Something, anything, to make her move her tortoise body a little bit. Half the distance to the line in the center of the highway would do.

If her mother were to see her now, standing along the highway, she would say: "Did you receive a postcard from that sister of yours?"

Emma wishes she could throw her postcards down on the highway so they would get run over by a semi at dawn. She wishes she could throw down her postcards on the highway so that all those places with Carolyn's handwriting would spring up in front of her, sprout like beanstalks in the middle of Kansas.

She hears a hum that is not locusts. Stands. Grabs her bag and postcard. Turns to face towards Lawrence.

From the valley rises light with a suddenness that is like a rip in cloth and Emma catches in the face the brights of a semi. Whiteness and noise pass her by, fall into the dent in the road beyond her. Her vision flashes with many white stars and Emma carries the image of headlight to the hills, to the pavement in front of her, to her suitcase. As if that sudden light was a camera's flash which can only come from semis when hills have hidden them. Emma gains an image of herself, an image so honed and true she could be looking at a postcard: A woman—brown hair, streaked already with gray, callused hands, aging body with particular sag and rumblings, no high school diploma or job training, money enough to fill a coffee canister, buy coffee, perhaps a train ticket, a motel room or two. This woman is standing on the side of a highway in the middle of Kansas in the middle of the night holding in one hand an old vinyl suitcase patterned with flowers, and in the other a postcard of the Grand Canyon.

In the leftover light of the semi, Emma sees the postcard of a canyon clutched by the hands of a tired woman in a glossy postcard. Standing next to the highway, Emma understands that identical postcards stacked in a rack that spins on an axis can be postmarked with many dates; the same picture can be mailed over and over.

Looking at the taillights rising on another hill, Emma thinks that perhaps there is only one postcard; one postcard which is written upon night after night, on many different dates, and all this desire for communication is layered in good handwriting, one night upon another, until the lines of text pile on top of each other, drape over other lines, overlap and weave words together until the ink runs like water, until all the holes, the white places between letters are filled, until the postcard becomes unreadable and cannot be mailed.

Hundreds of just one postcard, or only one postcard written on hundreds of times. Emma knows she still stands next to the highway in Kansas in the middle of the night with the Grand Canyon in one hand, suitcase in the other.

A. MANETTE ANSAY

July

I REMEMBER THE year it was rain that we prayed for, the death rattle of the crops our evening lullaby. Mornings, I rose to the dry catch of dust in my throat as the boys coughed themselves awake, rattling the bars of the divider that kept them from wandering out of their room and tumbling down the stairs into Alma's part of the house. I tasted the drifting fields in the damp folds of their necks, in Foster's sour kiss, in the second cup of coffee I drank after he'd left for work, a fawn-colored cloud of dust funneling behind his truck. At noon, we ate lunch with Alma in the coolness of the root cellar, gulping can after can of grape pop and pressing our toes into the damp, dirt floor. Alma owned the house outright as well as the sixty acres of land she leased to the canning company. "This heat don't bother me," she said. "I get paid whether they take the crop or no."

"I don't mind it either," I said. "It's like being on vacation in Florida or somewhere."

But each of us knew that the other had lied. There was shame in the terrible thirst of the corn, in the yellowing leaves and withering stems, the waste of it all, the wretched waste, and when the boys ran through the brittle rows at twilight, I shook with the sound of breaking bones.

"Come on out of there! You, Howard! Jamie!" They obeyed, my four-year-old tow-headed boys, born just ten months apart. *Still babies,* Foster liked to say, *too young for anything but belly-aching.*

"Aw, they ain't hurting anything," he said. The dust in the air had

25

kissed the sweat around his mouth; his lips looked made-up, like a woman's. "Crop's gone to shit, the world knows it."

"Don't say that word in front of them," I said.

"And which word might that be?" Foster said, his eyes shining innocent gold. The boys laughed because he was laughing. And maybe it was then that it all started, in the dusky heat, with the last faint bloom of summer curling up all around us. Now Howard's thirteen, sprouting hair along his jawbone. Jamie already wears a size-twelve shoe. *Foster's boys,* people call them, and it's true – they won't listen to a thing I have to say anymore. They nod, their flat stares scorching my face, but they know the right look from Foster will knock my words from the air like a flock of clay pigeons. "You leave them boys to me," he says, each word like the firing of a gun. And Howard and Jamie aren't about to wait around for me to pick up the pieces.

Today, they are both in a bad morning mood. Neither of them got their homework done, I can see it in their faces, though they both tell me different when I ask. They have to go to make-up class all summer long because they failed their regular school year. "Hustle up," Foster says to them. "I'm leaving at six-thirty whether you two are ready or no." They eat and they eat: toast and peanut-butter, toast and jelly, sugar doughnuts, cereal with milk, cereal poured dry from the box into their hands. "Manners," I say, but I'm no more than a mosquito's whine in their ear.

"*Man*-ners," Howard hisses to his brother.

"Lick me," Jamie says.

Foster says, "You two better hustle up."

I clear away their dishes, take the last of my coffee to the window where I watch the new sun bloom beyond the fields. It's the first clear morning we've had this month, and the flood waters shine like sheets of ice. I've always been afraid of water. As children, my sister and I took swimming lessons at the lake front park, but I never got in past my knees. I hated the idea of my foot coming down and not knowing what might be under it, the feeling that something might reach up and grab me. Now there is water everywhere I look, reflected sky and cotton-clouds spread over the ground. On Sundays after the homily, when we kneel down to pray for good dry weather, you can feel how much everyone wants the same thing, and how little we expect to get it.

"Let's go, let's go!" Foster says, clapping his hands, and the boys rocket down the stairs and into the front yard, jumping puddles and scattering the irritable flock of geese, another abandoned 4-H project. The truck is parked in two inches of water; Howard splashes Jamie, Jamie punches Howard. Foster comes up behind me, kisses me hard on the neck. He says, "Get some sleep, Marilee." There are those who envy me, married fourteen years to a man who never forgets to kiss good-bye.

But things have been bad between all of us ever since I started working full-time, five nights a week from eight until four-thirty, so Foster can go to school. I remember how I used to step into the day like an old familiar dress, and maybe it wasn't beautiful, maybe it wasn't the best I could own, but at least it was mine and I wore it well and I knew how to mend where it tore. By noon time, I'd have the house put right, and I'd go downstairs to Alma. "How're them weeds of yours?" she'd ask, proud of the boys as I was. They'd grown up in her kitchen as much as mine. Summers, they followed us around the vast garden we kept together, picking raspberries and gooseberries and strawberries for canning, running to the shed for a forgotten tool, climbing high into the apple trees to hang the pie tins that scared off birds.

Now I lose each day to a restless, dreamy sleep, and when I get up late in the afternoon, I'm cotton-headed from the drumming of the rain, disoriented, not quite real. It's as if I'm watching someone else fix supper for Foster and the boys, and carry a plate downstairs to Alma, and do up the dishes, and put them away–though of course it's me, who else? Then I drive fifteen miles of washed-out roads to the department store in Cedarton, where I stare at the flickering security screen and try not to think about being alone in the hollow belly of the building. I read magazines or write letters to my sister in Denver; when it gets really bad, I say the rosary. But all night long I hear noises–the muffled grunt of a window giving way, the thud of a man's heavy boot, the rain on the taut tin rooftop–wild as the beating of my heart.

Alma knows just how bad it is, but Foster tells me there's nothing to be afraid of. "Nobody's going to break in," he says. "You're there to keep their property insurance down, that's all." Insurance, profit, risk–these are the things he studies at school, but school can't help him understand this has nothing to do with being afraid and everything to do with fear. And when fear swallows your voice and drinks up your spit and hurts you deep in your privates, you let it have its way. It's what you feel during childhood nightmares, when outrageous things seem like honest possibilities: the two-headed monster, the six-foot-tall lion—they do exist, yes they do, wait here with me and you'll see. Howard and Jamie used to dream the same dreams, just like you hear about with twins. I'd go to their room, flipping on lights, tasting their screams in my own throat. When they buried their faces against me, I remembered the hot wet force of their births, how their crying mouths opened for my breast already knowing and it seemed to me then there was nothing I could teach them.

You'll ruin them boys with that babying, Foster warned me. Some nights, when they cried out for me, he held me down, playfully, not playfully, his tongue stuffing my mouth like a rag, his body inside my body. *Ma!* the boys screamed, I can still hear them. *Oh, Ma!*

Now, whenever I come into their room, they stop whatever they've been doing. Their faces are as smooth as the faces of the mannequins I pass on my rounds every night, ruddy complexions hushed by the artificial twilight, not quite real, yet close enough to be believed. Frozen mouths. Staring eyes. They don't even bother to ask, *What do you want?* They are endlessly patient, these mannequin boys with Foster's face and my own cold limbs.

At work, I know all the mannequins—the children holding hands in their back-to-school clothes; the twin hunters dressed in khaki with black grease paint under their eyes; the shapely young mother in Home Appliances; the teenage girl modeling swimwear on a sandy platform in Recreation. My favorite is the bride in the Young Miss department, unbearably fragile in her white-white gown with the sweetheart neckline, the pearly buttons, the lacy train coiled around her feet. I visit all of them, nights, on my rounds, touching their clothing, their hair, their long, smooth-jointed fingers, adjusting the little girl's knee-socks, smoothing the teenager's stiff blonde hair. Their mouths are half-open, puckered with worry, as if they want to warn me about something. Their eyes are fixed on it. They cannot look away; they are frozen with a fear I recognize. And then it's like the game I played as a child, imagining someone just behind me, and as long as I don't look I'll be OK. I force myself to finish my rounds before returning to the windowless office at the back, walking slowly, deliberately. The security screen never shows more than the quiet rows of merchandise, the mannequins holding their awkward poses, the vague outline of my face reflected back.

I've called in three false alarms since spring. Max Bolton, the day guard, makes fun of me for it. He phones me on the security channel, breathes heavily in my ear. Sometimes he talks filthy. Sometimes he doesn't say anything at all. *Just making sure the bad guys ain't gotcha*, he says when I tell him to knock it off. The tone of his voice lets me know he is smiling in a way that shows all of his sharp, yellow teeth.

When my sister got hurt in Denver last year, I flew down to stay with her at the hospital, where it took the doctors three weeks to fix all the things those men had done to her. She said, *I worry that after something like this I can't believe in God no more.* She said, *Don't let nobody tell you otherwise, this world is one terrible place to be.* Sometimes I feel like all it will take is one more thing–any small thing–and that will be it, I don't know what I'll do. It's the way I felt after Jamie was born, when his birth and Howard's had blurred together so I couldn't tell them apart and each day met the next day in a single, seamless scream.

This morning, arriving home from work at dawn, I found the front porch slick with goose droppings. And there they were, roosting on the lip of the concrete flower box, hissing those deep, nasty hisses. Their eyes opened wider, diamond-hard, shining over my too-tight uniform, the SECURITY badge sewn to my left breast pocket, the empty radio sling bumping my belly, the squeaky black shoes. *You look like a man in that thing,* Foster said the first time he'd seen me in it. But the geese were not fooled–it was me they saw, and they slithered down from the flower box, stretching their wide, white wings to block my path. I stared into their open mouths. Then I went around to Alma's side of the house, let myself in though the old mud room, and crossed through Alma's kitchen to reach the stairs leading up to where Foster and the boys were still sleeping. I set the table, put out cereal and toast and donuts, fixed a cup of hot, black coffee to wash out the ache in my throat. The sun began rising; one bloody knuckle peeked over the horizon and the flooded fields took up the color until the land around the house burned wild fire. And then there were the boys, stumbling into the kitchen with their eyes caked full of sleep. And then there was Foster in his fresh-ironed shirt and sweet cologne, telling them they better hustle up.

*　　*　　*

At noon, I wake up wet with perspiration, the bed sheets coiled around me and the smell of my polyester uniform caught deep in my hair. I shower and put on my robe, go into the kitchen where I make two grilled Velveeta sandwiches. The boys' old cat, Elephant, twirls between my legs, staring up at me adoringly with his single gooey eye. His stomach and paws are caked with field mud; there is mud beneath Foster's chair at the table, mud on the welcome mat at the top of the stairs, mud on the boys' tennis shoes, impossibly huge, with those wide, lounging tongues. The south edge of the lawn is still under water, and the fields reflect the scarred underbellies of the apple trees, the harsh coin of the sun rippling between them. A few straggly rows of corn grip the high ground, but for the most part the crop is gone, the season's seed lost to the sky. I cut each sandwich into four neat triangles, let a drip of cheese fall to the floor for Elephant. Then I grab a carton of milk, tuck a bag of cookies under my chin, and carry everything down the stairs to Alma.

The sound of Alma's cough, soapy and deep, hangs in the air like fine dust. Her heart and lungs are slowly filling up with water, and she spends her days at the kitchen table doing crossword puzzles, reading from the Bible, and listening to baseball on the portable radio. She no longer has the energy to pretend she isn't dying. Foster and I have rented the upstairs ever since Howard was born, and when Alma passes on I don't know what we'll do. But Foster doesn't seem worried. "An old woman like that," he says, "goes on for years and years." Last night after supper, while I got ready for work, he and the boys rode their dirt bikes up and down the long muddy driveway to the road even though Alma has asked them not to do this. Alma has also asked them not to lean their bikes against her altar to the Virgin beneath the chestnut tree; she has asked them not to walk through what's left of her perennial bed; she has begged them to pen up the geese which are eating her lawn and have taken to roosting in the shed. Mornings, they spread out beneath the old swing set, quarreling in their schoolgirl voices and tearing up tufts of drowned grass. I hate the smooth snake-weave of their necks, the pale slabs of their tongues. I hate the way they lower their heavy, white bodies into the watery hollows beneath the swings, overly careful of themselves, like rich people putting on airs.

Alma is sleeping in a straight-backed kitchen chair, her head dangling loose from her shoulders exposing the round pink cap of her skull. Her kitchen is just like mine, except that the walls are papered in blue, and last year she had new wood cupboards and a formica countertop installed to celebrate her seventy-fifth birthday. The old countertop was made of slate, and when the boys were small Alma would lift them up there so we could trace their bodies in chalk. Then we'd help them draw in their features–bulging muscles, mustaches and beards, bushy eyebrows–things that came to mind when we imagined them as men.

She wakes up when I set her sandwich in front of her. "Time to eat already?" Her voice is rusty, Elephant's tired mew.

"It is."

"You didn't have to go through the trouble."

"Easy to cook for two as one."

We pretend that these are not the same things we say to each other every day. When we bow our heads for grace, there's a commotion on the front porch, and I look up to see the cold eye of a goose gleaming through the window. "Amen," Alma says, and she turns to look, too. "Do you believe that?" she says. "Up on the back of the porch chair! Fixing to come in and grab our lunch, I would guess."

She pries open one of her sandwich triangles to scoop out a bit of cheese.

"It's the kind you like," I tell her.

"I like everything," Alma says, and she licks the cheese from her finger, but she puts down her sandwich without eating any more of it. It's hard for her to swallow; lately, even the act of chewing wears her out. But she drinks her milk in thick swallows, and when she finishes she says, "So how is Sarah Beth?"

Alma is the only person who still asks after my sister. With Foster, just like with my friends from our church, it's as if she has simply disappeared. In all the old stories about the saints, women died *protecting their virtue*. Saint Maria Goretti. Saint Cecelia. But my sister survived, and no one knows what to do. "She's taking a jewelry-making class," I say. "She's making me a pair of turquoise earrings."

"Turquoise," Alma says, her voice soft as the blue of the stone itself.

"She could make you something, too," I say eagerly, but Alma shakes her head.

"There's nothing like that I need. Though I wish there was." I watch the delicate flutter of the pulse at her neck. "I wish I could think of something."

Another goose has clambered up onto the back of the porch chair. It beats its powerful wings, thumping the side of the house. "You got to admire them," Alma says, twisting to see. "Once they get an idea in their heads, it don't shake loose."

"I'm still after the boys about that fence," I say, hating the high, defensive note in my voice. "Foster says they'll get to it."

"After I'm dead and gone, I suppose," Alma says mildly, and it hurts because it's probably true. More geese appear in the window, popping up like a bright-eyed garden of weeds, long necks swaying. The look of them makes me shiver. Last week they chased me all the way to the truck as Foster and the boys watched from the window, laughing.

"I get on them about that fence every day," I say, and with that the geese tip the porch chair with a terrible crash. "Ach," Alma cries. "I bet they broke that old thing!" She gets up, coughing, and moves to the window, clinging to the edge of the table for balance. I get up too, but then I sit down because the only thing I can think of is to go out there and shoo them off. I imagine how they'll fling their round white bodies at me, beating me down to the porch floor. I smell their hot, goose breath, feel the points of their beaks digging into me.

"Come look," Alma says. I can't believe she is laughing. "So many feathers! It's like a pillow fight."

I say, "I'm sure I'll see enough of them the next time they chase me around the house."

"They bother you that bad?" Alma says. "You just got to show 'em who's the boss."

"I guess I'm not meant to be anybody's boss," I say. "It's not in my personality," and I begin eating cookies, stuffing them down one after another, hoping that I won't cry.

Alma starts to cough, but checks it. Her face darkens for a moment. "You come with me," she says, low in her throat so I know she is serious, and I follow her slow walk out of the kitchen, through the mud room, and onto the porch. The geese flutter and hiss, but Alma has been seized with a strange, bright energy. "I know you don't like to hear it, but you got to stick up for yourself, Marilee!"

"I *do*," I say, knowing it's a lie. The geese roll at us like a terrible wave and I step back in spite of myself.

Alma grabs the broom from its hook beneath the awning. "Watch!" she says. She swings the broom into the side of the closest, plumpest goose. "G'wan!" she grunts, and the geese tumble off the porch, skittering through the puddles until they reach the edge of the fields. "Promise me," Alma says. "Promise you'll remember this." Then she begins to cough. Her mouth hangs open, purple-lipped, and I catch her as she goes down on her knees. The cough shakes her body, long twisting spasms that remind me of birth pains, how they get worse just when it seems they simply can't.

I help her back into the house, put her into a clean nightgown. "So tired," Alma says as I guide her into bed. I bring the radio in from the kitchen, but she says to shut it off, and my stomach falls into a hot, queasy pit that I imagine must be hell. I'm thirty-two years old, healthy and strong; it would have been nothing for me to run off those geese, but I couldn't do it, even for Alma. It strikes me that she could die right now, and for the first time I imagine how it will be to live somewhere else with Foster and the boys and miles of land all around us, and every night driving to work, and every day coming home, and my sister writing letter after letter saying, *I don't know that I can believe in anything now.* And the shame that I feel is worse than what I felt the last time I called in a false alarm, the time that I saw—*I saw*—someone outside the building with his pants down, his parts pressed against the glass. For weeks, Max Bolton wouldn't leave it alone. "What you got to worry about?" he'd say. "A man would pop one of those pretty mannequins before he'd take one look at you." It was Foster who heard from a friend in town that it had been Max all along.

I cannot bear the thought of going back upstairs, so I get into bed beside Alma, draw the covers up to my chin. Her body next to mine is like a child's, but the smell of her is different, sharper, strange. It's one o'clock, and if I sleep until five, I'll have my solid eight hours. I awaken at four-thirty to the sound of the geese beneath the bedroom window, fighting each other with their bright beaks, their blustery wings. And, still, I do not go back upstairs.

*   *   *

I get to work late, pulling into the flooded parking lot so fast that the water splashes up over my windshield. The department store is deathly hot; the air conditioning system is down, and without the big blowing sound coming from the vents, the building seems smaller. As I pass the mannequin children in their stiff new clothes, I notice the dust that has settled along the rims of their ears, the full, rosy bottoms of their lips. I lick my finger and try to rub them clean, but instead I leave a series of smudges, each one like a delicate bruise. The children's expressions are accusing now. I pull up the little girl's knee socks apologetically, rolling the tops the way I wore them at her age, confident in my own bright saddle shoes and already flirting with shy country boys like Foster. But I can see that she doesn't forgive me; her bruised smile is a sneer. I leave her that way, heading back to the windowless office where I drop off my magazines, my stationery, my purse.

The office always smells of Max Bolton: cigars, fried meat, English Leather cologne. There's a desk which we are supposed to share, a chair, a hot plate for instant coffee, and a TV screen that broadcasts three scenes: the front entrances, the fire door, and the central aisle that runs the length of the building like a backbone. The mannequin bride hovers at the far end, a frail white blossom, a ghost. I glance at the screens, but things look the way they do every night, fuzzy and grayed, like people in an old photograph. A second bride watches me from a single brass frame on the desk; she is Max Bolton's daughter, Elizabeth, married June 18th, 1987. I know because I have slipped the photo from behind its glass guard to read the back. I go through the pockets of the jackets he leaves on the hook behind the door. I jimmy the desk drawers with paper clips, rustle through shopping lists, sci-fi novels, half-written letters, unpaid bills.

You leave everything the way you found it, he told me when I first started work in January, and from the way that he said it, I knew he'd set traps, that he would be watching to make sure I obeyed. Foster had just started school, and I'd been lucky to get this job: no experience, a quick GED, my only reference written by Max as a favor to Foster. So I did not touch the centerfold of Miss July which was taped to the seat of the chair, her mouth open wide, her eyes pleading. I did not move the breast-shaped coffee mug, with its pointed red nipple. But I began to look for small secret clues I could chant like a spell when I ran into Max on the street, at The Fisco where Foster likes to drink, at the main office picking up our paychecks. *His daughter won't come home to visit. His truck got repossessed.*

I sign in, pick up my radio, and begin the first of my rounds. The department store used to belong to International Harvester, and tonight I notice the bitter odor of diesel underneath the new-carpet smell of polyester and dye. I remember the gleaming combines and balers standing in rows like animals as my sister and I walked between them, holding my grandfather's hands. How badly we wanted to climb up on the tractors! But he worried that we might fall, and he kept a cautious eye on us while he talked his business with the jolly sales rep, a skinny bald man who gave us each a sucker for being so quiet, so good. That same night my grandfather died of a massive coronary, and when the harvester he'd signed for arrived a week later, no one knew what to do. Sometimes, I wonder how often I've passed over the very spot where the three of us stood, my sister and I working our tongues around our suckers until we'd melted those hard, sweet stones. At the funeral, we were lifted up to kiss my grandfather's silent cheek, but we were not afraid. We knew it was the spirit of a person—not that person's body—which mattered, which was real.

In the hot, still air I hear the whisper of fabric brushing fabric—or is it just the sound of my own breathing? Perhaps it's my grandfather's ghost, watching me pass through Household Appliances into Lingerie. I imagine him rustling between the half-slips and bras, cracking the stumps of his broken-off fingers like he always did to make me smile. Alma's husband has appeared to her twice: once on the first anniversary of his death, once when she was tempted to re-marry. My sister has seen the men who attacked her standing at the foot of her bed, in broad daylight, plain as if they were real.

"You're not being rational," Foster said, after I told him that I planned to live downstairs with Alma till he and the boys got that fence put up like they'd promised. I'd already packed an overnight bag; I had my uniform, my purse, my keys. "Marilee," he pleaded, "it's supper time." I thanked him for the reminder, and then I cooked me and Alma Swedish meatballs and green beans and fresh corn muffins. I served her in bed like she was a queen, and together we pretended that she wasn't sick, that I wasn't afraid to go back into the kitchen in case Foster came down the stairs. We could tell by the thumps and the scraping of chairs that he was starting to get angry; several times, I heard him yelling at the boys. After supper, I shot out of the house so fast that the geese blew in all directions like pieces of a thick meringue pie. By the time I'd locked myself in the truck, I could see Foster in the doorway, but I looked the other way and drove off slow, as if I couldn't care less. Foster, with his easy walk, his shoulders slumped just so. Foster with his hands in my hair, his mouth over mine, speaking my name. Foster, when I wake up dreaming of my sister, saying, *Honey, I'd never let that happen to you.*

My heavy black shoes go screek, screek, but beneath that sound I still hear the swish of fabric–a man's trouser legs swiping against each other? I reach for my radio, but then I remember the disgust of the officer the last time he showed up to find only me and the empty night air. I force myself to walk extra-slow through Sports and Recreation, past the racks of hunting rifles, the display case filled with clever hand guns, neat as a row of hairdryers. *Don't look back!* I hear my sister say, and I plan to keep right on walking until I'm safe in the windowless office, but then I hear the soft click, click of a man's light tiptoe. This is no ghost. This is no game. There is someone else in the building, and my stomach gets small and hard and tight as I think about Max's pale body pressed against the window. Again I smell that acrid odor of diesel, stronger, too strong, I realize, to be left over from the past.

As I step out into the center aisle, the bride abruptly comes to life, the skirt of her white-white gown rippling hard as if she is walking toward me. Her arms embrace the open air; her fingers are sharp, naked bones. She is smiling like something out of a fairy tale, the good witch turned evil. As her skirt lifts again, I see the oscillating fan tucked underneath, its neck clicking like a tired joint, and there's the cord poking out from under the lacy layers. I walk around behind the bride's platform and kick the plug out of the wall socket. The fan's motor grunts one last time and quits, but it's hot, still heating, melting the rubber coating off the wires. *Max,* I think, *He must have thought to scare me.* And at that thought, the bride's dress catches fire.

In a single startling moment of clarity, I understand that if the fire alarm goes off, I will not be able to explain this. I knock the bride from her pedestal, grab her by the long flow of her hair and drag her, bouncing madly behind me, toward the wide double doors at the front entrance. My keys are a wild jangle at my hips; I fumble the right one into the lock and kick the bride into the entryway. She's smoking badly now, a harsh chemical smoke, and I hold my breath as I unlock the last door. Her head pops off, rolling end over end, so I pick her up by her slender neck and throw her, feet first, into the flooded parking lot. She lands in a hiss of steam. I turn her with my foot until she's wet on all sides, I kick her, I kick her again, and by the time the last of the smoke clears away, I have decided what I want to do next. I find her head just inside the door and carry it back to the security office, where I stuff it into one of Max's desk drawers.

But it's not enough. My anger has taken hold, its own sudden fire, gloriously out of control. In Denver, half-conscious, my sister used words worse than anything the boys would ever say, words I'd seen only in the sort of magazines that Foster keeps hidden at the back of our bedroom closet. She was one long broken bone, but when I touched her cheek, she bit my hand and then kept on cursing, even as I cried. Later on, when the priest on call talked about forgiveness, Sara Beth closed her eyes. "Anger will eat you up inside," the priest had said. But now I understand how it burns us clean.

I go back out to the parking lot and get what's left of the bride's body; I wrestle her inside and down the aisle and into the security office where I arrange her, scorched and dripping, in Max's chair. I wedge his nipple mug into the melted grasp of her fingers. And then I write FUCK YOU MAX on an envelope and pin it to what's left of her chest.

Suddenly I feel calm and good, the way I do after Mass when I almost believe that things will work out right, no matter how bad they seem. The building still smells of diesel, so I prop the front doors open wide and leave them that way until the last trace of smoke is gone for good. I mop up the messy trail left by the bride's wet gown, carry her white platform into storage, rearrange the racks of clothing and put the burned-out fan in the dumpster out back. By dawn, everything looks the way it usually does, orderly and cluttered all at once. I lock up slowly, knowing it will be the last time I ever do so. I'll get another job, I tell myself, a better one. Something during the day so I can spend time with the boys—*my* boys. Maybe I'll go back to school myself, become a physician's assistant or even a nurse, someone who knows how to help other people like those counselors in Denver helped my sister.

I drive home into the sun's rising eye with my windows rolled down, the wind singing in my hair. The flood waters stretch for miles, lapping and licking, that bright, wet sound of want. When I turn down the driveway leading to the house, the truck bounces over the potholes, shaking me like a mother's scolding hand, but I hang on. It's true dawn now, the dark limbs of the trees scorching the cherry sky. The silo hums with pigeons. Mourning doves coo on the clothesline. There, on the high ground beside the house, stands the new chicken-wire fence and, within it, the sleepy flutter of geese. Balloons of every color flare from the stakes, knocking their heads in the wind. And upstairs, the light in our bedroom is shining, faint as the first morning star.

LON OTTO

A Man in Trouble

"IT WASN'T wrong to stop," I tell her. She's fallen asleep, drugged by the grief and anger in her blood, leaving me to crawl around all night on the smoldering trash of our argument.

I say, "That part wasn't wrong."

"Didn't say wrong. Worse than wrong."

"Man flags you down, a man in trouble, you don't just check your door locks and floor it."

"A white man you never seen before."

"What's that got to do with it?" A white man, I mean.

"You haven't learned a goddamn thing, have you? That man in Florida they poured gas on and burned mostly to death?"

"This wasn't . . ."

"A little boy sitting in his car seat right behind you? My little boy, my first baby, buckled into his car seat for safety? For *safety*!"

That's where it bursts into flames. I can never get past that, hard as I try. I try. "Sara," I say, "I wanted to show him we could afford to be generous, stop and listen to anyone's story. Show him what it means to *belong* somewhere."

"Well, you showed him."

* * *

I showed him. A cold, overcast afternoon, the day after Thanksgiving. As we slowed for the intersection a block away from home, a man appeared suddenly, waving his arms, cutting across the frozen boulevard to intercept us. A tall, thin, white man, forty-five, maybe fifty, in a torn nylon baseball jacket too light for the weather. A face that looked like it was made in a hurry. He forced a smile through the tangle of dirty creases as he leaned down and said something through the passenger side window. Ike, my six-year-old, made an impatient noise from the back seat. I reached over and rolled down the window.

*　　*　　*

The day before, my parents, uncles, aunts, cousin and cousins' children, and Sara's grandmother, brother, and aunt had all joined us for Thanksgiving dinner. They'd driven in from Bloomington and Richfield and Burnsville and Eagan—suburbs south of Minneapolis and St. Paul—and crowded into this tall, old house in the inner city which Sara and I had spent the past fourteen months of our lives fixing and painting.

In the big kitchen where we set the kids' places and around the mightily-extended dining room table and later in the park across the street and in the living room watching the game, there'd been a lot of joking about "the 'hood." They kept calling me "home boy," as if the term were hilarious applied to me, applied to any of us.

My cousins especially were entertained by the eccentricity of our migration back into the once-decaying neighborhood my wife's family had fled twenty years ago; the same one which my own father and his brothers, up from Missouri twenty-five years before that, had had the good sense to avoid from the start in favor of the raw, pioneer suburbs. There, if they weren't welcome, they were mostly left alone, given plenty of space to fade into the blank-lawned developments.

My father wasn't entertained. He was permanently offended by my disregard for his advice and example. He thought my judgment had been bad enough when we bought a house in Merriam Park, a decent residential neighborhood of St. Paul that was about as white and middle class as his own suburb, but fifty years older, with more urban salt to it, houses two-storied, front-porched, alleyed. Drugstores and groceries within walking distance. When we moved east from there, straight into old Selby-Dale, he was almost struck dumb. He still identified it as the ghetto he'd so brilliantly avoided. The house is only blocks away from buildings he'd watched burn on television when I was in high school. Sara grew up in the neighborhood, and her family had moved away in 1976, when things were getting really rough. Afterward, it turned around again, but not in my father's eyes.

He was there when we first spotted the house, at Rondo Days, celebrating the mostly black community that had been ripped in half by I-94 in the sixties. Sara and I had been coming ever since we moved to St. Paul, but it was a surprise that my father and mother were there. They'd parked at our house in Merriam Park, and we drove them over. It was a church thing, I think, a sister congregation had a tent, selling bakery goods or doing missionary work, I can't remember. But I do remember my father complaining about the music pounding through the park, working on a plate of ribs and catching up with a man he knew from back in St. Louis who'd somehow recognized him. The man's son mentioned there was a good house across the street about to go on the market. We went and took a look, stepping over the tangles of electric cables running down the street to amplifiers and concession trucks. The next day, I called the owner.

*   *   *

An icy wind kicked in through the open window and I caught the man's smell, not awful, but brightly metallic, as if it originated in the tarnished silver fabric of his jacket rather than coming from his body. Over his heart there was a company or team name I couldn't make out, and a little below that a fist-sized hole had been burned and melted through the nylon shell, exposing scorched filler. His fingers, hooked over the car's door, were cracked and painful looking, the color of old radishes, and the frayed elastic of his cuffs curled back from his pale, thin wrists.

He stooped into the window. "Hey, my man," he said, not as jaunty as that sounds, even from a white guy. Tense, like his vocal cords had been broken once or twice. "Seemed there wasn't anybody in the world would stop for me," he said. "I about froze."

Looking past his seamed, wind-reddened face, I could see our icy park and in the distance swings swaying crazily from the playground equipment, and empty paths and empty sidewalks and not a single car, not a single moving thing except the swings and the desolate leaves of some crabapple trees the city had planted that summer.

I was taking Ike for an overnight with one of his classmates, glad to get him out of the house, where he'd been bored and whining. I had expected that there would be kids playing in the park on this school holiday, kids who would keep him occupied. But maybe it was too cold, too dark all day, the bloated sky wanting to snow but too half-hearted to get it going. It did seem like we were the only living things for miles.

"What's the matter?"

"Accident," he said. "I hate asking for help, but I don't know what else to do. Bless you for stopping." The car shook a little in a gust of wind. The man hunched lower, drew himself deeper into the inadequate jacket. "We blown out a tire on the freeway. My wife's hurt, they got her in the emergency room. I need to get back to Hudson. Over in Wisconsin? Wife got the diabetes, and they took her to the hospital. She's waiting for me. The cops said they can't take me home since it's in Wisconsin. They can't go there. Regular, they take you home if you have trouble. All my money's at home. I got to get home so I can come pick up my wife and take care of her."

I thought for a moment about the long, empty day, but said, "I can't drive you to Hudson. I have to get this boy somewhere. We're headed the opposite direction."

He nodded, sniffed, looked at Ike, then back at me again. His eyes were watery, and what I guess you call hazel—brownish, with fugitive glints of green and yellow. It's a sad color that makes me think of a Weimeraner our neighbors owned when I was a kid.

Another blast of wind struck the car, and Ike whispered, "Dad! I'm getting cold!"

"I know, honey, hang on. Look," I said to the man, "we're going in the opposite direction. Sorry." My neck was starting to cramp from the way I was leaning over to talk with him. It made me uncomfortable, too, to see him stooped so far, a tall man. I wanted to get going, but he had a hold on my car.

He stood there looking at me, seeming to struggle with something. "Well, listen, could you at least loan me something? So I could buy a used tire to get me back home?" I must have tightened up, because he rushed along, "I can get it back to you already this afternoon. You'll have your money in an hour. I just got to get back to Hudson where my own money is. I got enough, I'm working." The wind hit us again, billowing his jacket and riffling the pages of a paperback I had on the dashboard. After dropping Ike off for his overnight, I was going to a coffee shop and read for an hour or so.

"Dad! I'm freething!" Ike had a loose tooth that he was working on, and sometime he was hard to understand.

"Get in," I said to the man, "so we can close the window. Get out of the wind for a minute."

He scrambled in and cranked up the window. "Man," he said, "it is *bitter*! I like to die out there." He told me that he was a trucker, he'd just begun working for 3M. He would leave his pager with me for security, he said. He took the pager out of his jacket pocket and handed it to me. I took it reluctantly, looked at it. There was no 3M logo or anything like that. But would there be? "I don't have ID," he said. "My wallet's in my good jacket, in my car. I took it off when I had to get out and crawl around. If I'm leaving you my pager, you *know* I have to get that back, it's part of my job. You know what it's like to need a job."

I sat there, half-listening, and tried to think my way through a sludge of feelings that had risen up around me. He was probably trying to scam me. I'd felt that right away, must have felt it even before I rolled down the window. Except how do you ever know? Really *know*.

* * *

It was a familiar feeling. The first week we were in our house an old woman I'd seen around the neighborhood came by, asking for work. She needed to make five or ten dollars to buy food for herself and her granddaughter, she said. She'd do anything, they were hungry. Didn't we have boxes to unpack? Floors to scrub? We did, of course, have boxes to unpack, more than I could stand to think about, and we hadn't even begun to address the question of the floors. But not wanting a stranger in the house when we were in such chaos, I loaned her ten dollars and she promised to repay me as soon as she got paid by a lady she'd cleaned for that week. "I'm Maryanne!" she said. "Everybody know me around here, son. I live right around the corner, down Marshall."

Saturday, she came by with a personal check for twenty-five dollars to show me. "I'm taking this to the Unbank," she announced. "I'll buy some groceries and pay you back, both!" An hour later she returned with the check, her face distorted by confusion and anger. "They charging nine dollars just to cash it at the Unbank!" she cried. "What that leave me and my granddaughter, once I pay you off? Hardly squat!" Her voice dropped, became something small and pathetic. "I wonder, do you have a bank, sir?" (Sir. She was as old as my grandma.) "Could you possibly cash this check for me?" Before I could answer, she dug into a bulging vinyl purse and pulled out a state identification card, which she thrust at me, proving she was herself. I felt blood suddenly roaring in my ears, rage against the Unbank and the crazy bind she was in because she was too poor to have a bank account. I had her endorse the check over to me and gave her fifteen dollars.

A week later, while we were having supper, Maryanne came by, ecstatic, and showed me a check for eighty-five dollars her ex-husband had sent her from Illinois. "I can pay you back," she said, "and I'm going to buy me some *meat*. I'm headed down to the Unbank this minute and then I'm going to pay you back in full and then I'm going to buy me some *meat*." I reminded her that she'd already paid me back in full. She looked at me strangely, as if I were pulling her leg, but finally accepted it and put her skinny, loose-skinned arms around me in a quick embrace, then practically ran down our porch stairs and off to the Unbank.

At ten o'clock, just as the news came on, the doorbell rang. It was Maryanne again, clutching the check and a file folder. She made me look through it–certificates from community education classes in typing and accounting and household management and some letters from welfare and other papers I couldn't at a glance identify. She was agitated, almost in tears. "Unbank won't cash this damn check," she yelled. "Out of town, they say. It got to be local, or they won't do nothing." Her voice sank sickeningly again. "I wonder, sir, could you find it in your heart to take this check and write me out a local one they'll cash? I'll bless you all my life. I *got* to have this money. It's about the first thing that son of a bitch ever did good for me, he used to beat me, I had no choice, I *had* to leave him. I stuck with him nineteen years!"

She'd told me this about him many times. Sara came down to see what was going on, and Maryanne repeated the story until I finally stopped her and said, yes, I'd write her a local check. "Bless you, sir!" she said, "I'll pray to Jesus for you every day of my life! Both of you! Jesus bless both of you!" Twenty minutes later, the phone rang. It was the Unbank, calling to see if I had really written a check for eighty-five dollars to a Maryanne George. Yes, I said, of course I had, wasn't my name on it? I was barely able to choke down the anger I felt surging back up my throat like bile.

"That's the last of Maryanne, I think," Sara said, when I had hung up.

"Maybe," I admitted, looking at the pale blue check from Solomon George, Batavia, Illinois, with the memo, "for Gchild's Needs (Raye)."

"Why shouldn't it be good, though?" I asked.

Sara shrugged, "It's okay, baby. You're a decent man. Just so long as you know how it is."

"She looks so much like my little Grandma Magee."

"I know, baby. Come to bed."

It *was* the last we saw of her, though the check returned in a few weeks, stamped "Account Closed." I felt bad for Maryanne, as if the man had struck her one more time. Later, there was the man who'd come by offering to paint our garage and never returned from Sears, where I'd sent him with twenty dollars for primer, and the boy from down the block who borrowed a fishing rod I never saw again and who once scammed Ike out of five dollars birthday money, and the stream of kids selling overpriced candy and bad light bulbs. "You're like that brother from another planet," Sara said to me. "I bet they can't believe you're really one of us."

"I'll send those Walkathon kids to you, girl," I said. "You can carve up their lying butts for them."

"That's it," she said. "That's it. Recall, I'm from this neighborhood before it got nice again." She didn't really mind, though. She didn't mind that. But this white man. Why should that have mattered? We're hard enough on each other.

*   *   *

I said to him, "Look, you don't know this area. Why don't I drive you to a filling station. There's one at Selby and Fisk. You can get out of the cold. Call somebody."

He shook his head. "I got nobody to call," he said. "The wife is all I got, and she's lying there in the emergency room wondering what's taking me so long. What I need is just thirty dollars to buy me a used tire that'll get me home." He looked at me with that face that seemed to have ropes twisted underneath the skin, then stared out the window.

"I know what you're thinking," he said. "You're thinking, 'Who is this honky? Why should I help out this white mother fucker?'"

"Hey." I gestured angrily back at Ike, who was sitting there so quietly with his finger in his mouth, wiggling that tooth, the man might have forgotten about him.

He twisted around in his seat. "Sorry, fella, pardon my French." Ike just looked at him, and the man turned back to me. "Oh, man, I'm so upset, I don't know what I'm doing. I just really need that thirty dollars long enough to buy a tire and get home and get my money and come back. It'd take two hours, tops. You'd have my pager, man! You'd have my livelihood in your hand. You know what a job means to a man."

"I don't even think I have that much," I said. "Thirty dollars, I don't carry a lot of money around with me. I was just running my boy over to his friend's house."

"Couldn't you go to a cash machine?" he asked. "Couldn't you do that?"

I laughed, "No, I can't do that." I could feel Ike's impatience boiling against the back of my neck. When I turned to give him a reassuring smile, he mouthed something to me that I couldn't make out, probably "Let's go!"

"We will," I said to him. "Don't worry. We'll be going in a minute."

The man was trying to scam me, that was what I was still thinking. But I felt the need for the truth. If he was lying, I had to know it, I don't know why, nail him to it. And if not, I had to help him.

"Listen," I said, watching his reaction, "maybe I should take you back to the hospital, see how your wife is doing."

"Dad." A tight whisper I chose to ignore.

"That's where I just come from," the man said. "I walked all this way from there in this bad weather. I ain't going back until I get what I have to get. She'd think I was crazy."

"Your car's where, again?"

"Side of the freeway."

"Close to the Dale exit? Farther downtown?"

"It's where I left it," he said. "It ain't going nowhere, shape it's in."

I could have driven along the freeway and seen if it was there, but what then? "How about if I just drive you to the Phillips 66 on Selby, we can see how much they'd charge you for a used tire."

"No," he said, "that would be too much. I know a guy who'll sell me one for thirty dollars, just got to get the money together." He scoured his fingers into his shadowed eye sockets as if trying to root out migraine. He said, "I'm not asking for charity, man, just a little faith, a little human trust. You won't be out a penny, I swear. Loan me what I need and I swear to God you'll have it back before suppertime." He was getting sweaty and miserable, and I was torn between feeling that I had him, I'd just about nailed him, and that I was no better than the bastards who humiliated Maryanne George. He said, "You've seen trouble yourself sometime, I bet. You people know what it feels like, everybody thinks they can yank you around, right, man? Am I right?"

"Yeah," I said, "you're right."

"Dad!"

"Hang on, Ike. I'm trying to think, how can we help here." I turned to the man, wanting to gauge his expression. "I don't have much on me, over what I need for food, but say if I loan you that and give you a lift to the guy who's going to sell you the tire?"

He was silent for a minute, staring ahead. "Okay," he said finally. "How much can you loan me?"

I put the car in gear and swung around the corner. Motion seemed to clear my head a little. "So where is this place? A filling station?" There was still no traffic on Marshall, not a car had driven past while we were talking. I cruised along at a walk. He said something I didn't catch. "What? You got an address?" I was feeling better. I was moving, getting someplace.

"Other side of the freeway," he said. "Couple blocks north of University." He'd grown quiet, broody.

"Cross on Dale? Western? What?"

"Huh? Dale, I guess." He wasn't happy, but then the car's acceleration seemed to affect him, too, and without becoming any more cheerful or animated he slid into a kind of mechanical patter. "Knew that old retread was going to blow before it happened, knew it in my guts, but I was just praying it would hold till we got back to Hudson. Traffic-side front, bang, near dragged me into a semi. Big old Peterbilt. Slammed over onto the shoulder to miss it, good thing I know my way behind the wheel. Cop come by, he seen my wife was hurt, so he took her along to the emergency room while I went for a tire. I know this guy who's got one for thirty dollars. That's all I need, thirty dollars, it won't cost you a nickel. The cops, they can take you home, but not if you're from another state. Wish I lived here, I'd already be home." The machinery of his story seemed to run down. He whistled a few bars of something mournful, then turned to me. "You from here? This always been your neighborhood?"

"Yeah," I said, and half waited for Ike's picky correction. I glanced back at him. Strapped like a fighter pilot into a child seat he thought he was too big for, he met my glance with blank seriousness. He'd pulled his backpack up onto his lap, and one arm was slipped through the bungee cord that held his sleeping bag rolled. "My wife grew up here," I said. We stopped at a red light. The man was looking around now as if he were searching for a landmark. I looked ahead and saw what I should have thought of before, might have, except that another building still stands there in my mind's eye. "If you're lost, here's the place to get directions." I pointed across the street. "Might find your own cop."

I studied the man's rough profile as he looked across the intersection at the beige, blank-faced district police station that had been slapped up against the Lendways Lounge around the time they tore down the Belmont Club, with its "nood lunch" sign. The city had bought out the Belmont and the Notorious Faust and the nameless peep shows and porn shops near the corner and pushed the prostitutes a few blocks north, all to make room for respectable businesses that somehow still haven't materialized. Only new business I can think of, if you don't count the police station, is The Exstacy House, four blocks west, selling videos and more.

I had only to cross University, slide in among the shoals of cop cars that I knew must be parked behind the temporary-looking station house, and let the rest of it unravel away from me, outside my car, beyond my control. He'd get help, social service referral, maybe, or walk away. However it went, it wouldn't matter. We wouldn't even have to know. I'd say something to Ike about Officer Friendly, drive him to his overnight, then seek out the warmth of a coffee house and let the gray backwash of Thanksgiving Day evaporate around me.

"I ain't lost," the man said, expressionless. "Turn right here, couple blocks."

"Dad?"

I turned right, drove a block east, past Hong Phat Inc. and Auto Max, and pulled over to the curb. There was a tire place across the street that I'd forgotten about, Fred's Tires, big B.F. Goodrich sign. "How about this?" I asked. "They got retreads here."

He didn't even look. "Can't afford a place like that. I don't need just a tire, I need a whole wheel. Cop told me not to drive with that cut tire, it'd wreck the rim. It did, too. Anyway, we got it arranged, guy's going to sell me a used tire and rim."

I felt the warmth of grim confirmation like liquor burning inside me. I couldn't let it go. I needed to get to the end of it, prove something about him and us. Anything less felt unbearable.

"So, where?" I asked, pulling out again into the thin stream of traffic.

"Anywhere along here is fine," he said. "I can walk the rest of the way. I just need the money for that tire." He seemed down and disheartened, as if he were losing hope.

I didn't want him to lose hope. As I kept driving, past the thickening concentrations of Asian businesses, smoke from a kind of low fever seemed to mix intoxicatingly with the man's metallic smell. "We've come this far," I said. "Tell me where to go, we'll see can your guy give you a deal on that tire. Where do I turn? Mackubin? Arundel? Western?"

"Western." I turned north on Western Avenue, and again he said, "Here, this is close enough. I can get off here."

And I suddenly realized that he might be scared, some nigger had him in the car and wouldn't let him out. I said, "No, I'll take you all the way."

"Dad," Ike mumbled, working on his tooth again, "we tole Ethan's mom we be there."

"Hang on," I said, "We're almost finished with this." The steering wheel felt like a toy in my grip. I wished that Ike was getting it, how things had swung around. I drove slowly, letting the guy look for his tire seller. "Is this a store we're looking for?" I asked. "Filling station?" He shook his head but said nothing and wouldn't look at me.

Following his muttered, monosyllabic directions, right, left, right again, we were soon beyond the ragged commercial fringe of University Avenue and into a depressing neighborhood of asbestos siding and sagging porches, not just deserted, as our own neighborhood had seemed on a cold, dark afternoon, but abandoned. The rows of houses were gap-toothed, mismatched. This was the slum my father imagined when he thought about where we'd moved. Cracked asphalt driveways led past empty foundation sockets overgrown with brush and straggly saplings and bent, frost-burned weeds. One-story development boxes were spliced in between tall, old wrecks. The trees, where there were trees, looked like they might have been used for hangings.

"Here," he said. "It's right up the alley. You can let me off here." His voice had become dark, out of focus.

There was no alley. I drove around the block and turned east and found a dead-end alley running north and south. "Here?"

"Yeah." He didn't seem to care. I turned down the alley. About halfway into the middle of the block, among backyards that looked like they belonged to some failed industry, not houses where people lived, there was a caved-in garage, with an old Pontiac parked on the gravel and dead grass next to it. "Here," the man said without enthusiasm. And then, as an afterthought, "That's the car we're going to get the tire from." He didn't look at it. A wooden telephone pole leaning over the Pontiac's scabby vinyl roof seemed to have been chewed on, in inefficient fury, by some animal with teeth evolved for tearing flesh.

I sat there for a moment behind the wheel, cold dissatisfaction turning slowly in my belly. What had I been expecting? An overalled mechanic shaking my hand? We'd come this far. I'd obligated myself to put some money into this man's red hands. "Well, you'll need my address, I suppose," I said. Rummaging in the dashboard well I found a ball-point and a pencil and an expired Domino's coupon. Free cokes, free twisty breads. I tore the coupon in two and wrote my name and address and phone number on the back of one half while the man wrote on the back of the other.

"I'll give you my work number, too," he said. He was like a machine, his mind working on something else.

We exchanged the torn coupon halves, and I read what he'd written, Donny Jimson, and two telephone numbers, one with a 715 area code. "That's Hudson?" I asked. He said it was and got out of the car, leaving the door open.

"I think I'll just stay in the car," Ike said. He wasn't wiggling that tooth anymore. His sleeping bag was piled up against his back pack, you could barely see him.

"Sure," I said to him, "this won't take but a minute." I hadn't been thinking about getting out of the car, myself, but now it seemed awkward not to. I walked around the car. "So," I said, "where does your man live?" He gestured vaguely to the back of one of the houses, clapboard weathered to bare gray wood, windows puffy with sheets of cloudy plastic frayed and snapping in the hard wind. It must have been left over from last winter, maybe longer.

I could feel how close we were to something. The man was waiting.

Donny Jimson was waiting for his money. I took out my wallet. "I'll need about forty," he said.

"You said thirty. All along, you're saying thirty."

"Thirty for the tire. I need to get gas, too. Tire's no good to me without gas."

Standing there in the cold wind, sun dropping toward the old roof tops, I felt dizzy, drugged, blood pushing too hard behind my eyes. I hadn't gotten anywhere. I was just as certain as ever I was being scammed, just as incapable of saying forget it, turning my back on a man in trouble. I opened the wallet and rummaged a little, trying not to be obvious about how much was in it. We'd been paid before Thanksgiving. I took out a ten and a twenty. There was another ten, a five, some ones. I held the thirty dollars in my hand. "You're not going to cheat me, are you?"

"No, man, I'm like you, I'm a Christian. I know what trouble is." He looked down at the bills in my hand. "Couldn't you spare another ten, just to get me home and back? I really need forty."

Standing, he was half a head taller than me, even with his slouch, and younger than I'd thought. It was his bad teeth made him look old. Wallet in one hand, ten and twenty in the other, I felt something pulsing angrily, stubbornly, behind my eyes. I said, "I think maybe even thirty is crazy."

Blood darkened his face. "What is this? Why are you yanking me around this way?"

"Me? Shit, man, you say thirty, then you say forty." I shoved the two bills forward at him. He took them in silence and held them as if they were some spoiled thing. "There," I said. "That's the best I can do for you. I'm really going to need it back before tonight."

He shook his head, his face going purple. "Without gas, what good is the tire?" His arms lifted in a sudden gesture of frustration against the lowering sky.

"Ten dollars buy a hell of a lot of gasoline."

"Well," he said, "I need a lot of gasoline."

I stared at his dirty, badly put together face in disbelief and anger, then at the back of the wretched house, now sunk in shadows. "Maybe we should go in and talk with your tire guy," I said. "See can't we get you a better deal, so some be left over for all that gasoline you need."

He looked at me. "Maybe we should."

*   *   *

I wake before dawn and get dressed, with just enough light to see Sara's dark form lying tangled in what might be sleep, but looks nothing like rest. On the way to the bathroom I pass Ike's room, his empty bed, his toys still spread out all over from the mess he and his cousins made there on Thanksgiving Day. He should be downstairs watching television at this hour, cramming in his full allotment of Saturday cartoons. He's not, of course. It's quiet in the living room.

I make coffee, have no appetite for breakfast, try to work in my study. It's still too early to go. They won't have him ready for me. But I have to get out of the house, which is unbalanced and disorienting now, so I walk for a while.

The house where Sara lived when she was a girl is only a block away, though then it was three blocks west of where it stands now. Half the houses on this street were somewhere else, then—big two and three story frame houses that were moved when they plowed the interstate through or when they built the Control Data warehouse that now houses a multiplex of three grade schools, or in some other spasm of urban renewal. One of those schools is Ike's. Our house and the really old stone house next to it, pre-Civil War, where there were still ancient apple trees when Sara was little, were here all along, but the next three were uprooted and moved in. The row houses across the street were built about fifteen years ago when they'd bulldozed everything on that block, and the Martin Luther King Center is about that old, I guess, and the Lung Association building stands where Sara went to school.

Still, the neighborhood has a settled feel to it, solid, homey. Last year, when I built a fence to protect a bed of irises descended from corms brought north from Kansas by my mother, I built it low, neighborly, so passers by could talk across it comfortably. Some of these satisfactions were in the long, eloquent grace I spoke on Thanksgiving Day. I can't remember much of it, only isolated, well-turned phrases that now seem thin as eggshells.

I wait till nine o'clock and then I can't stand it any more and get into the car. I have to see my son. I'm thinking he won't be ready yet. It's earlier than they said they'd have him ready. But I have to see him.

We agreed that I'd pick him up around ten. However, he has his pajamas packed and his sleeping bag rolled when I get there, and before we're out the door he whispers, "How did it go?"

"What?"

"You know."

"Yeah."

* * *

It was thirty-three dollars, in the end. While I was hesitating, Ike had called to me from the car, "Dad, I have to pee!" and I gave it up. I gave the man the three ones from my wallet and said, "That's got to be it," and he turned and walked away, past the house, heading west when I lost sight of him. On the way to his friend's house finally, Ike asked me was the man going to give me the money back, and I said I didn't know. Maybe not. Ike said he thought the man wouldn't.

* * *

"I guess he scammed me," I admit now, as Ike dumps his stuff into the back seat. "You were right. He hasn't brought the money back."

And Ike finally breaks down. He cries out, "I told you! He was ugly. He could have hurt me. Couldn't you see how he looked?"

"He was furious with me," I tell Sara after we've put Ike to bed, and add hastily, "as he had every right to be." The house is no longer heeled over sickeningly by the shadow of disaster, though we have a ways to go before we can rest comfortably. What nags at me is that, even knowing how justified he was, how dangerous my niggling stubborness had been for both of us, I couldn't help trying to correct him. Said, you can't judge somebody bad for being ugly or wearing nasty clothes. And he just shouted at me, "I know that! Everybody knows that." So I shut up then. "I'm just glad he didn't see it as a race thing," I tell her. "It wasn't a race thing."

"That so?" Then Sara is silent for a long time, a silence I brace my heart against. Finally she speaks. She says to me, "You're a good man. You can't help that. Otherwise, you wouldn't be in my house, don't mention in my bed. But you, by God, cannot afford to be a fool. None of us so prosperous we can afford that. Not in this world. Not in this country. None of us."

ROSA SHAND

Sophie Was the King

GIRLS, OF COURSE, weren't Tsetse Flies. They weren't even Warthogs—
they were scared of things. It was the boys who organized the war between the Tsetse Flies and Warthogs, so it was the girls who chartered
The Wildebeest, Players, No Boys Allowed. The girls let Sophie in.
Sophie had scabby everything. She sucked her thumb and everybody
thought her ideas were a baby's, but Sophie read fairy tales and knew
ogre names and magic-sounding chants, and the Wildebeests were having trouble thinking up tantalizing scenes. Now they wrote a play.

The coup interrupted before they got the show premiered but The
Wildebeests No Boys Allowed understood a play went on—in spite of
massacres and shellings and no lights, no water, no petrol—and, anyway, they decided the coup was good. Kasubi View people were
strolling around outside asking where the war was and they'd rope in
an audience. They only had to change a line or two.

You could hear the real war all around you. Tanks were rumbling
and shells were bursting. You thought it was a Ugandan holiday. It
turned out to be a holiday because you couldn't go anywhere. You am-
bled in the sunshine. If you had good binoculars you could see across
the valley—people were crammed on tanks and Peugeot-tops. They
were firing machine guns and drinking waragi and waving palms. If
you couldn't find your binoculars, you watched smoke in banana trees
or sniffed sulphur in the frangipani. The Hungarian veterinarian said
those gun volleys were from howitzers. Will was nine and American
and he said, "Don't be a bubble-headed boobie, you can't tell how-

54

itzers from hand grenades," but that was what you said to girls, so Will said that to Sophie. Sophie and Amy were his sisters, but Sophie was the one who stared and sucked her thumb and never tried to get things right. Perry Wade, the seven-foot adventurer from the Isle of Man, said the shelling came from Wandegeya—which was the teeming settlement at the foot of the hill behind the Arab mosque. That was where they brewed the waragi. Ahmed Enyanju said No, the shooting came from Bat Valley, Bat Valley being the precipice beside the Indian mosque where bats hung in the eucalyptus trees and swarmed when the sky turned red. When the sky turned blue again, bougainvillea blazed out gold, and turquoise birds sang sweetly, so all in all you didn't believe it was a war. Anna—Anna was the mother of Will, Sophie, and Amy—Anna had seen old movies. She kept thinking wars were gray.

This was on the grounds of Makerere College, which was The University of East Africa in Kampala. If you didn't chase dogs or chickens or children, you didn't know your neighbors when the coup broke out. But when it did, you learned what you'd been missing. The neighbors were Ugandans and English and Indians and Americans and Nigerians and Hungarians and Norwegians and Kenyans and Germans and a lot of Jewish ex-South Africans. Canadians ran the Philosophy Department. Only doctors had telephones. The wires to those weren't normally connected. If you were the sort who thought of batteries, and if you'd dug up, at Patel's Electrics, the right size and the enormous quantities it took, you could switch on Radio Uganda for the flavor of things.

Or, when you had an enterprising son, like Will, you could make an attempt at listening. Will bought Sophie's two-inch radio for fourteen shillings. To turn it off you stuck a birthday candle in a hole, and if you caught words in the shrieks while it was on, the words were the title of the leader. When the brand new announcer gave that title the required respect, it took half a minute of air time and saved anybody from thinking up news. They just said "Uganda's Military Head of State His Excellency Major General Idi Amin Dada," and then a spot about the glorious victory of the people, and then they added another honorary phrase to Uganda's Military Head of State Major General Idi Amin Dada, like "Our illustrious eminent emancipator Uganda's Military Head of State Major General Idi Amin Dada," and you chanted the syllables over and over and over and that was updated coup news.

If you wanted more detailed instruction, you wandered up and down in sunshine and in and out of the hibiscus hedges. You spoke with Russians who had only frowned before, and everybody looked after everybody else, or Anna had the feeling that they did, the way they ran to tell you where to get a tetrapack of milk. It was a communal and a happy and a very educational time.

It was the Wildebeests Players No Boys Allowed who turned out to be the sneaky ones. Even the Tsetse Flies got in on some of their fishiness. Anna found out it had something to do with Sophie. She got worried. Sophie was sticky from sucked thumbs. Will made ugh faces if, by accident, he touched her. He'd hide snakes in her bed and tell her she was eating Number Two. But now Will left that off. Anna noted the way he watched his withdrawn sister, and she got genuinely scared. She asked.

Will said, "Nothing's going on." He was truculent the way he said it, like it was hard for him to get it out.

Amy was six and three-quarters. She said, "It's a very, very, very big secret."

Will said, "Shut up, Amy."

Amy said, "I know a bigger secret—the pork man has a brother who knows somebody who's seen a man with half a head."

Sophie, with a sudden squush, took her thumb out of her mouth and said, "There's a person on Kasubi View with magic boots. They can turn you into anything you want to be."

If Sophie had been a three-year-old, Anna would have smiled. But Sophie was eight. Anna didn't smile. She looked at Sophie. Sophie's hair was almost white, but mostly she saw scabs on Sophie's nose and understood: No wonder the child is scabs and cuts and bruises, she lives with trolls and fairies. She never sees where she is walking. She looks for magic potions in hollowed-out tree trunks. Anna's chest tightened. She needed to keep round, bruised-up, pug-nosed Sophie in her lap.

Will and Amy were thin and had straight, brown hair and sharp-cut features. They spoke emphatically. Sophie didn't seem to belong in Will and Amy's family, though being born when she was, she was jammed between these two as if between two granite slabs. It was Kai who tried to see where Sophie's eyes had gone.

Kai was Scottish-Ghanaian. At Wandegeya he'd seen a man cut off a woman's breast. Kai collected bullets and Sophie looked at the bullets when he held his palm out. Kai showed all his objects to Sophie when Will was somewhere else–but Sophie didn't care about coup objects. Her thumb stayed in her mouth. Kai twisted around to see what Sophie could be looking at. When Sophie was absorbed, you couldn't help but look–you felt left out. But neither Kai nor Anna ever saw what Sophie saw.

Boy-children now, observed Anna, had clear values. With Will, nobody counted but people who did daring things. Will and his friend Mengo invited a lot of people to the Tsetsie-Warthog war long before the coup. Their side was, of course, The Tsetse Flies. You could spot them by the cocky way they held their heads and by the elephant hair they tied around their necks. Mostly the Tsetses Flies perpetrated their atrocities on girls who didn't count, like Sophie, or on the "huh-huhs". Huh-huhs, as a generalization, were plump and freckled English girls who had to go in and sit at tables with their mothers in the middle of the afternoon and who had to take baths before it got dark and who didn't allow boys in the trees outside their bathroom windows.

Amy knew, she said, "a secreter atrocity" than boys in trees. It was from a vaguely tragic past. She'd learned legends of Kasubi View. Now Amy made everybody sneak around on snaky paths so a certain six-toed gardenboy would not see them–that gardenboy was going to whack their toes off with his poisoned scythe. The origins of this darkness Anna found out only decades later, when Kasubi View had vanished, when they were all on far-off continents and it was very late at night and Amy decided that Will–thirty, and lost somewhere in the Alaskan tundra–was safe at last from the poisonous scythe of the six-toed gardenboy.

Now the two-faced Players gave the Tsetsies Flies a purpose. Wildebeests were helpless without tools of persuasion, so they asked the Tsetsies to roam Kasubi View with hoes and scythes and, by this means, corral an audience.

The corralled ones folded themselves on mats, or leaned against flame trees, in the Enyanju's garden. Anna sat with Fatima Enyanju. She listened to the tanks and howitzers and she inspected sky–you wanted to know what was cloud and what was smoke. She was not waiting with an easy mind. She knew these child beasts were ganging up on Sophie. She knew the Wildebeests would expose her Sophie in front of everyone and Sophie would suck her thumb and think she was being a fine and funny clown.

The stage for the Wildebeests No Boys Allowed was the top of a terrace. Anna recognized the curtain. It was her own Indian bedspread tied between two jacaranda trees but with a sorry opening for play-seeing—none at all—because the curtain didn't slide. The eight-year-old Odaybea popped out from underneath it. Odaybea was American, born in Nigeria—her parents at the time were renouncing colonial names. The watchers laughed because Odaybea had on a baby dress so short it came to her crotch and she had a big red bow-ribbon in her hair. Elizabeth slid out around the spread. Elizabeth was genuine Nigerian. She had piles of beads around her neck and purple and orange scarves around her waist and wrists and ankles. It looked like Odaybea's and Elizabeth's lips were moving, but people kept talking and the tanks kept rumbling and Odaybea kept scratching her mosquito bites. Elizabeth shouted, "Why can't I keep my head?" The watchers didn't care sufficiently. They believed the tanks were on Makerere, right around the hill. Men trotted off. Odaybea couldn't decide what she should do. She scratched a while longer and escaped behind the curtain and got shoved out again, where she vowed to save her mother's head.

Metal burst. Something exploded. The watchers jumped. Babies cried. Soldiers! For a moment they thought it was soldiers—before the curtain shook. Now they smiled and were embarrassed for themselves. Anna felt the edginess around her, and then a creature yanked the curtain to the ground. It was a stocking-headed beast with polka-dot knee-britches and massive bloated gestures. It strode on stage, sliced the air with a plastic sword and roared, "Oh my people, your blatant immanent liberator has emerged. Oh my people, your lustrious mancipator has burst from his cocoon. Your glistening savior has come to waft you upward, ever, ever upward, and also to check you give the name the honor it is due we have invented some spying machines. You must repeat the name eternally and I forbid some tacky shortening. I am your blatant lustrious immanent glorious liberator mancipator savior Uganda's Military Head of State Major General Idi Amin Dada. Say it every bit or I'll lop off your head."

Anna's mouth hung open, in shock and happiness and fear. She'd spied her own boots on this liberator, and a scab. But she did not know this 'mancipated child—and she was not prepared for satire—shouted satire. Kasubi View was not so safe as they pretended and Sophie never heard of politics. Anna, and the jittery audience around her, studied this foreign imprudent creature. Anna dared not move to stop her child.

Odaybea popped onto the stage. Her legs looked ten feet long under her baby dress. She said, "Please, Sir, would you be so kind as not cut off my mother's head? Please, my gaudy mancipator, please Sir Idi."

The mancipator spun around. He bellowed, "I am your blatant lustrious immanent glorious liberator mancipator savior Uganda's Military Head of State Major General Idi Amin Dada and you dare say gaudy Idi. Off with your head."

Odaybea ducked and screamed, "I meant gorgeous Idi." The sword knocked off Odaybea's bow. A change came over her liberator. He picked up the bow-ribbon. He stared at it and rubbed it in on his stockinged cheek and smiled and stuck it on his stocking-head. He peered at Odaybea as if he saw into the child. He went soft, thoughtful. He began to stroke his bound-up chin, rub his mouth, look up through smoke at the circling hawks. Suddenly he dropped his arm and smiled down at the child. He said, "This is a problem. You, my sweetpea—you have given me beauty." He patted the bow on his head. "But your mother—she gives me a stomach ache. She never cleans her room—her floor is littered with underpants and Bibles."

Anna drew her breath in. The laughing she heard was uncertain. These were Alec's words—her husband's, Sophie's father's. She had, at one time, been studying translations. She now, at this time, felt not at ease with her daughter. While Sophie, the father-husband-mancipator, seemed to have sucked stage ease for milk.

The liberator froze, in character, and let the laughing settle before he spoke again. He said, "And what is more, my pumpkinpie, what is more, if you listen you will know the reason your mother's sorry head is such an obstacle—I will reveal to you a very ingratiating secret."

Odaybea grinned and squunched her shoulders up and said, "I like secrets."

The liberator said, "We all like secrets, honeybunch. But this one, now this one, you must promise me you won't tell anybody this one. I may desire your mother's head, but I do not desire your mother's shame."

Odaybea crinkled her nose and said, "Tell me a secret, tell me a secret."

The mancipator put both hands on his sword hilt, rested on it like it was a walking stick, leaned back, and said, "This is very difficult for me to say, but—but sugarpie, do you know, when Mister Silky comes to dinner—your mother *never* wears a bra."

The corralled ones gasped before they howled. This style from an infant! Anna knew the line too well because Alec didn't whisper well when they were fighting. Lord, what child was she sheltering? She prayed the Hungarian had never heard her wretched children call him Mr. Silky. She was glad she was in the front of this crowd where people couldn't see her face.

The eminent emancipator said, "But, my little pipkin, I have a plan. All I want—it's to sacrifice myself for my beloved people. My people have only to prove their worthiness, as you have to, my child. Let me meditate a moment and I will tell you how to manufacture valor." The savior strode across the stage, lost in speculation, until he slapped his knee, said, "Ah-ha" and roared, "Now my little cabbage—if you want your mother's ratty twitty head, you must bear to me, on the stroke of twelve midnight, under the sacred eucalyptus tree at the highest point of Kololo hill on the first full moon, the curly horns of an albino wildebeest."

Anna dared look up again—her child was safely back in the fairy woods where she belonged.

When the blatant illustrious liberator Uganda's Military Head of State Major General Idi Amin Dada came out around the guava bush to take his bow, the clapping audience jumped up and shouted Bravo. Anna forgave this emancipator. Her flesh, as a matter of fact, went goose-pimply and her cheeks got wet while the liberator never dropped his role nor glanced at her. Imperious, he waved mere Wildebeests to the top of the bank and disappeared himself. When the clappers yelled, "Encore! Encore!" Uganda's Military Head of State sauntered leisurely onto the terrace, stroked his stockinged cheek, caught a flash of an idea, ordered the audience to build a mountain of Smarties and aniseed balls—he flourished his sword to show how high—for all the hungry and sick and starving orphans on Kasubi View, and when he saw the mountain they would have a further episode in the underbelly life of their lustrous mancipator. He flourished his sword and he vanished back of the guava bush.

At once, as if he had been bursting with the news, Perry Wade, the seven-foot adventurer, reached the top of the stage-bank with one step. He'd heard the BBC—it was Obote's Special Forces holding out.

The listeners were jolted back to fretting: Were the British right? Had Obote been worse than this Amin would be? Was this coup good or bad? Perry announced it was the Special Forces who'd blown up the house by Nakasero School. No school tomorrow. The children jumped and shouted and next day had another play. They didn't need the Tsetsie hoes to round up an audience.

Odaybea, in this jerry-built new episode, worried about her mother's head and worried some more about what would befall the land. Then the mancipator burst out—the wheedling noises took life. He leapt down the terrace. He strutted through the audience. He lusted for harem, eyed Leah—Leah was his ayah. He strolled slowly around this woman who had raised "that sniveling Sophie." He inspected her. Leah stood in her long kiganda dress and hid her face. Leah's dress style—it meant a scarf tied kiganda fashion round her fanny—made her hip spread seem gigantic. The lustrious liberator said, "Nope, won't do, hips too little." Leah laughed into her hands. The gaudy Idi spied his mother, drew back, and twisted off, dismissing her. "I need a much more scrumptious-tasting woman," he said. The watchers threw hibiscus blossoms at him. Sophie was indomitable. She had burst from her cocoon. Sophie never sucked her thumb again.

*   *   *

Anna sat on her porch step. Amy was beside her with a book. The prism hanging from the beam was scattering gold and the lateness of the afternoon made Amy's skin and all the roofs and objects honey-colored. Frangipani hung sweet in the air. It was eerily quiet. No shelling. No distant motors. No people puttering in yards and kitchen doorways. The groundbirds' shadows stretched across the grass. The crickets were sleepy. Anna heard one isolated gunshot—and then Vivaldi, the Horn Concerto. That sudden burst was like the quick bright sound of happiness, gratuitous happiness. She grinned and Amy laughed. The power had popped on. The record had been playing when the power went dead days ago and here it was exploding from machines.

Anna twisted round to check the far side of the house, the bank-top patch of jacaranda trees. The sky behind the trees was orange. One tree limb did not look like a tree limb, more like a plastic sword, and Sophie was hanging on the high end of that sword—about to plunge twelve feet. Kai was behind her. He looked nervous. Anna stood up quickly. She called her daughter with a strained, pinched voice. Sophie cocked her head at her mother. She said, "Don't be a huh-huh."

Anna said, "Huh-huhs are alive."

Sophie said, "If you are afraid you are not alive."

Anna said, "Please, sometimes, be afraid. Please. Like now."

Sophie narrowed her eyes, looked down to consider her distance from the ground, flashed her dimples round on Kai, looked back at her mother, said "Kale" (that was *okay* in Luganda) and settled for standing up, jumping up and down along the limb, no-holding-on-allowed.

*   *   *

The nights were unnerving. Explosions rattled the windows. Most undermining were the waves of drunken shouting that pulsed from Wandegeya. In the day Perry Wade showed up–he'd reached Alec in Nairobi. Alec had inveigled his way onto the first flight coming to Entebbe, tomorrow morning. But, he'd instructed, if something were to happen and they had to flee, they were to go with Perry. Anna knew his worry was excessive. It wouldn't come to fleeing–this commotion was more or less tribal. She had petrol. She heard the Entebbe Road was open and she would meet the plane. Will and Sophie fought to come with her. She let them. She would not let Perry Wade come–his wife had typhoid fever. She would leave Amy with Leah.

Nubian soldiers blocked the road but waved their Peugeot through. They made it around some piles of rubble. In reeds, where the lake came close to the road, they passed a yellow shirt. It was wet with blood.

The airport building stood. But the windows lacked glass, the walls gaped open, and the surrounding cracked cement was strewn with metal and a burnt-out tank. It looked like a Muslim campground. Nubian cloth–red-yellow-black-orange squares and circles–wrapped bodies, draped heads, splashed bizarre brightness. Men wore fezes. Kohl-eyed women wore nose rings. An Arab with a long, white beard and a dirty-sheet turban slept against his bundle with one knee poking up. They were pilgrims, but they were not to reach Mecca. An Italian-looking monk with a wool beret and mud streaked down his cassock zigzagged through the crowd. Two monks followed him. All had machine guns roped across their backs. One told Anna: "Three monks shot–

two hour ago." In what had once been the lounge they picked their way over Arabs and Indians and Africans slumped against each other and on their lumps of bags, and the air was thick with heat and sweat and gunpowder and garbage and several pools of sick.

They watched the plane dip in across the lake. A pack of soldiers trotted over the asphalt, boarded the plane, and came back out in the blinding sun. They had a hand-cuffed African. It was Obote's publicity secretary—Will seemed to know that fact. Alec never appeared. To ask about him, Anna stood in queues she found. Some time later she got to the head of one and a man said, "No, Madam, we have not a list." "No, Madam, it is not known if more planes come." "No, Madam, we have not a message at this time."

They gave a lift to a ssaza chief from Kigezi and drove home. She was glad for the protection. The roadblocks had thickened. Soldiers fingered Sophie's hair. Sophie never liked that. Before, Sophie'd held still and sucked on her thumb but she had outgrown sucking. Now she held stiff under one soldier's hands, frowned under a second's, but by the third roadblock she turned on a glisteny recruit. She stared him in the eye and said, "Take your hands off me." The man dropped his hand and for a second said nothing. Then he burst out at Sophie in an incomprehensible language. Sophie sat with her lips pressed together. The soldier screamed louder and faster and crazier. The ssaza chief got out to negotiate. Anna said, "Apologize, Sophie." To the soldier she said, in Swahili, "She is a child, she is a toto, she is sorry." Sophie kept her lips together saying nothing. Will poked Sophie from the back. Sophie did not budge. A second soldier spoke sharply to the first and the chief got in and the soldier motioned them on. Anna's muscles slumped when they had passed. Will told his sister she was dangerously defective, they were almost shot. There was heat in his voice, but he didn't keep it up. He stared at Sophie with a kind of weary awe. Sophie kept her lips pressed tight.

Rain came, and it just as quickly went. Afternoons the showers stayed only long enough to make green sparkle in the sun and make Anna think about the rain in cypress trees in Carolina. Now she drove the ssaza chief up Namirembe Hill, and she and Will and Sophie drove on to Makerere Hill. Will and Sophie disappeared. Anna heard it would be days before Alec could get through. She grew more thoughtful. She organized the household better. Amy had a yellow sandbox bucket and helped her carry water. She had saved water in the tub—

always she'd laid up paraffin and candles and filled the tub with water when they heard about some restlessness, and now they carried water to the kitchen.

Fatima Enyanju called "Hodi" at the door. The mother said "Karibu." Fatima said some troops had sealed off Wandegeya. She said she'd bought some week-old bread from the pork-man-turned-bread-man and did Anna need some bread? Anna said, "Many thanks but no." The silky Hungarian came up the drive and said the explosives were coming precariously close and must have reached Wandegeya and had she heard they had sealed off Wandegeya? She said she'd heard. Perry Wade came to tell her they had sealed off Wandegeya an hour or so ago. He said some people thought this might be the stiffest pocket of resistance and maybe it was time to move her family in with them. She said, "Thank you but I'm not afraid."

Then she took Amy and they walked across the commons under the jacaranda trees and up through the hedges to check mail–internal mail could still be in the box, things were still that normal, Fatima had said. Amy was tired and sat down in the path. Anna sat on the grass near Amy. They watched weaver birds swarm out of hanging nests. They listened to the rush of wings. They heard the tinny pluck-pluck of a box harp. The wild-haired loco walked by them. He wore a muddy rag and he was barefoot. He thumbed the tin prongs on his box. It sounded monotonous and comforting.

They walked through the cassia grove behind the servants' quarters. The light was cool this time of afternoon. It smelled like woodsmoke. The smell belonged to cabins and cold mornings in the Kenya Highlands and if, Anna thought, the light and smell were good as this then things weren't very bad. And she had to be happy with a child who wasn't scared of things. If they managed to keep Sophie from leaping up on tanks, then Sophie might grow up; and who could know what things might come when Sophie was a woman. She thought and thought about Sophie. She had to think in a new way about Sophie, and she didn't yet know how to manage that.

At the edge of the commons the path stopped. They heard yelling. Will was running up with Mengo. He was crying. Will didn't cry. He was choking out, "Nobody believed anybody would do it." Mengo was interrupting that it wasn't Will, it was him, it wasn't Will–he'd dared Sophie because Sophie wasn't scared of anything but they never thought anybody would do it. Anna was saying "What? What? What?"

Will was saying, "Nobody would do it—nobody—they knew nobody would do it—they dared Sophie go get sweets at Wandegeya but they knew she wasn't that halfwitted and, anyway, the soldiers couldn't know their secret fence-hole. They knew nobody would do it, but Sophie did it—Sophie went to Wandegeya." Mengo was saying "It wasn't Will, it wasn't Will." Anna was sending Amy running to find Perry and she was running after Will and yelling "Where?" Mengo was saying, "Sophie was acting like a liberator and you couldn't believe Sophie so they weren't afraid when she ran off but when she didn't come back Kai got scared and ran and couldn't find her and they still thought she wouldn't go to Wandegeya and then somebody said they'd seen Sophie go under the fence and they got to the fence and yelled and saw drunk soldiers and tanks and not Sophie."

Anna was jumping over flowerbeds and ditches because all she knew was to head for Wandegeya. Already she could smell the fires and dust and hear the rumbling and shouting. Then she saw the noise was closer—a crowd on the path—and then she saw that straw-white head and saw it was Sophie and she saw Sophie flailing out of someone's arms. It was Leah's arms. Anna ran and she caught Sophie up. Leah was saying Sophie was hand-cuffed and shoved in a lorry and it was jammed with prisoners. Then the pork man, he saw Sophie and he found Leah and Leah she got that pork man's money and she paid those men and she got Sophie back.

People were collecting, trailing them. They were saying "Handcuffs?" They shouted. Sophie clung to Anna. Anna heard whispers—"prisoner," "brutalized," "kicked in a cage." Children thickened round them.

Anna reached their garden. She sat on the bank with her arms around Sophie. Elizabeth dared Odaybea to touch Sophie—Sophie had been a prisoner of war. Odaybea's finger brushed Sophie's arm—Sophie had been a prisoner of war. Sophie shuddered and drew tighter to her mother. The crowd kept staring. Anna felt it in her Sophie's muscles—the child was keyed to eyes on her.

Sophie straightened up, wiped her eyes, climbed out of her mother's lap. Sophie smiled at everybody—that was the gracious way that liberated personages acted. She thanked Leah. She said, "Webale, Webale nnyo" to Leah, with a formal nod. She walked toward the commons under the jacaranda trees. A crowd of children followed: Sophie was not a Warthog or a Tsetse Fly—Sophie'd been a Prisoner of War.

The children walked with chests out. They kept respectful distance. Sophie accepted. But if anyone but Kai got close she shook her arm.

Anna sat on the bank with Leah and quietly watched.

*   *   *

In the months that followed, after Alec talked his way back home, after the country started sliding into chaos, Anna still walked around the hill in sunshine and hibiscus. And when she glimpsed the liberated prisoner of war spearing enemies and giving courage lessons to the trolls, she was afraid. One day there wouldn't be a Leah to save her child, and one day her own lap would not help. She couldn't know, yet, how Sophie'd find her underpants bloodsoaked at far too young an age and hide the mess for months. She couldn't know, yet, how a bearded beauty of a trumpet player would beg her to love him when she had reached fourteen and how her mother would shout, "Slut! Slut! Slut!" and she'd reject the man she dreamed about. Her parents would divorce and she'd despair and plunge in darker sex and highs. How she would, at sixteen, counsel suicides on the Austin, Texas hotline. Anna couldn't know how Sophie'd find again, in Haiti, her sunshine and hibiscus, and how she'd be delirious with typhoid fever in a house with bucket plumbing and wouldn't leave that house because the people might be hurt. Anna couldn't know how far Sophie'd go to smuggle radios to Russia and give them to a family in the dark snow of Baku and never call for help—when she'd be raped outside a door—because the family could be jailed for knowing foreigners. Anna couldn't know, not the bleakest episodes of this pugnacious courage, not until years afterwards.

But she could know how it would be after they yanked their daughter from the garden and threw her, adolescent, in the New York sleet. Uganda slipped into nightmare, but it had been a cradle, with a Kai and a Leah and a Kasubi View. It had been sweet with frangipani and gold with bougainvillea. The thing was, ever since Sophie was a Wildebeest No Boys Allowed Anna knew, and was afraid, because she loved her daughter, and she never learned how she could let her daughter grow, and keep her safe.

KARIN CIHOLAS

Polraiyuk

ON THE HORIZON the sun flames up like ignited gasoline. I turn away from the window and look down at Sarah. Through the spots left by the sun I see the child splayed out like a rag doll, the fringe of her eyelashes matted against her round cheeks. Her black hair spikes around her flushed face like puffs of tundra grass. I look over at Aaka Ungarook. "I don't know what else to do."

Aaka reaches out and touches trembling fingers to her great- granddaughter's burning forehead. "In old days–" She stops and closes her eyes. "In old days shaman live right here with us. No waiting for doctor to come from Barrow."

"I know." In the old days virulent infections didn't fly in with the mail either. I think this but do not say it.

"Why scrape her throat? You can't remove sickness with this stuff." She looks at my sterilized instruments and wrinkles her nose in disgust.

"We will look through the microscope to see–" But already Aaka is shaking her head, and I lift my shoulders helplessly and walk to the window to look out again. The boats that left this morning are now mere black dots on the horizon. Many of the men and some of the women are out there hunting for the first whale of the season. Zack and Aalook are out there with their harpoons, hoping for a successful strike. Will they find Polraiyuk?

Right now I know they are scanning the horizon for the spouts that spray diamonds into the sun. The first sighting of the grey-black

mound that rises like an island in the sea is the most dramatic moment
in a whaler's life. He never tires of telling about it. I was supposed to
go with them and help. Ever since I was sixteen, I had always gone
along, ready to help with the tangle of ropes and cables. But I can't
leave the clinic when we have patients as sick as Sarah. I have to op-
erate the CB and wait for the message from Barrow.

The ice floes to the southeast look like a gleaming city of sculpted
walrus tusks sparkling in the sun.

I remember last year when the whale defeated us. This year has
to be better. We will find Polraiyuk. We will get him this time. We
began to call him Polraiyuk because he had swallowed a harpoon
and twisted a rope around so fast that Naulak was pulled overboard
as he tried to bring the boat around. It was Sarah's father who went
down. When we fished his body from the icy water, I began to ad-
minister CPR.

I press my lips against the cold window pane. I can still taste
Naulak's rough, salty mouth. All the way into shore I puffed and
pumped and pounded and panted, while the whale followed us, blowing spumes of foam in our wake. I can still hear the sound of his fluke
as he sliced the water before he swam away. He was angry with the
rope in his mouth.

When Cora saw her dead husband being lifted from the boat, her
face broke like brittle ice, and we had to hold her up during the funeral. People came from hundreds of miles away. They showed up from
everywhere—from Anaktuvuk, from Aklavik, from Inuvik. Even some
Chukchi steered across the date line to come sing their rhythmic song
at a fellow whaler's grave. We had to smile when they started their
chant just as the official from fish and wildlife began to speak. We
buried the pile of leaflets he handed out with Naulak. They kill trees
in the south to preach conservation.

Later we laughed about that. Our faces were streaked with tears
and our throats were raw from wailing, but we laughed.

In front of me the window is all fogged up, and I can no longer see
the boats.

*   *   *

We had no muktuk for the winter. So after the funeral we set out
again to find the creature who had demanded human sacrifice.

It was already dusk. The waves rolled by like scrolls of silver. Far to the north we spotted him. His foaming jet sprayed high into the air, as we revved our motors in pursuit. We knew it was the same whale by his size and the gash in his side. The second attempt failed. After the third harpoon hit home, my husband lifted his shoulder gun to load it, and the bomb that is supposed to kill the whale blew up in his hand. Zack lost his right hand, and we had to return to shore without landing a whale.

I stanched the bleeding and wrapped the mutilated hand in bandages. Zack refused an injection to deaden the pain and glared at me as though I had brought on his misery. The next day the doctor from Barrow cleaned up the wound and chattered happily about people he knew who had become as skilled with one hand as with two.

Zack said nothing while the doctor was there, but as soon as he left, he tore screaming through the house. He would not stop. "What good is a whaler without his right hand?" He kept yelling, until finally I yelled back at him.

And Zack started coming home drunk every night.

I can still hear Aalook pleading with him, his voice squeaky with eagerness, "I'll go and help you, father! I'll be your right hand!"

Zack had laughed at him, mocked his changing voice, and banged against the walls with his left fist until it was bloodier than his stump had been.

* * *

"Oh, Zack, get Polraiyuk! Please!"

"What you mumbling about, Edna Malik?" Aaka comes up behind me and studies my face.

"Polraiyuk."

"Polraiyuk? The sea monster? You believe in sea monsters? You with your modern medicines that smell funny?" She turns toward the sunlight, and I can see her dark eyes flare with their old fire. For the first time I notice the white ring that circles her irises, that curious nimbus that comes with age, giving her eyes the halo of the moon on a foggy night.

"We must get him this time. We must."

"You remember old shamans?"

"Yes, I do. There was an old Inuit from Aklavik. He used to invoke the great spirit–Inua." I grab Aaka's shoulders. "Why can't you do that now? Invoke the spirit for Sarah. For Zack. For Aalook."

"I have."

"And did Inua reply?"

"Not yet."

I look uneasily at little Sarah. "The answer had better come soon, or it won't do any good." I strain to listen for any crackle of static on the CB. Nothing. I would like to tune it to the frequency of the boats but don't dare, not as long as we have not heard from Barrow.

*   *   *

It was a long winter. Winters are always long. When the arctic storms blow and encase us in an overturned bowl, I always feel like I'm wading through frozen sheep's wool. Cora described it as breathing skimmed milk. This past winter was especially bad. Cora couldn't take it anymore. A widow at eighteen with Sarah crying, because she had no milk.

Through the nights of howling winds I would listen for Zack's footsteps. Sometimes he would come home. Sometimes they brought him home from the DEW Line station the next day after letting him sleep it off in a back room, too afraid to let him grope his way in snowdrifts. I would lie awake through the night, listening to the refrigerator kick on and off, still amazed that we kept it going in the winter when it was just as easy to keep everything in the kunychuk. But Zack and his father insisted it was better for the compressor to keep it running, and I didn't argue with Zack about that. We had plenty of other things to argue about.

Our world became a world of white lies swirling in whites. There was the lifeless white of the refrigerator, the stained enamel of our sink, the ivory curtains I made for the windows. There were the fresh-whites of swirling snowdrifts outside our door, the pure-whites of snow upon snow, the grey-rotten-whites of trampled mush, the milky-whites of melting floes, the green-whites and blue-whites of ice buckling up in a frosted sea. And there were the dirty-whites of the gauze bandages he kept wound around his stump long after the skin had healed.

A male voice fills the room. First the rasping of a throat clearing, then a tentative testing. "1–2–3– This is Prudhoe Bay 6. Kaktovik clinic, can you hear me? Over."

I grab the mike. "Yes, yes. This is Kaktovik clinic. When can the doctor get here?"

"He's picking up supplies at Nome. Had to stop by for some intestinal bug at Kotzebue. It'll be three days. At least."

"Three days! We can't last that long. Call back up there and get somebody." I shriek into the mike clutching the metal as though I could knead it to do my will. In the process I wake up Sarah.

Her eyes rove over me. They do not focus. She twitches her mouth but does not cry.

"Did you hear?" I yell into the mike.

"Yes."

"Is there someone else? Anyone else?"

"Have you tried Fairbanks?"

"No! We're supposed to get help from the North Slope Borough. You know that. Why isn't he there when we need him?"

"Kaktovik? You're fading out."

The voice becomes remote as I struggle to control my panic. Out of the corner of my eye I see Aaka pick up the baby and walk out the door. "Aaka!"

"Kaktovik? Kaktovik clinic?"

"Yes. Yes. Kaktovik here. I'll try to reach Fairbanks by phone. But you try Barrow again and tell them to hurry up."

Out on the tundra Aaka is walking slowly over the knobby tufts of grass. I call into the wind, but she does not hear. She passes the churchyard with its uneven crosses and kneels near a patch of snow. When I catch up with her, she is putting snow on Sarah's head and has already opened her blanket to set her down on her stomach in the snow. Sarah only whimpers, while I gaze down at her flushed skin blotchy with fever. Her Mongolian spot shines purple with feverish rage.

"Aaka! What are you doing?"

"We must scare fever away."

"But Aaka!"

"Hush, Edna! It's not cold that make misery, but warm sickness from the south. Her body's on fire. We put it out."

"Aaka, I've studied nursing in Anchorage. What you're doing is dangerous."

"Sarah creature of ice and snow. She need air. See, she already look better."

"For the moment. But tonight she will be worse. I cannot let you–"

"Her mother leave her in your arms."

"That's why I cannot let you do this."

"You want me tell Cora we watch Sarah die? We watch Sarah die without trying to scare fever away?"

"I have tried to bring the fever down."

"With vile medicines. She spit them out."

"I gave her an injection."

"It's no good."

"You don't understand."

"What Cora say?"

"Cora has nothing to say. She shouldn't have abandoned her baby." I am firm about that.

"Cora run away to hide."

"It was a selfish thing to do."

"She hide from death, death of Naulak."

"It makes no sense to abandon a child." I wrap the baby in her blankets and carry her back to the clinic. On the way, Sarah opens her eyes and gurgles through parched lips. She sees me. Aaka did lower her fever. I can tell by her eyes.

"Perhaps she will drink now." Aaka coaxes sugar water down her throat.

I switch channels on the CB. Out on the Beaufort Sea the boats talk to each other. Through the noise of the engines it is hard to make out the words, but the calm expectant sound of their voices tells me that they have not yet sighted Polraiyuk.

Rocking the baby, Aaka has rocked herself to sleep. There is a strange smile on her face. Sarah dozes quietly. I have to admit that she seems less agitated now. Quietly I let myself out the door and run to the long outhouse that has been transformed to hold the one phone of Kaktovik. After calling Fairbanks, I call the number Cora has given me in California, but there is still no answer. Her baby is dying, and she doesn't even know. I feel pity for Sarah, not for Cora. Cora has taken her share of the Arctic Slope Regional Corporation and run off to California. She has abandoned her baby. I feel that she has betrayed the dignity of all Inupiat women.

As I walk back to the clinic, I wonder about Aalook. Only thirteen years old and he thinks he is a man. He wants so desperately to be his father's right hand. Lately all he has felt is the sting of Zack's left hand against his cheek. I can wipe the blood away that trickles from his nose. I can tousle his hair and hug him. I can tell him how proud I am of him. It is of no use. It is from his father that he needs to hear it. How can Zack be so blind? I shield my eyes against the glare off the sea. Will he be too blind to see Polraiyuk?

When I turn around Aaka is standing at the door waving wildly. My heart is in my throat as I run to the clinic. "What's happened? Is Sarah worse?"

"Sarah asleep." She points toward the CB. "Agarik!"

The whale! I run to the CB and turn up the volume. Through the excitement I hear different voices confirming the bowhead's location. I recognize Zack's and can tell he is excited. Nervous. His voice is high-pitched when he issues orders for the boats to pursue.

"Polraiyuk?" I yell into the mike. "Is it Polraiyuk?"

No one answers. The radio emits the noise of the sea and men coiling lines, the metallic clank of the harpoon, the creak of the boat adjusting to men changing their positions. The spray of seawater that occasionally hits the open mike sounds like drums beating a deadly march. Beneath all that the hum of motors groans toward the mysterious monster of the sea.

"Did you see him?" comes hoarsely over the radio.

"He travels faster than I thought," is the answer.

Motors whine a higher rhythm, and I can't make out what they are saying.

I hold onto the table in front of me and see my knuckles go white. "Malik 2, come in!" I yell into the mike but no one answers. "Malik 2, this is Kaktovik clinic. Is it Polraiyuk? Have you gotten close enough to see?"

I stop breathing, straining to listen. Still there is no answer.

Aaka touches me on the shoulder. "It's all right, Edna. Everything will be fine. Just sit back."

My shoulders are in knots, and I let out a long breath. I imagine the vast form of the bowhead shooting lengthwise from the sea, twisting in a shroud of mist, hovering in the air, then splashing near the boats that could be knocked over by its wake. "It was easier when I could be on the boat with them. Now I imagine everything that could go wrong, and I see before me the giant whale, larger than life, winding the rope around Zack or Aalook and pulling them into the sea."

"It will be all right."

"How do you know?"

"Inua."

I sit up straight. "The Inua answered?"

"Yes."

"How do you know?"

She shakes her head and smiles.

"And Sarah?"

"I don't know about Sarah. Not yet."

We both look at the sleeping Sarah and then at each other. The sounds of the boats splashing against water are fading. Have they slowed down? Crackles pulsate irregularly over the speaker like damp firecrackers left over from the fourth of July.

I imagine the blind, reckless way in which their wild craft goes plunging toward its flying mark. Why don't they speak?

Over the next six hours I call Malik 2 over and over again.

Aaka holds Sarah and tries to distract her with the stories she used to tell us when we were small. Aaka told us they were stories she had learned from her Aaka. Stories of evil ice princesses and good snow queens and of little children lost in snowdrifts guided to the warmth by a spiral of whale oil smoke.

When Sarah's fever rises again, I call Prudhoe Bay to relay the message to Barrow. The calm voice from Prudhoe Bay offers no immediate help, and I switch back to the boats. No one answers their CB. I pick up dead space, like the sounds of the stars in winter or like the sounds that hum in my ears when I listen into the arctic night.

A doctor in Anchorage once laughed at me and told me I was hearing my own blood pulse in my veins. He claimed the stars and the arctic night made no noise. But I remember. I remember the sound of the stars in winter. It is the same with the northern lights. Some people don't believe they exist. Our eyes and ears must be on the right frequency to perceive. It is like the great Inua. The great spirit is visible everywhere, but many never see.

"Malik 2, come in please."

Minute by minute, hour by hour, the CB echoes through the night with meaningless clutter. My ears are so tuned to pick up the slightest variation of sound that I could hear a feather move or a snowflake fall. Sarah stirs, and we are both instantly at her side. Our awareness of her every breath underscores our ignorance of those who seem to have disappeared into the horizon where sky and water fuse into a rim of nothingness.

The morning sun stretches awake and starts on its low-slung arc. I have not slept and begin to imagine things. I look at Sarah's throat culture through the microscope and see angry sea monsters fighting each other. When I show Aaka, she shakes her head. "Looks like caribou on Brooks Range."

"It doesn't look good at all."

*   *   *

Toward late afternoon Sarah is thrashing around, whimpering, fighting the disease with her fists, railing wildly. Her temperature rises alarmingly. The women who have stayed behind stop by the clinic and make suggestions. One brings seal oil from her freezer. Sarah spits it out. We all have our CBs tuned to the same frequency.

While I'm on the CB calling the boats, Aaka returns to the patch of snow. I watch from the window as she kneels over the little form in the churchyard.

"Malik 2, come in please." I know they have turned it off to save the battery. I think of calling Prudhoe Bay to ask the doctor to fly over the sea on his way here.

I hear something. A response? It sounds like a voice, a whine that undulates. I shiver at the thought that it is Polraiyuk's voice, calling across the arctic sea.

I must have dozed off. Aaka is rocking Sarah back and forth. She is worse. She is no longer fighting the fever but lies limp and lifeless in Aaka's lap.

"Malik 2, come in please."

There is a faint crackle, and the pitch changes. Then I hear the other families calling their boats and waiting in vain for an answer.

*   *   *

In my sleep I hear: "This is Malik 2. We're coming in. Can you hear us?"

I open my eyes. At first I think it is wishful thinking, but then I hear others calling back on their CBs with relief flooding their voices like tears. For a moment I cannot speak. All I can say is, "Zack? Aalook?"

Then I hear Aalook's voice. Strong. Deep. Proud. "Tell Aaka we're bringing home supper."

From the jabber of voices yelling into the mike I make out that they are towing a big bowhead back to the village. Families begin to gather up and down along the shoreline to wait. They will party all night and put up the cook tent. Zack's father brings down his bulldozer and old Kupaaq bumps along the rocks on his bobcat. Both want to be ready to haul the huge whale ashore.

It takes the whole night for them to come in.

When I see the vast bulk of the whale beached on our shore, I fly from the clinic, forgetting Sarah's struggle in the triumph of the moment. Aalook and the other boys are dancing on top of the bowhead. Their arms gyrate wildly toward the rising sun.

Then I see Zack. I have not seen him in three days, but already I know he is different before he speaks. I see it in his shoulders, then his eyes. I pour him some steaming coffee, and he gulps it down without coming up for breath.

"Thanks!" He surveys the mighty swell of the bowhead with elation. "It was my harpoon that made the strike. He wanted to get away. It was obvious he knew what a harpoon meant. It was my bomb that exploded in him."

"Why didn't you answer the CB?"

"He ran north. We got out of range. He took us out for a whole day. The others wanted to turn around and give up but I refused to let him get the better of us."

"Is it Polraiyuk?"

"I think so."

Zack turns toward Aalook and hands him a long, curved knife. "You get the honor." He grins up at him.

Aalook scores the first line down his length.

Zack dips his fingers into whale blubber and reaches up and smears our son's face with blood. "Aalook steadied the harpoon," he brags.

All around us laughter and applause.

Then the cutting begins. There is nothing that smells quite like freshly butchered whale. It is overwhelming and strong. It fuses seaweed, fish, iodine, and salt with strong oil and raw, gamy meat. Some would call it rank. For me it has the sweet smell of a successful quest, of riches emerging from the mysterious depths of the sea. The essence of life itself.

* * *

By mid afternoon we have finished only half of the scoring and slicing and dividing up. The community always shares equally in the kill, and no one takes more than they can use. It is the unwritten law of the arctic. It is never questioned. Even Sarah will have her portion.

I run back to the clinic. Aaka is curled up on a seal skin fast asleep. The minute I close the door, she opens her eyes.

"Ah, you smell good!"

I laugh.

I study Sarah's little features. Her tiny chest hardly moves. Her lips have broken open with fever, and I rub fish oil over her parched face. Aaka drinks a cup of left-over coffee, while I try to make Sarah drink. She whimpers because it is too painful to swallow.

Aaka blinks glumly into her empty cup. "If only I go in Sarah's place."

"If only the doctor would come from Barrow. I've listened for the sound of his plane all day long. Now my ears hurt from hearing nothing."

Aaka doesn't pay attention to what I say. She gathers the limp Sarah into her arms. Her eyes have a far-away look to them. "Aaka old woman. I see enough caribou to feed the world. I sew enough seal skins to make blanket to cover the Beaufort Sea. I make enough mikitaq and uunaalik and ugaruk for all Inupiats to have grand feast. I carry ten children in my belly and forty-two grandchildren in my parka. Now I hold my great-granddaughter and not remember how many great-grandchildren I have. So I ask great Inua to let me die so Sarah live."

"No, Aaka Ungarook!" I say, but there is no arguing with her when she gets an idea into her head.

* * *

At dusk I hear the drone of a Cessna 180. It flies along the coast and lines up with our narrow runway to land in strong crosswinds. The doctor jumps out of the plane and waves to the whalers.

I run to meet him before the propeller stops turning. Breathlessly I enumerate Sarah's symptoms while he gets his landlegs and steadies himself.

"Quite a catch today, I see."

"I'm afraid she's no longer fighting back. She went into convulsions earlier today, and Aaka rolled her in snow. It seemed to help."

"How big? Looks like at least a fifty-footer." He fastens the tie-downs.

"The throat culture was positive."

"Is this your first bowhead this season?"

"I tried various medicines you brought last time. None seemed to work."

"How long did it take to bring him in?"

"Too long," I say.

When we open the door to the clinic, Aaka is sitting on the seal-skin on the floor, rocking back and forth, holding Sarah against her breast. It's the funny little noise that comes from her throat that lets me know Sarah is dead.

*   *   *

In the evening Zack's father finds a piece of Naulak's harpoon in Polraiyuk's belly.

We wait for Cora to come.

After five days we bury Sarah and the rusted harpoon beside Naulak. Cora doesn't come for the funeral.

She calls every now and then to ask about Aaka.

Aaka sits near the window and looks out. A sullen, white surf beats against the shore, and Cora doesn't come home.

CHRISTIAN DAVIS

The Wild Horses of Jerusalem

I DID NOT know them, except in that polite but hurried sort of way, as a neighbor who values the comfort of distance knows another, with the occasional comment about the weather, the summer heat, or the murmured greeting over the hedge. And I was surprised one evening, as I moved the sprinkler on the lawn, to hear the woman's voice coming from the camellias, from the green darkness of the porch steps next door, addressing me directly.

They were all three of them there, on the porch. The slender wife, standing, just visible past the trellis; the husband, sitting on the top step, cigarette glowing red against the bloom of his white shirt; and the little boy, his father's hand resting protectively across his bare middle as he stood between his father's knees. Peering up at them in the dusky light, I wondered how long they'd been there, observing me lost in thought and foolish under that splendid old canopy of trees.

Just then, the sprinkler caught me in its first shock of rain and I trotted breathlessly out onto the sidewalk. For those few stunned moments, as I looked off down the long avenue of lawns, too late to pretend I hadn't heard, standing there looking like a common fool, my hands wet from the hose, held out from my dress, I could feel it; I could feel it as a tangible thing. That shy attempt to connect with me was slowly turning to a fine mist, about to evaporate into the violet air.

And all at once, I thought, My God, Mary, will you never again come down out of yourself to know another beyond these soft evening pleasantries? What's become of you? The pity of it. The waste!

Finally, I felt I would suffocate if I did not say something, the silence pressing down on me so with its flat, public weight, and I turned, my jaw set in a resolute smile, not a thing in my head, and stepped firmly up to the low crumbling wall at the foot of their sloping yard.

"Why, hello there," I called, as that seemed as good a place as any to begin. "Hello!"

Although I could not have known it then, the events that led on from that perfectly ordinary encounter were to change something in me, or would at least prevent me from so easily resuming a life that, without my noticing it, had grown increasingly ethereal and detached.

You see, I have discovered something. I have found that you cannot be selectively in the world. You may bear witness from the riverbank, but sooner or later you must cast yourself into the flowing waters. I had been docked for a long time.

She was a Pickering, she said, next afternoon, reaching across the blanket to brush away a column of ants crawling up Rollie's little leg, but now she was a Thompson.

She'd married Avery Thompson five years before, when she was nineteen, (Would I care for more lemonade?), and little Rollie, Randolph Buchanon Thompson, had come along a year to the day from the wedding. Avery was going to school then, to study refrigeration. When he'd gotten his certificate, they moved up to Atlanta, where he was told he'd find a well-paying job, which he had. After six months, they'd found an affordable place not far from Euclid Avenue, a tall, white side-by-side, with a shared porch and a lovely catalpa tree in the yard. For a time, things had been wonderful for them there. There had been many happy hours spent with little Rollie beneath the shade of that tree, watching for Avery to come home from work, coming up the sidewalk, his jacket and his dinner pail under his arm.

She closed her eyes then, and I suppose she was thinking about that catalpa tree, she'd spoken of it with such rapture, smiling as though she were having a religious experience. When she opened them again, the sunlight streaming into them, making them an even lighter gray in her already pale, earnest face, I was struck with a rush of tenderness for how utterly plain she was. At first, with her hair drawn back in a tight bun, and the round, smooth expanse of her shiny forehead, I was concerned for her, as you are when you notice a one legged sparrow, or someone born with an unfortunate disadvantage. I imagined a diminished life, somehow; a life of dark floors, the smell of soap, and small careful rooms.

It was her voice that made you forget the rest. I had never heard its like. Shut your eyes and it was a river of murmuring water, a lullaby for the healing of faltering spirits. An intimate voice, resonant with concern, it had a breathy catch to it that underlined each note, like a saxophone. Beside her, on a pillow, I could imagine how a man might never again know despair.

By and by, the owner of the house had died and the surviving sons and daughters sold the property and the Thompsons had to leave. They had moved three times in two years. Though their present house was awfully big for them, she hoped they could stay there for awhile, for Rollie's sake. Someday, they would have a place of their own. It was a struggle. Avery wanted to buy a car.

I had the feeling that she would like to have said something more. A ripple of disturbance moved across her brow and, after a moment of quiet, during which she seemed like a woman looking about for a place to set down a heavy load of wash, she stared off over my shoulder and said, "Those were happy times."

I looked up and saw Avery Thompson approaching us with a cloud of cotton candy on a paper cone. Claris made room on the blanket and little Rollie thrust his arms up when he saw his daddy coming. From behind, with one of the straps of his coveralls folded under, and his cotton shirt hiked up in back, and the little tapering V of his hairline, the hair an appealing honey-white, he seemed like any other four-year-old tow-headed boy waiting on a picnic blanket, his mother beside him and his father bringing him a piece of the sky.

Avery Thompson came slowly up to the edge of the blanket, acknowledged me with a soft tug on the brim of his hat, a polite glance at his wife, and folded down to sit beside his boy, pushing his hat far back on his head, exposing shiny licks of dark, scented hair. Little Rollie opened his rosy mouth and bumped his face into the billowing tuft of cotton candy his father held out to him. With a clap, our laughter rose up out of us and hovered there a moment, suspended. Little Rollie stuck out his tongue and reached for it again as his father brought it close for him to taste, the boy smacking his lips loudly, plainly confused by the texture of this sticky cloud.

My heart went out to him. It took me by surprise. I am not ordinarily given over to such easily plucked emotion, but I felt a pull at something inside me. For a moment, I longed to gather up that silent child, to gather him up and find a special place for him in the exotic gardens, out along the edge of the world.

"He doesn't talk, yet," Claris had said, that first evening on the porch. "We hope someday he will."

After a time, with the afternoon drawing on and the sunlight slanting off the river, the water winking and splashing below the wide park lawn, Avery Thompson pulled his watch up out of his pocket. Studying the side of his smooth tanned face, I thought he had a Mediterranean look about him. With his heavy lashes and dark insinuating eyes, and the long expressive neck curving up from the buttoned collar of his soft white shirt, he reminded me of young men we'd seen on the bridges in Venice, leaning out over us with their loose smiles as we passed under them. Walter had said, "Mary, what do you suppose those men do for a living?" and he'd tightened his lip, stifling a grin, as we went on down the canal.

Avery Thompson turned to his wife with a quiet murmur about the hour and Claris and I began to pack the picnic things. Avery stood and took little Rollie up in his arms, moving off a little way, nuzzling his ear. I commented on how gentle a man he seemed. Claris bent from the waist and reached her long arms down for the corners of the blanket. "Yes," she said. "He's very gentle with Rollie," and then she motioned to me and together we shook the blanket clean. I made as if to take up the heavy basket, but she was firm and would not allow it, insisting that it was lighter now, anyway, and offered me the folded blanket, instead.

We strolled up through the park, past the wisteria hung arch, to the memorial fountain and the old iron gate. In the distance, we could hear the streetcar bell. It made me happy that I had held back the suggestion to take my car. They were young and I did not want to make them feel uncomfortable about their circumstances. By the time we came to the streetcar line, little Rollie was fast asleep, with the side of his cheek on his father's shoulder. From the extravagant curl of his thick lashes you could tell he had his father's eyes.

What a splendid, uncomplicated day it had been. I had slipped out into the middle of it and lazily let the current take me where it would, drifting through the afternoon without a care. I loved the ordinariness of it. And yet, that night, I found myself repeatedly walking the oval border of the big hooked rug on my bedroom floor. It was as if a latched door had blown open in the night, letting in a warning stir of air. Tying and retying my robe sash, stopping now and again to whisper words of advice to myself, I felt I was possessed of fever, searching among the patterns beneath my feet, as though I might find there a sign or a thread that would lead me through the sudden chill of apprehension that had overtaken me.

I knew what it was, of course. I knew exactly what it was. I already had a life. It was a good one, one I deliberately made for myself. I didn't want to change it or add to it; it fit me perfectly and I was happy and just wanted for it to go on. What possible need did I have for the complication of attachments? I had my mind, didn't I? My vision of the world? The black doves of night to sing beneath my eave? I spent forty-five years in the amiable anguish of compromise, loving and loved by a good man, and I would not trade more than half a dozen of them, at most, for all that. Still, it was a marriage, two bright souls in a single boat. Now, it was my turn to steer, and I wanted to go out beyond the edge of things.

When Walter died, I took the scissors out and cut up all of our address books and photographs. Out of grief, they'd said. I'd taken leave of my senses, is what I'd have told you at the time. But when I look back now, I believe it was something more. I believe I was resisting the role of the Bereft Widow, living out my days playing half of something that once was whole. I could not stand to be treated as if I were somehow infeebled, as if Walter had been the one thing that kept me afloat all those years. It's not that I did not love Walter; I loved him dearly. But, he was gone. So there it was. What we had was done. I needed to begin a new life and I wanted it brand new, from scratch. It simply was not possible to glide out on that same grand old pond without pretending to myself that people were not watching over me, waiting to throw me a line before I sank. Look at her. There she goes, poor thing, out beyond the limit. No, thanks. I wanted a complete change of course, and I wasn't interested in taking on any passengers.

Let them talk, I said. Let all of our friends, those good dear souls, go on with their merry rounds, but spare me, please, my widows' graceful entrances. What I keep of Walter now is what I always kept of him. The things we became together. The things we grew separately to become. With him gone, his gift to me was open water. I sold the house, much too large for me, anyhow, and came to live on this green street.

Oh, I love it so. In the summer evenings, with night blooming under these big trees, and the electric buzz of the cicadas tapering to a thin needle of sound, I climb the stairs with my cup of chicory coffee rattling on its white saucer, and enter my special room. I turn on the lamp by my open window. The green bowl of fluted glass casts a pool of warm amber light on the leather cornered blotter of my desk. If there is a breeze stirring and the wind is right, I can hear the faint clang of the streetcar bell. I look around me at my good room and I breathe air. This is my world. This is my life. I take down my pen, my canvas notebook, I turn to an empty page, and I begin to write.

I had not seen the Thompsons since that warm afternoon, all three of them together, I mean, for several weeks. Once in a while, as I gazed dreamily out of the window, my mind off on the wild horses of Jerusalem or the carved ivory tooth of the Emperor of Senegal, I would notice a light go on, or a light go off, or hear some domestic knock or clink, so I knew they were there. They were a quiet family. Avery Thompson spoke in a thin, wiry whisper, and was not given to talk, as it was, and Claris had only the boy to speak to and he spoke to no one at all.

One day, I had just come from the stationers with my new fountain pen. I was as excited as a schoolgirl and I sat at a corner of the dining room table to try it out, not even bothering to remove my hat. The deep ruby barrel of the pen fit handsomely in my hand and the polished gold tip gleamed in the afternoon light, moving effortlessly across the linen pad. I felt as a skater must, laced into a new pair of skates, streaking out on the ice, graceful and strong.

"My Dear Constantine," I wrote. "Dearest Hepzibah," the letters flowing out in a voluptuous Midnight Blue.

"Dear Rajah Pandragore Raj,

"Though I am touched by the sweetness of your princely generosity, regrettably I must decline the elephants."

I began a long sleeve of tight continuous o's and, following that, several lines of dolphine loops. Absorbed in the lyrical play of my pen, it was some minutes before I realized that the lines of ink flowering before me were not simply following the will of my imagination, but were, instead, a calligraphic tracing of a melody coming through my open window.

I stopped. I looked up from my letter pad and listened. It was Claris. I could not make out the words, but followed the shapes the syllables made as they turned and hung in the air. At last, I recognized it. It was an old church hymn, one I never particularly liked. She made it beautiful.

After supper, one night, I was looking down through the leaves, admiring the soft tide of evening as it slowly climbed the lawn, and I was so startled I had to reach around for my glasses, for I was sure there was a two-headed man coming up the sidewalk, one above the other. The figure came closer until I was able to see it was Avery Thompson giving little Rollie a piggy back ride on his shoulders. The boy's mouth swam all over his face with a wide rubbery grin and he had red candy in his hand. He wore his father's hat, which fitted down over his ears. Through the summer, I was to become disturbingly familiar with that hat. Long after the hour when children are tucked in their beds, I would see it come out of the house like a pale bobbing moon and disappear under the streetlamps, with Avery Thompson's lean solitary shadow heading toward town.

One morning, I was in back, spraying the roses with my sprayer, when I saw Claris hanging out clothes and little Rollie playing hide and seek among the wet laundry on the line. She waved and I came to the fence and little Rollie came up too. He grinned and blew bubbles. Claris came up then, slipping her hand down alongside Rollie's face, cupping his chin. "Roses are God's perfect work," she said.

"I believe he did a better job last year," I said.

"Oh, no, Mrs. Ford," she said. "Why, these are just beautiful!" and she leaned close to breathe the scent of a scarlet American Beauty hanging just over the wire.

"Try one of these," I said, finding an especially full Morning Star, growing by the gate. "The pale ones are ever so much sweeter. What they lack in color, they make up for in perfume." I clipped it and handed it to her.

She lowered her face into the ivory petals and closed her eyes. "Oh, my," she said, in a reverent hush. I began to select seven or eight more for her, reaching in carefully among the briars, when she said something that would come back to me over and again, all summer, with increasing poignancy, when I realized much later, what she had meant. Looking up at me, breathless, she said, "It's just too much glory for one to have it all, isn't it? Something has to be left out."

When I handed her the bouquet of flowers, her voice caught in a sigh of appreciation and she hurried into the house for something to put them in. Little Rollie stayed and pressed his face up against the fencewire. I studied his face awhile.

He seemed so like any boy, with his good looks and vitality. Those eyes didn't miss a trick. I had a peculiar feeling that, if I stood there long enough, he would eventually speak to me; that he could speak if he wanted to. I began to wonder what would possess a child to withhold himself so. He did not appear especially delicate or backward. What would make a child do that?

"You're going to be an awfully pretty husband, someday, Rollie Buchanon Thompson," I told him. "You're going to break a lot of hearts." He blew some more bubbles. I gave him a good squirt with my sprayer. He sucked in his breath and his eyes got bigger and then his grin got big and he stuck his tongue out through the fence. I gave him another squirt, pushing in the plunger. He turned round in a circle, wiping his eyes, then came back to the fence for more. "That's all now, Beauty," I told him. "You'll get your hair wet."

Claris came out of the house to show how pretty the roses looked in her grandmother's cut glass vase. Her grateful voice was breathy that day, throaty and vibrant like a reed. After awhile, she took little Rollie's hand and they went on inside, carrying the flowers, him looking back at me over his shoulder. I finished my spraying, emptied out the rest in a patch of mint, and took off Walter's gloves. I kept those, old and big as they were. I could never find gloves to fit me. His were big and sloppy and comfortable, though sometimes I'd catch a whiff of those awful chemicals he used in the garden. I never could stand those chemicals. I only use plain water. I know I must look ridiculous in those old gloves, but I like them. They make me feel I have paws.

It was a few weeks after that, when I awoke uneasily one night from a churning sleep. It was very late, I was sure, but when I put on my glasses to see the hands of the clock, I was surprised it was not later. The moonlight coming into my room was bright as paper, all across my bed and on the wall. My stomach churned and moaned something terrible. That afternoon, I happened to meet a woman I went to school with, getting on the streetcar, and she stayed on past her stop, we got to talking so, and we just kept right on downtown and had dinner at a Chinese restaurant. I thought it was the Chinese food. I got up and put on my robe and started down the stairs to get some bourbon and cold milk to settle my stomach, feeling my way along in the dark. I didn't bother to turn on a light. I know where my rooms are and I know where I put things.

Half way down the stairs, there is a small window with three tiny panes of beveled glass leaded in above that makes an interesting picture of sunlight during the day. As I came beside this window, all at once I heard from next door a crying out, a frightening sound, as though the world had come to an end. Then, there was a muffled sob and a slow angry shriek that trailed off, like a kettle pulled from a burner, with its pitiful little peeps of steam. My heart pounded. I was sure it was Claris. A light went on in their upstairs window, and immediately went out, then came back on again, then out. It came on a third time, staying on for a long moment, this time, then went out and stayed out, the minutes ticking by as I stood there on the stair.

I felt so alone. I felt as though the house had suddenly swollen up big around me. My first thought was that something had happened to little Rollie. I didn't know what to do, but it was plain I couldn't stay where I was. I got down the stairs and was on my way out back so that I could call to them from the yard, when the light came on in their kitchen. As I had not turned on my own light, I could see quite clearly into their window.

Claris was at the sink, in her robe, holding little Rollie. His eyes were enormous and he was sitting up tall in his mother's arms, struggling, looking all about him in the brightness of the overhead fixture. Claris herself was staring blank-faced out of the window, or perhaps at her reflection in the glass, distractedly coaxing him to take a sip of water, which he ignored. I wondered if he could have awakened from a bad dream. Could it have been Rollie screaming so? Was there a shape so terrible in the night that could finally break that mortared throat? Claris' face was bloodless pale, except for a mark of color high on her temple. Finally, she put down the glass of water and began to softly bounce little Rollie up and down, soothing him with steady pats on his back, her hand up inside his nightshirt.

I watched them for awhile longer, until I began to feel a delicate shame creeping over me - for what, I could not say. For witnessing too much, or too little, of their private lives? The crisis, whatever it was, had evidently passed.

I found the bourbon and fixed my potion in the dark, the residual light from the Thompson's window reflecting off the enamel of my cupboard doors. Slowly, I climbed back up the stairs. My mind was already turning, reluctantly beginning to rehearse discreetly phrased notices of my availability during times of trouble.

They say that you grow used to these summers, the long weeks when the sweltering heat hangs in the motionless air and your freshly laundered clothes cling uncomfortably to your damp skin. Even the nights, some of them, bring no relief, as you turn on the restless spit of the damned. And yet, they say that you learn to accept it, as an Arab accepts the sun, by covering up and letting it take a little of you. Personally, I do not believe it. I think that we never accept our condition, for we are not a stoic people, but merely learn to contain our rage. That, or go mad, and some of us do.

As the summer wore on, each month slowly opening onto the next, the incidents from next door continued. Afterward, there would come a period of silence, a calm which gradually ripened over the stunned and fragrant afternoons, until it burst, at last, into another episode. A shout in the night, a cry, the muffled thump of a door.

I know that there are men like that, but I have never understood them. What is it that gives them such desperate license? Perhaps I have been uncommonly lucky. Walter was always so temperate, so reasonable. I was never diminished by his anger, only amazed by it. Almost hopeful. Yet, Avery Thompson was so wonderfully sweet with that child! It hardly seemed possible that it was the same man at night with his wife.

Eventually, I succumbed. In the morning, after a night rent with stifled cries, I would post myself in the backyard with my gloves and clippers, so that I might be there for her when Claris, her thin proud back bent over the laundry basket, lifted her head, finally, with a loud swallow of air, and turned to me, coming brokenly up to the fence, her eyes swimming in a hot rush of tears.

I wish that I could say I gave unstintingly of myself on these occasions, with such comfort as I was able to provide, but I cannot. They were a distraction for me, after all, gnawing into my thoughts, seeping into the slow lavender nights beside my lamp and window. I am not a keeper of brothers, nor of string, and yet, how could I turn away? They did not involve me directly, of course, but I was troubled and could not pretend the Thompsons were strangers. And what if they had been? I felt terribly for them, little Rollie, and Claris, especially, with her raw, red-knuckled pride. Who else could she turn to, with every last soul of her family hundreds of miles away, and she without a penny to her name? And what of Avery Thompson? Brought down off the Cumberland hills, bred young on careless honey and drawn with his good looks to the temptations of an easy town, where would he turn when the music stopped and he realized what he'd lost? Would he crawl back, perfume on his shirt, to stand outside the window and howl at his slice of bachelor moon? And if he did, would I stuff my ears with cotton and righteousness? I hate to think it.

We are, after all, such imperfect vessels for the lives we might have had. Struggling on, we seem to pull along that which is least within us into a world so needful of our best. I suppose Avery's best was his love for little Rollie. In a way, it's him I think about—Avery Thompson. His hunger will haunt him longest. In the end, he will be easiest to forget.

When I consider my preoccupied nature, now, it strikes me as peculiar that I came so easily to monitor the Thompsons' house. So many times, returning from a walk, breathing in the excitement of wet shrubbery after a rain, my mind was worlds away, spinning with images. I might be lost in the orange glow of a campfire, the gleam of leather, listening to the sad pale whisper of the blue gaucho. I was often so engrossed in dialogue that I would find myself well down the block, past my own house, needing my full attention to get back. Once, I actually entered the home of a stranger. I'd stepped just inside the entry hall when I was stopped by the pungent smell of fresh baked cookies. Yet, later, climbing the length of my familiar lawn, my senses would seem to gather of themselves and sweep the vertical standing of my neighbors' house—its porch, its windows, its shadowy yard, skimming for the least sign of anything amiss—a lighthouse beacon probing the imminent dark.

I wish now that I had not been so loyal in my vigilance, for my heart, too, was broken a little. There are certain images in life that you take inside of you and keep there, all the rest of your days. Like the pages of an album, your memory carries the pictures of your experience, turning first from wonder, then to sorrow, and the long way back. It happened this way.

On the second floor of my house there is a window seat with a view into the back yards and gardens below. Built originally as a contrivance to hide some plumbing pipes, it had become a favorite perch of mine, especially in the stifling nights of August when my bedroom became unbearable. With my legs extended along the cushioned bench and the side of my cheek against the window screen, I became a kind of railwayman, sitting in his caboose, looking down the long track, into the night. Sometimes, I was able to drift away for a few hours, soothed by the faint puffs of an occasional breeze. When I could not sleep, it was still a restful place to be, and often I'd fall asleep without knowing it and awaken in the cool dampness of dawn.

It was one such morning in August when I awoke with the sky still dark and bright with stars. I looked down from my window and saw the figure of a child standing by the fence, at the end of the Thompson's yard. It was little Rollie, dressed only in his underpants and wearing his father's hat. Claris had said that he insisted on wearing that hat all of the time now, and he would not sleep without it. Rocking from side to side, his hands grasping the wire, he stared off down the alley. I looked for Claris but there was no sign of her, nor of Avery Thompson, whom I had not seen for several weeks. I suspected that I might not see him again. Their house was silent and dark. Little Rollie stood alone in the yard.

How my heart ached for him. The world sliding away beneath him and he unable to call it back. I tried to think what I might do. Perhaps I could go and bring him to stay with me, to wait in my kitchen until his mother awoke. I could fix him some cocoa, some sugarbread, get him something to put over his shoulders. I could talk to him, tell him stories, try and make him understand that when you've lost all you thought you had, there's still something left.

Drawing on my robe, my mind and heart in a flurry of anxious courses, I had to laugh at myself. There I was, Awakened Spirit, Sailor of the Night Seas, Guardian of the Palace of Dreams, about to charge off down the hall like a nanny, my maternal blood stirred by the plight of this poor abandoned child. What a combination of things we are!

Feeling around for my slippers, I heard a sound and looked to see that a light had come on in the Thompson's kitchen. There stood Claris in her robe, on the back porch, holding the door open, with the light coming from behind her, shining out into the yard.

Calling to him in a strained, plaintive voice, peering into the dark, she stepped down off the porch. For an instant, Rollie looked back over his shoulder to see his mother coming toward him, then turned again toward the alley and continued his rocking. Reaching his side, she squatted down beside him, trying to see beneath the brim of the hat into his tiny face. He refused to look at her and held fast to the fence.

As the sound of her voice rose and fell, nearly breaking, now desperate, now rich and flooded with compassion, she pleaded with him, attempting to draw him to her. Again and again she tried, but he shrank from under her touch until, finally, he began to shake the fence, violently pushing and pulling with his whole body. Sagging to her knees beside him, her face cupped in her hands, she let out a long, thin, heartstopping wail, then caught herself, abruptly, with an angry, determined sob.

I struggled to my feet as Claris wrenched herself up, standing over him, and for a moment, my hand clutching at my breast, I thought she was going to strike him. I was about to call out to her when she reached down and snatched the hat from off of his head, lifted her hand, and flung it, with a little cry, over the fence. Then, grabbing him up, she yanked his hands free of the fence wire and turned toward the house, hugging his silent, kicking body tightly in her arms.

I sat there in the dark for a long time. I thought of Walter and his practical wisdom. Of how he seemed never at a loss for knowing the exact thing to do, while I, in my own life, had become a familiar of inexactitude. Perhaps we complemented each other. I've never been attracted to exact answers. Besides, there's too much world for there to be an answer for everything. Sometimes you have only your heart to anchor you to life.

I went down stairs and turned on all the electric lights. Let them blaze. Dear Lord, what can it matter? Let there be light. I lit the oven and mixed up some flour and eggs and buttermilk. I have always made good biscuits, a talent I inherited from my mother. When they were done, I pulled them from the rack and breathed deeply of their heavenly smell. The pan was hot, even through the towel I'd wrapped them in, and I was surprised as I crossed into my neighbor's yard, to see the sun had come up on the day.

PAMELA ERBE

You Know What?

THERE WAS A TIME—I am not imagining this—when Dot loved Henry, my mother loved my father, when everything he did brought her pleasure and delight. I remember this like it was yesterday, but in fact it was long ago. It was the 1950s, when a wife's job was to adore her husband, so how she loved him was taken for granted, how extraordinary they were was overlooked. Nobody noticed but me.

I was fascinated by them, I could have watched Dot and Henry be in love forever. I watched them like TV, like I was crouched in front of our Philco, closer than I was allowed to be, in the zone where Dot always nudged my knee with the toe of her pump and told me, "Move back from the screen—you'll get radiation sitting that close." My mother and dad seemed to me then like TV lovers, like those shiny, polished-looking black and white couples in the old movies they showed on Channel 6, elegant types who had put on their satin and tuxedos and locked themselves in passionate embraces in the middle of the afternoon, who went to cocktail parties for a living, whose lives were about nothing but love love love.

I was always walking in on them kissing. It seemed I could not move from one room to another in our house, I could not turn a corner, without hearing the smack of lips, the purr and sigh. I used to feel embarrassed and duck out. Then I might stand just outside the door and clear my throat, or tiptoe back down the hall then turn and stomp my way loudly toward them, so by the time I got there, they'd be apart again and smoothing their clothes, Dot would be patting her hair, Henry rubbing the back of his hand across his mouth.

But after awhile I got used to how they were and I'd just pass on through. "At ease," I'd say, mimicking Henry's military talk. He had been part of the Army cleanup in Germany and France for two years after the war. "As you were. Smoke 'em if you got 'em." They'd step apart and we'd all laugh, and for a moment it would be the three of us together. But I could feel how eager they were for me to get whatever it was I'd come for, or get to wherever it was I was going, to leave them alone with each other.

This was so long ago it's like another world. It's only echoes now, it might have come from a story instead of real life. Sometimes, things being what they are, I mistrust myself, and though I know what I know, I wonder. Maybe they weren't like that through my whole childhood, maybe it was only one time, one scene I remember that I've stretched out over years, mixing it up with hours of Fred and Ginger and Clark and Claudette.

Dot swears the way it is now is the way it's always been. Henry, she says, has never been anything but the man he is, a muddler, a shnook, inept, spineless, a bore, a big snore, a bungler, a mope. A man who has made his bed on a rollaway cot in the second guest room—the second, not the first, because guests might come and need the room with the real bed and the bureau and the nightstands and the lamps whose bases are glass globes filled with seashells. He moved into what is little more than a storeroom because she told him to. Instead of putting up a fuss, he just did it, clutched his foam rubber pillow and went where she told him to go, and that was almost a year ago. A gutless wonder. Spineless. Nothing. A man all their neighbors like because he's always doing things for them, going out of his way for other people, but if they only knew, if they only had to live with him, a big nobody, a big fat zero, oh, would they change their tune!

"What happened to the two of you?" I used to ask her, and she always said the same thing: "What do you mean, 'What happened?' Nothing happened. I was never happy with your father. You have no idea, there are so many things you don't know, you'll never know, about what I've put up with, living with that man. You're imagining all this other stuff," said my mother.

* * *

Dot is complaining that she can't find her hat. "There are three hats hanging out here on the porch," I call to her. She is in her bedroom at the other end of the house. "Mother? Did you hear me?"

"Those aren't the ones," she calls back, and I sigh hard and flop harder down on the sofa to wait some more. I snap my forearm in front of my face and calculate from my watch how long I've already waited, I hiss air out through my teeth, I glare at the ceiling and jiggle my foot, as if other people were in the room with me and I were doing a per-formance for them, a one–woman show called "My Mother Is So Goddamn Annoying": I've been here three days and I've spent two and a half of them waiting for Dot. "You can sit under the umbrella," I call. "Mother?" No answer. "You don't really need a hat."

"I found it," she calls back, but does not appear. When she does, four more minutes later–a thirteen-minute wait for Dot to get herself ready to go into the back yard–she has on sunglasses and a straw hat with a brim that flops down to her nose. She has on long pants and a cotton top with long sleeves and she says she still has to put sun-screen on. "Get a hat, Margie," she says to me, and I tell her I don't want one. "Put one on," she insists. "The sun will kill you."

"I don't get enough in a year for a lethal dose," I tell her.

"At least put on some sunscreen, then."

She passes the tube to me, but I refuse. "What will my friends in the Midwest say if I go home from two weeks at the beach and I'm all fishbelly white?" I ask, hoping to jolly her out onto the patio with no more delays.

"You'll be sorry," she says, "but I never could tell you anything, could I?" She turns and gives me a big, cheery smile, as if what she had actually said was, "You are the most wonderful daughter who was ever born."

Finally we are settled on the patio out back, Dot in the shade of the umbrella, me in full sun, facing the narrow lagoon, a finger of the bay that makes a kind of alley along the back yards of the bungalows in their retirement development. Dot points a finger at my chest and makes circles with it. "If you're going to sit in the sun, at least take them down so you don't get, you know, strap marks."

Between us are a half–bushel basket of lima beans and a shopping bag to hold the pods. I hand Dot one of the two Pyrex bowls I have brought outside. "We can't stay out here too long," she says. She glances up warily at the sun, which has become another menace in her dangerous life, along with invisible pesticides on fruit, invisible radiation emanating from overhead electrical wires and the ground beneath her feet, invisible bacteria in the clams Henry plucks from the lagoon shallows, blobs of invisible cholesterol sticking to the sides of her arteries. "It will happen to you," she told me when I walked to the store for half–and–half to put in my coffee the first morning. "It won't be long now. It's from my side of the family, the cholesterol. You'll see. Soon it'll be skim milk for you." She sounded like she could hardly wait. Now she squints around the umbrella edge and frowns. "We're out at the peak. We should have come out earlier if we were coming out."

It smells so good by the water," I say, scooping furry unshelled lima beans into each of our bowls and handing hers back to her. We are making succotash this afternoon. After we shell the limas, we have white corn to husk. We will make two batches—one with only beans and corn and water, and another with a strip or two of bacon and a little butter and salt stewed in, succotash the way Dot always made it, for me.

"Your father will want some of your batch," Dot says, "even though he will probably not live out the year. So we'll make more of yours."

"What do you mean, he won't live out the year?" I ask. It is news to me.

She cracks a pod and detaches the row of beans from the inside with one long motion. "His triglycerides are over 300. He eats buttered toast," she snaps, as if I should have known, as if I were still living with them and could see for myself what my father ate for breakfast every morning, as if I knew all the daily details of their lives. Or as if I should still be living with them, instead of coming to visit once every five years, which is as long as I can last before she starts complaining that her neighbors say things to her like, "Do you really have a daughter?"

I blink stupidly at her, failing to get the gist. "What is it—does he have heart trouble? What has the doctor said?"

"Doctors," says Dot. She blows air out of her pursed lips. With a flick of her hand, she sweeps all doctors off the face of the earth. "If you waited for a doctor to tell you how to take care of yourself, you'd be dead. And his cholesterol! Did I tell you he won't eat breakfast with me any more? He said he'd rather sleep in. Then I come to find out he stops at a coffee shop in Ocean City every morning and has bacon and eggs. Bacon!" she says. "Eggs! He's lucky to be alive."

In her old age Dot has become a health nut. She describes herself this way; she is proud. She subscribes to all the alternative nutritional and medical newsletters and magazines, from the sober to the crackpot. We used to be big believers in butter. Dot bought one-pound bricks on sale by the dozen and stacked them in the freezer. She kept a canister full of bacon fat on the stove, and everything got fried in it–eggs, fish, potatoes, chicken, pot roast–because Dot said it was what gave fried food flavor. At other people's houses, food got fried in corn oil. "Poor Alice," Dot would say of my aunt after dinner at her house, "she couldn't fry a decent chicken if her life depended on it."

Now she has banished fat from her kitchen. She drives forty miles to a health food store. For snacks she offers stale-smelling chips of indeterminate origin. For breakfast there is grapefruit and skim milk and some awful flakes made with no salt, no sugar, no oil. They taste like something kept in the cellar too long–musty, damp.

"You aren't speaking to Daddy," I point out. "Why would he eat breakfast with someone who won't talk to him?"

"That's just an excuse," she says, her tone so bitter that I don't want to hear any more. We sit quietly for awhile, our fingers working at the tough pods, snapping them open and popping the slippery silver beans into the bowls in our laps.

It's a relief to be outside, where it's warm. Dot keeps the windows shut tight and the indoor temperature shivery at sixty-five dry degrees. Inside, I sneeze and rub my arms and long to be outside in the moist, salty heat. I am facing west with my legs stretched out to tan. Across the narrow lagoon a screen door on the back of a yellow cottage opens and a fat little spotted dog flops slowly down the three steps from the porch to the patio, where it sits down and pants. "That's an old dog," I say. "What is it–a fox terrier? A Jack Russell? It's too fat to tell."

Dot has her back to the lagoon and the house, but she doesn't have to turn around. "It's Peg," Dot mutters, "and that dog of hers. Bernie. Barney. Barney," she decides. "Wave to her, hon." It takes me a moment to see the woman behind the screen door. Dot turns in her chair and drapes an arm across the back. "Hi, Peg! Nice day, huh? This is my daughter, Margie!"

I am the only person I know who was named for a television show. *My Little Margie*, starring Gale Storm, my mother's favorite when she was carrying me. That's how she always refers to being pregnant—"carrying" me. It makes me think of myself as a big purse. Dot always says she hoped I would be as cute as Gale Storm. She says this in a tone heavy with disappointment. I am nothing like Gale Storm. Like my mother, I am tall and heavy-boned but I have Henry's English chin, which is to say none to speak of, and lank, dark blond hair and big hands and feet. "You were such a cute baby," Dot will sometimes say sadly, looking at the way I am now. "So tiny," she murmurs. "And sweet."

Peg calls something to us, but neither of us can make it out. Through her teeth Dot orders, "Wave to her, I said!" I wave and Peg and I call hello to each other, then Peg disappears back into her house. The little fat dog turns his head our way and sniffs the air.

"Well," Dot says, settling back into her chair, "You know what?"

"No. What?"

Dot smiles down at her fingers snapping the furry lima pods. "I don't know if I should tell you," she says after a moment.

"Tell me what?"

"You won't believe it," she says. Across the lagoon, the shadow of Peg's face appears in a window just over where the dog is sitting. Peg says something to the dog that sounds like, "Go on." She says it several times. The dog never moves. It sits and stares across the water at us.

"Tell me," I say. It is not like Dot to be coy. I can't remember ever hearing her say "you know what?" "What is it?"

Dot glances over her shoulder, leans slightly toward me. "A fella made a pass at me," she says, and there is no mistaking the pleasure in her voice. "He meant it too."

"Go on, now. Get it done," Peg sings out the window. "Get it done, now. Go on!" Like a mantra. The old dog struggles to his feet, steadies himself on his crooked legs, then gives himself a thorough shake and stares up at the outline of Peg on the window screen. The stump of his tail flips so slowly back and forth that I can count each wag, a doggy version of a Gary Cooper grin, a slow smile. "Go on," Peg sings. "Get done now."

Dot jerks her head backwards toward Peg's house. "This goes on all the time. It's like a game with them. She won't go out with the dog and the dog won't make unless Peg is with him. He's real old. Probably has prostate or something. Do dogs get prostate?"

"Who was this guy who made the pass, Mother?" I ask. This worries me, things between Dot and Henry being what they are.

Dot keeps her head down, apparently focused on the bean pods, although it's hard to tell where she's looking, what with the hat brim and sunglasses. But then she looks up at me and mouths a name without making a sound.

"John?" I say, and she shushes me hard, glances all around again, whispers, "Your voice carries over water."

I mouth, "John?" back at her and she nods. "John what?"

"Lumsden," she whispers. "We're on the beautification committee together. He's a good–looking man. Gorgeous legs," she says. And giggles. It is exactly the giggle you would think a seventy-year-old mother would make. Lummox, I think. John Lumpfish. Lumbering John.

The dog has made his way off the patio and is sniffing in the grass. Suddenly, he squats like a female dog and pees for a very long time. "Well, who is this man? How old is he? I mean, what is going on, Dot? And how do you know he was serious?"

"He's my age," Dot says, prickly like a thirteen-year-old, annoyed by the questions and pleased at the same time, dying to tell.

"Married?"

She nods and wiggles her eyebrows up and down, like we are in it together, co-conspirators, like we are sneaking a Salem in the girls' room before gym class. She scoops another handful of beans out of the basket and settles back into her chair. "His wife is something, a real character. Big yellow horse teeth in front. Smokes like a chimney and calls John 'Mr. Magoo' because she says he sounds like that funny guy who used to sell light bulbs."

"Cartoon," I say, a reflex. Dot has never switched to electronic lingo. A cartoon is a "funny," as in the Sunday funnies. I have corrected this quirk of hers fifty times if I've done it once, to no effect.

"Car–tooooon," she sings in a peckish, exaggerated way.

"Sorry," I say.

She goes on as if it doesn't matter. "Mr. Magoo. Do you remember that car–toooon? Maybe you were too young. John doesn't look anything like Mr. Magoo, but she says he sounds like him. I don't know. She's weird, the wife."

"So how do you know he was serious?"

"Oh, he would say things, he'd flirt a lot at the meetings," Dot says gaily. "He would say things. His wife doesn't go. Like your father. She sits home like a bump on a log. And then he came by and made himself clear," she says, as if this were nothing, as if men dropped by the house to take her to bed most days of the week. "When your father was at work. Of course, I sent him on his way. I didn't even let him in the door." From across the lagoon comes a low, yodeling howl. "I said to him, 'John, you are welcome here any time,' and as soon as he started grinning I said, 'as long as my husband's home.' You should've seen his face."

The dog yodels again, then woofs. He sits at the foot of the bungalow steps. "Oh," Dot sighs, emptying bean pods from her lap into the shopping bag, "now the fun really begins." The dog has arthritis, she says, and doesn't want to climb the stairs back into the house. He wants Peg to come down and carry him up, but Peg makes him walk up himself because the vet told her exercise is good for arthritis. "I told her the vet meant she ought to walk that dog," Dot says. "Can you imagine thinking going up a couple steps counts as exercise? She doesn't have the sense that God gave geese, Peg doesn't. I told her to give him some selenium."

"Some what?"

"Selenium. You don't know about selenium?" Her tone suggests that "selenium" is the word on everyone's lips but mine. "It's a mineral, excellent for arthritis. Better than these drugs they give you. Plus the dog is fat. And you should see her husband! I said to her, 'You overfeed your dog and your husband, and if you'd cut back on the fat, your dog could come and go and Clayton wouldn't snore all his time away in his lounge chair.'"

"You didn't say that!" I know she did, though. I'm sure she said exactly that.

Dot puffs air out of her cheeks. "I most certainly did!" She's always complaining that all that husband of hers does is sleep. But she feeds him nothing but fat and sugar—what does she expect? You know what she gives him for breakfast? Sausage cakes and Sara Lee! I asked her, Are you trying to kill him? And you know what she told me? She said, 'It's what he wants.' Unbelievable!"

I wonder how Dot knows what the man eats for breakfast. Maybe this is what they talk about across the lagoon. Peg comes out onto her porch, opens the screen door and stands two steps above the dog, coaxing him. "Come on–come on up–you can do it." She pats her palms on her thighs. The dog heaves his front paws up one step.

"Mercy," Dot mutters, "can you believe this?" She has half turned in her chair to watch the contest between Peg and her dog. "Mother?" I say.

"Hm?" She doesn't turn around.

"Are you encouraging this guy?"

Dot laughs. "Well, let's see. Do you think telling him he shouldn't be here when your father isn't home and sending him on his way qualifies as encouragement? I mean, am I missing something? He asked could he come in for coffee if that's all I wanted–if that's all I wanted! Can you believe the nerve? Anyway, why would I want another man? I've already got one I'd like to get rid of–"

"To punish Dad," I say.

She turns away from Peg and her dog. She peels her sunglasses off and squints into my face with an old, familiar expression, a mask of bitterness and disapproval, a pursing of lips, a glare of disgust. "Boy, you're really something! Just who in hell do you think you're talking to?"

Too late, I realize that what she wanted was for me to be happy and excited with her because a man–an attractive man–was interested in her. She is seventy years old and once she was pretty, she had fabulous legs and beautiful hair, the only woman I ever saw whose hair was actually strawberry blond–a sheen of pinky red-gold. I was maybe eight or nine when I heard her tell one of her friends over the phone that a man had asked her to dance at a party the night before, and as he clutched her to his chest, he said in her ear, "You make my mouth water." How she must miss that kind of attention. And instead, I'm worrying about Henry. I have let her down once again.

The fat dog pulls the rear of himself up and sits on the lowest step. The effort appears to wear him out. "I think your neighbor is cruel to that dog," I say to Dot. "I think it hurts him to climb the stairs."

"Of course it hurts," Dot snaps. "I told you—the dog has arthritis. You never listen to what I say, do you?"

*　*　*

What I remember is years of bliss. How once upon a time they went out every Saturday night. Henry in a suit with squared shoulders, his hat brim swooped down over one eye, his ties so wide they nearly covered his shirt front and they shimmered with big modern patterns—lightning zig-zags, atomic ovals over ovals, big turbine spirals. And his dress socks were so sheer you could see his skin through them, and he gave off after-shave from down the hall.

Dot wore dresses made of elaborate fabrics, something-on-something—brocade, pique, flocking. The skirts fanned out from her legs on layers of crinolines that made wonderful swish sounds when she moved, the bodice stretched tight over her bosom, and she wore black satin slingbacks with her red-polished toes showing at the front. She swept her hair into an up-do. Bunches of rhinestones dripped off her earlobes, her lips were red and shiny as patent leather. She was wreathed in My Sin.

They went to parties where the lamps were on low and the rugs were rolled up. They did the rhumba and cha-cha and the mambo. They drank cocktails, sidecars and Manhattans, dark and dangerous–looking in tiny glasses on thin stems, they smoked stubby cigarettes that left flecks of golden tobacco on their tongues, and Henry lit Dot's Chesterfields with the lighter she gave him for his thirtieth birthday, a gold Zippo with his initials etched in.

When the party was at our house, I got to help Dot in the kitchen, smearing pimento cheese spread on Ritz crackers, rolling slices of Swiss and boiled ham around gherkins and spearing them with frilled toothpicks, filling glass party bowls with ripe and green olives and mixed nuts and extra-thin pretzels. I got to take the guests' coats as they arrived and carry them up to Dot and Henry's bed.

Henry would make me a cocktail, ginger ale and maraschino cherry juice in an Old Fashioned glass with ice cubes and an orange slice, and I would sip it and hang around the edges of the glamorous adult world of Dot and Henry and their friends, eavesdropping on their conversations, taking in what the women wore, how they did their hair. I was allowed to stay downstairs until they had both finished their first cock-tail. When they gave me the whiskey–steeped cherries out of the bottoms of their empty glasses, it was time for me to go to bed.

At one of these parties, on a New Year's Eve, I sat off to one side, nibbling on salami cubes, and listened to what Dot told her friends about Henry. "He was trained when I got him," she said and sent him a look that had wings on it and flew straight at his cheek and raised a blush there. She flashed her eyes and crossed one leg over the other and kicked the top leg up and down from the knee so the shoe dangled from her toes. "Oh, what Henry learned in France," she murmured. Henry smiled and looked on purpose anywhere but at her, like he did not dare, and took one of her hands in his and kneaded it between his palms like dough about to rise.

I swear, she loved him then.

She says no, but Dot is wrong. How can she say I made it all up? Why are our memories so different? She says mine are not memories, but some infatuation, some dim conceit. It's all true, I tell her. Don't you remember? Remember what? she says, like a demand, like a threat. I reel off the details–how they used to do the cha-cha to Tito Puente and Xavier Cugat records, the day I caught them kissing in the cellar and she was embarrassed because her blouse was unbuttoned, my maraschino cherry from the bottom of her Manhattan glass. I remember the sweet, hot whiskey taste in my mouth.

You're dreaming, she insists. Maraschino cherries cause cancer. I never would have let you have them.

You didn't know that then, I remind her. It was the 1950s–nobody knew. Remember Daddy's gold Zippo? You had it monogrammed? Those swishy dresses you wore? She looks at me like I am a two-headed alien baby on the cover of the *National Enquirer* and always says the same thing: "You missed your calling. You should write for the television. With an imagination like that, you could make a fortune."

*   *   *

In the checkout line Dot scans the tabloids and reads the headlines out loud. "JACK RUBY FOUND ALIVE . . . 80-YEAR-OLD WOMAN GIVES BIRTH TO TWINS . . . MEXICAN INFANT BORN WITH PORTRAIT OF JESUS BIRTHMARK." She laughs and points to the pictures. "Do you read these?" she wants to know. Her hand flutters over one of them, then grasps it and pulls it out of the rack.

"No," I say. I grip the cart handle and concentrate instead on the contents of our shopping cart: the pound of butter, the package of bacon, orange juice and mineral water, coffee, and wheatberry bread. Dot tried to talk me out of the bread by pointing to palm oil on the list of ingredients on the wrapper and telling me, "Pure saturated fat. This stuff will kill you." And we fought over the bacon. She kept saying we only needed a slice or two, and I kept pointing out that pound packages were all they had.

"They have good information in them, health news. Foods that can cure cancer, things the doctors won't tell you. Don't you read them?" says Dot.

"I don't read them."

She flips through the pages. "This thing about Oprah's boyfriend," she says, shaking her head. "Do you think it's true?"

"That what's true?" We are stuck in this line. The woman being rung up is insisting that the checker used the wrong price on the plums. "If they were eighty–nine a pound, I wouldn't have bought them!" she is saying loudly. "They're sixty–nine. I don't care what your sheet says! I saw the sign!"

"That he's–you know." Dot holds her right arm vertically from the elbow, then lets her wrist fall in an exaggerated way.

"That he has a broken wrist?" I ask, refusing to accept her assumption that we see things the same way.

"Oh, you know." Dot lowers her voice. "Her boyfriend's supposed to have had an affair with a man. With her hairdresser. Oprah could get AIDS if it's true. I love Oprah. I think she should dump this guy."

"Geez, Mother," I say. "Don't believe that stuff."

"Well, they couldn't print it if it wasn't true," Dot says. "It's the law."

"Is it?" I say. "What law is that, exactly?"

Dot shrugs and begins paging fiercely through the paper. "I don't know. Some law," she says. She knows she has gone too far, but being Dot, she would sooner die than admit it.

"Mother," I say. "Look at me." My mother glances up at my face, which looks nothing like Gale Storm's. "Why are you pretending to be the expert on libel law, given what I do for a living?"

For a moment she looks utterly blank and I feel my heartbeat skitter a dangerous little dance. Dot knows nothing about my life. She never has, not since I left home for college. She never visits, and she not only doesn't ask me questions, but she doesn't listen when I offer details. She once introduced me to a friend of hers by saying I taught English to college students. I didn't know whether to correct her or just be quiet. When her friend asked me what college, and I said Northwestern, her friend said, "Oh, really? That's quite a good school, isn't it? And do you like teaching English?"

And I said, "Well, I teach journalism, actually," and Dot didn't even seem to notice.

When I was younger, when I was still trying to drum up some interest in my life, no matter what I told her, she always responded with something about herself. When I moved to Chicago from Michigan after my divorce, I tried describing my neighborhood. I said, "The apartment is right off the lake, Mom. You should see the view! From the twelfth floor, I can see the lake, the park, the whole skyline." I remember exactly what she said in response. She said, "I can't imagine why anyone would want to look out their window and see a city. I hate cities, all the crime and noise and dirt." When I was a little older and in a confrontational phase, I reminded her of that conversation, trying to point out to her that she never showed any interest in me, that she couldn't even describe the apartment I had lived in for eight years. She swore it had never happened.

I assumed that she lost interest in my life when I began choosing one that was so different from hers. But now I wonder: Is she sick? Is what I thought was self-centeredness actually early Alzheimer's? Does she really not know what my job is? Then she frowns and turns back to the tabloid. "You don't have to be sarcastic," she says. "I'm not one of your students."

In spite of myself, I'm relieved. But not mollified. "Why don't you just ask me, instead of lecturing? You could say, 'Are they allowed to print things that aren't true? Is there any law that prevents them from doing that?' You could learn something."

"Oh, just shut up," Dot hisses. "I don't want to hear this. Who cares about newspapers anyway?" She shoves the tabloid back into the metal rack and leans over the checkout counter. "What's the holdup?" she calls to the checker, who is holding the bag of plums and gazing off into the distance.

"I'm so sorry," says the woman who's holding us up. "They're trying to overcharge me for the plums, and I just want to get it straightened out."

"Good for you," Dot tells her. "You take your time. If you don't watch them, they'll rob you blind."

"Isn't that the truth?" says the man in front of us in the line. He turns to Dot and begins telling her about how he goes straight home from the market and checks the tape against what he bought and nine times out of ten he finds he's been charged too much. He is stocky and maybe sixty and he has on short shorts and flipflops and a turquoise and red Hawaiian shirt that is unbuttoned to expose the brown drum of his belly. The tip of a cigar peeks out of his shirt pocket. He turns my way and stares blatantly down at my legs. "Somebody got a little too much sun today," he says.

"Ha!" Dot says with a smirk. "I told her to put on sunscreen, but do children ever listen to their mothers?"

The man shakes his head like he has water in his ear and presses his fingertips to his temples. "Wait a minute, wait a minute," he says. "You don't mean to tell me you're mother and daughter?"

Dot grins all over herself. "Everyone tells us we look like sisters," she says, grasping my arm and striking a pose. I want to slap her. It's an effort to restrain myself, an actual physical effort.

*   *   *

When Henry gets home, Dot and I are in the kitchen, making dinner. Dot has *Wheel of Fortune* on the living room TV, angled so she can see it from the stove. I'm slicing vegetables for salad and Dot is preparing flounder fillets for broiling. The succotash is stewing in its two separate pots when the back door opens and shuts. I call hello to Henry.

"Evening, ladies," Henry says, coming into the kitchen in his stockinged feet. Dot doesn't allow shoes on her carpet.

"I know it!" Dot cries. "It's MISS AMERICA THE BEAUTIFUL!"

"Hi, Daddy," I say. I step over and kiss his cheek.

"So what did you gals do today?" Henry asks. He has a grocery bag, which he sets down on the counter.

Dot glances over her shoulder. "What've you got there?" she asks. Henry pulls a six–pack of beer from the bag, then a plastic bag of steamer clams, a brick of Parmesan cheese, and a package of bacon. Henry looks at me and grins. "We feast tonight!" he says.

Dot homes in on the bacon like she's been newly equipped with early warning. "Bacon! You bought bacon!" she cries. She lifts the package off the counter then throws it down hard and turns toward him, her arms stiff at her sides, her hands tightened into fists.

"It's for clams casino," Henry says. He looks at me, puzzled. "For Margie. They're her favorite."

"Great," Dot says, "now we have two pounds of bacon in this house! We bought bacon today to make your succotash because Margie insisted. And beer! Who's that for?"

Henry turns away from her and lifts a frosted bottle out of the carton. "Anyone who wants one," he says. "Margie?"

"You bet!" I say. I do want a beer, a beer sounds good, but I realize I've forced a dangerous amount of enthusiasm into my voice, like one too many puffs of air in a balloon. "Have a beer," I say to Dot. "Come on. Just one won't hurt you."

Dot acts as if I am not there. She stays fixed on Henry. "Your triglycerides sky high and you're going to drink beer?"

A hard look comes over Henry's face. He twists the cap off a bottle and hands it to me, then lifts another out of the carton. "Yep," he says.

"Well, go on and kill yourself so I can be a widow! See if I care," Dot says and turns back to the stove. "You might want to drape some bacon over this flounder while you're at it," she spits, "in case there isn't already enough fat in this meal. And there won't be time for any clams casino either. I have a meeting to get to."

Dot and Henry gather like storm clouds over by the stove and the downpour starts. It won't take that long to make them—there isn't time, her entire dinner will be spoiled—he's making them for me and if she's a few minutes late to her meeting it won't matter—how can he drink that beer with his levels so high? Finally Dot stalks from the room. Henry and I stand in the middle of the kitchen, clutching our bottles of beer. We hear her bedroom door slam. Henry clears his throat. "Well," he says, "guess it's just you and me. You ready for some clams casino?"

Henry pulls some oregano leaves from a sheaf of stems he has dried from his garden and hung over the sink. While he works on the clams, I finish the salad. There is not a sound from Dot's room. A baseball game replaces *Wheel of Fortune* on TV and neither of us is watching but we don't turn it off either. We finish our beers and start on two new ones.

We are just sitting down to eat when Dot appears, dressed in a pink pants suit and a seashell necklace with matching earrings. "There you are!" Henry says, rising quickly from the table and pulling her chair out. "Perfect timing. You look nice, hon."

Dot swings past the table, grabs her purse from off the sideboard, and is out the door without a word.

After a moment I say, "Daddy? What's going on here, anyway?"

Henry chews for a minute, then says, "Let's talk about something pleasant. The succotash is real good. I always loved fresh succotash."

"I don't know," I say, reaching for something to lighten the heavy atmosphere, "I think it could use more bacon."

Henry looks up, startled, from his plate, then remembers to laugh.

*   *   *

In the first guest room, I lie propped up against the pillows, reading a paperback mystery. Dot warned me that reading in bed would give me a stiff neck. When I told her I'd been reading in bed for thirty-five years without a stiff neck, she sighed, "Okay," and sealed her lips tight as an envelope. "You know best. You always did." In his little room down the hall, Henry snores softly, a reassuring sound in the otherwise silence. It's after eleven and Dot's still not home from her meeting.

My old radio, which still works, sits on the bureau by the window—the radio Henry gave me when I was about five, the year Dot redid their bedroom. Since before I was born the radio had sat atop a crocheted, star-shaped doily on the walnut nightstand next to their bed. Henry was in the Reserves, and when he was away, sometimes a week at a time, the radio kept Dot company until she fell asleep. First the serials, then the music—big bands and light classics were what she liked. Most mornings the radio would still be playing when she woke up.

One day the Salvation Army men came and hauled off the walnut spool bed she suddenly hated because it was so hard to dust, and with it the matching nightstands and vanity set—the "suit," she called it—

from Strawbridge's, and the chest of drawers that didn't match, it was oak and rickety, a hand-me-down, she said, from Henry's parents.

When the furniture was gone, the men rolled up the mouse grey rug that had maroon roses with yellow centers cut into the pile and was as soft on my feet as old socks, and they carried it downstairs like a log. "They've got the rug," I said, running to find her and tugging the hem of her skirt, trying to alert her to the mistake before it was too late. She made a face. "How I hate that rug," she said, how dull and old-fashioned that rug was, she said. That awful pattern, like bruises, it was never my choice, she said to the contractor, the man who was doing the work on the house, a man with big hairy knuckles and a five o'clock shadow, and he shivered all over and went "Brrrr!" like he'd fallen through ice, like he was drenched and freezing. "A ghastly thing," he said. "What a ghastly thing!" I thought he meant ghostly-spooky, and this made me wonder what was wrong with him, that he'd be scared of a rug.

Then he said, "And that spool bed!" and his eyes rolled like marbles on hard-packed dirt. They laughed together, my mother and the contractor. They kept saying "fuddy-duddy," can you believe how long I've lived with this "fuddy-duddy" furniture, and the contracting man went on making exaggerated gestures of disapproval and disbelief, smacking himself in the forehead with his hand, moaning and clutching his sides, and Dot laughing, like everything we had had, like our life up until then, was a hilarious goof, a *Candid Camera* stunt.

The contractor's men came in and sanded the oak woodwork and painted it shiny white, tore out the brass light fixture with the candle–shaped bulbs out of the ceiling, and put up some metal thing that looked like a flying saucer with cutouts in it. They ripped out the windows and enlarged them, they knocked down a wall, they added a bathroom, he called it a "bath," the master bath, with twin shower stalls behind ripply glass sliding doors that had cranes etched on them. They painted the bedroom walls pale orange. She called it "apricot."

He said men would come to install carpet. I asked her, "How do you install a rug?" She said it was wall-to-wall. They did a lot of cutting and hammering, and when they were done, the wood floor was gone and there was a big expanse of bright blue pile, right up to the white baseboards. Then the truck came with their new furniture, the new "suit," this one from Wanamaker's, six matching pieces made of ash, a pale wood, almost white, everything plain and spare, a breeze to dust.

My mother squealed and clasped her hands when it was all done, she loved how it all looked so coordinated. All but the radio, said the contractor. That old box has got to go, he said. But Dot said she couldn't go to sleep without it, couldn't sleep unless there was music playing. "Get your hubby to get you a new one," said the contractor, "something jazzy, more your style."   .

A few days later Henry brought home a sleek silver and black plastic Zenith that fit perfectly between the sliding louver doors of the headboard of the new ash bed. He came into my room and said, "Here," with a big smile, "this is for you, this will go just perfect in here." He set the old radio down on my bed, he dusted his hands against each other and left, looking over his shoulder, like the radio might be following him. My mattress sagged where the heavy wooden cabinet sat. Its cord, sheathed in plaid woven fabric, curled next to it like a tail.

There were little chips all around the veneer where it connected to the fiberboard back, like tiny tooth marks, like something had been nibbling at it. Maybe my mother had been nibbling at their radio on those nights when Henry was on the road, and there was only the static for company. But later, when she came up to my room to clear a place for the radio on a shelf of the bookcase next to my bed, and I pointed to the chips on the back and asked her, "What are those? They look like tooth marks. Are they your tooth marks?" she straightened up and scowled at me and shook her head as if I had suddenly moved beyond the reach of her comprehension, as if I were a strange fairy creature who had flown through the window and landed in that bedroom, my room at the back of the house, when she hadn't been looking. She said, "Where do you get these ideas? Why do you think these things? I can't imagine what goes on in your head."

I remember this so clearly, how she spun the radio around and pointed at the marks and insisted they were made by a screwdriver they used when the back of the radio had to be pulled off so a tube could be replaced. She sounded angry and upset, I couldn't imagine why. I remember that she came and stood over me, how loud her voice was. "It was a screwdriver. Do you understand? A simple tool to take the back off." I remember that this is exactly how it was.

KATHLEEN GEORGE

Maria

JOHN BARNES is afraid that this driver, this woman, Lynn Stroub, will hit a child or a dog because she turns back to face him much of the time, talking and talking, even when she turns down the steep cobblestone street in San Miguel de Allende. On the two hour drive from San Luis Potosi—it should have been three—she told him all about her sex life, or maybe it was actually a love-life, while creating a third passing lane between speeding trucks. Lynn Stroub has a pointed nose and spikey hair, eyes which stay open a fraction of an inch too wide. John Barnes thinks of her as some ancient spirit carrying him to a new place. But then, he's prone to romantic thoughts. She's actually only an American, like him, getting away from something. She makes a living by meeting planes, driving tourists, transporting baggage.

Moments ago she turned from a dirt road to a surprisingly wide tree-lined street, where he saw old cars, trucks, and buses spewing exhaust fumes, and then just as suddenly to this steep and crowded street of cobblestones. They must wait as one car squeezes around another. People actually carry things on their heads! At least one woman does—a caryatid with a table top of vegetables. Has she been selling them? Before he can see everything he wants to see—the groups of children playing, the stucco houses, the heavy doorways—Lynn Stroub has made her way through and past the people and the cars to the bottom of this hilly street where there is a tree in the middle of the road. Her Colt squeezes around it and there they are, before a door, a very newly painted, heavy door. His hacienda. For a time. For five months.

110

People have told him there might be anything behind these blank doors and stucco walls from mini-ghettos to elaborately-gardened estates.

"I've never seen inside this one," Lynn Stroub says, her eyes widening especially at this prospect, her curiosity at a greedy pitch. She wants to know what she is missing.

In the next moments, John Barnes meets two more women, Shauna, the expatriate owner of the property, and another woman, whom he knows—by the fact that she scurries under their feet—to be Maria. Shauna has explained Maria comes with the rental. Barnes is uncomfortable about having a maid at all, but to refuse her is a problem, too. It would deprive her of a job and him of needed time to write his book. Still, it dismays him to watch Maria lift his cases of notes. They are so heavy that he hates to lift them.

Meanwhile, Shauna Walters holds him with what she, no doubt, believes to be a line of polite social interaction. She drifts around the garden, dangling a set of keys and showing him what is what, as she asks him about his trip. He admires, quietly, the silk pants outfit she wears and thinks his ex-wife would have liked it. He wonders why Shauna is so decked out in the middle of a weekday afternoon. He tries to catch Maria's eyes to indicate that he is friendly and will treat her well, but she escapes him.

*   *   *

A week later, much settled into routine, Barnes looks glumly at the house from the table in the garden. It is just his luck to come to an exotic place and end up with a house that is pure suburban New Jersey. There isn't a bookcase or a reading lamp anywhere, not to mention a book or a magazine. Everything is perfect, predictable, blandly marble as if the owners have reproduced their formica, plastic, and pressed board in this new place, but with better materials. He sits among flowers, eating fresh tomatoes, a Mexican-made Brie, and crusty bread. As other Americans have hurried to tell him, he can find almost anything here, tucked away in tiny shops. He hears Maria tiptoe across the marble floors of the kitchen to peer out the screen door. Is it time to remove his plate? her look asks. No, he motions, a hand held up to halt her, he wants to linger over the last few bites.

And besides he is writing a letter. He is writing to his ex-wife, trying to give her the picture of a man who is not boring. He laughs at himself. Callie will probably read the thing in the company of some architect, some actor, some travel agent, who has the ability to fascinate her. He writes this letter, he tells himself, simply to report on the town she'd once wanted to visit. It's charming, he says–hot springs outside the town, clothing boutiques on every street, an incredible maid named Maria who washes clothes by hand and gets out all the spots no dry cleaner has been able to get out. He would like to tell her about the poverty around him, the difference in life styles between the Americans and the Mexicans, and ironically which of the two groups seems the happier, but he knows she is less likely to find him interesting when he writes about such things. So he gives her the tourist goods.

Yet, when he reads over the letter, he filters it through Callie's eyes, and realizes she will still find him boring. Boring, boring. The hell with it. She will never love him again. He gets up from the table, carrying his own plates.

"Maria?" he calls.

"Si, senor?" She runs from somewhere, takes the plates from his hands even though he is trying to hold onto them.

"Have something to eat. Sit out here if you'd like. There's chicken, brie, bread, tomatoes, whatever you'd like."

"Gracias, senor."

Maria is very small and square. She has a full face and not much of a waist. She might have been carved out of a rectangular block of brown wood. On most days she wears simple polyester pants with a shirt tucked in. These clothes are clean and pressed, not very colorful. Her long black hair is combed straight back and caught in an elastic band. There is something serene in her clean, plain, squareness.

He likes having Maria in and about the house. When he goes downstairs from the room he uses as his study, he finds her trimming the indoor plants, mopping the floors, giving the stove an extra wiping. If he reads outdoors, he might go upstairs to change a shirt and find her folding the laundry or ironing. If he needs to be upstairs in the late part of the day, he can hear her on the service deck scrubbing the spots out of his clothes at the old washing board. She is always on alert, always busy, always out of the way but still there. Yes, he understands that he is lonely. He wonders what her husband does for a living and imagines that because she is so orderly and her own clothes are well cared for, almost fashionable too, that she lives with an energetic man named Juan or Raul. He sees them sitting up late at night, budgeting, figuring. He determines to leave her a large tip when he goes home.

*   *   *

He has met yet another woman in this first week. He is on his way to see her for a late afternoon drink. Bibi Richter in many ways resembles Callie. It's almost the first thing he thought about her when he met her at a party he was lucky enough to be invited to on his second day in town. "Everybody has a favorite beggar," she was saying. "I give to the blind woman at the corner of Hernandez Macias and Quadrante." He shivered at her phrasing, and yet, in spite of himself, he found himself drawn to her. Maybe out of old habit. She had a strong confident voice which carried in crowds. One of his colleagues would have described her as a woman who had appropriated white male values in the feminine atmosphere of the third world. But Barnes thought there was more to her than that. He sensed a sweetness under some sort of discomfort. He planned to call Bibi and ask her to dinner or something, but one day, a few days after the party, he wandered up the hill, looking into shop windows at small boxes of Tide and muslin shirts, being jostled by laborers moving stones, smelling restaurant pizza and chicken along the way. At the top, he had just handed a few coins to the blind woman when he turned into another street and saw Bibi on her way to the corner, casually emptying her pockets as she walked. She called to him and asked him to join her for coffee at The French Place.

Bibi is blonde, cheerful, clothed expensively and with theatrical dash. Today she wears triangular hand-painted earrings in the Mexican combinations used for flower arrangements—red, orange, pink. A scarf dominated by those colors falls carelessly around her shoulders. Bibi, dawdling over the menu, watching others, reading flyers announcing an upcoming lecture, skimming the newspaper, acts as if she's known John Barnes for years. She is cozily domestic. This is like breakfast together between old marrieds. Given her resemblance

to Callie, it's odd, funny, intriguing. But how will it help him to ex-
orcise Callie?

It turns out Bibi knows something about Maria. "She has six children, last I heard. No husband, of course, they never do. Just babies,
one after the other. You'd think they'd learn."

Barnes is surprised but can't for the world figure out why he hadn't
thought of this to begin with. Maria works like a woman who has
never been cared for. He wants to buy her something. A scarf, a watch.
Something pretty.

"She's quite a religious girl, your Maria. Goes on pilgrimages, one
after the other. Ask her what she's doing on her day off and it's likely
to be a twenty-mile walk at midnight to see some Christ figure on a
cross. Amazing stamina."

"I'm impressed with her," he tells Bibi. "She's very alert, very re-
sponsible. Imagine how much she has to manage. And she always
looks perfect and she's always on time. Six children! To support!"

"Oh, I'm sure they fend for themselves. The girls learn to wash
clothes when they're seven or so. The boys are pretty worthless.
They're in training to grow up and leave women pregnant, just like
their fathers did. But by the time they're five, they stay out of the
house most of the time."

The croissants are amazingly good at this breakfast place. And the
coffee is excellent. Who would have thought to find them here where
girls of seven wash clothes instead of going out to play?

"I come here all the time," Bibi says. "Listen. I've got an idea. Would
you like to go to a full moon party—it's really a hot springs party just
out of town. I could pick you up. It's next Tuesday. Everybody brings
something to eat. I've been to other ones. They're fun."

But John has nodded acceptance all through her invitation. He
doesn't approve of Bibi's breezy tone, but he can't for a moment imagine not following this through. He's on a journey. He felt it when Lynn
Stroub drove him into town. "Would you like to go to dinner this
weekend?" he asks.

"Of course," she says. "Of course I'd love to go. John Barnes, John
Barnes. What does that name remind me of?"

"It's a very common name. When people want an alias to check
into a hotel or to open a fake account, they're as likely to come up with
John Barnes as anything. The FBI comes to visit me once a year or

so. It's a weird name to have. People assume you're a criminal. I'm always answering which John Barnes I am."

"And which one are you?" Bibi smiles, but her eyes dart away and back, checking on who has just come into the restaurant to be seated.

"I'm the one who's writing a book on the politics of upstate New York," he says.

"No kidding! You know about that?"

"Yes. Or I think I do. Otherwise I'd be a fraud. Like those other John Barneses."

"What's your book about?"

"The machines. The clubs. The organizations. A history of the changing terms for the same scratch-my-back operations. America. You see, we think the machines had to go, that they were a bad thing. And in some ways they were. But not all bad. In terms of grooming candidates, that kind of thing, not all bad. I've got a thousand stories to illustrate that."

"Interesting. Well, you mustn't work too hard. See some of the towns around here while you're here. See things."

At the moment, all he can see is her bright colors and Callie, always Callie, behind her, playing hide and seek with him.

*   *   *

"You're paying too much for this place!" Bibi says, a week later, as soon as she enters the house. "It's pretty good, it really is, but Shauna is over-charging you."

"Do you think so? Don't the houses on this row go for quite a lot?"

"Even so." She moves around, inspecting the kitchen. Barnes has no trouble believing Bibi. He goes out of his way to avoid Shauna and senses there is something of the cheat in her. Her face is sneaky. She parades around in her silks and satins, poses with her very large rump towards him, but she finds it difficult when they do have an interaction to look him straight in the face. Why can't she look at him? And she's always in a hurry, as if she's late for lunch at the Waldorf.

"Your plants are in perfect condition."

"Maria is fantastic." He opens the drawer of a cabinet in the dining room and takes out a silk scarf. "What do you think? I bought it for Maria."

"It's gorgeous, but what will she do with it? I hate to crush you, but she'll probably need to sell it. I mean, that would buy her groceries for a month."

"If she needs to sell it, fine. I just thought she should have something pretty, for once in her life." It's no secret that Bibi is looking at him skeptically. Yes, he romanticizes women. But isn't it true that under every hard-working, make-do woman, is a lyrical beauty? "Come," he says. "Show me your hot tub friends."

*   *   *

"Bibi," somebody calls. "Glad you made it."

Barnes slips into the strong-smelling water. The bright moonlight illuminates slabs of rock with plates of vegetables, chicken, dips, jugs of margaritas or bottles of wine. Bibi has brought barbecued chicken for both of them–in thanks, she says, for the dinner he treated her to over the weekend. The food all around him makes Barnes suddenly hungry but it would be impolite to dive straight for it so he joins a group of people who are engaged in a desultory conversation and who look at him as if he is unwelcome. Once among them, he doesn't feel like swimming away, so he stands his ground. Everyone wears swimming clothes except two men in the group Barnes joined. He sees their genitals lazily bobbing with the movement of the water. One of the men, surely drunk, is telling laconically how he left the rat race behind and brought his family to live down here. Barnes wonders what the family lives on. Bibi's voice rises shrill with laughter behind him.

There are three connected pools at this hot springs and Barnes, in swimming from one to the other, encounters Lynn Stroub as well. She and a man whom he doesn't know are eating something rapidly, desperately. "Tamales," she says apologetically. "Bill had his maid make them. We only have these two. Would you like a little taste?"

Barnes manages to refuse. He wants a whole tamale! And is afraid he will gobble as desperately as they do if they give him a little taste. For a moment he thinks he sees his landlady, Shauna, but then he realizes she would find this party beneath her. He finds it beneath him too, but hopefully for different reasons.

Bibi slips an arm around him and kisses him. Desire flares up and he knows he will follow it, can't help but follow it, he is so lonely and it's so familiar, her gesture, so like Callie, that it's almost as if Bibi isn't a stranger at all.

"It'll be a nice thing, this," Bibi says late in the night in her bed as they shelter against the night breeze. Her hair is still damp and it is matted, as his is, and they both still smell of sulfur. She is lovely, has a trim body and an eager look on her face. "Five months," she adds. "It'll be good for both of us."

Barnes doesn't tell her that he falls in love easily, or that he is almost too hurt already by the matter-of-fact temporariness of this affair to go on with it. He stares thoughtfully at the ceiling. Perhaps this is all part of whatever he has to work through, put behind him.

"How's the book?"

"Slow. I wanted to work eight hours a day, but I wear out after six. Still, if I keep at it, I should have a draft by the time I leave. Then I have a little time once I get back to do some revisions before the term starts."

"Are you up for tenure?"

"Oh, no, I have that."

"Will you have to look for a publisher?"

"I've got one." He laughs. "Nothing much wrong with my life, huh?"

"You're quite a success." Bibi shivers and snuggles down.

Does she think so? He doesn't want to give any false impressions. So he says, "I'm getting over a failed marriage. I only tell you because it might hit me in the face sometime when I least expect it. I want to get past it and all that. It's just that I still get depressed."

Uncanny. Bibi strokes his thigh just as Callie would have done, a comforting move which disconcerts him.

* * *

The only person with whom he does not feel boring is Maria. He gives her the scarf and she blushes and dips several times in bows of thanks. The blush is especially apparent in her eyes. She looks at the scarf, lifts it carefully, feels it with the back of her hand because, she indicates, her fingertips are calloused and scratchy and she is afraid to touch it. He has not seen anyone clean as hard as she cleans since he was a boy and his grandmother did everything—floors, windows, the pipes beneath the sinks–with cloths dipped in chemical solutions. He takes the scarf and puts it around her neck. She flushes again. He takes it up and shows her how it would look on her ponytail. He can feel the dampness of her hair where it's caught by the rubber band. She shakes her head as if to say, "Such a beautiful thing on my hair? Never!" She wears a pair of creased brown pants and a short sleeved red knit top which contrast with the colors in the scarf–Callie's complex purples, pinks, and blues, brilliant and shimmering with light. Where does she buy her sturdy clothes? How does she keep them so neat? He hopes she will wear the scarf.

But if she does, he never sees her in it. She continues to dress in the same way for work, to dip and bow her head as she passes him. Each morning, he tries to catch her with a friendly hello before she bows and then look back to his work so she will not greet him as a servant. One day she stands behind him and watches him work. At this point he is still writing his manuscript by hand. "Hay muchos papeles, muchas hojas," she says admiringly. Then when he begins to revise and type, putting the thing onto a computer disk, she stops every once in a while to watch the computer work. "Donde estan las hojas?" she asks, fingers to her mouth. In an elaborate pantomime, he tells her they are now in the machine, "la computadora," which "no olvida." She looks at him skeptically and laughs which makes him laugh.

He tries to tell all this to Bibi whose off-hand response is, again, just like Callie. "Oh, she hasn't seen one of those before. But she's smart, so I've heard. Don't think she'll forget it."

"How do you know she's smart?"

"These people I know, Mel and Linesse–they're artsy types, so I don't know whether we'll run into them at parties or not, probably not–but they're on a committee with me and I remember she used to work for them. Probably still does."

"Maria? She works for me six days a week."

"Maybe she squeezes in two or three more jobs, you never know."

Maria comes to Barnes ten to four o'clock some days and twelve to six o'clock on others.

"Mornings. I think she worked for them in the mornings."

*   *   *

He manages to ask Maria if she has "otro trabajo." After a while she understands that he means, "otro empleo." When she admits that she does, she looks frightened and he understands that she is worried he finds her work unsatisfactory. "No, no," he hastens to tell her in a mixture of pantomime, English, and Spanish. "You must get very tired, cansada. Six kids and all. Seis ninos."

She shakes her head.

Later that day she asks him if everything is all right. He tells her yes, everything is wonderful. He feels happy because Callie has answered his letter and because she has wished him well. And tonight her incarnation is waiting to serve him dinner and to take him to a lecture.

When he sees Maria look at her left wrist, which is bare, and then go to the kitchen to look at the clock, he understands that he has frightened her about keeping to exact hours. "No, no," he says, ushering her out. "Go." He tumbles over himself trying to tell her not to worry about time and also asking her why she has no wristwatch. "Ha olvidado su reloj?"

She explains in slow Spanish that her watch, a gift from her employer Shauna, has been lost. Lost. "Lo he perdido. Perdido." Her face shows distress. Somewhere on the street, she pantomimes. Her right hand shows the watch lifting off from her wrist and falling to the pavement.

"Terrible," he says, shaking his head. "Que color?"

"Negro," she says.

*   *   *

He cannot find her a black watch, so on the way to Bibi's house, he buys her a white one and slips it into his pocket. Perhaps by the time he leaves town, he will have found a black one somewhere. Then she'll have two.

"She probably sold it," Bibi tells him, not without a little pique. "But of course she can't admit it, she has to say she lost it. And she's probably afraid of Shauna. The whole town is, actually."

He, too, is a little afraid of Shauna without knowing why. "What would Shauna do to her?"

"Lord knows. She's a screamer. You should hear her at the school board, at the delicatessen, in shops. What a temper. She's always right, everyone else is wrong. She'd make your Maria miserable somehow, you'd better believe it." They don't actually go into Bibi's house to eat dinner, but settle at the table in the courtyard, surrounded by flowers.

"You seem to know everything about everybody," John Barnes says, sitting down. "I've never even seen Shauna's husband."

"Well, I've been here for twenty years, off and on. I do know just about everything. Her husband's a handsome guy. I remember seeing him around before she ever met him. Before my divorce, my husband and I used to come here on vacation. Then after the settlement, I couldn't afford much of a lifestyle in the States, so I came back. Everybody comes back. That's what they say."

He has wondered about her, wondered when she would tell him more than the simple fact of her divorced state.

"You live very well," he said.

"I wouldn't if I were in the States." She is between forty and fifty years old, as he is, and young looking as well, yet she refers to herself as retired. He can't imagine retiring. For Bibi, everything is stopped, settled. This a disturbing thing about her. For the first time he asks Bibi if she has children and he expects the answer to be no because that's what Callie would answer. But Bibi surprises him, with a "Goodness yes. Two boys. They're grown and out of college. Thank God! They're earning livings now and I don't have to support them." She starts into the house, motioning for him to be still.

"Didn't you ever think of working?" he asks a little loudly, calling after her.

"Living is work. Here. I've got a carrot salad, tomatoes, a beans and rice dish and a little chicken." She brings out two plates, already prepared.

"You shouldn't have gone to the trouble," he says.

"Oh, I didn't. I had my girl do it today. She does something with the chicken that makes it very tender." Bibi cocks her head, plunks down the plates, sighs, heads back inside before Barnes can find a way to tell her the way she talks about Mexicans grates on his skin. He wonders, during her brief absence, if he wants to go on seeing her.

She emerges again, brings a bottle of wine to the table, saying, "Actually I wangled myself a job with Bird's Eye for a while, but it was pretty unpleasant. I replaced a Mexican foreman and the workers there never forgave me. I finally quit."

Again it happens. Callie's manifestation. Something about Bibi's face–it is closed–keeps him from asking more. Callie too had had trouble at work, bitterness and difficulty making a place for herself.

He and Bibi talk about her marvelous garden and the tastiness of the meal, until they come around, once more, to Maria, who, he explains, does the most gorgeous flower arrangements, but has never cooked for him. For some reason her contract does not include cooking. "I wonder how old Maria is?" he asks. "Forty, I'd guess."

"Probably more like thirty-two. Her oldest son is about sixteen, so that makes it about thirty-two."

"A formulaic life," he comments.

"Yes," she laughs. "Predictable, at least. Listen. You're not thinking of dumping me for her, are you?"

"No. I'm just trying to understand her. I wonder about her circumstances. How many fathers do you think there were for the six kids?"

"Probably six."

"Really?"

"Don't be shocked. The guys just don't stick around. It's just how it is."

Is Maria sad, he wonders? Angry? Did she fall in love easily, get hurt easily? And how does she manage to raise six children on whatever she makes by cleaning? He assumes it is about a hundred dollars a week.

"Maybe some of the fathers provide support," he suggests.

Bibi shakes her head. She stands up and kisses him on the forehead, leaning over to do it. He feels foolish. She is leaning over him, rubbing lipstick off his forehead, so that all he can see is her hand which holds her brightly printed blazer away from the table so that it will not bump into any of the food.

"Sweet, foolish John Barnes."

"How much do you think Shauna pays her a week?"

"Oh, I think it's by the month. I think it'd be something like twenty-eight or thirty a month. I pay my girl thirty-five because she's been with me a long time."

"Ah! That's not enough! It's not enough."

Bibi nods. "But to them it's a lot."

All the way to the lecture, John reviews the prices of vegetables and eggs he's seen on the streets. No matter how he figures it, he can't get a week's order to come to less than four dollars. And that's just for a few basics. What about other things? Other food? Coffee? Clothes. Rent. Maria must have special merchants somewhere who cut her a break. He must make sure she eats more at his place. Maybe if he buys extra pastries and breads, she will take some home.

The lecture they go to is about the genius of the Mayan civilization. The lecturer says that he believes the expression caca and the word cocoa come from the same root.

"But these are English words," Bibi challenges the speaker in the question and answer session. One thing Barnes likes about her is her fearlessness. "How do you explain that?" she asks loudly.

"These two words are amazingly similar the world over."

John Barnes laughs quietly. "Caca is universal," he whispers to Bibi. "I always knew it."

"Cocoa too," she says. "That's a nice thought. At least to a chocoholic like me."

Callie was a chocoholic, so he knows what to do. "We'll have to go for a nice treat after this is through," he says. "Something chocolate."

"I can't say no."

Is it coincidence that the very persons Bibi said he would probably never meet at the parties she takes him to are at the coffee and pastry shop across the street from the Bellas Artes? Bibi says, "Oh, there are the folks Maria used to work for. Let's go in there and let me introduce you."

They are Mel Wechsler and Linesse Solomon, a married couple. Mel has a small goatee and wispy thin hair. He is slight but muscular. Linesse is a wide-hipped earthy woman with flowing hair. She wears a long cotton skirt and an almost-nothing cotton tee shirt which shows she wears no bra and does not shave under her arms.

"We have something in common," he tells them. "I think my maid was your maid. Maria."

"Gomez? Oh, you must be the man she talks about?" Mel says, settling into a seat at the table.

"So our Maria is your Maria!" Linesse says.

"She talks about me?" John looks from one to the other.

Mel answers. "She says you work very hard. She tells us about your big manuscript and your computer."

"It's the first she's seen a computer work."

"Oh, no, we have one. We've had one for years. She's seen ours."

"Well, she seemed to be fascinated by mine."

"She's fascinated in general."

"Oh. I see. She just humors me, huh?" He winces as a waiter begins to approach them. "Chocolate, of course, for you," he tells Bibi.

"You'd better believe it."

"Or caca," Linesse says. "I think that guy was full of it. I think he's working the Americans for money for his next dig."

"Oh, you were over there too. Listen, let me treat," Barnes offers because the Wechsler-Solomons look to be in reduced circumstances. And besides he likes them and hopes to get to know them.

"Thank you," Mel says, studying the menu. "We'll buy next time. We're bound to see you around town."

By the end of the evening, John Barnes discovers that Maria works for the Wechsler-Solomons and their family every morning for four hours before coming to work for him. He can't discover the size of the Wechsler-Solomon family, however, since sometimes they refer to two children, sometimes to sixteen. It takes him two months to sort it out fully. Bibi knows part of the story (that they are always surrounded by a brood), but the Wechsler-Solomons begin to tell him more as he runs into them at the cafe or at breakfast. It turns out they have two children of their own. But they also count a family of eight that has been orphaned when their mother—who lived next door—was run over by a car. The Wechsler-Solomons support these children, feed them, give them clothes, pay for their schooling. And then there are others: Intelligent children from the neighborhood who weren't getting much of a break until the Wechsler-Solomons came along and paid for their schooling. At first, John thinks this couple must be rich, the version of rich that dresses down. But Mel and Linesse are open about everything. "We have combined incomes from trusts of twenty thousand dollars a year. On that we travel back and forth to the States a few times a year and we buy whatever we need for us and the children. It's plenty, really. We don't need fancy clothes. Clothes are silly." Indeed they never wear anything but the few pieces he first saw them in. It turns out that four of the children they support are Maria's four youngest. "The two oldest boys are worthless," Linesse says. "They're going to be just like their fathers."

The generosity of Mel and Linesse appeals to Barnes enormously. He finds his heart opening around them. Maria's hard work and courage appeal to him too. He catches himself thinking about her. Wondering what she has to eat on Sundays.

One Sunday he sees her walking home from church with a little girl. The child wears a crisp, light blue, flowered dress with a lace collar. Maria wears a straight black skirt and a lacy blue blouse. He runs to catch up with her, to meet her youngest daughter, a beautiful child who smiles shyly and moves closer to her mother. "Lovely," he says. He wishes he could know them better. Why is that so difficult?

Later he finds out through Mel and Linesse that little Linda is Maria's favorite. "Oh, yes, there's quite a story there!" Mel and Linesse tell him over breakfast one brilliantly sunny morning at a restaurant a few notches down from The French Place. Their table is set up on the sidewalk where they can look down the hill to the stirring of people, traffic, exhaust fumes, or up the hill to a powdery brown mountainside with a cathedral at the top. Linesse explains, "Linda's father was a seventy-eight-year-old man with whom Maria had a relationship for a couple of years. Apparently a nice old guy. The man left Maria his house when he died."

"She has her own house?" John asks.

"By American standards it's hardly more than shack, a basic cottage. But Maria is the envy of all the women she knows. Having a house of her own. The old guy was ecstatic to have a child, his only child all his life, and he was devoted to Maria. But when he died, she was very matter-of-fact. 'He's dead,' she told us. And then she just put in a day of work."

"Oh."

"She's sworn off men," Linesse says. "She says they're not worth the bother. Now that she has a house and six kids she says she doesn't know what she needs a man for. She's quite a character. Our Maria."

"Maria?" John asks them. "I haven't seen that side of her." He tries to imagine her making speeches about her liberation from men. "Maybe she'll meet somebody good. Who knows?"

"I wouldn't bet on it," Mel says. "Although it would be nice of course."

"Look at it this way," Linesse says. "We all keep meeting the same people, playing the same scene, over and over again anyway. There were a couple of guys in there who beat up on Maria. I'm sure she doesn't want to meet up with them again." Linesse slides an elastic band from her thick hair and pulls her hair tighter before fastening it again.

"What do you mean about meeting the same people?" John asks her.

"I don't mean reincarnation or anything like that," Linesse says. "Only that we each have probably about ten people who matter to us—maybe less in some cases where there have been small families—and we keep finding them over and over again. Quite frankly, Mel here is my brother. The same type. All right, very incestuous and all that." She laughs and shrugs. "And Maria is my sister. And our kids are my parents. If you think about it, you'll figure it out."

When he first thinks about it, he can't find the resemblances—except for the fact that Bibi reminds him of Callie. But one day, sitting in the sun, he finds he can squint his eyes and picture one person through—almost behind—another. The faces and bodies and voices start to blend and chime in for him. Callie and Bibi are, after all, versions of his mother's sister who lived with them for a while. Shauna is his mother. It hurts to think this, but it's true. Mel and Linesse are cousins, the twins who always seemed so interesting, so emotionally advanced even when they were only five. And Maria would be his grandmother, his mother's mother, who had actually raised him for most of the years of his youth. He could remember his grandmother kneeling on the floor to clean, up on a ladder washing windows, a little too heavy to do either comfortably, but always busy, always active, a woman whose love he never doubted. All of his feelings of comfort go back to her. And his aunt, he remembers in this reverie, was glamorous, 1940s glamorous. She allowed him the role of her knight. And he fell effortlessly into it. While his mother was a social climber given to lies and stratagems, his aunt was secretly tender, sometimes whimsical. Yes, that was his world. It's coming clearer. His father had given up on his mother and left, although he had done his best over the years not to leave John as well. Long, long ago, John knew he couldn't please his mother. He has lately realized that nobody could.

This realization gets him through some of his interactions with Shauna which otherwise might have given him apoplexy. Shauna finds ways of charging him for things which aren't part of the contract—

heating oil, the basic phone service, a chipped toilet seat which he knows he didn't chip, a crack in a glass pitcher. And how has she found these things, anyway? She must have come to look at the house when he stayed overnight at Bibi's. It gives him the creeps. He took this place on the understanding that since he arrived on January tenth and was scheduled to leave on June tenth that he owed her five months rent altogether. She told him in mid-April that he would have to pay rent for all of June. "But that's not what we agreed to by phone," he countered. Then she flashed her silks at him and turned on her heel saying, "It is. By no means are you going to get away with this." And she rushed out the kitchen door, her shoulders at an angle as if he'd hit her. When he remembers his mother, he understands there is no pleasant way to resolve things with her. It's sad.

But he is all right. Because all of the love which John felt for his grandmother returns to him as he sits in his garden and plays the little game with vision that Linesse and Mel suggested to him. When he feels his grandmother's love, he can dismiss Shauna. He finds this very interesting.

Maria comes to the garden to say goodbye for the weekend. A little shock goes through him. He feels, in addition to everything else, a strong sexual current. He wishes he could bury himself in her squareness, that he could make her soft. He would never act upon such a thing. Still, he recognizes he's come to love her. His Maria.

On Easter weekend, there is a long parade through the streets which the Americans tell John he should see. It's more a religious procession than a parade. It lasts for hours and hours. Groups of women carry heavy platforms on which are papier mache scenes of the Easter story. The children carry a stage with the baby Christ, adult women carry a huge display of the journey with the cross, older women and teenagers do every thing in between. There are nearly a hundred displays; the whole town gets involved.

When Barnes takes his place on the crowded street, he sees that each group of women dresses formally and uniformly. Whole groups wear pink, or blue, or black. Women from the ages of twelve or fourteen on wear heels. Every group, no matter what the age, has to struggle to hold up its platform because the displays are so massive, and made of wood. Women relieve each other.

Barnes finds himself looking for Maria. And finally, after he has watched the slow excruciating procession go on for three hours, he sees her, walking with a group, waiting to take her turn at holding up a stage which shows the women at the tomb. She is dressed in white, as everyone in her group is, except for black high heels. She passes him without seeing him. After a moment's hesitation, he pushes through the crowd on the sidewalk keeping time with the part of the parade which includes Maria. He feels foolish, but when he sees her bid good-bye to the other women and begin to walk very fast through an arch-way, then an alley, he follows. He wants to know what kind of house she lives in.

She does not turn, she does not see him. He thinks it would have been a good idea to have an Easter basket, a ham, something to offer. But he doesn't want to lose track of her. Finally she reaches a crooked doorway in a small row of houses. Three small children stand at the door. She shooshes them inside and follows. Just as he had imagined– the small nest-like crowdedness of the place, the smell of beans, the warmth generated by seven bodies in a tiny space.

The next week he tells Maria that he has not had such an Easter in his whole life. He points to his heart to show that the procession evokes feeling.

"Ah," she says. "Bueno."

*   *   *

In his fifth month in Mexico, he wants to do something for Maria that will make her happy. Sometimes as he sits at his computer and taps away at his book, which is now coming along really well, he tries to figure out the right way to give her something. She is very proud. When he gave her the watch, months before, her face fell and she said, "No!" before she recovered and thanked him.

Shauna will be very angry if he spoils Maria, as will half the other Americans, since they have to go on employing Mexicans at the usual rate. He talks this over with Bibi and she tells him that, of course, he has to do what his heart prompts him to do, but she advises a tip of fifty dollars which is enormous in Maria's terms and amounts to two months pay.

He thinks about Bibi a good deal as well. They spend several days a week together and are thought of around town as a couple. And yet, what does it mean? When he tries to think of himself and Bibi in a future, away from Mexico—or even in Mexico (he had gone so far as imagining himself living the good retired life there)—the fantasy doesn't work. Nothing emerges. And the picture he gets of Callie through Bibi is frightening—a woman who doesn't actually do anything. And he, a man who respects work above all things. Wasn't it the work of holding up the platforms in the Easter procession that had touched him so much?

Besides, Bibi decided this was to be temporary from the beginning. What did she want him for? Bed only? And who said men always used women? It could happen the other way around, that's for sure.

When there are only ten days more to stay—the ten days for which he is paying thirty—John Barnes opens the door to Shauna who appears unannounced. "I've come for your rent," she says. It is only eight in the morning, but she wears high heels and makeup and a dress with a jacket. She is overwrought, or wants him to think so. She swallows hard, flips her hair about, and paces the dining room while he goes to get the check. Maria stands behind her in the archway, her hands folded, in attendance.

"Really, Shauna, I'm not going to cheat you! I don't have plans to skip town with your valuables," he says. He can't find anything very interesting or authentic in the whole place. He hands her the check.

She flushes, but doesn't reply, only reads the check as if there is something wrong with it. Maria waits with downcast eyes, surely embarrassed by the whole interaction.

"By the way, what about my two months security deposit?" Bibi had told him that nobody asked for two months! And at such a high rent!

"You'll get back whatever's left after I've deducted expenses like the phone bill and damages."

"Don't worry. I'm not going to have thousands of dollars worth of phone calls. I've called my publisher once. And I haven't damaged anything."

"I'll return the money to you two or three months after you leave."

"That's not very fair," he says patiently, "to hang me up for so long."

"I have to wait until the bills come in. I'll come by on the ninth to do inventory and check for damages." She pivots and goes out the door.

He stands and watches her walk to the gate. "Entendio?" he asks Maria when Shauna is gone.

She shakes her head no and goes back to work. And so does he, wondering why Maria is lying for she is smart and surely she understood.

When he next runs into Mel and Linesse, they have their own two children hanging off them and net bags of groceries from the street market. They invite him to a birthday party, a combined party for some of their kids, on the ninth, before he leaves. "You can meet Maria's children," they say. "And the rest of our gang."

So, his last day will be divided: Shauna in the morning, Maria and the children in the afternoon, and Bibi in the evening. He will take Bibi out for a nice dinner somewhere.

The ten days speed by as he packs his books, shops for this and that, looks at the bronze domed cathedral on the hill, and the street vendors and the beggars as if for the last time again and again. His chest aches to be leaving. How attached he gets to people and things. Even this plastic house he's landed in.

But most of all, Maria. Maria. He thinks about her all the time, looks forward to her arrival, regrets her daily departures. He knows her clothing better than he knows Bibi's. He's tried to ask her about her children, about her siblings, about her religious pilgrimages, and she's tried to answer. He's actually tried to explain his book to her. He's said there was actually sometimes a heart buried under New York's political machine–or at least that decisions sometimes addressed human being with kindness. Does she understand? In their broken Spanish, mostly what's communicated is that he cares about her. And she him? It seems so. They work during the same hours everyday, cheerfully, without complaint. And work is pure.

Sometimes he sits at his desk and just looks at the light coming through the windows and blocks out everything but its bright beauty. He thinks of Callie more and more as a woman from his past, a woman who expected excitement, security, joy, to be handed to her. He wonders if everything which comes to her will seem empty so long as she doesn't do anything to deserve it. He sees now that he loves life far more than she does. He thinks something tricky happened between them: he found her boring without knowing he did. She sensed it and called him boring and began to make her way away from him.

Then there are Mel and Linesse raising all those children! How he admires them. They aren't bored or boring. He vows to be useful to someone, somewhere, for the rest of his life. In the mean time, he buys small trinkets and toys wherever he finds them for the children's party. When the day comes, he will add a tray of pastries.

The morning of that day comes. It brings Shauna to his door as he knew it would. "Let's be civilized about this," she says.

"Certainly."

She opens a cabinet and using her finger to illustrate her count, counts glasses. "You've broken a wine glass," she says.

"But I bought another set to bring the number up again," he explains.

"One wine glass," she says as she writes it down.

"They were just inexpensive five-and-ten glass!" He almost bursts out laughing, but checks himself.

"And you've cracked the blender cap," she says, going straight to the blender.

This takes him completely by surprise. "I did?" He can't even re-member having used the blender.

"Yes." She shows him a hairline crack on the round plastic that connects the jar to the base."

"I didn't realize."

"Well, I did. Or I should say, Maria did."

Then she skips whole cabinets and goes directly from object to ob-ject which she considers damaged. So. She has already been here, snooping when he was out. "This wall," she points, has some pen marks from when you wrote the phone list."

"God! You can't even see them!" Now he is really angry.

She moves so fast through the house that he stumbles keeping up with her. Maria follows behind him, but when they get to a room, she moves past him and stands at attention, her gaze averted. In the sec-tion of the bedroom John uses as a study, Shauna points out, "I'll have to get the desk refinished. You've scratched it moving your computer mouse across the wood." In the bathroom, she says, "I'll need yet another toilet seat. You've chipped this one, too, from flipping it up too fast."

"Look, you said you wanted to be civilized about this. What is this really about? You can't be serious about these things."

"Maybe you just don't know how to take care of a house," she retorts. "That's the whole reason for a security deposit." Shauna finds nicks and scratches in her plastic house that he couldn't have known existed. He sees his whole security deposit gone, gone into her wardrobe. And how will he get it back? If he hires a lawyer, it will cost as much as what he's losing.

They go back to the kitchen. "You broke the glass on this table," she says.

"True," he steels himself. He once brought down a pot too hard and cracked the glass. "But I replaced it."

"But you didn't tell me. You didn't tell me. And even though you didn't tell me, I know you broke it. You see," she does another one of her stylish pivots, "Maria told me. She told me how you took the broken glass to the shop and tried to get the same thickness but they didn't have it and you settled on the thinner glass. So you see, I know after all. I have Maria. She tells me everything." Shauna takes a step backward to get Maria into her sights.

John has a moment of disorientation–something flashes very fast, a memory he can't catch, of some moment from childhood. What was it? His grandmother siding with his mother, maybe. To his horror, he loses his years, becomes three again, or four. He feels the blood drain from his face and his voice takes leave of him. It's not that Shauna is angry, that's not the worst thing. Or that she will take his money. Although that's bad enough. It's that she's claiming Maria. She's telling him Maria isn't his at all, but hers.

He tries to look at Maria but she looks away still, downward, as if checking the very clean floor. Her refusal to look up punches him in the gut, shortens his breath. Shauna says, pushing the list of damages across the table, "Do you agree to these things?"

He rubs a hand over his eyes. "How can I agree to them? You're attacking me for just living."

"If you'll sign this piece of paper," Shauna says. He sees the blur of Maria out of the side of his vision as he shakes his head no. Yes, she must have reported every little scratch for Shauna to be able to walk in and be so thorough in her castigation. He is a romantic fool not to have noticed that Maria is only Shauna's employee. And he can't re-member chipping or breaking anything except the table glass.

"I'm sorry you feel that way," Shauna says. "I'll leave the list here. You think about it." Then she tells Maria to look after everything while she is away, and she leaves.

For the rest of the morning, after Shauna is gone, he finds himself tiptoeing about the house. And Maria tiptoes too. She is quieter than ever. Even when she comes to remind him that she will leave early because of the children's party, she is down to a whisper.

He buys the pastries halfheartedly. But he can't not buy the pas-tries because he's had this idea for presenting them for so long. In the same uncertain and pained way, he hands over the envelope to Maria that he has had prepared for days. The equivalent of two hundred dollars and a note which tells her what a pleasure she's been. He can't not give it to her. She thanks him quietly twice without opening it, and leaves.

So, tomorrow, Lynn Stroub with her wild eyes and spikey hair will pick him up at six in the morning and spirit him away. He will not see Shauna Walters again. He will leave an unsigned list for her. At least there's that.

*   *   *

The good-bye evening with Bibi is more difficult than he imagined. They are both struck into silence. For entertainment he tells her about Shauna's sweeping tour of the house, and she tells him he should have yelled bloody murder. He feels the sting of criticism in her reaction.

The thing that surprises him is that Bibi cries. All through the night. "Oh, it's just foolishness," she says. "I hate partings." He holds her all through the night, hardly sleeping at all, and wondering how he could have thought their ailing relationship would cost them noth-ing. He's used her after all, let her be a way of saying good-bye to Callie. And then it's over. Five o'clock in the morning comes and he gives her a final kiss and goes home to check and recheck his bags.

He wonders if Maria will come in this dawn to say good-bye, knows she has thought about it, considered it.

But Lynn Stroub arrives early, packs him into her car. Her eyes look more alert than ever, but she is not in a mood to talk. That's fine. He's not either. He's tired and wants to concentrate on where he's going, to a new life away from Callie and to an as yet unknown woman with whom he plans to talk and argue and plan. Maria doesn't come. But it's all right.

He is all right. The party for the children yesterday was the best time he's had in his five months in Mexico. How happy they were with the pastries and gifts! Oh, he was a hero for bringing them. He drank wine and made conversation with the other adults there, aware, all the time, of the awkward silence which had come between him and Maria. She hadn't thanked him for the money. He hadn't told her he understood: she had her job to maintain, a life to maintain. He would leave, but she still had to deal with Shauna. He hoped for this exchange, but she was always across the yard, no matter how many times he moved.

All around him, children squealed with excitement, played games, marveled over the food (hot dogs); the hot dogs tasted good to John, too. All the children with May and June birthdays opened presents from Linesse and Mel. The toy truck and balloons and dolls made them so happy. And then the big surprise: a band of musicians arrived!

"How did you do this?" everyone asked Linesse and Mel, meaning 'how can you afford this?'

"Just for once," they said. They still wore the same clothes, the clothes they wore every day, clothes which Maria washed for them at some interval in the early mornings.

Eventually there was dancing to the mariachi band. The music was infectious. John wanted badly to dance. Mel and Linesse danced with each other. The rest of the people he didn't know very well. He'd invited Bibi but she hadn't wanted to come–"I don't know. Not to a children's party," she said.

Maria's little daughter, Linda, came up to John, tapped him on the leg and ran away. Somebody else pushed him into the circle and he found himself beginning to dance, not with anybody in particular, with everybody. He couldn't explain it, but he felt really happy. When he looked up, there was Maria, across the yard, nodding to him to go ahead and enjoy himself, nodding encouragement as if she knew him down to the depths. He could still feel where Linda had tapped him on the leg. Surely she'd been sent by Maria.

MARK R. GANEM

The Things You Get Yourself Into

SO MY SISTER Amy was all over me to cut the cake and I had to smack her hand away from the frosting like a little kid. We had to wait for Corey, I told her. Corey's my oldest, on his way up from Boston. I kept looking down at my watch, but with Amy at me like some tsetse fly, the music blasting, and me already with a wicked buzz on, it was like reading Greek. Fact remained, it was late–we all bust out with "Surprise" more than an hour before, when Gus showed up at the K of C hall thinking he was just going to hook up with the guys for a regular night out. That meant I'd been there a good four hours myself, hauling in the decorations, Gus's special nudie birthday cake, and the party platters, and setting everything up with help from absolutely no one–including the DJ, who sent me running all over the K of C looking for extension cords like I had nothing better to do.

It must be the snow keeping Corey, I thought. The radio said how it was coming down pretty hard in Boston, even though it was still falling in those big, lazy flakes up in Somersworth. At one point I was going to call him to say maybe he shouldn't come–I was hoping he'd insist–but it was enough he agreed to show up at his father's fiftieth birthday party at all. I didn't want to push my luck.

I heard a shriek and this high, birdy laugh from the table where the twins sat with their girls, and looked over in time to see Charlene, Johnny's girl, struggling under the "Happy 50th Gus" banner that had floated onto that teased, tarty hair of hers. I grabbed a roll of masking tape and marched over there, ready to give them all hell.

"Great party, Ma," Johnny said, tipping a bottle of Bud off his forehead to me like a salute. The others—mostly guys who'd been in and out of my kitchen since fourth grade—gave me the thumbs up. Jim's new girl, whose name I already forgot, kind of looked away—since the beginning of the party she'd made sure her eyes never met mine, like it made some kind of difference I knew she was doing it with my son.

"You guys expect to have the whole place torn down before Corey comes?" I wanted to know.

"Sorry, Mrs. K.," Charlene said, but I could tell by her voice she really wasn't. 'Mrs. K.' was what Johnny and Jimmy's friends all called me—guys who knew they didn't have to ask before pulling a beer out of my fridge. But she was just sucking up to me, I could tell—getting into that daughter-in-law mode just because John and her'd been seeing each other for all of three months. She took the tape from me and tacked the banner back in place. It leaned a little to the left.

"He bringing the wife?" Jim said, and the whole table of them snickered till I smacked him over the head. "You don't talk about your older brother like that," I told him, but I could feel a little defeat, just the way I did when I'd stepped back and looked at the hall after I finished decorating. Under the banner and the bunting and the confetti I threw all over the place, it was still the same old K of C hall with that skin-colored paneling, the nook with the statuette of the Blessed Mother, and the old photos of local slobs shaking the hands of these cardinals whose robes and pom-pom hats had faded to a sickly pink. I didn't know what to call this Ron of Corey's any more than Jimmy did.

Lover was the word they used on the talk shows, and it was like something sour in my mouth to think it. I made sure to invite Ron for Corey's sake, but I was glad when Corey told me he'd probably have to work that night.

I used to think of Ron like he was some dirty old man—he's five years older than my Corey. But on the phone he was kind of a scream, using all these different voices from the movies. He wasn't serious like Corey. I tried to like him, anyway, because Corey did, but I couldn't help wondering if it wasn't really this Ron's fault after all—if maybe I let Corey slip out of my hands somehow and right into his.

"Whatever floats your boat," Jimmy said, but this time only Charlene laughed, so I could have throttled her then and there.

When I came back to Amy, she was making to poke at the naked lady peeking over a birthday banner in the butter cream frosting of the cake. "I just want a piece of the boob," she said.

"You can wait for the boob until later . . . Booby." That was too much. We both bust our gut laughing like a couple of school girls, and I felt a little more like my usual fun self.

"But Traci, everyone's eaten," Amy said, putting her hand on my shoulder like someone died. "They're waiting for the cake."

"Everyone over there is waiting," I told her, looking over to where Gus's family and friends jammed together like they were afraid of getting raped or something. "And they can damn well wait. They piss me off."

"You invited them," Amy made sure to point out.

"Well," I told her, "we couldn't very well have a party for Gus without them coming along and ruining it, now could we?"

She let out that little titter of hers that gets on my nerves. Fact was, my nerves were just plain shot right about then. Gus's family had to be dragged to his fiftieth birthday party, which I had spent a month and two hundred dollars getting ready for, renting the K of C hall, calling around for the DJ, the food, the cake, the belly dancer, the wheelchair I rented as an old-age joke. All this plus Pa to take care of, laid out since Christmas with the prostate, and Ma barely able to take care of herself to boot. The things I do to keep this family together, I don't know.

I rearranged Gus's presents, putting the smaller packages on top of the big ones, and checked my watch again, this time staring at it until the numbers made sense to me: It was nine-thirty.

"I don't know why you even bother, Trace," Amy said. "Gus is a jerk."

I just shrugged, and finished off my white Russian. "He's the father of my sons," I told her, and just saying it felt like something solid I could lean up against. It should have been obvious to anyone, especially Amy, that I didn't love Gus anymore. His late nights and his women had just sucked all the feeling from me. If it weren't for the boys, I would have walked out on him years ago. Boys need a father, I always said. And it was true—at least for the twins, who got along with their father like old buddies. Jim was training for the police force, where a bunch of Gus's friends worked, and John was already on the line where his dad was supervisor.

The DJ put on "I'm a Believer," and I grabbed Amy's arm, going, "Let's show these guys how it's done." I was dressed for dancing, with these wicked bright floral stirrup pants under a big white sequined sweat shirt, and a pair of flats that made me feel like Mary Tyler Moore on the old Dick Van Dyke show. Most of the other women my age were dressed like frumps.

Just to let you know, I'm no Mary. I'd settle for being Rhoda, actually, since I'm a little on the heavy side. If there's anything I can't stand, though, it's those fat women who sort of curl in on themselves like they could just disappear. Reminds me of the elephant in the cartoon hiding from the hunter behind some spindly little tree, his legs crossed and his stubby arms covering his privates like a little girl who has to pee. I'm more like those dancing hippos in Fantasia. They weren't clumsy at all, but graceful and spry. That's me: I'm a good dancer, and I like to move.

"You'll be a beautiful swan someday," Ma used to tell me when I was a teenager, and I couldn't help but smile to think about it as I tapped the points of my feet and swayed my hips just so, doing this excellent Watusi. Corey was my beautiful swan. When he was a baby, his hair stayed pale, not turning brown like Gus's and mine, and his eyes were this clear gray. I would sit by his crib for hours, just watching him sleep and wondering where he'd come from. He was so precious to me it was as if he was a little prince who had been abandoned on my doorstep for me to care for, like in the fairy tales.

Stick-thin little Amy was huffing and puffing by then, trying to keep up with me. Amy could be a pain, but at least she knew how to have a good time, and I knew I could count on her to stick by me even though she moved out of town and married Mr. Cabletron Executive, who was too busy to show, by the way. A few people had followed our lead onto the dance floor, so by the time the next song came on I thought it'd be okay to hit the bar.

"I'm going to freshen my drink," I yelled to Amy above the music, holding up my empty glass and rattling the milky ice cubes at her.

She nodded, and I went into the barroom, where it was quieter and darker than the main hall. Four guys I didn't know were playing pool, and that 'achy-breaky' song was on the jukebox, competing with the thud of the Jackson Five coming through the walls from the party. Al

McKibbin was behind the bar, and he smiled at me when I took a stool by the register.

"Sounds like the party's going strong," Al said, giving me a new drink without me asking.

"Big success," I agreed.

During the day Al worked behind the counter of the parts section at the auto supply shop where I took phone orders and handled the stock. At work, he always wore these golf shirts and work pants that seemed to disappear into the browns and blacks of the place. The only other colors in the shop came from the girlie calendars–of women in bikinis holding up mufflers or fan belts, or standing in front of huge tool sets in red metal cases. When I got home from work, I couldn't wait to wash the smell of axle grease and cigarettes from my clothes, a smell that was just as black and brown as the stained, warped paneling of the shop. I felt sorry for Al–he seemed kind of lost since his wife died the year before, but lately he'd had a funny, hungry look in his eye whenever he talked to me.

"You sure know how to throw a party, Trace," he said, with a little more spark than he showed during the day.

"You know me," I told him. "Everything set back here?" I planned the whole party in advance: I'd haul out with the wheelchair so Gus would have to get his presents like some poor old cripple, and the belly dancer was waiting in the back room to come out right when I cued the DJ.

"All set," Al said. "Hey, feeling lucky?" he asked me, pulling a pair of instant lottery tickets from under the bar. For the past month or so, he'd been telling me I was going to bring him luck, and made me scrape off the tickets he brought into work every day.

I was feeling lucky that night, don't ask me why, so I nodded and he rang up a no-sale on the register and gave me a quarter. "Same deal," he said. "If you win, we'll split it."

I wondered what it would be like to split $50,000 with Al, who had this hairy mole on his chin but whose hands were white and steady as a glass of milk. I scraped the silver stuff off each card with the quarter. Zilch. It made me think about the chances I had in my life: with Gus, with Corey, with those night classes in accounting– maybe even with Al and his hungry look. Life wasn't as simple as a dollar lottery. There wasn't any easy risk, and sure as hell no big payoff.

Amy came tearing into the bar just then, saying Corey had shown up. I hustled her back into the hall and saw him hovering in the door-way, one hand jammed into the pockets of a bright red ski parka I'd never seen, a present in the other. He was holding the door open and talking to someone outside.

"Uh-oh," I said under my breath when I saw Ron step into the light. "The things you get yourself into, Traci K." I shook my head and sighed. Amy must have heard, because she let out this big "Amen," as we went to say hi.

I pulled Corey close to me and kissed him on the cheek. It felt cold on my lips and I stroked at the plush of hair on the back of his neck. For just that second, he was eight again and I was holding him tight after he fell off his bike in this stupid game he played with his friends, where they'd ride down the hill by the house, eyes closed and hands off the handlebar.

He pulled away and said, "Sorry we're late. We had to wait for Ron to finish work."

I remembered my manners and shook Ron's hand. "Go ahead, blame it on me," he said, smiling at me. He wasn't nearly as good looking as Corey. He was tall and stooped a little, and he kept this goofy grin plastered to his pale face. When he talked, he rolled his eyes up like he didn't believe a word he was saying. His hair was slicked back and he was wearing a white turtleneck with a blue blazer, like he was some foreigner from France. It made me wonder what Corey liked about him. What attracted him to him? It still sounded so strange to me–the words were topsy-turvy, like the Dr. Seuss stories I read to Corey when he was a baby.

"How are you, Mrs. Komeski?" Ron said, just a little too chipper, maybe.

"Mrs. Komeski's my mother-in-law," I said. "I told you how you should call me Traci."

Ron made this stiff bow, like a butler. "How are you, Traci?" he said with this English accent, acting wicked formal. I got a little tickle from that, like he was putting on a show for me.

"Good, and yourself?" I said, and gave a little curtsy.

Then Amy butts in with, "I'm Corey's aunt," over my shoulder. She shook Ron's hand while I just sat there soaking in my Corey. I could never get over this strapping, full-grown man of mine with those hard gray eyes that softened up just for me. He made me a little nervous, even, but a good nervous. People were looking at him even though Corey just stood there in that bright, noisy, smoky room like he was the only person in the world.

Amy was working Ron's hand until I thought it'd fall off. She'd been way too interested in meeting him when I told her he might be coming. She was always going on about all her gay friends from up by Ogunquit. "They're so interesting, Trace," she was always going. "They're so artistic, and they have this flair for decorating." One of them was doing her house, turns out, and she would rave, "he has such an eye for color." I didn't want Corey to be interesting like that to anyone. Not like he was some animal in a zoo. He was special. That ought to be enough.

"You two are just what this party needs," Amy was going on to Ron, and I wasn't sure what she meant, just that I was glad Corey was there.

"Ron's the party animal," Corey said, taking off his jacket. "I'm a little tired myself." I noticed the lift ticket on the zipper and wondered when he'd learned to ski. When the boys were growing up, the closest they ever came to skiing was standing up in the toboggan as they slid down the slopes at the golf course.

I had good times with my boys. That's something nobody can take away.

I didn't want Amy getting all the attention, so I said, "Guys, have something to eat," and led them over to the buffet.

"Jesus K.," I joked when I saw my nice display all half-eaten. "It looks like the Viet Cong got here before we did." Really, though, I was disappointed, after all the work I put into it. People could have been neater.

"That's okay," Corey said. "We ate something before we left."

But Ron was going, "Pimento loaf! I haven't seen that in years. Corey, your mom's a pip."

Feeling like a dope, I asked him, "Don't they have pimento loaf in Boston?"

"I guess," he said, pulling a piece of meat from the tray and rolling it into his mouth. "But the really classic luncheon meats are hard to track down in our neighborhood. It's all prosciutto and smoked mozzarella."

I had a feeling Ron was pulling my leg over the buffet, but before I could say anything, Corey said to him, "Stop acting like such a faggot."

I winced—okay, partly because I was thinking the word myself—but partly because the way Corey said it, it sounded so much like some old married couple bickering, which was just too weird for me. I could never stand those awkward silences between people, so I jumped in, going, "Oh, guys, we were just about to give your dad his presents and cut the cake."

When I brought Corey and Ron over to say hello to Gus, he stiffened as soon as he saw Ron, whom he'd never met.

It was just like Gus to ignore the whole thing with Corey. Even the time Corey came home from college in Boston the Christmas of his junior year and said how he was living with another boy, Gus just stayed in the front room watching TV; I knew he could hear the whole thing. When Corey told me, I just held on tight to my coffee cup, not wanting to look upset, even though I felt like my eyes were going to burst out of my head and a few tears got stuck on the tip of my nose before plopping one by one onto my hand. Finally, I just couldn't help myself, though I wished to God I could, and Corey turned away from me, slouching over the counter. I didn't want to make him feel bad, but like I said, I just couldn't help it. Still, Gus stayed away, and the only thing I remember hearing were the cheers and whistles from the Patriots game floating in from the next room.

I told Gus what Corey said a week later, after Corey left, and he just kind of shrugged. "Always was a mamma's boy," he said, which made me mad. But deep down, secretly, I was pleased about what Gus said and knew it was true. Corey had always been my little boy. What I found out that Christmas, in my kitchen, was that he would stay that way. The twins were turning out just like their dad, with their cheap girlfriends they wouldn't bring home and their big pickups with the lights on top. I loved them, of course, but they weren't mine the way Corey was.

Gus was sitting with some of his buddies, guys from work, a couple of cops—guys he went to high school with. As we got closer, their eyes lifted halfway to meet us, and they looked at each other almost like they were sizing us up for a fight. Corey made like he hadn't noticed, but the muscles along his jaw tighten into little ridges.

He gave Gus the package, and said, "Hey, Dad, happy birthday."

Gus took it, not bothering to get out of his chair, and said, "You're old man's getting older," but he was looking right at Ron, dressed in that fruity French outfit, so I knew exactly what was on his mind. Careful Gus, I was thinking, trying to make my thoughts loud enough for him to hear. Careful what you say.

Corey introduced Ron, who held out his hand. Gus hesitated, and I thought for a second he would ignore it. It was one of those silent times that usually makes me go "Well!" just to hear a voice, but Gus took Ron's hand finally and gave it one shake—up, down—then dropped it.

"Pleased to meet you, Mr. Komeski," Ron said. "Happy birthday."

I wanted to say something about how Ron was doing wicked good in real estate down in Boston but I just kept my mouth shut.

Gus was already looking back towards his buddies—just kind of daring them to say something, when he said, "You two guys get yourselves drinks? Bar's in the next room."

"Good idea," Corey said, and he put his jacket down on an empty table, where Amy had planted herself and was watching the whole thing like it was *Days of Our Lives*.

Gus just sat there with the gift box about to slide off his lap. I couldn't believe even he would be so rude as to not open it, so I opened my big yap, going, "Aren't you going to see what Corey got you?" Both Gus and Corey looked at me like death. Why did everything have to fall on me? Gus pulled the wrapping off while the others at the table looked on like they weren't interested and Corey just kept staring at the box. Gus lifted off the cover and spread the tissue so you could see a sweater, with this design in these earthy colors, the kind you see in the catalogues my sister got. I wondered if Corey had the same eye for color as Amy's decorator.

"A sweater," Gus said. He looked up at Corey, who hadn't moved from his spot. "Thank you."

"Happy birthday, Dad," Corey said again, and he raised his hand so I thought he was going to pat Gus on the shoulder, but he wound up scratching his own chin and asked, "Can I get anybody anything at the bar?"

All the guys just kind of mumbled and shook their heads, point-ing to their half-full drinks, so I held up my own and said, "I'm all set, Honey. Your mom's on cruise control tonight."

After Corey and Ron were gone, I pulled the sweater out of the box and held it up.

"A John Weitz," I told him, reading it off the label. "Gus, it's beau-tiful. Isn't it beautiful, Amy?"

Amy just nodded. She wasn't being much help.

"It's just a sweater," Gus said, giving a quick look over at the guys, who were pretending not to hear.

"But it's a wicked nice one," I said. "I saw one like this down at Filene's for eighty dollars. I hope he didn't spend that much on it." I was trying to interest Gus in the gift. It really was a nice sweater. Not what Gus would have bought himself-but he only knew how to buy jeans and work shirts. Whenever he tried to dress up he would go over to Chess King and come out looking like some kind of gigolo.

I was wondering what was taking Corey and Ron so long, but then I saw them coming back from the bar with beers. Ron had a tight smile on his face like he was trying to enjoy himself, but Corey only scowled.

I'll be the first to admit I never knew how to deal with Corey when he got in one of his moods. I could feel something harden around him like a shell. Once, when he was ten, he stood in the kitchen, re-fusing to go to school because someone or other didn't like him. His fists were clenched so that the knuckles turned white, and his face clamped shut until the tears squeezed out of his little eyes and collected on the tips of his eyelashes. It scared me. I remember holding him by his shoulders, which were stiff as a dead animal, and going, "Please, Corey, please." When I pried apart his fists, there was a line of little red half-moons along the bottom of his palms.

*   *   *

With Corey there and all I figured it was time to get the festivities under way, so I clapped my hands and signaled the DJ to turn the music down. "Okay, people, let's cut into this thing," I called out. "Corey, Honey, come take a look at the cake I got your dad."

I pulled him over to the cake and presents and he seemed to get a kick out of the naked lady. I saw Gus starting to come over and re-membered the wheelchair. "Wait a minute, wait a minute, old man," I said. "Not so fast." I ran into the bar where Al had the chair ready and waiting, bless his heart, while the belly dancer sat at the bar in her green Genie costume.

"In this," I said, wheeling the chair into the hall, and everyone went nuts. Gus gave me this look, but I ignored him.

"I've got you right where I want you now, Gus," I joked as I wheeled him over to the cake.

I made a big production out of giving him his gifts, and everyone was hooting and yelling with each one. Even Gus was having a good time, I thought, taking his ribbing like a man. There were bottles of Geritol, and bikini briefs, a hot-water bottle, and Secure diapers, every-thing to get him ready for old age. Finally, after he opened the last one, I gave the DJ the signal and the belly dancer came out on the floor. The guys in the crowd whistled and the girls rolled their eyes while the woman danced around Gus in her bare feet with the ankle bracelets, chinging her little finger cymbals and wrapping all these colorful silk scarves around Gus's neck one at a time.

Boy, that belly dancer sure took command of the situation. She seemed like someone who didn't take crap from anyone. I wondered how old she was. She wasn't pretty—she had yellow teeth with a big gap right in front—but there was something wicked sexy about her. She had one of those dark, foreign faces, with big round eyes and bright green shadow. Her boobs were pushed up into that Genie bra so you could almost see the nipples, and she had this wide belly with a green jewel planted right in the belly button. I practically got hypnotized, watching that green jewel gyrate slowly around or ripple like it was hit with an electric shock.

I wondered if guys really liked having a girl take over the controls like that. They were just like fish on the hook with her, and she teased and played before reeling them in. I never had that power over Gus—he always seemed too good for me. When I started seeing him in high school, I was everyone's favorite—the chubby girl with all the per-sonality—but no one anyone would come back to for seconds. Gus was this great big mystery to me, with his creased brown bomber jacket and sleepy eyes. He was twenty-four—Corey's age—but everyone knew him from his job at the Esso station downtown.

I looked over at Corey, but he and Ron were ignoring the dancer, sitting alone, talking and taking tugs at their beers. She didn't have the same kind of control over him, and it made me proud of him, some-how. The last veil that the dancer pulled out had "Happy 50th Gus" written in sparkles. She teased him all around with it like she did with the others, and then raised it into the air so that it floated down over his head. The guys at his table whooped and clapped. One of the twins—Jimmy, I think—yelled out "Careful of the heart, you old geezer."

Gus raised the veil and yelled, "Fifty nothing. She just took ten years off of me."

The belly dancer barely even smiled at all the commotion. She just ching-chinged her finger cymbals and swept off on her toes into the bar while everyone applauded. It said just the way I wanted. After a second, the DJ had cranked up "Mony Mony," which was one of my all-time favorites, and the twins and their girls moved out onto the dance floor, along with some other people. I yanked Gus out of the chair and started to dance around him the way the belly dancer had done. He was a stiff dancer, but a good-looking man at 50, with his trim brown hair and neat mustache.

That mustache was one of the things I fell in love with that summer between my junior and senior year. I was working in the drug store across from the Esso, and he would come in every day around two and pick up a pack of Dentyne. Even then he had his hair cut close to his head, not like some of the kids in school then who you couldn't tell if they were guys or girls. He told me how he wanted to enlist but how he was kept out of the Navy for his asthma. The only other per-son I knew who had asthma was this pale, sort of hungry-looking girl who was excused from gym class, and it was like I saw this frail little girl in him that made him seem even sweeter to me. When I got preg-nant, he told me he would marry me, and I cried just knowing he was that good. Believe me, I've wised up since then.

The DJ played "Devil With the Blue Dress," and I was working up a sweat, rolling my shoulders to the beat and singing along, "Fi fi fie fie fo fo fum, Look out baby, here I come," twirling around Gus, who held his ground, mostly nodding and shuffling to the beat the way guys do.

I was getting sweaty, so I finally bagged it, sat down next to Corey, and pulled my sweat shirt off to the t-shirt I had on underneath, not even caring about showing off the chicken skin on my arms. I remember seeing Ma's arms, pale and dimpled, when she washed dishes, thinking I'd never be that old and tired-looking. But I've given up being shy about things like that. "How's my hair look?" I asked him, knowing it looked like crap. "Oh, well," I said before he could answer. "Who cares?" I felt the cool air on my bare arms and shivered. I turned to Corey and said, "Your mom's a party girl."

"I know, Mom," he said, and the hardness in his eyes softened again. It gave me a little leap in my chest, as though someone tickled me there with a feather. It made me feel kind of daring. I looked up to where Charlene was leading everyone in the Electric Slide. "Just look at that Charlene, wagging her bony ass out there," I said, and turned back to Corey and Ron, like we were a bunch of gossipy girls. "Now I've got an ass that'll get me across the floor. Like a freight train. You will know when I am moving my ass across that floor."

Ron and Corey looked at me with their jaws just kind of hanging open.

"Oh, come on," I said. "She doesn't like me anyway. I don't see why I have to be nice."

Ron scrunched up his face like a gambler in a western, going, "I agree," in a deep voice.

I slapped him on the forearm. "Good. She's just plain trash, as far as I can see." Well, that was too much—she was John's girl, after all. Just then I felt guilty and mean. I looked at Corey, into those steely gray eyes, and told him, "I stopped off at your Memère's today. She's so tired, poor woman. Set your Pepère up, turned him around for the bed sores, changed his bag. I don't know how she thinks she can take care of him herself though the home care lady's not much better. Can you imagine? She's there forty-five minutes a day and Memère says she spends half of it complaining." I shook my head at the thought of it. "Nobody takes any responsibility any more."

That's what I had wanted to say, I think, even when I was talking about Charlene. I wanted to say how hard I've been trying, giving everyone all the love I could, and how it didn't matter—Pa was still sick, Gus still ran around, and Corey, even my Corey, never gave living the right way any kind of a chance. Why couldn't Corey have tried harder, I wanted to know. Just because it felt better with another boy.

When did I ever decide on something because of how much better it made me feel? I gave him the right kind of love, but he took it the wrong way, somehow.

Those were the same ideas that would crowd in on me at night and wouldn't let me sleep, until I wanted to hit someone, only there was no one there but the pattern of flowers on the wallpaper that, in the dark, kind of hung there in space. I didn't know how to tell him all that and still love him the same way I always have, so I just repeated myself: "Nobody takes responsibility."

"How is Pepère?" Corey asked me, quiet.

I thought of Pa's gray face, once so burly and red, pressed into the starched pillowcase of the hospital bed we'd set up on the ground floor of their house. "You should go see him," I told him.

"I will," he told me, glancing over at Ron. "This weekend maybe. Sunday."

I leaned over and took his head in my hands and kissed him so that he squirmed to get away like a little boy. "Thanks, Honey. He'd appreciate it so much. Listen, though, tell me how things are going for you? How's work?"

He told me about how he'd been given more responsibilities with this book that could get him promoted out of the position he had, which sounded well and good. When he'd gone to college, I couldn't keep myself from thinking he'd be a doctor or a lawyer. But something about what he said that Christmas his junior year told me it wouldn't be like that. I just couldn't fit the pieces of the picture together anymore so that they made sense. He got a job as some kind of editor in a book company, and hardly made any money.

"They like you there," I told him, to encourage him. "You're moving up." He gave me a weak little smile so I thought maybe I'd said something wrong. I had to be so careful around him I never knew where I stood. I'd tell him how he was going to be a famous lawyer or other, and he'd turn into that angry little boy again, telling me it wasn't what he wanted, so that I would back off.

And that's just what I did. After all, we were at a party, and I'm not one to dwell on the negative side of things. "Corey, baby," I asked him, trying to chipper us up, "Are you having a good time?"

"Sure," he said, but I didn't believe him.

"I'm having a wonderful time," Ron chimed in, though I hadn't asked him.

"Good. I'm glad," I told him. "Corey, why don't you dance with your aunt Amy," I added so he didn't think I meant with Ron. I've seen that kind of thing before–pairs of guys two-stepping and holding hands like some circus side show–on *20/20*.

"I don't feel like dancing," he told me flat-out.

"What about karaoke? The DJ's all set up for it. Come on. We can do a duet. I was flipping through the catalogue. "Here's 'Don't go Breaking my Heart.' Do you know that one?"

"Not right now." He face tightened into this tense smile. "Thanks, Mom."

"I just want you to have a good time," I told him. "What about your dad? Did you have a chance to talk to him?"

"Mom," he said to me, "I came here because you asked me to."

I could tell he was getting annoyed and I didn't think he was being fair. "Don't do me any favors," I told him. "You don't have to do me any favors." I tried to think back to when the party was working, when people were having a good time. All of a sudden it was beginning to sour, and who's to blame? Traci K, every time.

"You've got a lot of your father in you," I said, and it was true. The two of them were a pair of stubborn mules.

"I don't want to have a lot of him in me," he said.

I wondered just how much of me he had in him, too. Not much, I figured. When he graduated from college, Gus didn't bother to come, but me and the twins made it down. It was a struggle, shaking hands and making small talk with the parents of Corey's friends, the fathers in important-looking suits and the mothers wearing pearls and smelling like cinnamon and lemon. It was the kind of smell you think of when you look at those ads in the magazines, the women in their beautiful homes. I could tell my clothes were too bright, and the twins' hair was all wrong–long in the back, spiky in front. They stuck out in that crowd, but Corey fit right in. Still, I wondered how many of those people knew about Corey–knew about how my good loving got twisted around the wrong way. One woman let out this big sigh when I told her where I lived. "We go to the lakes for the summer," she said. "It must be lovely to live there year round."

"It's just a town," I told her. Just a town with a roofing factory and an auto parts store and a K of C hall. It was the wrong thing to say, I could tell, but it was true.

It was like that at Gus's party: always the wrong thing. The party seemed like it was spinning out of control, as though everybody depended on me and what I did would make everything all right or all wrong. "Sorry, Hon," I said to Corey. "I'm a little gone."

"I know, Ma." He wrapped his arm around me and pulled me close. "That's okay. You're doing fine."

When he and Ron got up to get another drink, Amy came and took the seat next to me.

"Are Corey and Ron having a good time?" she asked me. "Don't you just love Ron? He was telling me that the real estate market in Boston is starting to look up a bit. He seemed interested in the idea of cross-listing a couple of properties on the seacoast."

I looked up at her, not really clear on what she was talking about. I was thinking instead how all these people–Corey and Ron, Amy, Gus, the twins–were helping themselves to whatever they wanted in life, while I was left behind, tending to things.

"Why don't you go see Pa?" I said, trying to look hard into her eyes.

"I'm busy," she practically mumbled, so I could hardly hear. Busy. She didn't know what busy was, with her one little girl and a husband who made it home to dinner every night. Try raising three boys on your own, knowing people are talking behind your back about your husband, then your son, then you, like you're some poor pathetic creature for putting up with them both. People have got nothing better to do than to talk. I thought of Amy, going to real estate school and then working in that firm on the seacoast. Try going back to work because you have to pay the rent and have the car fixed even though you really need a new one, and then find out your oldest wants to go to college. Try all that, I thought. Then try and find out your special boy has taken your love and run with it where you never intended.

"Just for an hour, every once in a while," I said instead. "He asks about you."

"I don't know, Trace. I don't deal with sick people well."

I felt my patience snap like a dead twig. "He's not 'sick people.' He's our pa." The word came out like a sob, so that I couldn't stop the rest from coming out. "And he's dying."

"I know that," she said, her head down, her fingers poking at the special birthday confetti I'd spread over the tables, separating the little 50's by color, stacking them into their own little piles. "Don't you think I know that?" Suddenly she looked up past me and smiled. "Loading up, huh?"

I got myself together again before turning to see Corey and Ron balancing their beers on plates full of Ritz crackers and cheese from the buffet. "Come on, Corey," I said. "Let's dance with your old mother."

"I don't know, Mom."

"Oh, Corey, you old poop," Ron said, in a wavering, old-lady voice that made me laugh.

He took a bow and said, "Ladies and gentlemen, Miss Katherine Hepburn." Then he looked at me, going, "Traci, will you dance with me?"

I looked at Corey, who shrugged with a little 'why not' smile, and then at Amy. But I didn't have time to answer before Ron was pulling me onto the dance floor just as "Shake Your Tail Feather" came on.

"I love this song!" Ron yelled out to me, beginning to twist like a madman, singing along, "Do it right . . . Do it right . . . Do it right!" as he took the twist right down to the ground. I followed him down, ignoring the pain in my knees until I couldn't go any lower. When the song came to "Twist it!" he bounced up, and was practically running all over the dance floor like a crazy man. Well, I caught the bug and kept right up with him, doing the twist and waving my hands over my head so you'd think I totally lost it. When they said "Come on, let me see you shake your tail feather," well, I did just that, shaking my tail and working my arms like a demon. Ron was right there with me, clapping and whooping it up, basically clearing the dance floor, as you might imagine.

The song ended, and I was just about winded and ready to call it quits. The DJ put on "I Can't Help Falling in Love" which is a slow song anyway, so I said thanks to Ron and started to walk off the floor. But instead, he grabbed me and pulled me close like the other couples who came out to dance. I was a little surprised, but I figured, all in good fun, and let it go. He put one arm around me and held my hand in the other, and before you know it, we were doing a real, old-fashioned waltz.

I was having a hell of a time trying to keep up with him, but he said, "Relax, I'll take care of it," so I did, and pretty soon it was like my feet knew just where to go, with him leading. We were twirling so slow and nice around that dance floor, like a fairy tale ball, and it was like Elvis was singing right to me in that beautiful deep voice. I felt like I was sixteen—sad, but a good sad, if you know what I mean. The kind of sad you feel when it rains in the summer, and you can smell the steam rising off the street.

Ron was a good dancer, strong and gentle, and I thought it would be okay just to rest my forehead on his chest. He didn't seem to mind, and we danced slower, but still in that old-fashioned way. Maybe that was what Corey liked about him, the way you could just rest your head on his shoulder and he'd let you keep it there.

"I'm glad Corey has you," I said, and I meant it, all of a sudden.

Ron didn't say anything, and I wondered, for the millionth time, if I just stuck my foot in my mouth again.

"He's going to leave me," he said.

I didn't know what to say. It was really too weird, so I didn't even look up. Right then, I felt like Ron was just like me: a couple of rejects, taking care of other people with no one else to take care of us.

"He hasn't said anything yet," Ron said. "But I know." I thought about Corey's hard gray eyes, about that way he's got, like his father-stubborn and hard and sad—and I knew, too. For the second time that night, I was mad at Corey, and I wanted to know the answer to what had been bugging me. I figured Ron would know.

"Couldn't he," I started to say, but I stopped, nearly chickening out. Still, I wanted to know, so I asked. "Couldn't he have tried just a little harder?"

I felt Ron let out a big sigh, and he stooped a little more.

"I mean," I said, "just because it feels good with a boy . . ."

Ron jerked straight. His arm tightened around my waist and he pressed me closer. We were moving in slow circles, and I could feel the warmth of his chest against my ear.

"It doesn't feel good," Ron said, so quiet I could barely hear him above the music. "It doesn't feel good at all."

CAROL K. HOWELL

Defying Gravity

For my uncle Robert Mendler, once Roman Reibeisen: #B5188

LUCY GOT THE JOB in the first place because when Maxine asked why she wanted it, she said: "I need the money." All the other girls from the Temp agency had talked about what an honor it would be to work with–they never said "for"–the author of *Back To Dachau*. Maxine couldn't stand being venerated; it oppressed her, she told Lucy, adding: "I know too much about human nature, including my own." Lucy, who'd never read *Back To Dachau* although she thought her parents owned a copy, was too oppressed by her own problems to do any serious venerating. It took Maxine very little prodding to get her to spill the details.

After living with her for nearly a year, Lucy said, Jason had finally been accepted to law school in Colorado and had packed and moved out, just like that, the same day the letter came. For a while Lucy struggled on alone in the apartment and thought about changing her major yet again, but since the prospect of a career, or any life after college, seemed improbable, one night she simply packed her own bags and came home. Since then she had been taking the train into the city each day to work Temp jobs, saving up for a new apartment. Living at home again had turned out to be a very bad idea. This was the first summer of her life that was not a vacation: while her younger brothers lay about the house savoring their leisure, Lucy dressed up and went into the hot city and sat in stale offices all day. Her parents were embarrassed to have a drop-out daughter; her friends were all getting ready to go back to school; Lucy could not explain what had happened to her; and she could not plan any further ahead than finding a new apartment.

Maxine listened to all this, then gave a short dry laugh, stubbed out her cigarette and said they might as well get started.

Lucy was mystified. This was the oddest interview she'd ever had, but apparently she was hired. She was to be paid five hundred dollars for a week of helping Maxine catch up on correspondence, sort through her papers and belongings, and pack up what needed to be stored. At the end of the week, Maxine would enter the hospital for surgery. She would not be coming back to the house. Since it was such a long way out of the city, she wanted Lucy to bring her things and stay the entire week. Lucy thought briefly about her birthday coming up on Saturday, but five hundred dollars was good money, and it would be a relief to get away from home.

And so the next morning she again took a train and a bus, then lugged her suitcase down the dirt road to the modest property which Maxine insisted on calling a farm, even though the fields had gone wild and the barn had stood empty for nearly a decade. At one time the farm had been Maxine's permanent home—Ben's, too, Lucy gathered. She was intrigued by Maxine's relationship with the journalist Ben Kanin. Why had they never married? But thinking about them reminded her of Jason, which made her unhappy. Not that she'd expected to marry Jason. But he was her first real boyfriend—her first lover—and she didn't understand how something so momentous could just *end* like that, as though it had run into a brick wall.

Maxine's relationship with Ben Kanin had lasted thirty years and ended with his death. Since then, she told Lucy, she'd spent her winters traveling and only visited the farm in fine weather, poking about the garden, sitting on the porch at night to watch the sky. But now her cancer had come back and the farm had to be sold. She would move in with her nephew and his family in Brooklyn. They were all the family she had left—born-again Jews, she called them, because Yaakov, who used to be Geoffrey, had married an Orthodox girl and gone to live among the Chassidim. They would take care of her after the surgeon removed her vocal cords.

Lucy thought Maxine was remarkably calm about it all. Each morning, no matter how early Lucy rose, she found a fresh pot of coffee in the kitchen and Maxine waiting in the garden, her face tilted serenely toward the sun. Lucy brought the coffee out on a tray along with the mail, which she opened and read aloud. Each day brought new requests and invitations. Maxine said no to everything, even to a university which wanted to award her an honorary degree. She told Lucy to plead ill health.

"Besides," she said in a raspy voice that broke like a boy's. "I've got my degree: University of Dachau, Class of '45."

Lucy wasn't sure how to take this. She'd never heard anyone joke about concentration camps before. *Back To Dachau* wasn't at all funny, she gathered–it was about Maxine's return to the camp where, seventeen years earlier, she had arrived with liberating troops and discovered what Hell was. The book had made Maxine famous, even more famous than Ben, and had won almost every award possible. What Lucy didn't understand was why, between 1945 and 1962, Maxine had written nothing except a few ordinary news stories. She knew from Maxine's old press clippings that critics had wondered the same thing.

The clippings, along with mountains of old papers, photographs, and mementos, filled nineteen boxes. Lucy thought they should go through the cartons systematically, cataloguing each item for storage, bequest, or disposal, but Maxine kept pulling things out at random and carrying them with her as she wandered through the house. There were piles of leaflets about the Scottsboro Boys, the Lincoln Brigade, strikes and Pinkerton scabs, and a dozen political buttons with bleached-out slogans that made Maxine utter her short dry laugh.

"Were you really radical?" Lucy asked.

"Are you kidding? There was a Depression. People didn't have shoes; they didn't have food. Of course I was radical–I was your age." She tried to pin a button to her blouse, but time had blunted its point.

"What made you stop?" Lucy asked, not sure how anyone stopped. Did you give back a membership card? Take out an ad in the paper?

"Spain," said Maxine. "The purges. The pact. Only dolts believed in Uncle Joe after that. Fascism is fascism, no matter what it likes to call itself." This seemed to tire her, for she leaned back and reached for the coffee pot. Not a drop came out.

"I'll make some more," Lucy said, jumping to her feet. She was glad of the distraction, for she could think of no reply that would not reveal her ignorance. She was not sure what the purges or the pact were, though she knew Uncle Joe meant Stalin, a tyrant who had murdered a lot of people. What she didn't understand was why anyone had followed him in the first place.

When she brought the coffee out, she saw that Maxine had spilled a pile of photographs on the floor and was holding one up. It was old, brownish, showing a woman in long skirts, a small boy, and a young girl sitting in the rigid poses of the period. "My mother," Maxine said briefly.

Lucy took the photograph to study. The mother's hand lay heavily upon the girl's shoulder as if keeping her in place. "None of you look very happy," she said tentatively.

"We weren't. My father died when my brother was still an infant, leaving us to the mercy of a woman who was essentially an infant herself. She was completely self-absorbed–still working off the effects of her own upbringing, I suppose, too wrapped up to see what she was doing to us. Of course, I didn't understand any of this till much later."

Lucy nodded uneasily, thinking of Jason and that last confusing term at college. The suggestion of a wide gap between experience and understanding depressed her. "What did you do?" she asked to keep Maxine talking.

"What else? I rebelled. Any kind of authority was fascist to me. I ran wild."

"Were you for Communism even then?"

"For?" Maxine ran her fingers through her short raggedy hair, and Lucy wondered if chemotherapy would make it fall out. "I don't think I've ever really been *for* anything. My whole life has been one long anti. Anti my mother, first and foremost. Then capitalism and the bourgeoisie. Then totalitarianism." She grinned suddenly. "But the joke's on me, isn't it? Death is the greatest totalitarian of them all."

Lucy caught her breath, but Maxine only tossed the photograph aside and fished out another. In this picture there were no people, only a steep mountainside ending abruptly in a sheer drop. Many feet below the cliff was a thicket of bare, sharp, angular branches standing up like spears.

"I remember this," she said softly. "This is something I still dream about. I was camping with friends and we experimented with peyote. First I got sick. Then I felt wonderful and began to climb the mountain. It was night, and I had a strong conviction that when I reached the top, I could just step out into the sky, walk right up into the stars. My friends stopped me. I took this the next morning."

"Wow, I didn't know they had peyote back then," said Lucy, fascinated, then blushed when Maxine laughed.

* * *

During the afternoons Lucy typed letters, then took Maxine's car into the village to mail them and buy a newspaper and groceries. Maxine ate the canned soup and sandwiches Lucy made for lunch, but grumbled about their blandness. One thing about wandering all over the world with Ben, she said, was discovering exotic dishes she learned to reproduce at home.

"You should taste my Goanese Pork Curry," she said. "Fifteen red chiles and fifteen cloves of garlic, all soaked in vinegar and served with green tomato chutney."

Lucy shuddered. "Sounds great."

Maxine pushed her plate aside. "What *does* your generation consider `great'?" she asked. "I haven't noticed much in the way of a common ideal."

"You mean great food?"

"I mean what do you care about?"

"I don't know," said Lucy. "Happiness, I guess. Peace, liberty, justice for all." She stopped, embarrassed. She hadn't meant to recite the Pledge of Allegiance.

"Tell me what you're against."

"AIDS," Lucy said warily. "Pollution, drug abuse, homelessness."

Maxine scowled. "Straight off the six o'clock news. Tell me, do you know anyone who's in *favor* of AIDS?"

"What do you mean?"

"I mean your generation seems to have no passion. When you talk about the things that matter most, it sounds like satire. What do you intend to do with your life?"

"I don't know," Lucy said, staring into her alphabet soup.

"People don't even have love affairs anymore—they have 'relationships,'" Maxine went on irritably. "It's all so damn correct."

Lucy willed the tears in her eyes not to slide down her face. But they obeyed the law of gravity, and Maxine noticed.

"Oh shit," she said, laying her hand briefly on Lucy's. "I didn't mean you personally." She gave the hand a pat. "Listen, why do you think they're cutting out my vocal cords? It'll make a lot of people awful happy."

She tipped her chair back against the wall, lit a cigarette, and elaborately unfolded the newspaper. Lucy just stared. She had never heard a woman over seventy say "shit" before, and she had never heard anyone speak so lightly of cancer, especially their own.

*   *   *

While Maxine tried to nap, Lucy went through a carton alone, sorting things into piles: a chewed rawhide bone, a red and gold silk scarf, a dirty green knitted cap, photographs of a man she took to be Ben Kanin–a long bony man who never looked straight at the camera. He always seemed sleepy, stretched out in a hammock or rowboat, though Lucy knew from the clippings that he'd been a prolific journalist who traveled all over the world for stories. She wondered whether Maxine had always gone with him and whether that continual adventure was what kept them together so long. It must have been a very passionate affair to last thirty years without marriage. She laid out the photographs like a game of Concentration, studying them. When Maxine spoke behind her, she jumped. "I was just trying to put these in order," she said.

"What for? I like them mixed up."

Lucy felt a little burst of exasperation. "Then what did you hire *me* for?" she said, and was rewarded by Maxine's raspy laugh.

When she came back from the kitchen with fresh coffee–Maxine drank more coffee than anyone she'd ever known–Maxine was wearing the scarf and green cap and turning the rawhide bone in her fingers. "I can still see his teethmarks," she said.

Lucy sat on the floor beside her. "What was his name?"

"Karma. And we had a cat named Dogma. Ben named them–he was clever. This was his." She tugged the cap from her head. "He always wore a hat indoors, a red or green stocking cap. They made him look like a big grouchy unshaven elf."

They both looked down at the array of pictures. In none of them did Ben Kanin look elfin or grouchy or even unshaven.

"He got the scarf from a gypsy," Maxine went on. "She stopped him on a street in Paris in 1939 and told his fortune for twenty-five cents. She said he would live a long time." Maxine held the scarf up to the light as if to read the faded pattern. "Well, I guess he did. Longer than she did, anyway. I thought of her when we learned about the liquidation of the gypsy camp at Auschwitz." She pronounced the name as a German would, making a "v" of the "w" and running the "a" and "u" together so they sounded like a cry of pain.

"Why did she give him the scarf?" Lucy asked. She had never heard of gypsies at Auschwitz.

"Because he had green eyes and she thought that was lucky. Maybe she foresaw her own future." Maxine took the scarf off. "He always sneezed three times before going to sleep. I'd count aloud and he always came through. He used to lie on the couch, staring into space, his hands under his head and an open book laid flat on his stomach. He called it `reading.'" They both laughed. "He never went to college, but he knew more about history and politics than I could discover in a lifetime of reading to catch up."

Lucy was silent. She was thinking that the only photograph she had of Jason was his formal graduation portrait. What would she do when she was Maxine's age and wanted to remember? But then it wasn't the pictures of Ben that made Maxine remember–they didn't even look like him.

Maxine glanced at her. "You know, when I was twenty, I was still a rash little girl, running about, furious with everyone. No man could tolerate me for long."

"Why was it different with Ben?" Lucy asked, though what she really wanted to know was why they never married.

"*I* was different. Everything was different. I met him in Europe after the liberation, after I'd been to all the camps, seen the bodies and the ovens and the walking skeletons. I was reeling. The only good thing about that time was meeting Ben–he steadied me. And," she added ruefully, looking into her empty cup, "he taught me to drink. What I remember most from those years is bottles. Bottles, smoke, noise, arguments, and typewriters." She smiled faintly. "From that time on, everything I've ever written has been written for him."

"How did he die?"

"Same thing that's got me, only his was in the lungs." Maxine leaned back against the couch, sipping her coffee. "He'd had the cough for years. One day I caught him shoving a handkerchief in his pocket just as I came in, but he was too late–I'd already seen the stain. That night he couldn't sleep; he got up to get a drink. I heard him coughing in the kitchen. Then I heard choking. I ran downstairs and saw him leaning over the sink, the blood just pouring out of him, all over the dirty dishes."

Lucy shuddered. From where she sat she could see both the stairs and the kitchen sink, and she imagined Maxine standing there, watching.

Maxine took a bottle of brandy from the sideboard and added a splash of that to her cup. As an afterthought she offered the bottle to Lucy, who shook her head.

Maxine grimaced. "Are you even of age?"

"My birthday's Saturday," Lucy said shyly.

"No kidding? Want the day off?"

Lucy shook her head. "I'd rather be here. Twenty-one, you know, my brothers think it's great, but all my friends are graduating this year, and I'm living at home, working menial jobs." Then she reddened. "I didn't mean *this* was menial. This is the best job I've ever had. I just wish it wasn't–" She stopped in time.

"Temporary?" Maxine gave her a wry grin. Then she said: "I tell you what. We'll have our own celebration, and I'll cook you Doro Wat–the national dish of Ethiopia."

Lucy smiled. "I don't think I've ever had a national dish."

"Well, you won't forget this one." Maxine lit a new cigarette and coughed. It was a bad cough. Seeing Lucy's face, she said: "I know, I know. But it really doesn't matter anymore."

"But won't you–aren't they taking it out?"

"If it was only in my larynx, you think they would have let me postpone surgery? Damn fools must think I never heard of metastasis." She pointed the cigarette at Lucy. "But that's a word I know from the inside out."

"You mean because of what happened to Ben?"

"No, I mean what happened to me." Maxine added more brandy to her coffee.

"When I went back to the camps. When I finally broke my own stasis." She rummaged through a carton and pulled out a notebook, handing it to Lucy. "Adolf Eichmann," she said as if performing an introduction.

Lucy was relieved that she recognized the name. "The one the Israelis kidnapped and put on trial?"

"His crowning achievement was Hungary," Maxine said in the same placid voice in which she spoke about her cancer. "They gassed twenty-four thousand in one day alone. He told the court it went like a dream."

Lucy opened the notebook and flipped through pages covered

with faded blue scrawl. The number was like a headline, too big to take in. She thought about twenty-four thousand people going to their death one at a time, but the line was too long to imagine.

"A few months after his capture, the Germans got busy and arrested his henchmen: Baer, Richter, Zöpf . . . I can't remember the rest. They were all in Europe leading successful middle-class lives." She paused to regard the lengthening ash of her cigarette. "Not one of them had found it necessary to live under an assumed name."

"Were they executed?"

Maxine laughed. "Heavens, no. Five years here, ten there, time off for good behavior. But for the first time in twenty years, the papers were full of stories about Nazi mass murder."

The back of the notebook was stuffed with old clippings, some in German. Lucy wondered why they used so many capital letters–did it reveal something about the German psyche?

"We followed it in the papers," Maxine went on, stretching out again, perfectly composed. "Eichmann admitted his crimes but acknowledged no guilt. 'I never killed a Jew,' he said–I suppose he meant with his bare hands. He said that repentance was for children."

"How could anyone believe that?"

Maxine did not answer the question. "He spoke entirely in cliches about duty, orders, law," she went on. "At first we thought he did it on purpose. But gradually we realized that this inability to speak reflected an inability to *think*, to understand. As Hannah Arendt said, he was banal. The chill of that is what got me going again."

"Who was Hannah Arendt?" Lucy asked, then reddened when Maxine looked over and said: "What *did* they teach you in college?"

"Well, that's why I dropped out," she replied, forgetting that this wasn't strictly true. "All anybody cared about was getting a good job, being a success."

Maxine smiled at the ceiling, linking her hands behind her head. "Eichmann said that no matter what you thought of Hitler, you had to be impressed with his rise from lance corporal to Fuhrer of eighty million. He said: 'His success alone proved to me that I should subordinate myself to this man.'"

Lucy found a clipping with a photograph. Eichmann was balding, middle-aged, with a bland expression. He looked like her seventh-grade geography teacher. "What happened to him?"

"They hanged him," Maxine said. "Much too quickly."

Lucy stared, wondering what would have been slow enough, as Maxine got up and wandered over to the screen door and pushed it open. Then she followed.

Although the day had been summery, the air was cool now, more like fall. There were still streaks of pink and orange in the west, but above Maxine's garden the sky was deep violet, like spilled ink slowly spreading. They walked down the dirt road, looking at the dark shapes of trees. Lucy thought how familiar all this must be and tried to imagine how it would feel to know you were seeing it for the last time.

"So I went back," Maxine continued without transition. "Dachau was still intact. You could buy postcards of the ovens and send them to your friends."

Lucy tripped over a root. It was getting increasingly difficult to see, but Maxine seemed to know the road by heart. Lucy drew closer and matched her footsteps.

"I took a taxi to Auschwitz–imagine. The mud was covered by grass, and the wooden huts had mostly disintegrated, but the gates and barbed wire were still there. I stepped on bits of bone among the weeds. There were big glass cases full of shoes, dentures, hair. We toured the ovens. The tour guide, a girl about your age, told us the manufacturer had had the design patented. He'd also designed a smaller oven, for burning children more efficiently."

Lucy rubbed her arms. "I don't understand. They must have had children of their own. How could they do things like that?"

"That's what I went back to find out."

They both came to a halt, staring down the dirt road into the darkening woods. Lucy waited as long as she could. "Well, did you?" she asked finally.

"Of course not," Maxine said, her voice cracking. She had used it too much today. Then, putting a hand on Lucy's arm, she added: "Let's go back now and feed you. I don't want your mother accusing me of wrecking your health."

*   *   *

In the middle of the night, Lucy heard a soft thump and crept downstairs to find Maxine lying on the living room floor, legs raised over her head with a knee resting beside each ear. She did yoga whenever she couldn't sleep, she told Lucy, who walked all the way around her in wonder. Maxine stood up and bent forward easily, laying her palms flat on the floor. Lucy tried to do the same but couldn't. It was embarrassing.

"It's not a contest," Maxine said. "Relax, stop when it hurts, relax a little more. It feels good to stop fighting gravity."

Obediently, Lucy let her head and arms dangle, feeling the muscles in her back lengthen and pour slowly forward. It did feel good. It made her want to breathe slow and deep.

"That's it," said Maxine. "Just give in."

They did a few more positions and each was the same: relax, give in, let go. Afterward they lay completely flat on the floor, eyes closed, breathing deeply, and Lucy had the oddest sensation of floating up toward the ceiling, like a balloon whose anchoring rope had been cut.

*   *   *

The boxes they got through the next day contained old manuscripts and reviews of Maxine's work. It seemed the critics had loved the first book and hated the rest.

"Didn't that depress you?" Lucy asked, studying a newspaper photo of a younger Maxine.

Maxine coughed, then turned it into a laugh. "Writers are too egotistical to believe their own bad press."

"Still, I wish I had some kind of work like that. It must make you feel like you know what you're here for."

"Absolutely," Maxine said dryly. "Work makes free."

Lucy didn't understand the dryness, but she did recognize the words from the inscription over the gate at Auschwitz–they'd been quoted in some of the articles–and realized Maxine was making fun of her. "Then how come you quit for seventeen years?" she said a bit sharply.

Maxine glanced at her in mild surprise. A few moments passed before she spoke. "In 1945," she began leisurely, as if telling a story, "you could smell Dachau long before you could see it. It was the end of April, a beautiful day. There were clear blue skies, roses just coming into bloom, cobbled roads, stone walls–the Europe of Grimm's fairy tales. Except for the smell. We entered the camp through handsome scrolled gates. There were bird houses, fountains, gardens, a moat.

Spring had no trouble returning to Dachau. Someone said it looked like a girls' finishing school."

Lucy took another cup of coffee, though her stomach was roiling from caffeine. For some reason she thought of the child-sized ovens.

"But we followed the smell into the real camp. Behind the barbed wire, the soil of the execution grounds was literally soaked with blood," Maxine said thoughtfully. "I'd always thought that was just a figure of speech. The warehouses, the gas chambers, the ovens, the barracks were stacked to the ceilings with bodies. Stacked like logs. I was with two other journalists, all of us Jews. They said Kaddish. I threw up."

Maxine paused to light a cigarette. Lucy watched nervously. This was like telling ghost stories at pajama parties, like watching a scary movie. She tried telling herself it was real, but who could envision whole buildings full of bodies? She had never even been to a funeral.

"The prisoners lay together with corpses," Maxine went on. "You could scarcely tell the living from the dead. When you touched them it was like touching bones. There were bodies with wounds showing where starving men had cut out the kidneys and livers."

Lucy's stomach lurched. It couldn't be real. How could Maxine sit here sipping coffee if it were?

"The only parts of a starving person that don't shrink are the head, hands, and genitals," Maxine continued. "Their bones rub through their skin. They shuffle rather than walk, big bald heads bobbling like those toys you see in the rear windows of cars." She paused to fill her cup. "Civilians from the town of Dachau were brought in to dig mass graves. They began saying then what they would spend the rest of their lives saying: they didn't know, they hadn't heard."

"Couldn't they *smell?*" Lucy burst out.

A faint smile crossed Maxine's face. "You might think so," she said. "It didn't smell like rubber or coal. It smelled like large quantities of roasting meat. So, I decided to collect testimony. Everything was very chaotic then, people wandering between DP camps looking for relatives, trying to get home or away from the Russians or out of Europe altogether. There were going to be trials, we knew, and I thought the material I gathered might help, and I . . . I thought . . ."

Lucy looked up in surprise. Maxine, who chose words with such precision, was stammering.

"I wanted to get a book out of it," she said finally. "I wanted to beat the others to the punch."

"But you didn't," said Lucy. "You didn't write it for seventeen years."

The faint grin reappeared. "No. Joke was on me, wasn't it?" And she slowly pulled herself up and started up the stairs for her nap.

*   *   *

It was lunchtime, but Lucy decided that what she needed more than food was motion. Speed. She hurried into her shorts and shoes, not bothering to warm up. Outside she ran hard, feet slapping the road, fists chopping the air. She ran until she was winded and had to throw herself down in a meadow and wait for the strength to run back.

She meant to reflect on what Maxine had said, what it revealed, what it required from her. It was like decoding a poem. "Even the sunshine at Dachau seemed part of the lie," Maxine had said: "Two days later there was a blizzard." What did it mean? How did it explain why Maxine had waited so long to write her book? She closed her eyes against the field of brilliant goldenrod, trying to envision the moat, the gardens, the warehouses full of dead. But the warmth the earth held drew the thoughts out of her, drew the pictures right out of her head, and she fell almost instantly asleep.

*   *   *

When she came downstairs after her shower, she found Maxine sitting on the floor, surrounded by a pile of old-fashioned notebooks with thick cardboard covers. Her face looked grim and gray, as if she hadn't slept at all. The sandwiches Lucy had set out for her were untouched.

"You should eat," Lucy said.

Maxine ignored her, gently turning brittle pages splotched with old coffee stains. "This is the testimony."

Lucy looked at the heap. "You talked to a lot of people."

"I wrote down everything anyone would tell me. I thought to leave a detail out was to diminish that person's pain, as if it didn't matter as much as someone else's."

"But you must have left things out when you wrote the book."

"Yes indeed," Maxine said softly. "But not then. I hadn't seen many corpses before, but after the first week corpses were nothing. It was easy to understand how prisoners lived so intimately with the dead.

Listen." She turned a page and read: *"The prisoners want to show us how the poison gas was dropped through the ceiling of the gas chamber. They wedge a ladder into a pile of corpses to keep it steady and climb to the roof."* She looked at Lucy. "As if corpses were bags of sand. And why not? Although," she added thoughtfully, "now and then you'd see a hand twitching and realize that some weren't quite dead." She stopped to pour herself some coffee and Lucy took some too, suddenly cold again, sick again, as if she hadn't napped in the sun and eaten ham sandwiches only an hour ago.

"In Birkenau," Maxine read, *"before they built the great ovens, they buried the bodies in mass graves. But there were too many, and soon the ground began to heave and break as if in protest, the bodies bursting from the earth. The prisoners had to dig them up again and burn them in great fire-pits. They used the pits again in later days, when there were more corpses than the ovens could burn. They had to stoke the fires constantly with long forks. There were channels at the bottom of the pits which collected the rendered fat, which was then poured back over the bodies as additional fuel. The man who thought up this ingenious method was named Moll. He often killed infants by hurling them into the boiling fat, making witticisms at the same time about the Kosher proscription against cooking a kid in its mother's milk."*

The coffee boiled in Lucy's stomach and she pushed the cup away. Then she pushed herself back, away from the notebooks, but Maxine didn't seem to notice.

"The heat was so intense," she continued, *"that it made the bodies stir and writhe as if straining to leap up and escape, as if even now they could not believe the truth."*

"*I* don't believe it!" Lucy shouted, startling herself. She was almost too furious to speak. "How could anyone *do* that?"

"Oh, they did much worse," Maxine replied, as if to provoke her further: *"The Polish town where there was a fine hospital: one day the mothers in the Jewish ghetto were ordered to bring their children in for typhus shots. The children were taken from their mothers, drained of their blood and stripped of their skin, which was sent to be used for wounded German soldiers."*

Lucy was shaking her head. "I don't understand. I don't understand."

"No," Maxine agreed, turning a page. *"The transport where prisoners were told they were being transferred to a work camp: they were suspicious because they knew all about S.S. treachery. But they were bathed and disinfected, given better shoes and food rations, and the train they boarded was pointing away from Birkenau. They sat waiting hopefully for a long time in darkness, and then finally the train began to move . . . backward. They backed towards the chimneys and death."* She turned another page. *"The Polish Kapo who requested–and received–the suicides of six Jews in his block as a Christmas present. The pregnant woman who somehow escaped selection: when her labor pains started, the Nazis hung her from a tree . . . by her feet."*

Lucy burst into tears. Maxine put the notebook down and gave her a napkin, waiting patiently.

After a moment, Lucy said: "It's too much."

"That's what my editors said. People don't want to hear horror piled upon horror. It doesn't sell books; it doesn't win prizes." She looked at the heap of notebooks. "But it happened; all of it happened to *someone*. So people don't want to hear. What should I do–burn the notebooks? Bury them?" She gave her dry laugh. "The Nazis would have recycled the paper."

Lucy began to cry again. Maxine poured some brandy into her cup. "Drink this."

She drank. It tasted like lighter fluid and made her tear up all over again, coughing.

Maxine thumped her on the back. "Wait, I've got something better."

She went into the kitchen and came out with a bottle of red wine and two glasses. "All right," she said, easing back down beside Lucy. "Let me try this again." For a moment she studied her folded hands as if they controlled her flow of words. "When I left Europe, I was numb for seventeen years, as numb as liquor could make me. I couldn't repeat the stories. I couldn't even open the notebooks. I kept picturing scenes straight out of Dante, straight out of our collective vision of Hell: prisoners poking burning corpses with pitchforks, infants kicked into the pit as though they were footballs–"

Lucy clapped her hands over her ears.

"Sorry," said Maxine. She poured the wine. "I kept thinking that the surreal *absurdity* of such scenes should have stopped them all in their tracks, slave and master alike."

"But it didn't."

"Because they were numb, like me. At first I reacted like you did. But as the list of abominations grew, each more inconceivable than the last, I lost my outrage; I lost my passion. And finally I realized that this is how it works. This is what made it possible for people to participate, to cooperate. You get used to it. You can get used to anything."

Lucy, tasting the wine, remembered what Maxine had told her last night: relax when it hurts, give in, and then you can take a little more. The taste soured her mouth, but she kept sipping.

"When I left Europe, I felt as if I'd been held by the feet and dipped in a latrine. I didn't want to spare myself–I didn't want to spare anybody–but I could not write about it. I was ashamed of being warm and well-fed, of sleeping in my own bed with Ben safe beside me. I don't think there's been a time I've baked bread that I haven't weighed the loaf in my hand and calculated how many lives it would have kept going just a day or two longer." She lit another cigarette, holding it up for Lucy to see. "This alone would have bought two day's bread."

Lucy felt the wine easing the turbulence in her belly. "I don't understand," she said. "If it were me, I'd want to tell the world. Why couldn't you just report what you saw?"

Maxine shook her head. "No words for it. You have to rely on ordinary language. The Nazis knew that. Think of the grotesque mockery behind 'transport,' 'selection,' 'process,' 'solution.' I'd like to believe they ruined those words forever for us, but, of course, they didn't."

"But you did write about it. You didn't stay numb."

Maxine smiled faintly. "Not entirely," she admitted. "Life has a way of distracting you. One minute you're contemplating Absolute Evil, and the next you're rinsing out your hosiery and checking the roast."

Lucy, getting up to use the bathroom, blushed guiltily at this but proceeded nonetheless. An awful joke had come back to her, something comparing urination to death–the punchline was: when you gotta go, you gotta go–but she did not laugh. In the bathroom mirror she looked like someone else–flushed, with reddened eyes. On her way back, she paused at the window and saw that it was almost dark already.

"That reminds me," said Maxine. "Yaakov will have to put up the storm windows."

Lucy heard the irony in her voice. "What will it be like there?"

"At Yaakov's?" Maxine coughed, crushing out her cigarette. "Crowded, noisy, strict. A Kosher kitchen, no lights on Saturday, that sort of thing."

She got up and they took the wine out onto the porch, where they sat in rusting lawn chairs, watching the last of the glow above the trees. Down by the pond the frogs were twanging like banjo strings. Soon they would die or hibernate or do whatever frogs did during winter, and the pond would be silent.

"I guess you don't believe in God, do you?" Lucy said.

Maxine lit another cigarette. The smoke blended into the purplish dusk and disappeared. "Let's put it this way. You'd better hope there is no God. Because a God who presides over Auschwitz is either evil himself or psychotic."

Lucy, who considered herself more or less agnostic, was shocked by this remark. It had never occurred to her that God, if He did exist, could be anything other than benevolent. But this was too harsh; there was too much it failed to take into account. She tried to tell Maxine about how it felt to run, about the tender warmth of the sun on her eyelids, the field bursting with yellow flowers. Maxine listened, but Lucy could no longer see her face, only the tip of her cigarette glowing red, intense.

Soon she stopped, exhausted. After all, what argument could refute the image of the pregnant woman dangling upside down from a tree while the child inside her tried futilely to batter its way out? This was blasphemy of life itself. She leaned back and looked at the deepening sky. Out of the corner of her eye she caught a brief silvery streak, but for the first time in her life she could not think what to wish for.

"Tomorrow's my birthday," she said. "I've waited all my life to be twenty-one. I'll be *of age*. Why don't I know anything?"

Maxine laughed her scratchy dry laugh and stood up, grasping the bottle in one hand and Lucy's elbow in the other. "Come on," she said. "Let's get you a sandwich and put you to bed. You're about to have your first hangover."

Lucy did wake with pounding head and dry mouth the next morning, but instead of going back to sleep she did some stretches, then went for a long run. The air was cool, almost cold, and a white mist hung over the road that followed the pond. She spread her arms and ran through it like an airplane cutting through clouds. By the time she got back, her head felt fine.

They spent the morning packing Maxine's old leather suitcases with her clothing and personal articles. Lucy was touched and embarrassed to see the famous author's lingerie, limp and gray from too many washings. They went through the mail for the last time, then

Lucy loaded the car with boxes that were destined for the dump and the Rescue Mission. The errands took most of the afternoon. It felt strange to be acting as Maxine's agent at the post office, the bank, the library. People stared at her for a moment before attending to the business at hand. Perhaps it was because she didn't look like a professional secretary. Perhaps they took her for a niece or even a granddaughter.

In the supermarket she bought walnuts and chicken and tiny hot peppers for the Ethiopian national dish. At the liquor store she stood self-consciously in line, hoping the cashier would ask her for I.D., but he barely gave her a glance.

Her last stop was the dump, where she unloaded crates of papers and mementos which Maxine said served no purpose. She stood at the edge of the pit looking down at them, the artifacts of a life, mingled now with abandoned mattresses and blown-out tires. The pit made her think of the mass graves at Auschwitz, of the earth heaving to yield up the corpses. She shivered and got back in the car, knowing that these images, a gift from Maxine, were now fixed in her mind like tatoos.

Back at the house, Maxine put her to work picking the last of the tomatoes from the ruined garden and shelling the walnuts, showing her how to crack them by squeezing two together in her hand. They worked together in the sunny kitchen until the frying peppers drove Lucy, coughing, into the living room, where she fell soundly asleep on the couch.

It was dusk when she awoke to an intriguing blend of smells. Maxine was sitting at the table, eyes closed, a cup clasped in both hands. Lucy knew without glancing at the clock that by this time it contained mostly brandy. The living room had been put in order, the remaining boxes stacked neatly by the door along with Maxine's suitcases. No wonder she looked exhausted.

"You should have woken me," Lucy said reproachfully, turning on a lamp.

Maxine's eyes opened. "You sleep like an infant. Wish I could do that."

Lucy stood up and began to stretch gently, cautiously, the way Maxine had taught her. This was her third day of doing yoga, and although her muscles were a little sore, she already felt the urge to extend and relax them, to bear down gently on the exquisite ache and let gravity do the rest. She linked her fingers behind her back and bent at the waist, lifting her arms high in the air.

When the telephone rang, Lucy answered. It was Yaakov. Maxine refused to come to the phone.

"He wants to know how you are," said Lucy, covering the mouth-piece.

"Tell him I'm singing *Carmen* at the Met."

Yaakov heard and gave a short laugh. "She's a joker, my aunt. But she is very ill. She mustn't strain herself."

"No," said Lucy, guiltily. "I won't let her."

"Won't let me what?" Maxine said irritably.

"We shouldn't have postponed the operation," Yaakov was saying. "At this point even a day or two can mean–" He hesitated.

"Life or death," Lucy supplied.

"Yes." His voice became cool. He would arrive about nine tomor-row, he continued. He hoped everything would be ready to go, as he had to get Maxine to the hospital by noon.

Lucy hadn't realized the surgery would be so soon. This was so shocking that she forgot to listen to the rest of Yaakov's lengthy instructions.

"Above all, don't let her drink," he was saying when she tuned in again. "It was a mistake to let her come back, but she is so stubborn, so de-termined to do things her way, even at the expense of her health–"

"Don't worry," Lucy interrupted, watching Maxine twist a corkscrew into a chilled bottle of wine. "She's a tough old broad."

Maxine laughed, raising the bottle in thanks for the tribute. Yaakov's voice went from cool to icy.

"Please inform my aunt that I should be there by nine. And then I think we can dispense with your services, Miss . . . ?"

"Okay," Lucy replied, hanging up. It seemed very important to be rude to Yaakov. Maxine, grinning, handed her a glass of wine.

"This one won't give you much of a hangover," she said.

The wine was light and crisp and left no sour aftertaste in Lucy's mouth. She decided that white wine would be her drink. It was good to know what your drink was.

"He seems kind of stuffy," she told Maxine. "How are you going to stand it?"

Maxine shrugged. "Don't have much choice. It's either that or a nursing home."

"Maybe the home wouldn't be so bad. For a while, I mean."

"I don't want to die in an institution," Maxine said sharply. "I saw what Ben went through. The doctors wouldn't release him, not even to me–because I wasn't his wife, the bastards. They knew he was dying. Why did he have to be tortured?"

Yaakov had said not to let her get upset, to steer her away from dangerous subjects. Lucy looked at the empty bookshelves. She looked at Maxine sitting in the room and then imagined the room empty. The only subjects that mattered were dangerous.

"Will yours be awful too?" she asked.

"Of course," Maxine said calmly. They were going to cut her voice out; she would no longer smell or taste; she would have to breathe, cough, and sneeze through a hole in her throat with a tube sticking out of it. There was some gadget she could hold against her throat to project a mechanical "voice," but she wouldn't consider using it. "It would scare Yaakov's children to death. They'd think I was Darth Vadar," she said.

She poured them some more wine. This time Lucy thought it tasted even better, tingling on her tongue. She breathed in the rich peppery fragrance coming from the kitchen and wondered how it felt to smell and taste for the last time.

"But you'll still be able to write," she said. "You'll still have your brain and your hands."

Maxine looked amused. "I haven't written anything for ten years. Not since Ben died."

"Then why–" Lucy paused to gulp wine for courage. "If you feel like that, why have the operation? Why stay alive at all?"

"What a good question!" Maxine mocked her lightly. Then she relented. "There are two reasons I think of. One is the Law of Inertia. The other is Yaakov's children. I've never lived with children. I've never lived with children. Ben and I–by the time we settled down, it was too late. We were bitter; we let those years go by. That's the main thing I regret; all the time I wasted. How's that for originality?" She roused herself, sitting up straight. "Anyway, Rachel is pregnant again. I want to live long enough to hold the baby."

The kitchen timer went off with a sharp ping. Maxine, getting up to check the chicken, glanced at Lucy's face and gave her shoulder a pat. When she came back, she brought a little package wrapped in newspaper. Lucy looked up in astonishment. She had forgotten it was still her birthday. Everything she had done this morning seemed like part of yesterday. And last week–when she was still getting weepy over Jason, over college and summer vacation–seemed a year or more ago.

The present was a Swiss watch, all delicate gold with numerals that looked as if they'd been painted with a calligraphy brush. It seemed old but also new, already ticking with the correct time, cushioned in a red velvet case which had faded to rose.

"Ben gave it to me while we were still in Europe, but I've never worn it," said Maxine. "Too fragile for the likes of me."

Lucy held out the box, very conscious of doing the adult thing. "I can't take Ben's gift to you."

Maxine just laughed at her. "Sure you can."

"Then, thank you," Lucy whispered, clasping the watch around her wrist. "It's beautiful."

But Maxine was already back in the kitchen dishing out the Doro Wat, which looked like red chicken stew and tasted like fire. After the first bit Lucy hastily reached for her wine, but Maxine pushed it out of reach, saying "Take bread," and she was right–the bread absorbed the burn. The trick was to take small bites of each. Seeing the whole eggs that had been cooked with the chicken gave Lucy a bad moment– they reminded her of Moll and his witticisms–but after a moment she got used to those too.

"This is wonderful," she said. "Will you teach me to make it?"

"There isn't time."

"I could come to Brooklyn."

"I don't think so."

"Why not?"

"For one thing, I won't have any voice."

"You can show me. You can write things down."

"I'll be taking chemotherapy. I'll be weak, maybe sick."

"You can sit on a stool. I'll do all the moving around."

"It's Rachel's kitchen."

"She can learn too."

Maxine stared at her, then let go her sudden bark of a laugh. "I *would* love to see Yaakov's face when he gets Doro Wat for Shabbos dinner."

Lucy reached for the wine, triumphant. She had just won a major battle: there was a future.

Dessert was walnut birthday cake–no candles, but Lucy said candles were for children–and then they piled the dishes in the sink to soak until morning. Maxine opened the second bottle of wine and tipped her chair back against the wall. Lucy liked lingering this way at the table. She liked the warmth of the wine in her blood—it didn't make her dizzy, only fearless, ready for anything.

"What I don't understand," she said, adopting Maxine's habit of picking up where they'd left off, "is how they got away with it. Why didn't we stop them sooner?"

Maxine shrugged. "A lot of people tried to keep us out of the war. Father Coughlin had a big audience; there were rallies of Brown Shirts, swastikas and all, in Madison Square Garden; heavyweights like Joe Kennedy were telling us America should mind her own business."

Lucy wondered who Father Coughlin was and what qualified a boxer to dictate foreign policy. She added the names to the list of things she had to look up.

"We knew it was genocide by 1942," Maxine went on. "Sources in Switzerland, including our own ambassador, kept sending Roosevelt cables till he told them 'No more.' He wanted to concentrate on the war. And there was strong opposition in this country to mass emigration. The War Refugee Act admitted one thousand. That was it. Eichmann was burning millions."

"But how could they do it?" Lucy asked again.

"You talk as if genocide were unknown to human history," Maxine said, irritated. "This is not a civics lesson. Evil is evil. The Nazis institutionalized it, made it cost-efficient. But it goes on and on, everywhere. You must know *that.*" Her voice cracked and she began to cough. Lucy jumped up to get some water, but Maxine waved it aside and went to lie on the living room floor.

"I'll tell you what *I* don't understand, " she said when she could speak again. "The trains full of prisoners who were loaded up and locked in during the Nazis' retreat and then left to starve. Why? Even from the Nazi point of view, why not just abandon them, let them fend for themselves? What possible end could it serve at that point? Did they really think no witness would survive? Did they imagine the corpses wouldn't speak for themselves?"

"They were monsters," Lucy said, conscious that her answer answered nothing. What made monsters of men?

"If they wanted slave laborers to produce for the glory of the Reich," Maxine went on, "why did they keep poisoning their soup? And then why, for God's sake, give them a dental clinic? And why, when the war was so clearly nearing its end, did they step up their slaughter of Jews? Why did they take hundreds of trains and troops badly needed at the front and use them for transporting prisoners to other camps?"

Lucy shook her head. Maxine lat flattened on the floor as if a giant magnet had drawn all the tension from her body. What made her look so tranquil whenever she discussed the most terrible things?

"You see, we have the same question," Maxine said. "It happened. It was permitted to happen. And all our outrage, in the end, means nothing. Because there is no High Court, no ultimate justice."

"They got Eichmann," Lucy pointed out, but Maxine just laughed, clasping one leg to her chest.

"That's why I don't write anymore," she said. "There's only one thing to write about, and it yields no relief, no enlightenment."

Then Lucy had a thought that made her scramble onto her knees, spilling wine on the sofa. "Why don't you write about Ben?"

"I don't know." Maxine said after a moment. "I don't think he'd like it much."

To Lucy's ears it sounded like a possible concession. Encouraged, she went a little further. "How come you never married him?"

Maxine looked into her wine glass. "The short answer is he never asked me." She glanced at Lucy's face. "I guess it had to do with the drinking and the restlessness and the refusal to discuss certain sentimental subjects. A way of registering the shock of 1945. Like wearing a permanent black armband. I had an uncle who lost a young wife and wore that armband for years. Everyone said it was morbid. But it was a protest, a refusal to forget."

"What happened to him?" said Lucy. "Did he die of a broken heart?"

"Hell, no, he got married again. Life is the problem, but life is also the solution." She emptied her glass. "Of course, if we'd had children, that would have been another story. Children always are another story, aren't they? I would have liked a daughter."

"I'd like a girl too. I've got three younger brothers, and each time I wanted a sister."

"Well, maybe you'll have better luck than I did."

"I think you were pretty lucky to have Ben," Lucy said. "And I think you were lucky to be where you were in 1945 and see what you saw. It made your life worth something–it gave you something important to say."

"And what difference has that made? A book might entertain or appall, but in the end it's only a book. People put it aside and go about their business. None of the stories I told have made one bit of difference in what men do to each other."

"But books last," Lucy argued. "Future generations will hear those stories. That has to give you some satisfaction."

"I know it's supposed to–the great legacy and all that. But it's really a crock. Dead is dead. It doesn't matter what you've done or who you are: the light goes out, that's it–nothing. The babies thrown into the fire ended up just as dead as the monsters who put them there. Death is the great leveler. There's your justice."

This speech made Lucy's throat ache. "You make it sound so awful."

"It is," said Maxine. She poured the rest of the wine into their glasses and raised hers in a toast. "But let's drink to the future anyway," she said. "Tell me what yours will be."

"I don't know how I'll end up."

"Then tell me how you'll start out. What's next? Not another Temp job?"

"Back to school, I think."

"School," Maxine repeated. She did not seem as thrilled by the prospect as Lucy knew her parents would be. "And what will you study?"

"I don't know," Lucy said, then scowled. She had forgotten she was not going to say that so often. "History, I think. German history."

Maxine nodded. She was grinning a little, but if she had doubts she kept them to herself. "To history, then. Perhaps we'll learn from it yet."

Lucy raised her glass and swallowed the wine, which tasted as bland as water. Maxine began to do slow stretches. Lucy lay on the couch and watched, remembering what she had said the other night. You bent down, let your arms hang, gave up the breath in your lungs and poured forward, letting go, giving in. The mind emptied, or rather filled, concentrating completely on the slow extension of muscles. You countered the effects of a lifetime of straining against natural law, against the incontrovertible force that sucked all living things into its center. And it seemed to Lucy as she watched that at last she understood Maxine's tranquility: it was a kind of petrified bitterness, enforced by long contemplation of horror, by rage beyond words or gestures. It was her way of giving in. But it would not be her own way, Lucy decided. She would search and understand. She would find words for the unspeakable.

This thought made her happy and she wanted to tell Maxine, but Maxine was concentrating on the simple fact of air passing in and out of her lungs, and besides, Lucy's lips had gone numb. Just before she fell asleep, she heard Maxine's voice inside her head saying again with perfect clarity: *Life is also the solution*, and her numb lips curved into a smile.

*　*　*

Maxine was right about the hangover. After Lucy showered and dressed and had some breakfast she felt nearly fine, except that she couldn't quite remember her revelation of the night before. Perhaps this was due to the ephemeral nature of revelations. On the other hand, perhaps it was due to the second bottle of wine and the way it had slipped down her throat like water. She decided to become the sort of person who sipped wine slowly in moderate amounts. If she had any further relevations, she wanted to remember them.

Maxine had not slept well. Lucy could tell by the stillness of her posture as she sat at the table with coffee and cigarette. She looked as if she'd been sitting there a long time. Her face was gray and sagging, her shoulders slumped, as if gravity were exerting more force on her than usual this morning. Lucy remembered that in a few hours she was going into the hospital. She wished she had the courage to touch Maxine's hand or shoulder, but Maxine was not the sort of person you touched casually. Lucy did not wish to seem patronizing. She was quite sure Yaakov would be patronizing enough.

Instead she said: "He'll be here soon."

This seemed to rouse Maxine a little. "Then you should get going."

Lucy was going to protest but then remembered her phone conversation with Yaakov. It also occurred to her that Maxine might have her own reasons for greeting Yaakov alone. She went upstairs and packed her bag. Maxine's room was empty and neat, the bed stripped, a fine haze of dust already coating the furniture as if the room had stood empty a long time.

Downstairs, Maxine was waiting by the front door. This was not to be prolonged. Lucy's throat felt thick and sore. She wondered is this was how Maxine's throat felt all the time. Before she could speak,

Maxine thrust out a square but lumpish brown package. It was heavier than Lucy expected, packed tightly. In a flash she knew.

"The notebooks! But shouldn't these be in a library or something?"

"Hell no," Maxine rasped. "I want you to keep them."

Lucy nodded, clasping the package. Her throat was unbearable now. "I'll come and see you," she managed to say.

"That might not be a good idea."

"I'll come and see you," she repeated firmly and was rewarded by Maxine's familiar grin. Then, courageous enough after all, she hugged her hard, the package caught between them, and walked straight out of the house. Good-byes should be swift and direct, she decided, wishing she had known this when she said goodbye to Jason.

The edges of the package were digging into her breast and she loosened her grip, studying the blank brown wrapping paper. Who could guess what it concealed? She thought of Maxine stacking the notebooks, blinding them, wrapping them, pages covered with faded ink describing evil beyond comprehension, a world where anything could happen, a universe ungoverned by any justice or compassion greater than the puny efforts of individual men. She thought of Maxine lying on the floor, calmly reciting horror upon horror—and, this time without benefit of wine, understood that counting up the horrors was both participation and protest. The notebooks were Maxine's testimony, her obligation to remember and tell. In giving them to Lucy, she was also passing on the obligation.

Lucy put down her suitcase right in the middle of the road, tempted, despite what she had decided about clean goodbyes, to go back and tell Maxine that she understood, that she accepted. But a big black car was approaching and she had to move out of the way. It passed her in a little flurry of dust, and she saw that the driver was a bearded man in an old-fashioned black Homburg. She glanced at the delicate watch, Maxine's other gift. Right on time. That would be Yaakov.

For a moment she remained looking after him, undecided. But then, hearing the rumble of the approaching bus up ahead, she turned swiftly, clutching her burden, and hurried to get on board.

JULIA ABBOTT JANEWAY
Above the Apothecary

THE LONGER SHE remained in Haworth, the more its smell repulsed her. Exactly what made it disagreeable was hard to discern—perhaps the combination of the coke-burning Victorian past and, illogically, liniment oil—but Greta hated the way it clung to her, cloyingly fingering her dress hem, her skin, the silver undersweep of her hair. Sometimes, while she waited in the cobbled street for her husband to buy *The Times* or take a photograph, she wondered if the smell was more of an essence. In a guidebook, she had read all about the terrible history of this place: the Victorians had no sense of water sanitation, several families had shared a single privy, and disease had made the average person die at twenty-four. A stone-jumbled graveyard, sequestered between the Brontë Parsonage and the Church of St. Michael and All Angels, held too many skeletons. It was only after Charlotte Brontë's father was buried, hoary-jowled and mean, that the town officials finally declared the graveyard at capacity and sealed it off. Too late, Greta cried inwardly. She stood in the street, imagining the decay that seeped into the flinty ground, the bones and filth of many ages, capped with industrially cut stone. A traveler of the twentieth century, she possessed the luxury to see the profitless mistakes these people had made, the folly of constructing a town on a shrunken hill, the absurdities of blood-letting and hoop skirts.

Yet, when she viewed her own life, Greta claimed no superiority. It had been her idea to visit West Yorkshire, after all, because she wanted to relate Brontë country to the Great Books Club back home.

178

Recently admitted, she considered herself unprepared; in her imagination, the wealthy faces of the literary ladies followed her everywhere, assessing her struggling intellect, her clothes, the impropriety of Andy's globe-shaped stomach. In London, Greta had insisted Andy wouldn't be sorry if they rented a car and drove up here. Her suggestion contained many expectations. Like the ladies in Great Books, Greta believed one could shake out landscape and material remains and read them, like fortune sticks, for clues about genius. She had never been to Haworth, but presumed the countryside would be enchanting.

At first, as their mini chugged up the cloistered streets, circumventing tourists and a few other automobiles, Greta thought she had chosen wisely. They arrived at twilight, when Haworth was at its best, and even the air seemed fine to her then—spicy and romantic. Parking near the Black Bull Inn, the fender of their Englishy car kissing the graveyard wall, they tugged their suitcases out of the trunk and struggled across the street to their bed and breakfast. From the guidebook, Greta had purposely chosen lodgings with atmosphere. She asked for room number seven because it was directly above the old apothecary where Branwell Brontë used to purchase opium for his addiction. Supposedly, Room Seven was also haunted by a ghost.

Up the narrow staircase, they filed behind the owner's son, Andy listening to instructions about keys and curfew times, Greta blinking in the moldy dimness, suddenly unsure of what she had asked for. The owner's son was cheerful. While he unlocked the door to the room with a long-toothed key, he told a joke about an Englishman and an American meeting in the rain. Greta never heard the punch line because the door opened effortlessly, not what she had anticipated. The room was stale and pretty. Crossing the rose-trellised carpet, the owner's son pulled aside the lacy curtains to let in what was left of the day. Outside, a streetlamp was already lit and glowed, a perfect circle of gold, against the squared and foggy panes.

"Will you be needing anything else?" the young man asked. Andy held out his palm for the key.

"Well," the young man said, "There's tea if you'd like." He gestured toward the bedside table on which was set a tray with an electric kettle, a copper tin, and two translucent teacups.

"One more thing," Greta said shyly. The young man paused in the doorway. "Will we see the ghost?" She was trying to make a joke but the young man laughed the wrong way, taking her question as a friendly dismissal.

"Oh, the spirit," he said. "She's a nuisance, but I'm sure you won't be bothered."

Smiling, he left them alone.

Through the thin door, Greta heard the tremor of footsteps heading back down the hallway and a tune, half-wild and whistled intermittently. Carefully, Andy unpacked and rearranged his clothes in the broken-footed bureau. His habit annoyed Greta. In a corner, her own suitcase usually sprawled open with her belongings piled high in view. She was afraid of leaving her things behind—the odd glove, a silk scarf her children had presented on a birthday long ago. When he took time to organize his things as though he were at home, Andy sometimes pointed out, he never lost anything when it came time to leave. In a drawer with a tiny scrolled handle, he positioned his socks, balled into pairs.

If Greta had pinpointed her first moment of discontent, it would have been then—watching Andy bend over his suticase with his glasses fallen down the bridge of his cold-reddened nose. Over the double bedspread what appeared to be a lace tablecloth, scalloped where it brushed the floor. Near the window, a T.V. jutted from the end of a mechanical arm and, to the side of it, crouched a pay-per-view movie box. This was not the type of place a ghost haunted. Still, as she changed into her evening shoes and took a sequined wool sweater from her suitcase, Greta felt uneasy. A darkly-stained wardrobe bulged against the far wall; there was barely passing room between its doors and the foot of the bed.

Greta buckled her shoe and sat up. On top of the wardrobe perched three hideous dolls. Two were pink-skinned, one was chocolate brown, and all three wore Victorian dresses and bonnets edged with frills. They were the size of real infants but, as if to make their skin more atrocious, their gowns were the outlandish colors of tangerine, canary, and emerald. Their lashes were cemented to their lids like miniature black razors. Their eyes were filmy and unblinking. Tattered bows knotted stoutly beneath their chins and, from their bonnets, their hair escaped like whorls of spun glass.

Greta thought the owner's wife was crazy to presume her guests would fall asleep under the watch of such creepy things. In the dolls' immobile fists dangled wee purses of potpourri—the same perfumy woodchips, Greta suspected, that filled the decorative basket set on the nightstand. Impulsively, she considered draping a blanket over the dolls to hide them but quickly rejected the idea. She didn't want to admit she was afraid. Finished with his unpacking, Andy was reclining on the bed. He leaned back against the starched pillows, clicked on the BBC with the remote, and rested his arm along the wrought-iron headboard. Sweat bloomed in the curve of his arm, changing his powder-blue Oxford into a deeper blot of indigo.

Greta frowned. "Shall we go eat?" she asked.

Tired, Andy barely changed expression. On the TV flashed pictures of people crushed against the chained gates of Hillsborough Football Stadium. More people sprawled on the brilliant green turf, clawing for air. "Now?" Andy asked. "I think it's too early."

"We can walk around the town first."

"All right," Andy said, closing his eyes. "Give me a few minutes and I'll be ready to go."

*   *   *

When Greta and Andy stepped out on the street, they breathed in the incense of the coming rain. Smoke swelled from the Haworth chimneys and cascaded, in visible gray spirals, down from the edge of slate roofs. In one direction, the central street sloped downward to disappear in the haze. Because shops had closed and cars had been parked elsewhere for the night, the space seemed older, hemmed in by blackened buildings and shambling storefronts. On the door of the old apothecary hung a CLOSED sign. Through its dirty window, Greta strained to see, over the displays of tea towels and scented soaps, the shelves hidden in the shadows at the back of the shop. Scraggy bunches of weeds hung from the ceiling beams; herbs, Greta corrected herself. Squinting, she could make out immense wooden vats and the distant sleekness of bottles.

"We'll have to come back when it's open," she said.

Andy was out of earshot and standing on the sooty steps of the Church of St. Michael. Contrasted with the grimness of the pediment, he looked fragile in his tweed cap and London Fog. How Greta had begged him not to buy a London Fog–she noticed English people never wore them–but Andy said he wanted to be prepared for the rain. If he was a tourist, he had reasoned, there was nothing wrong with looking like one. Nonetheless, Andy could be accused of making a mockery of their first trip to the Isle by hackneyed dressing. With her newfound recognition of clichés, courtesy of the Great Books Club, Greta should have replied that Andy might as well wear a hat of bobbing corks on a visit to Australia. Not that he would have listened.

Greta walked toward the church and the soft tocks her heels made on the burnished cobblestones echoed between the dimensions of the street. Below the yellow streetlamp, moisture swirled like dust motes, forewarning the coming drizzle. The air was murky. They had left the bedside lamp on in their room above the old apothecary and as Greta turned to glimpse a comforting glimmer behind the lacy curtain, she remembered how a room could appear warmer from the outside. Andy sneezed. His tweed cap fell from his head with the sudden movement and landed across the toe of his sneaker. Picking it up, Greta placed it back on his head and, in the process, deftly smoothed a wisp of his snowy hair. When had he become so old? she wondered, and she linked her arm through his to steer him toward the Black Bull and dinner.

Settled on red velvet cushions amid brass-covered walls, Greta and Andy ordered drinks and sat for a while in silence. The ceiling felt near, crossed with thick beams, and a fire crackled in the hearth at the end of the pub. From the laughing group near the bar, a blue plume of cigarette smoke drifted over Andy's shoulder to settle in Greta's hair. Discretely, she tried to fan it away with her menu. She had forgotten her guidebook in the trunk of the rental car and couldn't remember if this was the inn where Branwell Brontë had drunk himself to excess. From appearances, it seemed like a good place—close and gleaming—and she guessed boredom in Haworth had driven Branwell to extremes.

Andy took a sip of whiskey and stared idly at a brass stamped with the image of Wuthering Heights. He didn't ask Greta about it, he wasn't the least bit curious, and he'd forgotten her recent passion in research. His unconcerned expression made Greta want to drown him with a barrage of facts: Wuthering Heights was a farmhouse Emily Brontë walked to on the moors; Mrs. Gaskell found the graveyard romantic by moonlight; after her sisters died, Charlotte continued to walk late at night around the parlor table, the steady quakes of her footsteps overheard by a servant in the kitchen below. "You know," Greta began, but was interrupted by a sallow-faced English girl.

"Are you together?" the girl asked, hugging a red-bound menu to her flat chest, and Greta was taken aback. Of course they were, otherwise they wouldn't be sitting at the same table, sharing drinks. As if to answer, she gazed stupidly at the girl, thinking that such a simple question must be more complex. Were they together? Andy nodded and, carrying his whiskey delicately between his thumb and index finger, followed the girl into the dining room. He had ordered the Yorkshire Pudding and asparagus, as Greta predicted he would. Still, as Andy disappeared through the cavernous doorway, he appeared to her a stranger.

*   *   *

That night, Greta slept fretfully under the oyster-colored bedding and waited for the ghost. Wool blankets scratched her legs, the stiff pillow elevated her head at an uncomfortable angle, and she kept opening one eye to glance at the dolls on top of the wardrobe. Though their terrible baby-toothed smiles blended into the dimness of their faces, Greta sensed them awake, scrutinizing. The owner's son, she remembered, had mentioned the ghost was female; for this reason, Greta assumed herself particularly vulnerable, lying in bed, laced helplessly in her granny nightdress. Warily, she noted the angles of the dolls' arms, the tilt of their seedy bonnets. She would know if they moved. The room smelled like the ointment her son used to rub on his knees after running, but Greta was too apprehensive to rise and crack the window. Instead, she huddled next to Andy's sleeping nakedness and was surprised at how hot his skin felt. Sweat covered the curve of his spine, glistened at the nape of his neck. Troubled, Greta rolled away to find a cooler place near the edge of the bed. Part of her was upset with Andy; although she was certain the ghost would appear to her alone, she was dismayed her husband could sleep without a flicker of fear.

When she awoke in the morning to the sound of Andy brushing his teeth and the feathery sunlight across the rumbled bed, Greta's jealousy was replaced by disappointment. The ghost hadn't come and as she rose and dressed, she realized what annoyed her was a new detectable stench to Haworth, seethingly sweet.

*   *   *

Andy arrived at breakfast, clutching Greta's guidebook and bleeding lightly from the center of his forehead.

"Oh, Andy," Greta exclaimed. Around them, the other breakfasting couples glanced over with mild curiosity. At the end of the room, out from a maroon curtained doorway, stepped the owner's son, carrying a breakfast tray.

"Looks like you nicked yourself," he said and, after situating a toast rack, pointed to his own forehead.

Puzzled, Andy touched his wound. A smudge of blood rubbed off on his fingertips. "Oh," he said, startled, and then related to Greta what had happened: he had heard a bird call from beyond the graveyard wall. The cry sounded surprisingly human, somewhere between a yodel and a moan. Otherwise, Andy claimed, he wouldn't have paid attention. As it was, he had looked away at the exact moment the trunk of the rental car had sprung up and cuffed him on the forehead. The pain passed quickly. Slightly dazed, Andy went on searching for Greta's guidebook because he hadn't realized he'd been hit hard enough to bleed.

"If my mother was here, she'd know what type of bird it was," said the owner's son. He added, for the benefit of the newly-arrived guests, that his parents had gone on weekend holiday and would return tomorrow. Issuing forth from the curtained doorway came the reek of burned meat, and the young man laughed, nervously explaining how he and his elder brother had been left in charge. Setting a plate of ossified eggs before Greta, the young man was apologetic. He knew his brother's breakfast was inedible. He was sorry about his ignorance of birds.

"Shall I get you a sticking plaster?" asked the owner's son.

Andy waved him away. "It's nothing," he said and, sitting down, began to butter his toast.

As with Haworth's oppressive smell, Greta was irritated by Andy's mark. It was shaped like a bloody thumbprint and, positioned in the exact center of his forehead, it could have been purposely made. Disregarding her offers to bandage it, Andy examined his wound in the mirror after breakfast and decided it was insignificant. He declared that wounds healed better if left in the open air. Greta tried to ignore the conspicuous mark, but was herself ambushed many times that morning. Peering through the closed door of the apothecary, buying a map, or changing her money at the Bureau de Change, Greta would turn in time to see her husband bumbling into someone, not paying attention, the bloody spot bright on his brow.

By early afternoon, exhaust-spewing buses parked on the other side of the hill and the visitors descended. English pensioners. German, Italian, and French. These motley crowds accompanied Greta through the parsonage, straining against the crimson ropes that barred the wallpapered sitting room and the Reverend's study. They mobbed the back kitchen to see the board where Emily had kneaded bread and jammed the staircase to scrutinize Branwell's portrait of his three mousy sisters; pausing, they tried to discern the shade between the sisters, where Branwell had painted out his own dissatisfying figure in an ascension of yellow ochre. Greta headed past the grandfather clock and dodged an unattended foreign child covertly licking the wall. Upstairs, around Charlotte's diminutive brown dress, a troupe of Japanese clustered, snapping pictures.

In the latter rooms, Greta forgot all about the Great Books Club and the fact that her viewing these things–the inch-high handwritten novels of early juvenilia or classic first editions–would elevate her place among women better read than she. Simply, Greta couldn't shake the feeling that she was rummaging. Some objects were too personal: Charlotte's square-toed slippers, her necklace of carnelian beads, her calling card, her mourning brooch preserving a plait of Anne's hair. Behind polished glass, Charlotte's gloves were folded over one another, so sad and brittle they could have been fashioned from the skin of a fish. Yet these pieces were inadequate proof of Charlotte's imagination. They gave no clue as to what she pondered during ordinary days. And who could guess what any of them believed but never articulated in writing–quiet Anne and dark-browed Emily, Maria and Elizabeth who died early, Branwell who burnt out his mind with a million teaspoons of drink. The nursery windows in the Brontë parsonage overlooked the mouldering graveyard. Shivering romantically, visitors and scholars often conjectured the effect such a space must have had on the children. But perhaps the Brontës' house, their books and dresses, were only those trappings that everyone had. Why do we preserve such things? Greta wondered.

Andy, with his petal-shaped wound, loomed behind her, nudging. Being here, speculating about such matters, was like falling in love with someone already out of reach. Only tokens remained–a wedding bonnet trimmed with green leaves and white flowers. A clean sheet of paper one was about to use.

"I'm hungry," Andy said.

"I'm not ready," Greta told him. But she was finished and found it hard to linger. All that remained was the gift shop, the most popular room. Students rifled through the postcard racks and bookshelves and a Japanese man, scrutinizing a bad sketch of Haworth's main street, pondered whether to buy it. Three argyle-clad English women were waiting in a line. As Greta passed, she heard one coo, "Ah, lovely." The woman was holding up an engraved bookmark for the inspection of her companions. "A nice addition to any collection," agreed another with beady bird eyes, and the third cackled in agreement. Above the hum of discussion peeled the electronic voice of the cash register, tallying up more postcards, stamps, film, Yorkshire cookbooks, flowered coasters, key chains, pencils, and crystal plaques imprisoning Charlotte's profile in smooth and limpid planes.

Opening the exit door, Greta expected the stench again and instead stepped out into a clean wind. Andy was waiting near a stone wall. When he saw her, he smiled and pointed in the opposite direction, away from the graveyard path from which they had entered the parsonage. The place where he pointed was open. Hills oscillated into a gray horizon and the clouds were strung out thin and spare.

*   *   *

Later, while they ate lunch in a tea shop adjacent to the closed apothecary, Greta read from the guidebook the description of a little walk across the moors. Words like "heath-bound" and "stern mystery" rolled from her tongue and the hope of escaping from Haworth and enabled Greta to bear her present surroundings: the plastic tablecloth that was like a yellowed membrane, the congealed bowl of shepherd's pie, the flowers that rotted in a vase near her elbow. Above Andy's head, a collection of china dogs begged and skulked across a cobwebbed shelf, and across the carpet were the crumbs and grease slicks from previous diners. Andy was tucking into a large plate of sausages–bangers, the English called them–and mash. Greta wrinkled her nose and read: "Your destination is a farmhouse known as Top Withens, which may have been Emily Brontë's inspiration for *Wuthering*

Heights." Reaching across the horrid table, she creased open the guide-book for Andy's examination.

"Looks like an old barn," Andy said.

Jerking the guidebook back, Greta studied the photograph. He was right: the roof of Top Withens was a sagging blot of charcoal, and the walls were uneven, seemingly weathered. The photograph was ambiguous; there was a door in the side of the farmhouse, but apparently there were no windows.

"We should see the moors," Greta said firmly. In the photograph, the land buckled away as if to mirror the furrows of gray clouds. From her reading, she knew it would be clean there, flushed by wind.

"I could use a walk," said Andy with his mouth full. "And I think I read that book in school."

"*Wuthering Heights?*" Greta was shocked.

"Was that the one about everybody dying?"

"I don't know what you're referring to." Greta sniffed.

"Yes," Andy said and his eyes had a faraway look; Greta wondered if he was making fun of her. "They made it into a movie, too. Laurence Olivier and Merle Oberon. She kept whining at him to open the window so she could smell the heather once more before she died."

"How romantic," Greta said, but Andy shrugged, his moment of inspired conversation gone.

"I don't think heather even has a scent. She must have gone berserk." He sliced off another obscene-looking banger, speared it with the tines of his fork, and rubbed it in the clotted gravy. Greta couldn't help but comment. "You'd better watch your heart."

"My heart's fine," Andy said and took another bite.

*   *   *

Away from the parsonage and graveyard, the path conducted them past a series of garden plots containing red-feathered chickens, roses, and tomato vines prodded into tidy rows. The directions were easy; up a cobblestone walk, over a road and stile, and out onto the darkening plain. Mild sunshine parted the stringy clouds and glinted off the puddles in the trail. Although it wasn't raining, the ground was boggy, scrubbed with brown heather. At times, Greta and Andy had to walk on top of tangled branches because the track fissioned out, too muddy from use. Greta unbuttoned her jacket, loosened her paisley scarf, and let taintless air converge over her chest and burrow through the knit of blouse. Tenderly, it cleansed the creases of skin Haworth had invaded– her armpits, her throat, the sweaty crevice between her breasts. When they passed a few returning tourists, Greta smiled with the natural ca- maraderie she felt meeting other people coming back the way she had yet to travel. She located a wooden sign which stood on the next hill. TOP WITHENS THIS WAY it proclaimed and, underneath the English, the same information was carved in graceful Japanese characters.

Despite all these attendants, the returning people, the road sign and guidebook, Greta and Andy soon became lost. Somewhere, Greta was sure of it, they descended a hill they shouldn't have. The path dwindled off into an open field of rocks and peat. Purple-specked crags flushed into sloped farmland, and they waded through wheat fields and grass- lands full of ubiquitous sheep. In every valley, stone walls sectioned off pastures and impeded their progress. Because Greta and Andy could- n't climb over a wall without a stile, they roamed from one corner of a pasture to another, searching for an opening. Once, as they hesitated near a fence, they were inspected by a shining black plow horse. Andy held out his hand and, timidly, velvet lips nuzzled his palm, searching for sugar. When the plow horse found none, it jerked its head irritably. Its mane was a sudden spray of black. "This isn't the moors," Greta said. But she and Andy persevered and did not retrace their steps.

They ended up along the paved road, walking the verge between the yellow line and weeds. In a little village called Stanbury, sidewalks appeared again and close-together roofs. Some houses they passed were obviously derelict, the steps sprinkled with glass shards, the windows and doors boarded over. Other places, like the Wuthering Heights Pub, seemed to be waiting for another time. From its open doorway, shaded in maroon depths, came a low murmur and the clink of coins. Continuing down the center street, Greta and Andy thought they would stop and ask directions but villagers were scarce. Laundry flapped from nearby clotheslines–evidence of occupancy–and gaudy roses grew riotously in a few front gardens.

Finally, Greta spotted a fat woman leading a menagerie of small, scruffy dogs. The woman was too far ahead to ask directions–so they followed her from a distance. Because Andy was slow, they lost the woman with the dogs near the village outskirts; but there, like a gift, they found a familiar sign.

When she reached Top Withens, Greta stood still with shock and thought she was in the wrong place. Gone was the intact farmhouse she had studied in the grainy photograph; in its place was a ruin. Where rooms should have been were depressions filled with decaying lumber and rock. There were no doorways, only openings between the stones, and the remaining walls slouched, fused with a reckless layer of cement. Still, as she looked around, Greta knew this was Top Withens because of the hill that rose up behind the foundation and, more importantly, because of the single tree that grew close, gnarled by the wind.

As she sought the leeward side of the ruin, Greta surprised a black and white goat. Alone, it had been resting out of the wind, with its side pressed against the cold stone, and its forelocks curled prissily against its breast. When it saw Greta, it bleated mournfully and scrambled to its feet. Following her, the goat seemed to expect something. Greta turned and stared unwaveringly into the opal-colored eyes, the vertical black slits of pupils that tapered at the ends.

Andy's cold had flared up. By the time he neared Greta, he was wheezing deep within his chest. Removing his cap, he sat down on the rock beside her and she noticed how the edge of his cap had worn a sweaty groove in his plastered hair. From the side of Andy's bulb-shaped nose stretched delicate wings of chafed skin.

"Are you feeling bad?" Greta asked, sorry she had suggested this walk.

Andy asked, "Is this it?" Vaguely he waved his hand, taking in the ruins, the rustling heather, the goat, and gathering gloom.

"Yes," Greta said, wondering if she could trick him, tell him the real Wuthering Heights was much nicer and over the next hill—but it was too late to walk farther. Andy pulled two plastic-wrapped scones out of his pocket. From his other pocket, he extracted a hunk of cheese and a compact bottle of cranberry juice. Greta wanted him to be angry with her, to be as unsatisfied in their destination as she was. Complacently, Andy handed her a scone. His pale eyes took in the overcast sky, the rain clouds that were bearing down on them and threatening to spoil their rest.

*　*　*

Back through the rain they went, hurriedly following the signs, careless of the mud that slopped over their shoes. Mostly, Greta kept her head bowed to make sure she didn't slip, but now and then she lifted the rim of her hood to look toward the horizon. In this country, the rain was as fine as needles, and Greta watched it move across the moors in vast and silvery sheets. Because they had strayed from the right trail the first time, Andy and Greta now encountered unfamiliar objects: a stile shaped like a spiral staircase, an access road, an abandoned Yugo minus its tires and windshield wipers. Under the eaves of a barn, sheep huddled. Their haunches were stained a brownish green and they chewed their cud with awkward, sideways jerks.

The presence of the sheep barn panicked Greta–she thought she and Andy might be lost again. "Come on," she cried, quickening her pace. On the slope of a hill she fell. Instinctively, Greta flung her arm out to break her stumble and her hand sunk into a pile of manure. A foul lick of mud stained the side of her leg and coat. Helping her up, Andy plucked a sodden hanky out of his pocket and briskly wiped her palm. Greta wanted to cry. Her hair clung in sticky tendrils around her face, her feet were drenched and chilled, and she realized she had lost her guidebook. Beneath his plaid cap, Andy's forehead was bleeding again. A curtain of rain billowed and then, like a mirage coming toward them, Greta saw someone carrying an colossal red umbrella. He was a stocky Japanese man and he wore a London Fog exactly like Andy's.

"Haworth?" Andy asked as he approached.

"Haw-wart." The Japanese man said, smiling broadly. His hand left the shelter of the umbrella to point through the falling rain at the hill in front of them. "Haw-wart," he repeated, and Greta and Andy trusted him.

*   *   *

Beneath the watchful dolls, they went to bed, exhausted. It was still early and Greta could hear sounds fluxing through the walls from other rooms–people talking, booms from a television or radio, the squeak of someone settling into a hot bath. Behind this noise continued the hiss of the rain. Ever since Greta and Andy had hurried back through the graveyard and into the bed and breakfast, the storm had never faltered. Water trickled over the edges of slate roofs and jangled down the gutter pipes. Beaded and cold, the windows of their room refracted frost-colored squares of light across the rose carpet. Greta, too tired to sleep, let her fears about the ghost return. It was a perfect night for a specter to emerge, wavering coolly in some corner where light met shadow.

Feverishly, Andy slept beside her, mumbling under his breath, the way he often did when he was ill. Greta was concerned. By the time they had entered the graveyard gate, Andy was leaning heavily on her arm and, although they were close to home, Greta had made him rest beneath the low bowing branches of a tree. Above, in the wet leaves, a flock of crows quarreled raucously, their warring black wings beautiful among the vibrant green. "I never thought I'd be glad to see this old graveyard," Andy puffed.

Greta smiled weakly. "A silly old graveyard, isn't it?" she answered, neither a question or a declaration. Compared with the wild moors, the graveyard had become a welcome sight to her. Throngs of tomb slabs swelled unevenly from the ground. Many of the gravestones held a list of chipped names, familiarly compressed. Taking Andy's hand, Greta had led him toward the main street. A layer of green mold covered the flagstones, and she guessed how slippery the path could be.

Sometime—it must have been the middle of the night because the room was very dark—Andy cried out. Turning over, Greta discovered his face oiled with tears. He stared at her and his bewilderment made her remember the nights she had awakened, unsure if she had protested some awful dream, such as her mother leaving her or her own child killed. For Greta, tears were proof she had shouted out in fear. Though as fine as spider's filament, they were the durable cord between the dream world and the real. Gently, she wiped her husband's face and asked, "What do you want me to do?" But Andy pulled her close and his stomach grumbled. His skin was hot again. "I was burning in a fire," he whispered into Greta's hair. Then, he fell asleep and, letting him hold her, Greta continued to listen to the muttering voice of the rain.

*   *   *

The owners had returned; Greta could tell by the pleasant aroma of frying ham and eggs that floated up the stairwell in the morning. When she and Andy entered the breakfast room, miniature glasses of orange juice were set at their places and warm toast awaited in the toast rack. The maroon curtain parted and, this time, a tall gray-haired man stepped out, bound in a crisp white apron.

"Hope my boys didn't kill you off," he said, jokingly, as he shook Andy's hand.

"Oh, no," Andy told him.

"Segments?" the owner asked and, when Greta nodded, he disappeared behind the curtain and emerged with two bowls of pink grapefruit. The windows in the breakfast room let in an airy light and, as Greta spooned apart her grapefruit, she actually felt sentimental. Would she ever return here? She didn't know because a dual emotion settled within her, aversion combined with pleasure. Perhaps it was the same way she felt about her husband—Andy had habits that annoyed her, but she couldn't imagine living without his predictability. Look at us, she thought, here we are, two old Americans having breakfast as if nothing cataclysmic is happening, as if our lives are not spinning out from beneath our grasp, as if we have all the time in the world to return to any place we choose.

On the shamrock-patterned walls of the breakfast room hung miniature oil paintings of Haworth. The constricted amateurish scenes had annoyed Greta yesterday but now they were charming because she finally understood them. Someone had painted the village not for profit or honor, but out of love.

Lingering after the other guests had retreated to their rooms, Greta spread jam over a piece of crustless toast while Andy buried his nose in *The Times*. Finished with her cooking, the owner's wife brought them a second pot of tea and asked if Greta had enjoyed her breakfast.

"I know it's not what you Americans are used to," the owner's wife confided. "All those sugar pastries in the morning."

"It was delicious," Greta said.

"I'm sorry if my sons caused you any inconvenience," the wife continued. "When we called yesterday evening, we were appalled to find they'd given you room seven."

"I asked for it," Greta told her.

"Why?"

Greta smiled shyly. "I read in my guidebook there was a ghost." In the bland morning light, the confession was outrageous, conjured up by a foreigner with evidently no sense of reality. As if to regard Greta better, the English woman put on her reading glasses.

"I'd love to see that guidebook," she said, and the golden chain, attached to her glasses and looped around her neck, trembled.

"I don't have it," Greta said. "I lost it on the moors in a rainstorm."

"Ah, what a pity," the old woman said. She took off her glasses and rested them on her flowery bosom. "And you don't remember the title?"

"I'm sorry, I don't."

The owner's wife sighed. "Well, I was just asking because we like to keep track of who writes us up. Maybe this book was by that cheeky fellow who visited us last spring–yes, it must have been him because he was certainly more interested in our haunting troubles than my breakfast."

"Well, for Americans, a ghost can be an attraction."

"Pah, she's nothing but a worry. We've even had the vicar in, to put her at peace, you know. He did whatever vicars have to do–opened up all the windows to let out the spirit, dashed around the holy water and prayed a bit. The night after he exorcised our house, I was so happy. I thought, well that's that. But then . . ."

She interrupted her own story to call her husband out of the kitchen.

"Gordon, come here. I'm telling this lady I don't believe in ghosts."

"My wife has never been what you'd call superstitious," the husband said.

"That night," the landlady said, turning back to Greta. "I sat on the stairs, certain she was gone forever. But then, I don't know how to describe it, I felt something rush over me, like this . . . " she passed her hand over her blue-tinted hair. "Whoosh, and she was here."

"But why is she here?" Greta asked.

"Half of this house burned to the ground in 1640," the owner answered, as he untied his apron. "This woman was trapped upstairs. She perished in the blaze."

Startled, Greta remembered Andy's fire dream and waited for him to say something, but instead he smiled and folded his paper. "Well, Greta," he said, apparently forgetting. "We'd better be moving on."

"You aren't a guidebook writer?" the owner asked, nervously.

"No," Greta said. "I only wanted to come to Haworth to . . ." She hesitated. What had she come here for–to impress the Great Books ladies, to get away from noisy London, to see if she would be chosen by the supernatural? The wound on Andy's forehead had dried into a tight little scab. Across the breakfast table, Greta stared at him with astonishment. He was the one who had been sensitive to it all–not her, with her ruminations on the Brontës or her dread of a ghost. And still Andy had no idea it was he who had been chosen. His fire en-

counter was submerged deep in his mind as a nightmare or a side effect of fever.

"We wanted to see some of the country," Andy finished for her.
He pulled out his traveler's checks.

"Well, we're glad you weren't bothered," the owner said.

"Yes," his wife agreed. "The poor soul only runs up and down the
hallways, trying to get out, I suppose. And our son is terribly affected
by frightful dreams. He can't sleep in the room above the apothecary."

* * *

They packed their suitcases. Methodically, Andy cleaned his shav-
ing kit and retrieved his clothes from the three-footed bureau. Greta
sealed her muddy shoes within plastic storage bags. Outside the rain
had ceased. The remaining water drops clung to the windows of the
bedroom and trickled, now and then, in crazy angles down to the sill.
Without looking at the cloudy sky, Greta knew their drive back to London would be a confusing obstacle course of wet lorries, tour busses,
and baffling roundabouts. Still, she was ready to leave and, as Andy
closed the door to room seven, Greta didn't glance back. Down the
narrow staircase they descended, bumping their suitcases against the
walls. They shook hands with the owners, said their good-byes, and
moved across the street. Smoke rolled from rain-slicked roofs. A shop-
keeper across the street was sweeping her stairs. Near their bed and
breakfast sat a wooden cart draped with commemorative tea towels.
The door to the old apothecary, was wide open.

"Wait," Andy said as she continued to lug her suitcase toward their
car. He was standing next to the tea towel wagon, his brow worriedly
creased like a child's.

"Didn't you want to go into the apothecary, since this might be our
last chance?"

Through the door, Greta saw a long, varnished counter. The
apothecary didn't seem like it was of this century, but of a previous
one, a time Greta knew very little about. "No," she said, and kept
walking toward the car.

When she had come to West Yorkshire, Greta had been too busy
studying the effects of industrialism and had missed the land. But now,
as they drove down the hill, out of Bradford and through the countryside, she felt as if she could see each quiver of grass and tree branch,

every individual turn of earth. This space, Greta realized, is what was haunted after all. Not the house or the room above the old apothecary, but the very place where tragedy had happened. Beside her, within the tight air of the car, Andy hummed between sneezes. Back lit by the stain of the rainclouds beyond the window, his profile was illuminated. His white hair glowed like an aureole. With both hands curled around the steering wheel, he drove carefully, as he always did, and Greta smiled. What secrets he held! And did love, as well as sorrow, sink far in the bones, remain intact until the end of time beneath the cities and stone and peat? Rolling down her window, Greta thrust her hand into the rush of moist air as if she was about to wave, and the essence of Haworth dissipated, fell away like ribbons through her fingers.

TODD LIEBER

Haying

THE TRACTOR was backed up to the mower-conditioner, but they weren't hitched. Keith picked up the power take-off shaft and found it hadn't been greased either, though the grease gun was on the ground beside it. He found his son, Roy, bent over the hoodless front of his primer-gray sixty-five Mustang.

"I swear," Keith said, "You got to be doing this on purpose. No human being's that scatterbrained."

Roy stood up, blonde hair falling over his eyes. When he brushed it aside with the back of his wrist he left a smudge of grease on his forehead.

"Huh?" he said.

"The mower."

"I didn't figure you'd be back so quick." He stared at the machine shed as if he could see through it to where the tractor and mower were parked. "You want me to get it now?"

"I can get it myself now."

"Whatever." Roy turned back to his car.

Keith had taken a week's vacation from his job at the Conoco station to mow his first cutting of hay, but yesterday afternoon, just after the implement dealers closed, the reel belt on the mower had snapped. This morning, with an extra-long day's work ahead, he'd gone to town first thing for a new belt and asked Roy to have everything else ready to go. Now Roy's butt, raised in the air as he leaned over his engine, taunted him.

"I ask a hell of a lot of you, don't I?" Keith said.

Roy grumbled something that sounded obscene.

"What?" Keith snapped.

"Nothing."

"Stand up. I don't like talking to your back."

Roy removed himself from the cavity of the car. "Okay, I'll grease your damned mower. I didn't know it was such a big deal."

Keith had the new belt–fifty-four inches of fiber-enforced rubber–in his right hand. He'd never struck his son, never even spanked him, but it took a concentrated effort to keep that hand at his side as Roy edged past.

He replaced the belt while Roy greased the machine. Neither spoke, but the tension between them made the silence hum. From the time Roy was eight and showed his first steer at the county fair, Keith and he had worked as partners. But lately, anything Keith wanted done, Roy had a reason for not doing: he was late for work, or his arm hurt, or he *had* to work on his car. You could fill a book with his excuses. If he didn't have an excuse, he'd argue that whatever it was Keith wanted didn't need doing. It seemed as if he'd lost half his brain when he turned sixteen, and the half that was left couldn't think about anything but girls, baseball, and that damned sixty-five Mustang Keith wished he'd never loaned him the money to buy.

Roy finished and tossed the grease gun in the tool box behind the seat of the tractor. "Was that all, then?"

"That's it," Keith said. "That there's your whole day's work."

For a moment they locked eyes. Then Keith climbed on the tractor, sent a puff of black diesel smoke up the exhaust, and pulled away.

He's seventeen, Randi kept saying, he'll grow out of it, be patient with him. But Roy kept pushing. For what, Keith didn't know. But he sensed his son would keep on pushing until somebody pushed back hard enough to find out.

*   *   *

At the gate to the hayfield, he stopped and pulled his shirt over his head, folding it on the tractor seat, neatly so it wouldn't bunch up beneath him. Then he eased the power take-off into gear and lowered the sickle into the waist-high meadow. At first he was tense, brooding about Roy and listening intently to the noises of the mower, concerned that some other problem had caused the belt to break. But after he'd made a round and opened up the field, he began to relax. There was something hypnotic and soothing in the humming of the tractor engine and the rollers on the hay conditioner, the back-forth clicking of the sickle, the rapping of the one broken tooth on the reel each time it came around. With a rhythm as strong and regular as a heartbeat, the machine devoured the crop and left it behind in high even windrows.

He loved being in the field alone, with his shirt off, immersed in the bright summer colors of earth and sky: the purple blossoms of al-falfa and clover, the occasional yellow of sweet clover and trefoil, the dark green of the meadow set off against the lighter shades of the bor-dering trees and the patchy white clouds that, despite the high blue sky, he kept searching for signs of gray.

The mowing was the first step in a process that had come to be almost a ritual for him. Like his neighbors, he rolled the bulk of his hay into fifteen-hundred-pound round bales that one man could han-dle by himself with a fork lift on the tractor, but each year he did some of his first cutting the old way, in small square bales. The sixty-or-seventy pound bales were convenient for feeding his bull and other cattle that needed to be fed individually, but mostly he did it in homage to his grandfather and the other farmers he and his friends had worked for all the summers of their teens. It kept alive the memory of being young and strong with a body so hard and lean that by mid-July he had to punch extra holes in his belt to keep his pants up, the memory of neighbor families helping each other; of the jokes and the teasing, al-ways some kid pulling a snake out of a bale and dangling it around another kid's neck, always the crazy competitions to see who could throw bales the highest, who could load a rack fastest and tightest. And afterwards, sprawling on a piece of lawn, his arms scratched and cov-ered with leaves, shivering as sweat dried from his body in the near dark, waiting for a supper the wives would cook. That was haying.

* * *

When he got home, hot and grubby from his afternoon in the sun and ready for a beer and a shower, he found a note from Randi pinned to the refrigerator by a magnetic cow: "Got called back to work. Meet you at the game. Hamburger to fry or leftover chicken."

The game. Jesus, he'd clear forgot it. He did some quick figuring and realized it was Roy's turn to start. He skipped his shower, found a clean shirt, grabbed two pieces of cold chicken, and headed back out.

The game was in Northwood, seventeen miles away. By the time he got there it was the bottom of the second, and Warren, their team, was ahead two to nothing. As he'd guessed, Roy was on the mound. Before climbing into the bleachers, Keith paused to watch a few pitches through the diamond-shaped wire of the backstop.

He could tell right away Roy didn't have his best stuff. His fast ball was flat, and he was missing with the curve. But the first hitter Keith saw lined out to left and the second ended the inning with a hard grounder to third. Northwood was one of the weaker teams in the conference. If Roy kept throwing strikes, and the team didn't make too many errors behind him, Keith thought, maybe he'd be all right.

He scanned the bleachers for Randi and found her beside Marcia and Joe Bagley, the parents of the first baseman. She slid over to make room for him and gave him a perfunctory kiss.

"Get my note?" she asked. "Did you get something to eat?"

He nodded. Joe Bagley jabbed him with an elbow.

"No hitter so far," Joe said.

Marcia smiled hello and quickly returned to a conversation she was having with another woman. Most of the Warren parents had known each other all their lives, and the ball games on summer nights were an occasion to socialize. Keith rarely enjoyed that, and tonight he was in no mood for it at all. Joe tried to start a conversation on several subjects, and Keith gave him nothing but monosyllables.

"Bad day?" Randi whispered.

"Just tired," he told her.

Roy kept throwing strikes and had a no-hitter through three innings, but in the fourth, with the score still two-nothing, the Warren shortstop booted a routine grounder and Roy threw the next batter's bunt into centerfield. When the ball came back to him from the second baseman, he snapped his glove at it. The glare in his eyes when he stepped back on the mound made Keith's stomach turn.

"Go out and settle him down," he thought, but the coach, fat Eddie Higgins, watched imperturbably from the top step of the dugout.

Roy reared back and fired fastballs at the next hitter—four of them, high and wide, to load the bases. Higgins nodded his head at the little lefty, Billy Brater, and Brater hurried down the left field line to warm up.

"That damn Higgins," Keith said to Randi. "That's the worst thing he could do. He oughta just go out there and settle him down."

Roy went to three and nothing on the next batter.

"Come on, kid," Keith urged silently. "Just relax. Rock and fire. Right down the middle."

Roy threw two strikes. Keith hunched over, elbows on his knees, hands clasped together. "Come on, one more."

From where they sat, the full count pitch looked good, but the umpire called it low. Joe Bagley jumped to his feet and shouted at him to wipe off his glasses. The runner from third clapped his hands in the air and trotted home. Roy remained in his follow-through, bent over, staring in at the ump. He snapped his glove at the ball again when the catcher threw it back, and without pausing he toed the rubber and stared in for the sign, though the next hitter had yet to leave the on-deck circle.

"Come on, Roy," Randi cried, "You can do it."

"Stick a fork in him, he's done," someone from the Northwood bench called.

Keith knew it was true. Roy wouldn't be pitching anymore, just throwing as hard as he could, the ball a weapon, the opponent anything that might get in its way. "Get him out of there, Higgins," he thought. But the coach didn't move from his perch on the dugout step.

The next Northwood hitter put Roy's first pitch in the trees beyond the Martin Implement Company sign on the centerfield fence.

Higgins popped out of the dugout, motioned to his reliever, and started for the mound. Roy didn't wait for him. He tossed the ball over his shoulder and walked toward the dugout. Higgins stopped halfway, waiting with his hands on his hips as Roy walked past him. To jeers from the Northwood crowd, Roy threw his glove at the bench.

Keith spat at the ground under the bleachers. The back of his neck felt hot, as if all the Warren parents were staring at him. Randi touched his knee, a gesture he knew was intended to be comforting, though it only made him angry. What he wanted to do was go haul Roy out of the dugout and smack him. Even more, he wanted to just go the hell home and get his shower and a beer. But he knew he couldn't leave now.

He suffered through the rest of the game, his anger at Roy swelling each time he glanced at him in the dugout, laughing and exchanging elbows and shoves with his friend, Doug. Warren came back with lots of runs in the sixth and seventh, and the reliever, Billy Brater, pitched credibly, so that when it was over they'd won, nine to seven. As Keith and Randi joined the parents trooping to their cars, Joe patted Keith on the shoulder.

"Get 'em next time," he said.

Keith scowled. "Get 'em yourself."

"Keith!" Randi took his arm to guide him away from the crowd.

"What's he saying that to me for?" Keith said. "I'm not the one made a horse's ass of himself out there."

"You're about to," Randi said.

He spotted Roy walking with Doug to his car and waved him over.

"Don't," Randi said. "You'll just make it worse."

"I'm sorry," he told her. "I'm tired of this shit." She still had hold of his arm, and he shook her loose.

Roy sauntered toward them, cap pushed back on his forehead. His spikes were tied together through the strap of his glove and slung casually over his shoulder.

"Tough game, son," Randi said.

"Hell, we won."

"So. What kind of act was that out on the mound?" Keith said.

Randi swung away from them.

"What act?" Roy's blue eyes were unyielding. They both watched Randi go to her car, deliberately, not stopping to visit with anyone.

"Look," Keith said. "You know I don't care if you win or lose. I never have. That doesn't matter. But damn it, conduct yourself with some dignity."

They had walked toward Keith's pickup, and Roy leaned against it, scowling.

"All you did tonight," Keith continued, "is make yourself look like a horse's ass." He softened his tone. "You're better than that."

Roy pursed his lips and swallowed. Suddenly Keith felt the futility of his anger. He wanted to say something about more than just tonight. He wanted to find some way to pull Roy back from what he saw him becoming. But how? They stood, not looking at one another, until the silence became oppressive.

Finally Roy said, "Was that all, then?"

"Yeah," Keith said, "that's all."

Roy elbowed himself off the truck and rejoined Doug. They would be going out, as they always did after games.

"Hey!" Keith called after him. "Don't forget we got hay to bale soon as the dew's off."

Roy raised his arm halfway and waved but didn't turn around.

* * *

Randi was sitting on the sofa watching television and shelling peas. She looked up when he came in but didn't speak and didn't interrupt the rhythm of popping peas into the bowl on her lap, dropping the pods into a paper sack at her feet. In the kitchen, water was simmering in a pan, and a strainer full of blanched peas was cooling in cold water in the sink. Keith got a beer and took it in the living room. He took a handful of peas, shelled a couple, then put them down.

"What?" he said. "What did I do that's so terrible? Try and talk some sense into my son?"

Randi shook her head and kept snapping pods.

"Tell me."

"Keith, I don't want to talk about it. The two of you are driving me crazy."

"Is it so terrible to tell him when he's being a jerk?"

"He knew he was being a jerk. He didn't need you to tell him. At least not in front of his friends."

"Oh, hell," Keith said. "I didn't. I didn't even . . . "

He left his beer half-finished on the table and went to shower. Afterward, he stood naked in the kitchen where Randi was still blanching peas.

"You coming to bed anytime soon?" he asked.

"When I finish."

He took the newspaper upstairs, intending to read until she came, but the first time he shut his eyes to rest them, he felt the bumpy motion of the tractor and the steady vibration of the mower lulling him to sleep, and he didn't try to resist.

* * *

When he woke—with the first daylight, as always—he felt mildly surprised to find Randi asleep beside him, to look out the window and see Roy's car in the driveway. It was as if, by sleeping so soundly, he'd missed a night of comings and goings he should have been aware of. Behind Roy's car, the tin on the shed roof was dry, which meant no dew had settled and he'd be able to get an early start raking. This pleased him. Unlike the mower-conditioner, the rake was almost noiseless and required little power, so he could run the tractor at half-throttle. It was a job that matched perfectly the stillness of an early June morning.

He brewed coffee and took a cup with him to check the alfalfa he'd mowed two days ago before the reel belt broke. He loved the sweet smell of alfalfa drying into hay and the almost blue color it turned as the sun baked the moisture out. The top of the windrows was almost ready–fluffy and not quite crisp. He flipped one over to check the underside. There it was still cool and limp, but he thought if he turned it and threw two windrows together, the wind and sun would cure it perfectly by early afternoon. It was not yet six–he could be done raking by ten and go to town for breakfast before he started baling. The prospect of the morning made him happy.

Roy's car was blocking the rake, and as soon as he opened the door to move it, the smell of stale, warm beer assaulted him. The floor of the back seat was littered with Old Milwaukee cans.

The one promise–the one goddamn *promise*–he and Randi had asked of Roy when they loaned him the money for the car was that no one ever drink in it. Keith knew this wasn't the first time Roy had broken that promise. But by God, he thought, it will be the last.

It was nine-thirty when he finished raking. Randi had gone to work, and Roy was still in bed. Keith banged on the closed door to his room.

"Get up," he said. "We got hay to bale."

"What time is it?" Roy groaned.

"Just get up."

He swallowed a quick half-cup of coffee and went out to get the baler. After he greased it and checked the twine, he tightened down the cranks so the bales would be as heavy as the old New Holland could make them. He hitched a rack behind it and pulled around the drive by the back porch. In a few minutes, Roy stumbled down the steps.

"You're crazy!" Roy said. "That hay won't be ready."

"Get on," Keith said.

Roy hopped up on the rack and stood against the back rail with his arms spread wide. He rode that way to the field.

Keith eased the baler into the first high windrow. The tractor strained as the plunger packed hay into the bale chamber, and he dropped it down a gear. Roy didn't move until the first bale was almost off the chute. Then, slowly, he put on his gloves and grabbed the strings.

"Holy shit," he gasped. "You want me to bale hay or wrestle elephants?" He lugged the bale to the rear of the rack. Another was at the end of the chute. "At least slow down a little!"

Keith didn't. In a little while, he hollered back over the noise of the baler, "You know, sometimes you're just plain stupid."

"What?" Roy challenged.

"First, you're under age. Second, you know damn well about drinking in your car. Third—"

"That's what this is about, huh?" Roy said. "That's why you're baling green hay."

"Third," Keith said, "At least don't leave the damn cans laying around in plain sight."

"I didn't," Roy snapped. "They were in my car." He was breathing hard, his white tee shirt already soaked with sweat. "Teach ol' Roy a lesson, huh, that's what this is about?" He balanced a bale against his thighs and pushed it ahead of him.

"Just work," Keith reached the end of the windrow and turned.

"I'll tell you one thing." Roy said, as the baler moved again into the hay, "This is the last year you get any help from me. Next summer I'll be out of here."

"That's next summer," Keith said.

"That's right." Roy panted. Bales were piling up around him at the front of the rack. "Will you slow the fuck down!"

"Watch your language."

Keith pulled sharply on the throttle and the rack jerked ahead, toppling Roy over one of the bales. When he got to his feet, he glared at Keith a moment, then jumped off the rack and started across the field.

Keith stopped the tractor. "Where do you think you're going?"

Roy didn't answer.

"Roy!" he called.

But Roy never turned. Keith knew he'd pushed him too far, but to his way of thinking, a father should be able to do that without his son walking away. For a moment he considered going after him and hauling him back—having it out once and for all right there. Instead, he sat listening to the steady ker-wumph, ker-wumph, ker-wumph of the baler, ringing out in the still morning, while Roy crossed the hayfield, climbed the woven wire fence, and made his way over rows of ankle-high corn to his car.

All right, Keith thought. To hell with you then.

He unhitched the baler and drove the tractor back to the house, thinking he would call Pat, the clerk at the Conoco station, who'd mentioned several times that her fourteen-year-old was looking for work.

The boy was gone at Bible Camp, but Pat gave him the numbers of some others he might try. By noon, he'd been on the phone nearly an hour and all he had lined up were two boys whose mothers said they might call back when they got up. The last one he tried was free but didn't feel like working.

He couldn't think of anyone else to call. The energy he'd been going on since dawn was spent, and he felt discouraged, burdened by the pressures of time and more work than one man could do alone.

"Son of a bitch," he said aloud, thinking at that moment of Roy.

But he was through fighting Roy. For what felt like the first time, he acknowledged that he disliked his son and was helpless to change him. Roy's life was his own.

To hell with him, Keith thought again.

He poured a glass of iced tea and sat for a moment staring at the kitchen table, at the wood grain like arrowheads growing out of each other across the surface.

He could finish baling. At least he would have that done, so if he did get some help they could just pick up the bales. But when he went outside, he thought he saw in the distance the thin gray edge of an approaching front. The weather forecast hadn't mentioned rain, but the last thing he wanted was baled hay in the field getting rained on. He decided to wait an hour. Maybe one of the kids would call back, and if they didn't want to work, maybe they'd know someone who did.

*   *   *

He was still sitting in the kitchen when Randi came home.

"I saw the baler in the field," she said. "Did you break down?"

He shook his head. "How come you're home?"

Since she'd worked late the night before, she explained, she'd left early. "Where's Roy?" she asked.

"Gone."

"Gone?"

He fidgeted with his empty tea glass, uncomfortable under her gaze and embarrassed to tell her what had happened.

"Maybe I shouldn't tell you this," she said eventually, "but they're talking rain now for tonight."

He got up and peered out the west window. The day was still bright, but the clouds on the horizon were now unmistakable.

"How much is left?" Randi asked.

"Nearly all of it."

"I could drive the tractor for you."

He turned to her, surprised. He'd gotten used to the separateness of their days. They'd been dividing work so long—his crops and cattle, her house and garden—that it never would have occurred to him to ask her.

"I'll go change," she said, before he could reply.

*   *   *

The atmosphere in the hayfield had changed palpably since morning. The sun, high overhead, glared off the hard-baked ground, and the humid air was heavy and still.

"Jesus," Keith thought, as he pulled the first bale off the chute. Then he remembered he had the tension on the baler cranked tight, and he made Randi stop while he loosened it.

They made their way slowly around the field. Sweat rolled off his forehead and stung his eyes, and as he looked across the field at the windrows left to bale and behind him at the clouds massing thicker and darker, the thought of the work ahead made the work they were doing seem even harder and slower. Though the alfalfa was top quality, bright blue-green and leafy, he felt none of the pleasure he'd taken in it that morning. Now it was just dead weight that scratched his arms and wore out his back. A few more years, he thought, and he would be too old for this kind of work.

It took most of an hour to load the rack five bales high; then they pulled it to the side of the field and hitched on to another. The second rack had weak tires, and after he'd loaded it four high, he waved at Randi to shut down the baler. When the noise ceased they could hear the faint rumble of distant thunder.

"Better put what we've got in the barn," he said.

Without slowing, Randi swung the tractor out of the windrow and eased to a stop. Keith jumped off the rack and pulled the pin to release it. Randi drove the tractor and baler to the side of the field where he dropped the jack and unhitched the baler. Then she backed up to the rack, easing the draw bar between the straps of the tongue he held up to her. They did this wordlessly, anticipating each other's movements, knowing what had to be done and doing it as smoothly as if it had been days, not years, since they'd worked together in the fields.

Resting on top of the load while Randi drove to the barn, more exhausted than he would have guessed, Keith felt momentarily displaced. The humid air, heavy with the fragrance of blooms and of the storm surely brewing in the west, the hayrack gently rocking as it crossed uneven ground–this might have been any June afternoon, any year of his life. Watching Randi on the tractor, hunched forward in concentration, he had a sharp memory of her–a girl with a slim athletic figure and dark brown hair blowing loose behind her. That would have been twenty years ago, before they were married, before Roy, when he was just back from Vietnam, full of dreams and energy, working in town all day and farming nights and weekends. What time he and Randi had together as often as not was spent in the field, but neither of them minded. They'd imagined themselves building for the future.

At the gate to the barnyard, Randi stopped and let him drive so he could position the rack just where he wanted it beside the elevator. For a moment they stood awkwardly beside the hay, as if suddenly they didn't know what to do next.

"If you can get 'em on the elevator," Keith said finally, "I'll stack."

The bales were interminably slow coming up. He pulled one off the elevator, climbed with it to the back of the barn, pushed it into place, then returned to the small door to wait for the next bale. It was dusty and airless in the hay mow, and it was more draining to work slowly than it would have been to handle the bales continuously. The

hardest thing was to watch helplessly while Randi wrestled a bale
loose from the top of the rack, pushed it to the ground, then struggled, using all of her strength, to get it up on the elevator.

He was waiting at the door, bent over with his hands on his knees,
when he saw the swirl of dust rising from the gravel road. Roy's
Mustang, moving fast, skidded to a stop, backed up, and wheeled in
the barnyard gate. Two other boys were with him.

Keith braced himself in the doorway as the three of them approached. Roy spoke to his mother, who gestured toward the hay
loft. Roy looked up and said something Keith couldn't hear over the
clatter of the elevator. He waved at Randi to cut it off.

"Doug and Glen said they'd help awhile," Roy said.

Keith's pride told him to send them all away, to let the hay rot in
the field before he accepted Roy's help on Roy's terms. Let the hay
turn to dust. Let Roy go from his life. Keith knew it was in him to do
that, and the knowledge frightened him.

He stared at Roy and Roy stared back–blankly, innocently. The
other boys stood with arms folded, scraping their feet in the dirt.

"You want two up and one down here, or what?" Roy asked. His
eyes did not yield or soften.

Keith felt beaten but knew he would only lose more by refusing.
"All right," he said.

Roy stayed on the ground and lifted onto the elevator the bales
Randi toppled off the rack. Upstairs, Doug tossed them to Glen, who
hoisted them to where Keith was stacking. As the thunder came nearer,
the boys instinctively worked faster, and Keith pushed himself to keep
pace. The bales rode up the elevator as evenly spaced and uniform as
the markings on a clock, and the chain rolled continuously over the
head, each link clicking in time as it passed the sprocket. He gave
himself up to the repetition of his task, taking the bale at his feet, shoving it into place, turning and bending for another, filling a row across
the barn, then up and across again. He moved as if his work were a
kind of primitive dance, and the rhythms he danced to–the rhythms
of his body, of the elevator, of the thunder–were the measure of earth's
own relentless music.

JOSIP NOVAKOVICH

Tumble-Weed

SLEEPY FROM spending a night at a truckstop near Rapid City–in dull debate with a couple of hairy pot-heads about whether there could be another Prohibition in the States and another Revolution in the Soviet Union–I stood on the shoulder of Interstate 90, sticking my thumb up. My arm began to hurt, and after an hour or so I sat on the side of the road, propping my arm on my backpack. Two hours later I lay on the shoulder and lifted my right leg, barefoot, sticking up my large toe.

I was standing up when a pick-up braked; its tires squealed and smoked, painting gray asphalt black. I climbed into the truck, and faced a drooping blond moustache and weathered skin under a leather hat with a snake brim. A black gun on the seat made me shrink back; I didn't shut the door behind me.

"What you waiting for? You aren't an Iranian, are you?"

"No." My feet crunched through a bunch of empty cans and stepped on a hunting rifle.

"At first sight, I thought you were. I'm not gonna stop for some Iranian shithead. But then I thought, so what if he's an Iranian, I could blow his brains out–do a service to the world–but you aren't Iranian?"

"No, I'm glad to say."

"Have a beer then. Where you going?"

"New York."

"That's a sick town. If I was you, I wouldn't go there. I could take you to Iowa, to I-80, how would that be?"

209

"Tremendous," I said.

"I'm driving to Missouri, to visit my ol' man. It's lonely down there, so I'm taking him a toy." He pointed at a gray snowmobile in the back of the pickup.

"It's summer," I said.

"So what? Soon it'll be winter. For old folk time passes fast. But for us fuckers on this freaking road, it's different. Man, I hope you're fun, because I hate being bored."

I glanced at the gun.

"Oh, this thing, don't worry about it, it's for rattlesnakes. Hypnotizes them; Just keep it circling in front of their eyes, their heads follow. Once the sucker's got the rhythm, you pull the trigger. Head busts like a tomato. Thirsty?" He offered me another can.

I slid my thumbnail beneath the opener, and the smell of yeast popped out. For a while we didn't speak. On one side of the road a field of wavy alfalfa seemed to spin clockwise; on another, a field of Angus cows rotated counterclockwise. Not all the cows faced the wind.

Brown clouds of dust made the horizon hazy. Little dry, wiry, round bushes, like skeletons of globes, bounced over the road and collected on the fences alongside.

"What are these weeds?"

"Russian thistle. Hum. You've got an accent. Where did you say you were from? You aren't from Iran?"

"I didn't say I was from anywhere. Yugoslavia."

"How do you like it here? Much better than Czechoslovakia, isn't it?"

"I imagine it is."

"I've never been to Czechoslovakia . . ."

"Neither have I."

"Man, don't you joke like that with me, you just told me you're a Czecho."

"Yugoslav."

"Well, how'd you get out?"

"Simple," I said. "Cut these electrical wires with a pair of scissors, swam across a river into Austria, took hot gunfire the whole way." I was about to pull the sleeve of my tee-shirt to pass off my small-pox vaccination scars as bullet wounds, except I didn't have the energy it takes to sustain such bullshit.

"At least in this country we have democracy," he said.

I leaned over the speedometer, staring at the hand that trembled around ninety.

"Don't worry," he said. "I don't believe in cops. Dig me a beer out of the cooler. Grab one for yourself."

We drank more than a case of beer, and then, for refreshments, stopped at a pitch dark country bar and had a couple of shots of Jack Daniels. He kept laughing that he was on the road with a commie "from Yugoslovakia." "It's pretty cold in Yugoslovakia, isn't it?"

"No, Yugoslavia's on the Mediterranean," I said. Or used to be, I might have added.

"Oh, the Russians have got so far." He took off his hat, wiped his white forehead with a red handkerchief. About half a dozen Minnesotans at the bar insisted that I have a double shot of vodka, so I wouldn't feel too far away from home.

Back in the pickup, the sunlight was unbearably bright. Hawks floated on the updrafts over grassy pastures nursing placid ponds. The gray and the blue of the sky winked at us from the ponds. A hawk dove into the grass, and slowly and heavily rose from it, with empty talons.

He swallowed a white pill and gave me one too. "Amphetamines, a good invention, helps you drink more." A black Corvette passed us. Mike sped up to 110 mph, and passing the Corvette, made the international "fuck you" sign to the driver. "Nobody passes me, I mean, nobody. Not even a cop car gets by with that shit."

"Have you ever got a ticket?" I asked him. Instead of answering, he opened his right palm; I popped a can and placed it in his hand.

"So how come you don't got no wheels?" he asked me, sympathetically, perhaps imagining that I was stripped of my licence for heroic driving.

"Too much time at school," I said. "Hoped I'd save some money this summer, working the oil fields, except, I couldn't find enough work. I'd heard you could make tons here."

"You should've run into me before. I run rigs up in Montana. What work can you do?"

"Just a worm."

"That's O.K.–you could make a derrickman pretty fast if you aren't scared of heights. A little overtime, you'd be cracking fifty grand a year. I make about eighty grand, more than a fucking dentist in L.A."

"It must be a great feeling. All the bucks."

"Better than getting laid."

"I couldn't compare. I haven't touched tits since Ford was president and I haven't ever made real money."

"Shit, as a drummer in Chicago, I got puss every night with a different woman—sometimes two, three at a time. We'd go into a hotel room, smoke weed, and bang! I screwed more in a year than a hundred average men in their lives. You'll never lay as many women as I did, I don't care how much education you got."

A green and white IOWA sign loomed huge above us. A small black and white sign appeared on the side of the road—"Speed limit 55. Mobile homes 50."

"So you study in New York?"

"Yeah, Columbia."

"Don't crap me. That's a school for rich kids—all you got is your dick, which I hear you don't even use it."

"I do study there, what can I say? The rich kids are the undergrads."

"So you think you're smart? Can't get laid, can't do better than work as a worm." He laughed. "A pinko at Columbia, you tell that to my gran'ma, not me!"

For a while we didn't talk. Then he said, "Well, I'm gonna crash somewhere around here, I don't know about you, but I'm wasted. Why don't you get out here?" He braked suddenly and swerved on the shoulder and nearly into the cornfields.

"I thought you'd get me to I-80," I said.

"Out!" he said.

* * *

I had barely enough time to get my backpack out of the rear of the pickup. My notebook fell out and slid under the snowmobile. The pickup started quickly, the tires shooting gravel and soil in low trajectories fifty yards down the shoulder. The red sun was sinking into the cornfields. I realized my notebook was gone, and with it my novel of two hundred pages, a romance of sorts, which I was sure would be published by Second Chance at Love, Inc., and make me a sure fifteen-thousand, maybe twenty.

Unsteady, I stuck my thumb up and looked around. A green LEMARS sign with a couple of rusty holes from bullets; a low and long

building, like half a dozen mobile homes put together–MOTEL; a
CONOCO gas pump with half a dozen junked cars and an oily repair
shop.

A truck siren hooted at me like a lonely cargo train–as if I hadn't
calculated there was enough time for my walking across the road to
the gas station, where I asked whether there was a bus stop around
so I could get up to I-80. The attendant ignored me while pumping
into a large Chevy filled with wide ruddy cheeks of an extended family. "Is there a bust. . .eh, bus stop around here?"

No answer, so I shouted, "Are there any Christians around here?"

The husky gas attendant looked at me. "Christians? Listen, man.
If you don't leave the premises pronto, I'm gonna call the cops. They'll
tell you about Christians."

"But, you must know Christ's teachings. He may even be your
Lord, your own personal savior?"

"Get lost, ya hear!" shouted the man, while a Chevyload of sun-
flower faces looked at us like at a television talk show.

I staggered into the motel and asked about the bus terminal–three
miles down the road, a little too far for me; and about a single room
for the night–twenty ninety-five–a little too much for me.

Stepping out, I was blinded by bright lights. I missed the last step,
sank, jolting my back with its slipped disk–potentially a capital injury
if I'd promptly sought workmen's comp from the construction company where I had hurt my back. There were two police cars there, three
or four cops with beer paunches protruding authoritatively into the
darkness outside the scope of the beams of light. Not happy with the
limelight, I sidled sideways.

"Sir, stay where you are. There's been complaints about you."

"About me? How do you know it was about me?"

"Driver's licence, please."

"But, I'm not driving."

"I need it to identify you."

"I've got a green card."

"No driver's license." The cop's tone made it sound like grounds
for execution. "We've got to test you. Drunk as a skunk, seems to me."

"I don't want to be tested. I am drunk, isn't that good enough? Isn't
the freedom to get drunk at the root of democracy?"

"Come now, it'll be better for you. Close your eyes. Bring the tip
of your index finger to your nose."

"I don't want to, I *am* drunk, and so what? I'll bet you lift one your-self now and then, when you get home after a dull day of work, with your wife in pajamas. . . ."

"Bring that finger to your nose!" The cop was shouting now. The other one clanked his handcuffs melodiously. So I followed orders, and it seemed to me I did a pretty good job, damn near hitting the nose, and only once my right eye, so that my eyeball hurt, but not badly.

"All right, now walk the straight line—put one foot right in front of the other." I did that too, and didn't fall, so I thought I must have done well there too. My assessment of the test results must have differed from theirs: the handcuff melody-maker put the cuffs on my hands, and two cops shoved me into a car. They turned on the siren and drove me around the town several times to brag about having caught a menace to law and order. I felt honored. That was attention, certainly more of it than you get standing on the shoulder of the road for hours, passed by all sorts of vehicled people.

They led me into a police station, doing a pretty good imitation of TV scenes of cops escorting robbers. In a room, a thin investiga-tor sitting behind the desk asked me to empty my pockets. He examined all the things on the table, one by one, as if he hadn't seen the likes. He found my registered alien card especially fascinating, though I for my part didn't think much of my photo; I had a large pimple right on the tip of my nose from heat in Miami where I had immigrated.

He asked me what I was doing in Iowa, and I told him I was a part of the labor force in retreat. We were defeated near Laramie, Wyoming, because of the oil glut, no doubt an Iranian swindle. My anti-Iranian comment didn't seem to placate him. He asked, "Didn't you know it was illegal to be intoxicated in public?" I said I didn't. "Didn't you know it was illegal to hitchhike in Iowa?"

"But how else are you going to get around if you can't afford a car? That's discrimination against the poor."

"None of our business. We're not the welfare department. For your own good, to protect you and others, we'll put you in jail for the night, until you sober up." He now talked in a friendly voice, like a doctor sending a patient to a hot-springs spa in the Alps for a cure against rheumatism. That made me feel pretty good, thinking I'd have a free night.

"And, in the morning, you'll have to go to court and pay a fine."

"A fine? I have hardly any cash. I just have this check from working on coal-mine silos in Wyoming. . . ."

"Maybe you can get someone to wire you money," he said, turning my student I.D. over and cleaning his nails with it. Now I felt humiliated and hurt. So far my emotions hadn't been involved, and it all seemed sort of fun, so much bustle and bright activity, but now on account of thirty bucks, tears welled up in my nose so that I sniffed and sniffled, clearly under severe emotional strain. Another cop came by and said, "Give me your belt and your shoelaces."

"Shoelaces?"

"So you don't kill yourself."

"I am not depressed," I said. "Besides, my shoelaces are rotten." To demonstrate, I tugged at one, which instantly snapped. "See, you couldn't even hang a cat with these."

But there was no arguing; I had to surrender my shoelaces.

Holding my biceps, a cop led me into an empty cell. Neon light emanated from the edge of the ceiling. The faucet water was hot; I couldn't drink it to alleviate my dehydration and headache. Although even the stool was hot, I sat on it and remained in that philosophical attitude for hours, as if posing for a making of a post-modern replica of a gloomy sculpture by Rodin. Then I lay on a hard wooden bench in the middle of the room—I guess it was supposed to function like a Spartan bed—and tried and failed to sleep. I was nauseated; my bones, eyes, kidneys, and unidentified internal organs hurt.

When it seemed it must be at least noontime of the following day, I began to bang against the metal door, staring through the little barred window. Soon some other admirable citizens joined me, and we hollered, screamed, and kicked the doors of our respective cells. I hurt my toe kicking the door and wondered whether I could sue the U.S. government for compensation.

After a quarter of an hour of that jam-session, a guard appeared and asked us what we wanted. We all wanted to drink and to eat. The guard brought us some frosty donuts with orange juice. The donuts were sticky and the orange juice tasted of flour.

A guard led me into the courthouse, a large room with some kind of wood panelling. A well-fed woman showed up in a black gown, took a small polished wooden hammer and banged with it on the table and asked me to raise my hand and swear. I swore all the judge wanted, and even thought of contributions. I had to keep my right arm raised; my left was employed in keeping my trousers from sliding down. The cops had forgot to give back my belt; and, judging by the appearance of most of the cops and the judge, belts were not a necessity in Iowa, with trousers looking like they would burst any minute. The judge asked me whether I was guilty of public intoxication.

"I am not guilty. It's pretty natural to be drunk."

"Answer my questions straight, to avoid further inconvenience."

She repeated her question. She seemed persistent, so I agreed to plead guilty, to get out of the tiresome place. I had to pay thirty bucks to a cashier—a cheerful woman behind the glass partition who slid me half a dozen papers to sign, with the joy and generosity of a person distributing prizes after a golf tournament. I varied my signatures to break the monotony.

I got back my belt and my shoelaces. I tried to pass the tip of the shoelaces through the appropriate holes in my sneakers. My hands trembled from the hangover, and I couldn't pass the laces—like an old man who cannot pass a thread through the eye of a needle. A policeman observed my struggles, and I looked at him angrily to mind his own holes. With my saliva I pointed the tips of my shoelaces between my forefinger and thumb—the faithful thumb that had got me so many places—and passed the laces through the hole.

It was cloudy, humid and awfully bright outside, so that the streets glared as if coated with ice. I got to the Greyhound bus terminal, bought a gallon of spring water, and sat, gulping the water loudly and waiting for a bus to Sioux City. An old man sat next to me and started chatting, "How much rain did we get last night?"

"I have no idea."

"Not enough, not enough. I sure hope it rains some more."

Since I didn't look worried about the submoisture of Iowa soil—I had enough worries about my own submoisture—the old men scrutinized me, and concluding I was an alien, asked, "How long are you staying here?"

"Half an hour longer, just passing through," I said.

"Oh, that's too bad. Our town is small, but we got some things worth seeing—the most beautiful courthouse in the whole state of Iowa. Its interior is panelled in polished oak. Just beautiful." he sighed, his voice growing gruff with local patriotism. "But of course, you wouldn't have seen that." I stood up, shaking hands with the fellow-drunk for about half a minute; and so, with the sensation of welcome, I climbed onto a steely bus, where about a dozen babies screamed for milk (or, maybe, for beer and speed).

Through the tinted glass, I beheld quite a sight before the I-80 exit: a mobile home lay over a crushed pickup, and an intact gray snowmobile stood beside them, like a faithful dog waiting for its drunk master to get up from the ditch.

EPHRAIM PAUL

Cargo

MOST FAMILIES I knew were like constellations: Stars connected by strong imaginary lines, patterns emerged from the chaotic sky. A bear, a hunter, a little dipping cup for water. No one was particularly happy with their family, but they stuck together anyway. Each star burned on its own, big and self-sufficient, yet it made more sense as a pattern. The only way to locate a star was to fix it to another. But as far as I could tell, there was no constellation when I tried to connect the Fines. We were diffuse, clustered without cohesion, like the Milky Way. I only saw vague formlessness, a lack of relation, each one going their own way. Perhaps we were a happy family once–I don't remember, but I doubt it.

But I do remember the day things fell apart. The day my mother disappeared. Thirteen years ago. . . .

It was a drizzly morning in March and she wasn't there and my father wasn't talking. Of course, I thought, she has an appointment—her hair, her teeth, her eyes—but my father looked dazed as he fumbled half-heartedly with our breakfast and smelled of alcohol, which was highly unusual. He put the bread in the toaster but forgot to push it down. Then he pushed it down but neglected to get it when it popped back up. He made eggs without buttering the pan. He left the room and took more drinks from a bottle in the dining room buffet; I could hear the smooth slide of the teak doors and the low kiss of the cork coming out. Then he disappeared for a while, taking a long shower while Jerry and I toyed with the notion of burning down the kitchen in protest until Sherry took charge, poured my mother's Shredded Wheat and skim milk in three bowls and said, "Eat or else," as if eating our absent mother's cereal would bring her back.

My father came downstairs dressed in a business suit, shaved, showered, trying to be as fresh as he could, and said, "Get dressed, kids, we're going out. Bring a toothbrush and a change of underwear, bring a fresh shirt. Dress nicely, we're visiting someone special."

Well for all the cutting up that Jerry and I would normally do, for all the joking and jiving that we'd impose on any family activity, we were silently obedient. My father's voice contained some hardened tool in his larynx, some tightness and fear that we unconsciously respected and knew to obey.

"Mom's sick," she said, "Mom's dead. I can feel it in my stomach. The way Dad is acting. She's dead."

"A car accident, I bet," Jerry said. "Wiped out on the highway. A head-on collision with a truck driver on downers who skipped the median strip."

"Shut up, Jerry," Sher said. "You are such a creep."

"Let's get going," my father shouted. "We don't have all day." He was standing in his overcoat by the door, a briefcase in each hand, the incarnation of Grim.

Into the city our father drove, in his inimitable hoggish style, just under the speed limit, straddling two lanes. Sherry sat up front with him, holding her head high, having concluded that our mother was a mess in the morgue and that she was both expected and entitled now to take her place. Would she sleep next to him in bed, I wondered. Jerry and I shared contorted faces with each other, mangled mouths, cauliflowered noses, crossed eyes, silent laughs, faked cries; we had no idea what was happening.

In due time we were downtown, in an old neighborhood crammed with shops whose customers seemed to be different from us, that is to say poor, the sort of place my mother would avoid or if she had to pass through, would instruct us to roll up our windows and lock the doors. Here in Old City, at the east end of Philadelphia, smack dab on its main artery, in view of the Delaware River and Camden across it, amid the ninety-nine dollar suits, the two-for-twenty ties, the no-iron silk-polyester blend shirts, the jaunty hats, the lizard skin shoes; in the middle of the jeans discounters, leather shops, wholesale drygoods merchants, newsstands, diners, bus terminal, just a block away from Ben Franklin's house, post office, and printing press–was my grandfather's store. Fine Bargains. The junk shop, our father called it when he was in a generous mood. The shit house, he said when he was not.

Paint the color of ancient chocolate peeled from the upper floors, revealing blotches of red brick far more appealing than that flaking dead brown, but cheaper to paint brick than to point it. On the first floor, a large picture window the width of the building teemed with jumbled merchandise from the four corners of the tri-state area, and behind the display case the half lit interior of Fine Bargains, oldest sundry store in town.

"Grandma and Grandpa's place," my father mumbled. "Everybody out."

"Grandma and Grandpa," Jerry said whispering to me in the back seat, his face shiny with sweat. "Who the fuck are they?"

"Bubba and Zadie," Sherry said in a starched self-righteous voice. "What are you guys, idiots?"

"Oh I remember," Jerry said. "You mean the two old people who we see once a year for the holidays? I keep thinking they're Mom's parents."

"Mom's parents are dead, jerk," Sherry said. "For twenty years."

"I have to go to the bathroom," I said.

"Shut up," my father growled. "You know exactly who they are. And if you're not careful, I'll leave you with them permanently. How would you like that, Jerry-boy? You pay some respect or else. They're going to watch you a few nights while Mom is away."

"I wanted to ask you about that, Dad," Jerry said. "Where is Mom?"

"Dad," I asked. "What do you mean they're going to watch us. Watch us what?"

"Out of the car now," he barked tightly, like our little repressed Schnauzer Puff used to yap before he was run over by a drunken joyriding teenager.

"Careful crossing the street," Sherry said.

When we walked in some bells jingled dissonantly on the door which didn't close by itself. The air inside was old air, coming from the basement, cool and musty, recirculated too many times within the confines of its interior. It had little do with the air outside - this was the smell of yesterday, or the day before that.

As dreary as it was outdoors, a cold and unnaturally dark Saturday morning in March, it was even worse within. I'd never been to a mausoleum, but I imagined I was in one now. Nothing seemed to happen; a few people stood around the room. The floor was streaked with dirt, the punched-tin ceiling needed painting, the walls were lined with shelving crammed so tightly with merchandise I couldn't distinguish one thing from another. The two aisles were flanked by long tables with bin dividers holding things of little or no value—to me anyway. I was used to clean stores in the malls, bright lights, and expensive, well-kept merchandise.

There we stood, a middle-aged man in a wrinkled double-breasted suit with three kids in tow, the boys' clothes mismatched, the girl in a party dress, each of them carrying a small pack of belongings.

Looking us over, Bubba's face had ancient rivers of worry etched deep. Her large head seemed to grow heavier as she considered our condition. A gnarled liver-spotted hand propped up her whisker-strewn chin. Behind his darkened glasses and half-smile, Zadie remained serene and unmoved. When my grandmother raised her arms to smother us into her full and sagging bosom, he stood behind her staring at my father and probing him for an explanation.

"It's my busiest season," my father muttered softly into his hand. "Tax time. And I completely forgot that she was going to visit her cousins in Scranton this weekend."

"She never told me that," Jerry said. "She was going to buy me sneakers today."

"She must have forgotten then," my father said.

Zadie now spoke sharply to my father in Yiddish, a good tongue for bitterness and scorn, and my father answered back in English, short crisp answers, the kind a lawyer instructs you to make in order not to incriminate yourself. "Yes . . . no . . . I told you what I know . . . She'll be back tomorrow night . . . no she didn't leave a note, I told you that already . . . I can't . . . You must . . . What are grandparents for if they can't help their children once in a while? Please . . . Here," he said, pulling out his wallet to hand Zadie money.

Zadie laughed so loud as to crack a bone in his jaw, I could hear it echo off the tin ceiling and around the store. "What am I?" he asked in English. "The baby-sitter? Keep your money, you might need it for a divorce."

My father stood angry and silent, humiliated. Bubba, who had shepherded us toward the back of the store, approached him and looked him over. "What kind of a man are you anyway?" she hissed. "You can't keep a wife at home, and then you can't watch your own children when she leaves."

"She hasn't left," my father said. "I keep telling you, she'll be back. It's just for a weekend. I know where she is."

"Why don't you go get her then?" Bubba asked. "For the children, at least. A woman may leave her husband, that's no big deal, but her children? Never. What did you do to her?"

My father smiled at his mother, a cool slippery gash in his face that said he wasn't letting her in on any secrets, and replied, "I did nothing, nothing at all."

"Perhaps that's the problem, Howie," Bubba said. "You do nothing, you get back nothing."

"She's in Scranton, for Christ's sake," he bleated. "Let me out of here. I'll call you, all right?"

And then he left without kissing his own mother good-bye, panicky instead to get out from under the harsh light of his parents' interrogation. He didn't look back either. And he didn't say anything to the three of us, his children, massed in the back of the store like immigrants at a port of entry, seasick from the roiling upheaval we'd already endured, as if he were the captain of the boat and we merely the cargo in steerage.

Out the door, and off to his gleaming erect office tower on the other side of City Hall, the bells on the door clanging after him, those goddamn high-pitched defective sleigh bells, as jarring as a siren, and perfect for some rainy winter's ride to a chaotic and empty Christmas, the kind particularly celebrated by the Jews of North American—my clan of birth—Hanukkah bush and all. It was months after Christmas, and yet the store was chockablock with cheap and cheesy red and green stuff for every purpose—tinsel for the tree, cardboard reindeer for the window, dime a dozen ornaments, napkins with holly, paper plates with a Santa that looked drunk and lecherous, the ugliest wrapping paper in the world. And no one had bothered to put the goods away.

Bubba approached us greedily, hands clasped together, ten years of pent-up grandmothering unleashed in a fury, looking like old Golda Meir more than anyone in the world: thick yellow hair like unspun wool in a bun, heavy-soled schoolteachers' shoes, a nose that seemed to be fashioned by a child out of Silly Putty.

"Children," she said, "let's go upstairs for a while. I'll fix you something to eat." And she led us into the dark back office and up the rickety stairs to the apartment. We'd never been here before, none of us, in how many years, only twenty minutes drive from our house. Suddenly we were going to be eating and sleeping here. Where was Mom? Kidnapped? Car wreck? Scranton?

"I made some apple sauce," she said, beckoning us into the kitchen. Old enamel fixtures, stove, sink, refrigerator. There in a dented aluminum saucepan, some chunky off-white mixture with traces of peel in it, certainly unsweetened, awaited us.

"Smells great," Sherry said, hope in her voice. "I've never had home-made applesauce before."

"I know you'll like it," Bubba said, unwrapping a loaf of moist brown cake and slicing thick slabs on to a pink glass plate. She poured hot water into a cracked teapot and brought out three mugs. Mine read, Irving's Hot Dogs, Good As They Are Long, So What Are You Waiting For?

"Sit down, sit down," she said nervously, "and eat something." How kind she wanted to be to us. "Here is some hot tea, there's lemon or milk–we only have skim–honey, if you like it. I have sugar cubes, if you want to drink the old fashioned Russian way, the cube in your cheek. And tell me, each one of you, what you are doing. In school and out. Tell me everything. We'll drink tea and talk."

Nobody said anything: Jerry seemed furious, Sherry was on the verge of tears again–she was sure Mom was dead–and I don't now what I was sure of. I was there, taking it all in, in a low-level state of shock. I could hear the clock humming on the wall, its frayed cord dangling down to an outlet near the sink, and what sounded like mouse feet scratching on the ceiling above us, nibbling and skittering above. The refrigerator compressor clicked on and overtook the small kitchen in a loud rhythmic drone. Bubba fingered the honey cake and watched us not touch our applesauce, not drink our black tea, not devour the sweaty brown cake glistening with oil.

"Doesn't anyone tell you?" Jerry asked. "They don't tell you on the phone what we do all day? Don't you talk to them?"

"Of course I do, Jerry honey," Bubba said. "Of course I do. But your parents are modest about these things, or maybe they don't think your grandfather and I are that interested. Mostly your father asks me how I am feeling. And talk of the weather. With your grandfather, it's business conditions, I guess. I don't really know. Don't bother your-self over these things."

These things, she repeated, pushing the plate of food closer to us. Suddenly she was frightening, like the woman who lived in the gingerbread house, or the old lady in the shoe who beat her kids. These things–like what our parents thought of us. Something not al-together small. Other kids we knew, Jewish kids mostly, were the sun around which their parents orbited. Now maybe that is not such a great thing, but still, why were we barely mentioned to our grandparents?

All at once Bubba cleared away the food and wanted the dirt on my parents. She could see we weren't going to recite our good deeds like well-behaved children, so instead she asked, "What about your parents, what on earth is going on with them? Do they fight all the time? Do they do things together?"

Sherry started to talk. "Yes," she blubbered, then, "No"–and Jerry kicked her to shut up. He was the oldest, and as long as we were to-gether he was in charge. At age sixteen, he was not about to trust any-one, including some old woman who brought our father into the world.

You expect us to know? I wanted to ask the old lady. You expect us to understand what marriage is like? Christ, I didn't even know what Shredded Wheat tasted like until this morning.

Bubba saw she was getting nowhere with the three of us. She stopped pushing, and seemed to make a conscious decision to sepa-rate Sherry from Jerry and me. "I have to clean," she said. "It's Satur-day. It's my day to clean the apartment. You want to help me, Sherry?"

And before Sherry could answer, she said, "Sure you do. Let's get a broom, let's get a bucket."

Sherry burst into tears again, but seemed more than happy to help. It was something to do, something to get her away from Jerry and me, who were probably starting to veer dangerously into violence. She had on that silly party dress, though, to look her best, so with a doo-rag on her head, a broom in one hand, she looked like some crazy kind of witch.

Exiled, Jerry and I were hoodlums, slacking down the back stairs. I pinched him, he dragged me down in a headlock. More than ever before we were brothers, unglued and unhinged together, knocking and rubbing and shoving, endlessly kidding and cutting up, a St. Vitus' dance of nervous laughter and horseplay. I kicked over a shoebox and out spilled hundreds of check stubs and deposit tickets, from 1958. They littered the steps and floor, the last of them floating down to the foot of the steps into Zadie's office.

"Shit!" I hollered, and blamed Jerry for being careless and rowdy. And I went from step to step stuffing papers in the box all the way down, a step at a time, until I came to the bottom where a pair of perfectly polished brogues confronted me foot to face.

Zadie towered over me, stern and tall. He cleared his throat but said nothing. Then I heard the gabardine of his pants gather as he crouched down to my height, his dark glasses showing nothing of his eyes, his face stony and calm. Damn, I thought, he's going to kill me. He seemed to be looking into my eyes, and I looked right back, seeing only myself in the reflection of his glasses. We were fixed to each other like that for I don't know how long, some kind of magnetic gaze of recognition and lack of recognition. We were blood, and we were strangers. Then, as if a trigger went off inside of him, his fierce visage bloomed into a smile from ear to ear, and the old man began to laugh, his yellow eroding teeth clattering up and down.

"1958," he said taking the box from me. "For Christ's sake. Who the hell needs those anymore?" And he dumped them back out onto the floor. "Got a match?" he asked, giggling. "No wait, we shouldn't burn the place down, should we? Then you won't have anywhere to sleep tonight."

I found him a little scary but Jerry laughed insanely along with the old man, forcing a giggle out of his chest.

"You kids hungry?" Zadie asked. "So what do you say we get out of here and eat? Let me finish a few things here, then we'll dash across the street to the diner."

In the store it was better than before, things were happening. Dozens of people crowded the aisles, rubbing up against each other in order to fill up the small plastic baskets with no handles. A man with a goiter the size of a baseball and blotchy skin carried a suitcase up and down the aisles, grinning stupidly. Three old women congregated near the sewing needles, and a shabby middle-aged man in a mangy shirt stood by the register, trying on a dozen sizes of reading glasses with generic prescriptions, unable to decide.

A red-eyed bum wandered the store, and I feared he might explode and hurt someone or steal something. But no one seemed to bother him, because the bum wasn't a bum. His name was Reggie. He drank too much, and he didn't have a job. He smelled. Other people came in, the likes of which I'd never seen. My grandfather treated these people with complete equanimity, showing neither warmth nor disgust toward anyone. Everyone got the same polite respectful attention.

He locked up and we left. At the Snow White Diner, the air smelled of hamburger grease and burnt coffee. Large pink and chocolate cakes sat on plexi-covered platters on the lunch counter. Plate glass windows lined both sides of the corner of 2nd and Market, and I could see everything: buses, trucks, beggars, businessmen, all from the comfort of inside. It was like watching a movie. Riveted to my surroundings, I was struck by how different they were from my home life, the silent manufactured hush of the suburbs, the distinct suppression of bustle.

The waitresses in black and white dresses all seemed to know my grandfather, and he them, and one rather pretty one opened the spigot of the coffee urn and let forth a cup of steaming thin diner coffee into a large mug.

"Who are these two charmers, Jacob?" she asked, plunking down the coffee in front of him, fixing her eyes on me. A woman who loved children always excited me.

"My accountant here on my left," Zadie said. "And my lawyer across from me. Meet Ruthie, boys. A fine woman, despite her bad reputation."

"So these are the kids you never see? Why, they're cute. Real cute."

"Now, now, Ruthie, what would Sherman think of you ogling the customers?"

"Put a lid on it," she laughed, backing away from the table. "I got grandkids too, you know. Let me know when you're ready."

"We haven't got all day, Ruth. Bring them turkey clubs and a milk shake. Put it in the express lane too."

"But I don't like turkey clubs," Jerry said.

"It's the only thing to eat here," Zadie said. "You're getting it."

Jerry stared at me across the sea-foam Formica, apparently stumped. As the oldest he was always the ringleader, always the one with the snappy comeback, always understood the spin of the top first, and was first to say so. But I could tell that Zadie had him mystified. I could tell, because his eyes looked foggy and isolated from the rest of his face. He still smoldered with indignation for having been dropped off here like a package from a mail truck. For me, well, I was used to following Jerry's cue for everything, but not this time. I was utterly captivated by the old man, so mystified by his grubby little store and the world it occupied.

The milkshakes arrived. Jerry took a sip and gagged. "What is this?" he asked. "Brown crayon dipped in sugar water?"

"You want something else?" Zadie asked. "A soda maybe?"

"I want to go back home, I don't like it here, I can take care of myself. I'm sixteen."

Zadie chuckled then began stirring his coffee urgently, peering into the black eddy as if to divine an answer. A gentle light came into his eyes, a kind half-smile took to his craggy face.

He said, "Look, I'm sure you're confused about this. Don't ask me what it's about. I have no idea what goes on in your father's life. He doesn't talk to me, I don't talk to him. I wouldn't be surprised if when you grow up, you'll be in the same boat.

"But let me tell you about what it was like for me," he said slowly, in a low gentle voice, like a pigeon's chortle.

"When I was your age, I struggled and I fought while I wandered around Russia, an orphan. My parents were murdered, murdered in their beds, you hear me? Because it was Easter and there was a crazy story about my parents keeping all the Jews' gold under their mattress. I was lucky enough to hear the peasants coming in the night, I could see the shadows of their flickering torches in my room. And I ran into the chicken coop, and while the chickens slept, my parents were butchered and quartered and our house was burned down. The peasants were too drunk to think of stealing the chickens, which after all, were the real source of my parents' so-called wealth.

"Then I was alone," he said. "My older brothers and sisters had all left for America. I wandered the small villages and towns of Russia with no one calling my name for dinner, no one turning my ear for misbehaving, no one bringing me to account, no one suggesting that I be bar mitzvah'd. I was an urchin, a rat digging in other people's garbage, until I lucked into becoming a peddler of rags and other things people took for granted. I had no money, but I learned to take things from the trash in the nice parts of town, clean them up a little and sell them in the poor parts. It was pure profit. And I went from small village to small village, working my way past the hovels, sleeping in barns, abandoned shacks, counting houses, wherever I could sneak in when the sun went down and the last candle was snuffed out. And you know what? Despite the fact I was lonely and cold and longed for warm water on my belly, I loved the freedom of it. I loved not needing to sit with anyone in particular, not having to say please and thank you and sorry all the goddamn time.

"And everyone knew me, and no one knew me. I would visit each village once a month, and people began waiting for me. I developed a clientele. People started asking me to bring them things and I delivered. As I got older and the hair sprouted on my chin, it got so women would take pity on me, or find comfort in my youth, in my rambling ways. This was by far the best part, and I learned to love them in the hours that their husbands were on the road selling like me or praying at the shtiebele or working in the fields or sleeping drunk in the doorways. Then a Rabbi caught me with his wife, cursed at me like a fishmonger, and threatened to kill me with or without God's help. I knew then it was time to leave and make my way to America."

The turkey clubs arrived and Zadie ordered more milkshakes because Jerry and I had drained ours while listening to him. The bacon was all fat, and the turkey warm in some spots and cold in others. The mayonnaise was an unfamiliar shade of yellow. But we ate it all, because the idea of Zadie in the arms of lonely shtetl housewives transported us out of our misery.

"You're going to love it here," Zadie said. "More than you think. Since it's time I did some spring cleaning, I have plenty more files back at the store for you to destroy. In fact, I thought that might be fun for you to do. You could go up to the top floor of the building and make a mess. Tear the place apart, whatever you want you do, you do. We'll clean it up later. Look at today as a vacation, maybe the beginning of something new for you. Something good is in all this."

"But do you know where Mom is?" I asked him.

Zadie looked at me glumly and ran his hands over the table as if to divine an answer from an invisible Ouija Board.

"I don't know," he said. "But I don't think she's in Scranton."

Jerry and I were silent.

"Hey," he said knocking our heads together. "I was an orphan, and I didn't turn out so bad. Did I?"

"But we're not orphans," I said. "We still have our father."

"Yes, you do," he said standing up. "Yes you do. Let's get out of here."

Zadie paid the bill, left a large tip, winked at Ruthie, and stuck a toothpick in his mouth on the way out. Jerry and I had toothpicks in our mouths, too.

Bubba stood at the door to the store when we walked in, and she started to yell at Zadie in Yiddish, something to the effect of where the hell have you been. "Kinder, kinder"–that's all I could understand. "Children. They're only children." Zadie barked back at her–"They're not children anymore, they're refugees"–and she retreated to the cash register.

Then he led us up the four flights of dusty stairs to the top. Sherry was apparently taking a nap, drained from Bubba's interrogation and the scrubbing of walls and windows in their apartment. The fifth floor was an open loft, a big mess of pigeon shit, cigarette butts, and piles of wilting boxes in the corners. Out of one stack, Zadie pulled some old roller skates and dumped them on the floor.

He said, "I forgot about these for years until I saw you two, I never could figure out a way to sell them downstairs. Anyway, find your size and fool around. I got to go downstairs before your grandmother has a stroke. The only rule is: don't kill each other."

Jerry started to laugh again, that crazy annoying laugh he forced whenever he wasn't sure what was going on. And for the first time that day, I began to cry. Little boy's tears squirted out of my eyes like the sprinkler on my parents' lawn. It just didn't make sense to me, it was all too strange. The idea of roller skating while my mother was missing was like falling off a swing and landing on my stomach. It knocked the wind out of me, and left me in that suspended state of waiting for my lungs to work again, of panic and despair that something I took for granted, like breathing, like Mom, might never return.

I imagined my mother was dead, perhaps she really was. What would I do with myself? Who would I do things for? Who would I do things against? Suddenly I felt like a planet without a sun. Gravity was gone, light was gone, warmth was gone. I was an orphan star, weightless and drifting, in search of something large enough to fix me to a path. All was lost, the stars were shifted against me forever.

Jerry stopped laughing and considered my tears. He then whacked me on the back of my head. "Cut it out," he said. "That's not going to make you feel better. Here, put these on, put these on right now, they're your size, and start skating."

His whack had a surprisingly calming effect upon me. I slipped the skates on and wobbled onto my feet.

"Watch this," he said, and zoomed headlong toward the back of the loft. "Pigeon shit, here I come!" he shouted, and the roar of the wheels became deafening. He came this close to hitting the wall when he crouched down and turned around, just like they did in roller derby on TV. Then he came careening back at me and stopped on a dime inches in front of my face.

"Come on, Murray, let's skate!" he screamed.

I wiped the tears from my eyes and began slowly to push myself around, my ankles shaking from the stress of keeping balance.

"Go faster," Jerry said. "Go faster and you won't fall down. Going slow makes it hard to stay up. Push harder."

And I did, dammit, I pushed as hard as I could. I pushed each foot down against the warped floorboards and up again and began to go faster than I ever had on a bike. I flew toward the back of the loft, with Jerry right beside me, even though I had no idea how to stop or turn or do anything that would prevent me from crashing. I didn't care though, the thought of smashing up only made me push more, and the next thing I knew I plunged headlong into a pile of boxes. I heard the sound of old cardboard crumpling and my own groaning, and what fell out but brightly colored kickballs! Happy blues, reds, and yellows, they bounced everywhere and Jerry began booting them with his roller skates as I lay on the floor in a pile of them, stunned. The kickballs spread throughout the loft, moving in all directions, according to the skewed pitch of the floor. Then I began to laugh, too. What the hell, I thought, we're sailing on our feet in the middle of nowhere, in heaven for all I knew, with big balls around us.

I jumped up on my skates and gained maximum speed for another soft collision into the unknown. Boom, I hit boxes of party hats. Boom, wind-up toys. Boom, fly-swatters—crashing everything, feeling the rush of destruction, the thrill of not caring who watched us or who would punish us.

Jerry found two brooms and we became fierce warriors, knights in clanging armor, charging each other at full speed and clashing our broom handles like jousts, the sparks thick in the air, the cheer of the crowds everywhere around us. It was like the movies. It was our best hour ever. We were finally free.

VARSHA RAO

Traveling by Train

AS UMA WALKED briskly down the unpaved road to catch the train to work, she passed a construction site. The barefoot workers moved in perfectly synchronized motions: one loading gravel into a vessel, one balancing a vessel on another worker's head, one carrying it to the work site and another one emptying it. Their lean bodies were black and ashen, layered with sand and dirt and grime. She wondered how they withstood the sun's torture all day, every day.

It was only eight am, but already the best hours of the day had come and gone. The sun beamed brilliantly, baking the earth below. The air was thick and heavy, laden with moisture from the Bay of Bengal. Uma could feel perspiration forming on her freshly powdered face, on her forehead and above her upper lip. Dark patches had formed under the arms of her fitted sari blouse and she could feel sweat trickle down her bosom. Her fair cheeks were flushed. She stopped in her path to dab her forehead with her cotton handkerchief, taking care not to smudge her kum kum, and then tucked the kerchief back into her sari at her waist. She looked down at her sari as she adjusted her pallu. Her brother Ravi had sent her this cotton sari from Bombay as a gift after having received his first paycheck in his new job three months ago. It had been accompanied by a letter in which he had assured his younger sister that soon he would be back to join her and Appa in Madras. Uma chuckled to herself recalling this promise and said aloud, "Good for Ravi. At least he has escaped this unbearable Madras heat."

Uma looked at her watch. The electric train would be arriving in

231

six minutes. She began to walk quickly, knowing that if she missed the
train she would have to ride standing on the bus for over an hour. Her
slippers made putt, putt noises as she walked quickly and the heels
rhythmically hit the dirt road. Uma's eyes focused downward to steer
her through the cow dung that had not yet been removed from the
streets by peasants.

Once in the ladies' compartment, Uma secured a seat by the window. She sighed a breath of relief knowing that as the train entered
the city and working women, peasants and beggars crowded onto
the train, she would have the sanctity of her own seat. Uma stared out
of the window as the train pulled away from the station and young
boys whistled at her.

*   *   *

It had still been dark when she had been awakened by the ringing
of the milkman's bell this morning. Mechanically, she felt her way to
the kitchen and found the tarnished milk vessel. She made her way
through the depths of blackness to the veranda, unlatched the front
door and handed the brass vessel to the milkman. He was waiting
patiently just outside the compound wall holding onto the rope that
secured his cow. The cow chewed at the stunted grass that grew along
the edge of the unpaved road just outside the sewage gulleys. Uma
straightened her worn sari, smoothed her mussed hair and yawned
as she watched the milkman squat next to the sacred animal and
manipulate its pink udders. Milk squirted out, missing the vessel initially, and the milkman cursed to himself for having lost potential rev-
enue. Her mind still in a sleepy haze, Uma wondered how this scrawny,
dark-brown, half-naked man managed to feed his cow enough for it
to have the strength to keep producing milk.

As she sat on the steps waiting in the darkness with the branches
of the mango trees swaying in the balmy morning breeze, she felt the
eerie twinges of déjà vu. She thought hard and finally, it came to her.
It had been on a morning just like this, years ago, perhaps fifteen years,
that Ravi and she had stood on these same steps and had said good-
bye to Amma. Uma had been terrified. Amma had been coughing up
blood-mixed sputum all night, and Appa had waited until the early
morning to leave their remote town and take her to the city hospital.
At that moment Uma had known that Amma would never return

home. It wasn't until a few years later that Uma learned that Amma had died of tuberculosis. Now there was a cure for tuberculosis.

Uma paid the milkman two rupees and began her banal routine. The sky was a dull gray now—the sun setting in some other world, slowly making its way to wreak havoc on hers. She walked to the kitchen and placed the vessel full of milk on the kerosene stove and struck a match to light it. She lifted the heavy kerosene tank in a pivot-like motion and heard a distinct swishing sound. "Almost empty," she thought; she made a mental note to tell her father.

Uma tried to walk silently to the back of the house, but in vain; her feet revealed her.

"Uma?"

"Go back to bed, Raju," she whispered to her half-brother of nine years. After Amma's death, Appa had remarried and fathered three more children. Raju was the youngest. Now they all slept silently on the bed mats that lay one next to the other on the floor. Raju closed his eyes again and rolled into the space where she had been sleeping. Above them, the turning Bajaj ceiling fan circulated the warm air and helped to allay the torture of mosquitoes. A thin stream of smoke from the burning mosquito repellent coil flowed from the corner of the room. Guided by the faint morning light while her father, step-mother and step-brothers slept soundly, Uma continued to make her way to the back of the house and went outside.

Uma held the weathered rope in her hands and lowered the bucket into the well to fetch water for her morning bath. She held the rope steadily until she could feel that the bucket had filled and began to pull the bucket up methodically, hand over hand. As the summer had progressed, she had had to let more and more rope into the well to reach water. The water level in the well was the lowest she could remember. All over south India, crops had died in the drought. Food prices had shot up; the price of rice had doubled in six months. Everyone in the village was looking forward to the monsoons—everyone except for her. This year, by the time the monsoons arrived in late July, she would be married.

*   *   *

The train jolted suddenly as it arrived at a station, rousing Uma from her semi-conscious state. At the stop, two young women about her age entered the compartment and sat down facing her. She recognized them; they were from the same locality. She nodded "hello," and they returned the acknowledgment.

Above the drone of the train moving over the tracks, Uma could decipher the young women's conversation: "Found a boy," "engineer," "Aiyer." The woman from whose mouth the words had spilled—her name was Shanti, Uma now recalled—was beaming with joy and pride and satisfaction.

Uma did not need to hear any more. She could fill in the rest of the dialogue and knew her compilation wouldn't be far from the truth. After all, in India, in 1965, most everyone had arranged marriages. That she had accepted. "Love marriages" were only for film stars.

Lulled by the motion of the train, Uma stared intently at Shanti's feet as the bride-to-be continued to describe the details of her wedding. The slipper-clad feet surprised Uma. They were cracked, calloused and dry. They were not ornamented in any way; there were no mehendi designs around the edges or nailpolish on her toenails. Shanti's feet looked old, as if they belonged to a woman not of her twenty-some-odd years, but perhaps a woman of forty. Uma could tell that these feet had never been enveloped in Western shoes; rather they had walked barefoot along sunbaked roads and supported a body that did housework. When Uma looked down at her own, she was surprised to see feet that looked no different from Shanti's.

For the first time, the other young woman dressed in a bright peacock blue sari began to speak, drawing Uma's attention. The train slowed to a steady trot and now she could hear them better.

"Speaking of marriage, did you know Ramesh has called off his marriage?"

"No, don't tell me?" The shock enlarged Shanti's pupils.

"Yes. I can't believe it myself," the peacock girl said. "Her family is crazy. They are very provincial," she said, shaking her head back and forth in disbelief. "When Ramesh mentioned that he may want to move to Bombay or the U.S. to get a job, they forbade it. They refuse to let their daughter go to those places. Now my parents will have to go back and look for new matches."

Shanti shrugged her shoulders. "At least he found out now. I'm sure everything will be good for your brother." Shanti sighed. "But thank God he is a boy."

*   *   *

Uma disembarked from the train and joined the throngs of people who risked their lives each day by crossing the train tracks to reach the station exit. She made her way through the crowded streets, unaware of the honking of buses, cars, autorickshaws and cycles. She lifted the pleats of her sari slightly to facilitate her agile movements between the bullock carts and the herds of people. On her way, Uma passed by her grandparents' house; they were her mother's parents. For a moment she contemplated going inside, but decided against it. She would come back to see them.

Outside the State Bank of India office an old, blind beggar woman stood with her hand outstretched to all who passed by and cried "Amma, Amma." The whites of her eyes had turned yellow from constant nutritional deprivation. The treacherous tropical sun had coated her black pupils with a greyish-blue film, the tell-tale sign of cataracts. Uma hesitated momentarily in front of the woman before side-stepping into the bank.

She went to the teller and instructed him to withdraw her savings. Since graduating from engineering college two years ago, first in her class, Uma had been working at British Petroleum, saving her money. This evening, her aunt and she would use this money to purchase saris to give as gifts to Venkat's family at the wedding. Uma handed the teller her passbook and he made the appropriate entry and stamped both the branch log and her book with the official SBI seal. The teller pointed to the cashier located at the opposite side of the room and directed her to go there to receive her money.

There was a queue of five people in front of the cashier. Uma took her place and stared down at the mosaic floor quietly. When she reached the front of the queue, she handed the cashier her passbook. She had never seen this man before. He had a pencil thin mustache that reminded her of her father. He counted the money in front of her and handed it to her through the hole in the security glass. She placed the thick stack of bills inside the vinyl State Bank of India pouch and placed it into her purse carefully. She looked around to see if anyone was paying too much attention to her. As she left the bank, she took out a one rupee note and gave it to the beggar woman.

Uma ran up the steps of the British Petroleum office just as the company bell struck the last note of 9:00 A.M. She opened the heavy glass door and was whisked into a vastly different world by the cold rush of air conditioning and signs of India's progress everywhere. It took her a few seconds to adjust to the change and gain her composure. She then lifted the pleats of her sari and hurried up the stairs to the third floor where the engineering department was located. She closed the door to her newly acquired office, sat down at her desk and immediately locked her purse inside. On her desk was a note from Brigette Stevens, the British engineering consultant for the gas project on which Uma had been working for the past eight months. Fifteen years her senior, Brigette had become Uma's mentor as well as friend. Brigette had been sent from the U.K. and, after having spent a year in the BP Bombay office, she was very experienced in the field. Her stint in Madras was coming to a close, however; at the end of the month she would return to Bombay. Uma skimmed the note quickly. Brigette wanted to see her as soon as she got in.

*   *   *

Uma appeared at the entrance of her office at the stroke of 1:00 P.M., having worked the Saturday half-day. From the top of the stairs, she spotted Appa standing by the curb. He was flagging an autorickshaw for them.

"Hello Appa," she said as she carefully stepped into the auto, taking care not to wrinkle her sari. Her father said "hello," to her and "Tambaram," to the driver in the same breath. The driver nodded his head, recognizing the place, and pulled the shaft on the floor towards him with vigor to start the engine. As the auto picked up speed, Uma could feel the heat of the engine radiate through the soles of her slippers. The vibrations of the vehicle shook her body.

Above the drone of the engine, Uma spoke. "It is too hot for you to wear a full-shirt." He was wearing the shirt that Ravi and she had given him for his fifty-first birthday last year. They had bought the material at Binny's and had it stitched.

"Not if I'm going to visit my future son-in-law. This old man can stand a little discomfort for his daughter."

Uma smiled uncertainly.

"What is wrong, Um?"

She hesitated for a few seconds before answering. "It is the same thing, Appa. I don't know if I am really ready for this marriage."

A warm smile spread on her father's face. He looked directly into her eyes.

"Kootty, you are just nervous. Every girl is nervous before her marriage. It is natural. But Venkat is a nice boy, and the time is right to get married. You have just finished college and you are still young."

"But Appa, did you send me to college just to get married?"

"Uma, these days no one even looks at uneducated girls."

Uma was about to object more vehemently, but stopped as she looked into her father's weathered eyes: eyes that had married for the first time at the age of twenty to a fourteen year old girl; eyes that had studied as far as SSLC, the Indian equivalent of completing high school. Were they eyes that simply viewed the world differently than she did? And what were her alternatives anyway? If she didn't marry Venkat, wouldn't she just remain her father's burden?

Uma nodded her head slowly. "Alright, Appa."

Her father said "Good," and patted her on the back warmly. He looked out the side of the autorickshaw to gauge their whereabouts. "We are almost there. Remember, we have to finalize all the details of the wedding today."

"Oh, look. I almost forgot." He pulled out an envelope from his worn leather carrying bag. "I picked up the invitations this morning." He held the ornately decorated card out to her. "Beautiful, no?" Uma reached for the card hesitantly and then held it in her hand carefully, holding it only on the edges as if it were a photograph. "Yes. It is," a smile covering her lips just as the auto stopped in front of Venkat's house.

*   *   *

Uma sat quietly next to her father as he showed the groom's family the invitations. Venkat's mother cooed in delight. She had never seen such beautiful invitations. Uma stared at her future mother-in-law as she spoke. She was about the age of her own father. She wore a traditional silk sari and the bright red lipstick of a youngster. Her fleshy arms jiggled as she raised and lowered her tumbler filled with coffee. Next to her sat an older woman to whom the invitation was passed next. This woman wore a darker silk sari and did not wear the large red kum kum that her daughter did. Her hair was tied in a tight bun that uplifted the loose skin on her face. Venkat's father sat in the background quietly and listened.

Venkat sat next to the old woman, his grandmother, opposite from Uma. She looked at him intently, directly into his eyes. It had been almost eight months since this courting began–about the same time that she had begun the gas project at work, she recalled. First there had been the exchange of her photograph, then a few months later a meeting. Venkat had not been the only boy they had contacted; there had been a few other boys initially. They were all intelligent, well-mannered and handsome. But having met them all, Uma told her father that she wanted most to proceed with Venkat. At that first meeting, Uma had observed a passion in Venkat that she hadn't sensed in the others. It hadn't been from anything that he said, but in his eyes. There was something fiery in his eyes, a strength that signaled to her that he was his own person, a defiance that excited her, that made Uma believe their marriage would be different and that she would fall in love with this man. And she would relieve her father of his parental responsibility.

Now as she stared into his brown eyes, she saw traces of the same zeal that she had detected so many months ago. She could not help but smile, though hesitantly. In all the months that she had come to know Venkat, she had never seen an exhibition of this passion, this strength. And the few times she had sensed that the smoldering ebbs of Vankat's defiance were about to burst into flame, they had been extinguished by his mother's will.

"We have made arrangements to go to Tirupathi the week after the wedding to celebrate this auspicious occasion," Venkat's mother announced suddenly, having finalized all the details for the wedding. "Venkat has taken the week off from the office. We would love for you and Padma to join us." Before her father could respond, Uma interrupted.

"No one told me. I cannot go at that time." A look of horror overcame Venkat's mother's face. Venkat raised his eyes to Uma's in astonishment.

Her soon to be mother-in-law interjected, "You must, Uma. Why do you say this?"

"I cannot take anymore leave from the office. As it is, I am taking two weeks leave to prepare for the wedding. Our project is already behind schedule. If I ask for any more leave, they will give me a permanent holiday." A few seconds of silence permeated the room. Uma looked to Venkat for support.

Venkat did not speak immediately; when he did, it was in a controlled tone. "Amma, we can go on the weekend so that Uma will only have to miss a half-day of work," Venkat offered in compromise. Uma smiled in her heart. That was reasonable.

"Oh Venkat, Tirupathi is so far away. The trip will be rushed if we have to go on Saturday and come back on Sunday." She paused for a moment and began to smile at Uma's father knowingly, as if they knew each other's thoughts. She turned to Uma.

"Why so serious, dear? You are young, you should enjoy." She took Uma's hand in hers and looked directly at her. "In a year, Uma, you will have a child and you will have to leave your job anyway. This is your wedding. You must go to Tirupathi and get God's blessings."

Uma looked to Venkat to support her position but saw him looking toward his mother, nodding his head ever-so-slightly, as if to say, "She is right."

*   *   *

A cool breeze swept through the iron-barred window as the Madras Mail sped through the plateaus of the Deccan. Four hours had elapsed since she had boarded the train in Madras and now people were settling into the long overnight journey. Uma sat quietly next to an old woman and her son, and across from her sat a woman with two young boys. In the moonlight, Uma could make out acres and acres of land that bordered the train tracks. The drought had left the land dry and sparse with vegetation only in limited areas. The cool air numbed her face. In disbelief, she recalled Venkat's nod earlier in the day.

Feeling the sensation of touch, Uma turned to the old woman next to her. The woman was offering her some idlis to eat. "Oh, no thank you," Uma said respectfully in Tamil, gesticulating this response with her hand. The woman smiled and asked her where she was going. Uma responded, "Bombay."

"Do you live there?" she asked.

"Yes, I do," Uma said with certainty, as if she had lived all her life in the place–the place where she would not be anyone's burden.

ELIZABETH SEARLE

Another Spineless White Girl

SHE WAS as good as she was beautiful, Alice recited silently in the rain. And what does this mean? she asked the unborn unimaginable baby she hoped she wasn't carrying. Not all that good, not all the time. Splashing through the gray New Haven green, Alice ducked past a JJ-sized body asleep beneath a bench. She hunched lower under her bubble umbrella. Good, say, depending on the light.

*   *   *

"No, I'm not."

Half an hour before, hidden in drizzly dawn window light, Alice had made her voice firm. *No*, she was preparing to tell workshop workers. Don't drool, don't rock, don't bang your head. Her neck tightened. And she bent over her husband cautiously, as if he had turned, overnight, into one of them.

"You are, y'know." JJ's sleep-swollen lips, still and always sexy, barely moved. "But listen, Alice. Even when I was all-the-way crazy, even back in Mass. Mental, I never hurt myself and I never hurt anyone else." He rolled over, giving off a whiff of thick unwashed hair, then added in almost his usual tone of bemused thoughtfulness, "No wonder I'm so screwed up."

Rain rattled glass. "I'm not, I swear, Joseph Jerome." Trying to smile, Alice knelt beside the fold-out mattress. "I'm not scared of you."

His head stayed still, his profile noble and bony. But y' know the truth? she imagined telling him in some future talk when he was back to his old self. I said that because I *was* scared you might—as we say in Special Ed—go off.

And they'd laugh, she thought, self-consciously poignant, moving her eyes up and down his long curved body. Ten years before, a Mass. Mental doctor had told JJ his hyperactive eighteen-year-old body was manufacturing its own Speed. And now? Its own—what would be the opposite?

"I mean, I'm *scared*, sure, but not of you. More of . . ." Her eyes passed over the shadowy fold-out mattress, the three-legged Goodwill desk, the orange crates filled with books. " . . . this. Living like grad students, but—for good." A beat passed, JJ's new three-second satellite delay. Drizzle and traffic sounds were thickening.

"Look, I'm sorry. Sorry 'bout all this, Al." JJ rolled on his stomach.

"I gotta go," Alice mumbled. But she stayed on her knees on the cold linoleum.

"'T' work?" JJ raised his head from his pillow as if from a plaster mold. "'T'day?"

"Sure." Hope stiffened her spine. He realized, maybe, how weak she was feeling. "Guess it's a, our, real job now. Our only paycheck. Right?" She met JJ's blue-green-grey eyes, wanting him to say no. "I mean yesterday, I could walk out if any assignment got, y'know, dangerous. But now I'd stay. Now each job'll be a real—test." He kept up his unblinking stare. "An' I've been wanting to see if I'm tough enough for Special Ed, really. See what I'm made of. I mean—the truth."

"No, no," JJ told her, his head sinking back down. "You're like me. You only *want to* want to know the truth."

She mimed a smile and leaned forward in the dimly flickering light. Her tender breasts strained her bra under her T-shirt. Wondering yet again if she was carrying his baby, she touched JJ's warm bristly chin. Afraid not so much of him, the gentle JJ she knew, as of the other him. The JJ who'd informed her so calmly the night before that he hadn't been attending graduate computer classes, that he'd been hiding out all day at the New Haven Public Library re-reading certain science fiction novels. *The Blue World, The Faceless Man.*

"You *are* scared of me, Alice in Wonder," JJ told her now, sleeptalk slow, his heavily lidded eyes already closed. Would he stay here all day, asleep? In his new, flattened voice, he added: "You're looking at me like you don't know who—no, what—I am."

*   *   *

A man? She stopped because she thought it was a man. Half hidden in the drizzle, halfway down deserted Manslaw, aka Manslaughter, Street. University-protected turf had ended along with Alice's faltering fairy tale; downtown New Haven had begun. No Haven, JJ called it. Sooty brick walls dripped. Cannibal pigeons pecked a red-striped box of fried chicken remains. And what *was* that, further up? Alice peered out from under her bubble.

Chopped short by his own umbrella, the long-legged figure stood where she estimated 101 to be. Today's Helping Hands assignment, 7:00 A.M. sharp. Through the rain, the fist that gripped the metal umbrella stem was brown.

Ever scared to show any shameful fear toward anyone not white, Alice took another step. Her neck tensed up as it always did when she approached or fled these Helping Hands jobs. Two eyes weren't enough, she'd begun to feel. You needed eyes all over, front and back.

Under the black umbrella, the darkly clad legs stood steady and stick-thin. A fellow worker? The doors opened at 6:00 A.M.; why didn't he go on in? Alice inched forward in wet grit. Maybe not a worker-worker but one of the Workshop workers gone beserk—no, that would be normal—gone beyond beserk, holding everyone else hostage. The fist tightened. Dark chocolate, not milk.

Slowly, the figure took a step. Alice's throat tensed with the scream that always waited there. She tilted her umbrella against the wind, its stem straining. A plastic shield. Blurred into an advancing amoeba, the figure took another step, maybe five sidewalk squares away. As she bent both arms, baring her face to the cold rain; as she raised her umbrella over one shoulder like a baseball bat, Alice glimpsed on the figure's chest a shadow, a certain round soft presence.

She broke into a sheepish smile. Her arms and spine relaxed. With her next quick steps, Alice glimpsed under the black umbrella the face above the breasts. Foolishly, she beamed her smile straight into it. The face stared back unamused: carved from brownest clay. Alice halted. Pale, she felt, with shame.

"Scared you?" The mouth wore a coating of purplish lipstick, frosted. The long fingers on the hand wore nails—how could Alice have missed those?—of the same chilled-plum color. Rain filled the space between them.

"Scared you." Stripped of its questioning rise, the *you* came out contemptuous. Alice closed down her smile. "Had us some break-ins so we keep this locked now." Serious keys jangled. "Can't hear no knocks way down in the workshop."

Alice blinked through streaming plastic, her throat tight not with a scream but with a desire to burst out like a kid: *Pretend that didn't happen, OK?*

"—yer Supervisor, Ms. Sticks."

"You are?" Alice raised her umbrella, meaning You're saying you *are* Sticks? But it came out different, disbelieving. The key clanked into 101: a peelingly painted door so flimsy-looking its oversized lock alone seemed to hold it up.

"Tha's what I said." Supervisor Sticks glanced over her slick purple raincoat shoulder with regal indifference. Her strong-boned brown face shimmered. "An you're the girl from—" Sticks shouldered open the door. Even through the rain, Alice caught her deliberate mispronunciation. "Helpin' Hams?"

* * *

No, I'm not, Alice had first answered the night before when JJ'd asked if she was scared. Just 'scared,' not scared of him. No, she'd repeated as she'd paced the cramped living room that JJ had for weeks referred to as the Surviving Room, the Getting By Room. And of course, JJ flatly informed her, he wouldn't receive any more fellowship stipend checks, starting this month.

Then I'd better get my *period* this month, Alice had blurted out, halting and turning. JJ on the couch jolted to attention.

Just what we'd need, huh? she had asked shakily, thinking it might be what JJ, anyhow, needed. Shock Therapy.

Not that she was all *that* late, she reminded herself now, dripping and plodding behind Supervisor Sticks. The cardboard-colored concrete floor sloped for wheelchairs: a bumpy ramp descending into the gym-sized workshop. *OK,* Alice told herself, her feet trying to catch Sticks's purposeful beat. *It'll be OK.* A less catchy chant than her usual but no longer plausible: *It's OK, It's OK.*

"We got it all," Sticks told Alice over her shoulder. "Some D.D., some E.D.—"

"De-velopmentally, E-motionally—" Alice murmured, ticking off the 'Disabled's, eager to show she knew at least this after months of Special Ed. temp. assignments. A little something to supplement JJ's stipend, at first. A little dare to see if she could do, not just wistfully want to do, some good.

"Tha's what I said." Sticks halted at the bottom of the ramp. Uncovered, her short-chopped hair formed stiff peaks, brushed back angrily.

"S-so they're all here under Observation, pending—" Alice almost rolled her own eyes at her Goody-good voice, her Helping Hands terms. "Placement?"

Ms. Sticks gave a one-shouldered shrug. "You could say that." You, not me, her no-nonsense walk implied. Her boot heels clicked on the concrete workshop floor. "'less you count this as a *place*."

Struggling to keep up, Alice hurried past stacks of mildewed junk mail refolded so often the folds had split. Empty bins rested in rows on six tables; no workers filled the metal chairs yet. No windows here, no sound of rain. Alice bowed her head, the fluorescent tube lights making her face feel bare.

"Course—" Supervisor Sticks clanked her keys onto the central table beside two new-looking plastic-covered bins. "Some stay f'r years. You take Eric now."

"Yeah, take Eric," a hoarse cheerful voice echoed. "Please." Chewing gum at a furious rate, the woman waddled over from a far corner, her orange-brown face aglow. Her rabbity front teeth glinted like rapidly repeated winks.

"Morning, Vi. Gonna show this Sub our Eric." Sticks pivoted on her high-heeled boot and gripped the handles of a wheelchair that faced the cinderblock wall. A grey-blond crewcut head showed from the back. Releasing the brake with one pointed boot toe, Ms. Sticks swung the chair around to face Alice.

"Hi Eric!" Alice's voice strained too high again, echoing in the wide, nearly empty workshop. "Hi there." She touched Eric's rigid shoulder, patted it.

"Ooh, ain't she sweet?" Ms. Sticks murmured to Vi. "Always so sensi-tive, when they do drop in."

Vi gave a cough or maybe a laugh. "Not like us, huh, Eric? Us full-time witches?"

Smiling uncertainly, Alice bent to meet Eric's eyes and found none. One black patch, one deflated eyelid. Only a sliver of eyewhite showed through the lashless slit. A flattened eyeball afloat under his lid. This can't be my life, Alice thought numbly, staring. Eric's crewcut head bobbed like—no, not at all—a nod.

"Don' let him scare you, hon'," Vi rasped, bending so close Alice breathed her tobacco gum. Vi's stomach gathered in rolls under her sweatshirt. Gratefully, Alice gave that soft inviting stomach her first unforced smile of the day.

"He blind, he deaf, he crippled—" Vi shook her frizzy hennaed head. "Makes you wonder what He—" Alice caught the capital 'H' "—wants to pull such tricks for. But Eric's got the face of a baby, don' he?" Alice had to nod. A thirty-year-old baby, his dry skin unlined. "I would too," Vi announced, "if *I* didn't have no worries left, like him—right, Eric? Not much more this world can do to you, right?"

Alice widened her tentative smile, running one hand over Eric's bristly greasy crewcut. His head kept bobbing.

"We're lucky." Ms. Sticks raised her voice to Supervisor volume, stepping over to the bins. "We got a new Contract Job, t'day."

A puffy-faced white woman drifted to the center table. "Oh joy." Light, this woman looked. Swollen so round with air?

"T'day—" Using one plum fingernail as a knife, Sticks stripped plastic off the newest-looking bin. "The workers gonna be stuffin' this—" She forked up a handful of shredded brownish green paper, a dirty distinctive color. "Into these."

She tweezed between her thumb and index nails a plastic bag. Small, oblong. Eric jerked his head hard, knocking her hand off. He must be a—what was it called?—head-butter. Alice took a step back, wiping his hair grease on her skirt.

"Want *ev-* eryone watching," Sticks intoned. Alice stepped around the table, closer to the opened bin, avoiding Ms. Sticks's narrowed stare.

"'scuse me, but—what is this?" Alice poked a finger into the shredded green paper, it's familiar worn texture. "Didn't it used to be—money?"

"An' *then*—" Sticks notched up her Supervisor voice. "*Staple* the *bag.*"

Between her purple nails, she pinched shut the plastic, stuffed with shreds of George Washington, the all-seeing pyramid eye. Hypnotized, Alice asked: "Why?"

"Why?" Sticks's frosted-purple lips curved derisively. "'cause they say."

Eric lurched forward in his wheelchair and banged his head on his

wooden tray. Alice jumped. Then, at the second thud, she made herself hurry back around the table behind Sticks and Vi.

"–get it off–" Sticks gripped Eric by the shoulders, shredded money
floating to the floor around her. Vi crouched before Eric with a grunt.

"Guess we all know what he needs–" Vi struggled to unfasten the
tray and Eric knocked it askew. Wood cracked on concrete. Alice
froze, staring over Vi's head. Eric's upper body flailed like JJ's when JJ
danced. But no grace, no control.

"Watch out, Sticks, or we gonna wind up on Channel 8." Vi gripped
Eric's strained arm. Sticks took hold of the other, rolling up Eric's
sleeve. "That's t'day, right?" Vi chomped gum no faster than before.
"The camera guy?"

"So they say," Ms. Sticks mumbled, sounding elaborately bored.
The puffball woman drifted forward in her white dress, wielding a
hypodermic needle.

"He'll look like he cryin' but he's not–" Vi's tooth winked over at
Alice.

Staring down, Alice crouched to grip the flung tray. Unmistakably,
Eric laughed. A phlegmy full-throated man's laugh.

"See?" Vi demanded. Gritting her teeth, Alice looked up as Sticks
eased the needle out of Eric's bare arm. Eric laughed harder, his eye-
patch slipping. Vi patted his shoulder, hard too. "He like it, see? Likes
that needle, likes boilin' hot water, likes bitter-black olives, th' saltier
th' better–"

Vi lifted the wood tray from Alice. Eric slumped forward, still laughing, his head hanging between his knees. Hefting the tray that held
him upright, Vi added, "Guess if something's gonna get felt by him at
all, it's just gotta be *strong*–"

Alice nodded, still crouched.

"Want this Helping Ham girl t' work with the Prez," Sticks decreed,
looking mercilessly skinny as she wrapped the used needle in a paper
towel.

The main workshop door thumped; a slow-motion army began to
shuffle down the wheelchair ramp. Alice jumped to her feet, her breasts
aching with her motion. Her pulse thudded with the steps of the
workers. Multiple pulses.

"Here comes the Prez," Vi murmured, kneeling to re-fit the wood
tray. Alice stepped forward and took hold of Eric's warm, slimy wrists.
It's only spit, she told herself, keeping Eric still. "That's James Carter

in front." Vi nodded over her shoulder at the workers. "Get you a look at his hands. They found him a couple months ago tied up in a closet in some empty apartment. His fingers tied, see; they don't know for sure how long. Don't know what all his problems be–"

Alice shot a glance at a slouched crowd of twenty workers filing in. A decidedly un-slouched man walking to one side of the crowd, winking one eye shut. A video camera perched on his shoulder like a robotic hawk, sweeping over the room, its lens eye as blank as the green, triangle-encased eye on an unshredded dollar bill.

*　　*　　*

Watch out with him, Alice's mother had warned from the first in her mannish long-distance voice, deepened by the cigarettes she'd taken up again immediately after her divorce. *What's he been doing with himself all this time, this JJ?*

Smelling smoke through her dorm-room phone receiver, Alice had kept her answers bland. She'd wanted to protect him: her JJ, six years older than she was. JJ with a secret month in the Massachusetts State Mental Center in his past and a chronically depressed Dad as his only family. JJ's silent cipher of a Dad, whose mere mute presence made Alice tell herself, clearly: Do not marry this man's son.

Hit by a wavelet of delayed shock–*was* JJ headed for another breakdown, for real?–Alice swayed now on her feet. The white light roved her way. And a stooped-over man veered from the worker crowd and began to lurch toward her.

"Here he come." Vi nudged Alice, jarring her. "An we gotta steer him *away* from that camera–"

"Who?" Alice blinked. The Channel 8 light fixed on the stooped milky-brown man who halted in front of Vi, wobbling.

"James Carter." Vi took hold of his scabby elbow. He wore an old-man style short-sleeved shirt so thin his tank top undershirt showed through.

"Don't he look like he's from somewhere else?" Firmly, touching both their elbows, Vi began herding Alice and Carter toward a corkboard partition, camera lights warm on their backs. Carter lurched along, his jaw jutting out over his caved-in chest. "Told you those hands. See what I say?"

Carter's hands swung, his fingers unnaturally stretched. The fingers of his left hand were swollen like long balloons tied in knots by a sadistic circus clown. These fingers puffed out from joints thin as bone, ringed by dead white.

"See where th' ropes dug in? Musta been tied up who knows how long." Vi stopped in front of the partition. Alice dared a glance over her shoulder. The camera man was talking to Supervisor Sticks. A second man balanced the long-necked light and wore headphones attached to a radio contraption strapped on his waist. Alice turned back to Vi and nodded, theatrically slow.

"They're doin' some sorta in-vestigation on this place," Vi was telling Alice in her own raspy stage whisper, still holding Carter's elbow. "For—you know—"

"A-buse?" Alice pictured herself led into a police car in front of all America, her head ducked under a coat but her name afloat beneath her, seen only on screen.

"For TV," Vi answered matter of factly, as if that explained all. "Channel 8 at six."

Carter gave a wheeze like a laugh, rocking on his heels. Glee shone behind his glasses.

"And Carter—" Alice pointed her chin at him. "He's likely to—?"

"Go off." Vi nodded like a sympathetic executioner. "So Sticks wants you two back here."

"But shouldn't someone else—?" Alice planted her heels. "I mean, not me—"

Her eyes flickered around the crowded workshop, the camera nowhere in sight. Isn't it against the law? Alice used to demand of her dad when they'd watch *60 Minutes*, her voice quavering with a sense that someone even more powerful than Dan Rather wielded some larger scale *Candid Camera*.

"I mean." Alice met Vi's eyes. "Es-pecially today, this time of month, I'm kinda, y'know—"

"Cramps?" Vi hissed companionably, still holding Carter's elbow.

"I *wish*, " Alice whispered back, and she was rewarded by a sym-pathetic tooth glint. A few firm, steadying pats on her back.

"Take it easy." With a final pat, Vi nudged Alice halfway behind the partition. "You're not much more'n a baby. Had my first when I was sixteen. But you . . ." Vi gave her an appraising yellow-flecked glance. "What're you doin' here, anyhow?"

Working my husband's way through grad school, Alice usually

answered, making her voice offhand. Now her voice came out flat on its own. "Just working."

Something whirred. Abruptly, ducking her head like it *was* covered with her coat, Alice stepped behind the corkboard. James Carter lurched in after her.

"–ESL training, they say Carter need: English as a Second–but we don't even know 'f he got a first!–Language." Vi filled the partition entrance. *And Lead Me Not into Temptation*, her faded sweatshirt read. *I Can Find the Way Myself.*

"He can't do much," she told Alice, her front tooth winking. "But you're s'posed to make him do something. Use his–good hand?"

"Yeah, right." Alice glanced down at the table holding two bins, one empty and one filled with shredded dollars. "But wha'd you think these're for–?"

Vi rolled one round shoulder, leaning in. "Beats me, baby doll." Her broad back must have formed a wide tempting target. Still, no lights swung that way. Safe here, behind the corkboard. Hidden, anyhow.

*   *   *

First thing, Alice fished out her pocket compact. Her fine-boned twenty-two-year-old girl's face stared back, her skin wan and shiny in the harsh light. She powdered her nose, snapped the mirror shut, looked up and jumped slightly. Carter stared, maybe offended that she'd done this as if he wasn't there. Guiltily, she slipped the mini-compact back into her cotton skirt pocket.

"OK." Alice raised her voice above the blood beating in her ears.

Carter wheezed at her across their small table. A deeper mean-old-man wheeze though he looked, up close, no more than forty. His face was heart-shaped, like her own; only his heart was turned upside down. His forehead low, his jaw broad as a pit bull's. And it held, this tough brown face, a trace of something Asian: a mandarin slant to his wary black eyes. His nose was too flat to support the glasses strapped around his patchy-bald head. The nose-pads of the frames gripped air, the glasses afloat over Carter's suspiciously narrowed gaze.

"OK, now." Alice looked at the heap of plastic sacks. A clipboard held a chart to record how many he filled. A stapler waited. "We gotta start." Carter heaved a sigh.

"See?" Alice fingered one sack open, remembering how JJ fingered open and then puffed air into his condoms. Back when he called her his duckling, newly hatched. Imprinted—as he'd put it—on the first creature she saw. Shyly now, Alice blew into the plastic. Smirking as if he saw her memory, Carter lifted his twisted left hand, dropped it into the bin. Dead weight, a muffled thump.

He closed his swollen fingers around the shredded dollars, lifted his hand again. Clumsy as a bulldozer, he spilled the clumped shreds over the plastic, only a few curls falling in. "Other hand, please," Alice said in a low, even voice he showed no sign of hearing. As Carter lifted another slow-motion fistful, Alice's ears began to separate words from the murmurs on the other side of the corkboard.

"That new one . . . 'nother Helpin' Ham." This was Sticks. A bin clomped.

"Uh huh." Vi. Another clomp. They must've been stacking the bins.

Now Sticks again, a little louder and a lot clearer. "Another spineless white girl."

Alice sat still, holding open the silly sack with her fingertips. She stared at its dirty-green paper curls. They could sit here all day, filling one. I can't, she thought, meaning more than this job. Vi outside gave a hoarse, considering "Mmm." A bin clomp. "–Eric had his fit, she *did* come on over t' him."

"Nn." Sticks allowed the briefest of reprieves. "But she didn't do nothin'."

True, Alice thought, holding the sack steady, waiting for a third voice: an impartial judge rendering a final verdict. *She was as good as–*

"I–" Carter raised his less swollen right hand: not pointing, reaching. His scrawny neck strained. Alice turned. On the ledge of the partition's upper corner lay a pipe. A reward: in sight but out of reach? "I–I–"

Supervisor Sticks poked her head around the corkboard, her angrily brushed hair rising now to higher peaks. Choppy waves. "No–" Sticks addressed Carter. His glasses gleamed from the light of her eyes. "No smok-ing." Her nail pointed. "Not til one hour wortha work, you hear?" Then, to Alice: "I better not smell nothin'."

Carter fixed his eyes on the space where Sticks's vivid dark head had been. With a wheeze of a sigh, he lowered his head to the crook of his arm. "Shush," Alice whispered the way JJ did when she woke from nightmares. Then she sighed too.

Years before, in that same voice, hadn't JJ warned her about his history, her head resting on his chest so each word vibrated? Hadn't she nodded solemnly, impressed to be taking a real–though deep down she felt as safe as ever–risk?

Alice stared now at the limp sack and its few paper curls, remembering how abruptly she'd run out on JJ this morning. But I was still in shock, she told herself, shifting uneasily, trying not to reconstruct those last fumbling moments.

"Pie–" James Carter raised his head, dollar shreds sticking in his hair. He stared up at his pipe: his glasses askew, the lenses gleaming. And he lifted his bad hand, then–Alice gasped–stuck one swollen fingertip in his mouth. As he bit down, she winced, half expecting the finger to burst like a blister.

"W-wanna *chew* the pipe?" She stood hurriedly. Carter's strong jaw worked, maybe stirred a smile. He released his finger, watching her turn. She stood on tiptoe and reached for the plasticized corncob pipe but not the matches. *Spineless, spineless,* she thought, fumbling as if she was the one in need of this pipe's fix.

"P-pie– ee–" Carter wheezed, beginning to rock in his seat.

One day before, Alice might've decided the one-hour rule was silly, might've risked smoke and done what she thought was right, really. She was always slipping favors to patients back when this Helping Hands job was a novelty, not a necessity.

"Here." Stepping forward, she stuck the chewed-looking stem between Carter's eagerly parted lips. His teeth bit down on it. And he rocked in his seat gleefully. No smoke. Bins clomped and voices mumbled. Alice's heart rose. Was she going to get away with this slight safe risk, her favorite kind?

Then Carter sucked in hard: a hollow sound. He slumped, staring up at her, betrayed. Alice sat down. "I *can't*–" she whispered, and–aware of a muffled whir–she turned quickly in her seat. The partition opening was empty. But was the camera watching somehow, invisible? Alice swung back around and gave Carter's misshapen left hand an awkward, apologetic pat. His skin felt rough and dry, not all that strange. Self-consciously–*was* the whir real?–Alice let her hand rest on his, her own fingertips avoiding his swollen fingers.

Carter chewed on the pipe, staring with interest at her hand on his. OK, as long as she didn't touch the fingers. Just dry brown skin, scales like fleshy tobacco shreds. Flickering in Alice's mind was an image of herself on TV, nobly holding his hand. Or–her hand stiffened–herself in a misty, vaguely imagined Mass. Mental ward, holding JJ's. Carter's hand stiffened with hers, turning under her palm. His reddish brown blister-swollen fingers curved, about to take hold of her hand. Straightening fast, Alice pulled it back.

"Eee–?" Carter patted the table where their two hands had been. Spilled dollar shreds jumped. Sucking extra hard on his pipe, he fixed his bewildered melted-chocolate gaze on the hand Alice still held up, suspended between them.

Hours before, hugging JJ goodbye, she had let his hands run down her body, the body he had discovered for her. His strong, calming hands. But as Alice had buried her face in his chest this time, he had gripped her ribcage tightly as if he was suddenly dropping, dropping fast with her lying on top of him, dropping too. And she'd pulled herself, abruptly, up. *Gotta go.*

She stared along with Carter at the hand she'd just yanked away from his. Behind her, the camera's muffled whir moved closer, maybe ten feet from the partition. Alice's spine tensed. "But lis-ten," she whispered to Carter, lowering her hand so it rested beside his curved, swollen fingers. "I- I'm not scared of you . . ."

The corners of Carter's mouth began to twitch. Behind his glasses, his eyes glinted. A derisive chuckle rumbled deep in his throat. Could he–with no First Language even–have understood her foolish words? Carter's pipe quivered, clenched between his crooked tobacco-tinged teeth. Only after his chuckle died down did he suck in again, even harder. A piercingly hollow sound.

"It's–it'll be OK." Alice did the dumb thing. She tilted her wrist. Was it running backwards, her watch? Her tense voice rose with false Special Ed. Teacher cheer. "Only forty-five minutes til pipe time!"

Behind the corkboard walls, a bored man's voice began to speak. "–over there for me please," he told someone. Nearby workshop murmurs had quieted down. "Yes, right there." Definitely a few feet away: that whir. Carter sucked his unlit pipe urgently, a child straining for soda in an empty glass.

"OK, calm down now," Alice whispered, trying not to draw attention.

"Ee-*ee*–" Carter whimpered louder, his pipe falling from his mouth with a hollow *thwock*. Outside the partition walls, the camera man's voice stopped talking.

"W-w–" James Carter rocked up to his feet, wobbling, his glasses knocked further askew. The lenses gleamed down at Alice. Behind, his eyes gleamed too: rheumy bright with an old man's, not a child's, confusion. "–ee?"

"No, please sit," Alice hissed, not only hearing but feeling the camera whir, only slightly muffled behind her. She stood shakily, suddenly aware of Carter's height and weight. A man. "Please–" She held up one hand to keep him away.

Hope you are, JJ'd told her as she'd stared back at him after stumbling to the bedroom door. She'd turned to go, wondering with a chill if he meant *Scared of me.*

"Nuh–" Swaying on his feet, meeting her eyes with a plea of his own, Carter reached for Alice's hand. His swollen blister-stiff fingers crackled as they bent, closing over her fingers. His skin rough as fiberglass.

"No–" Alice's knees braced against his grip. She drew a quick breath, ready to let loose her scream.

"Wee?" Carter choked. *We?* Alice wondered breathlessly, meeting Carter's darkly unreadable eyes. "Wuh–" Bowing his head so his glasses jumped, Carter stared at his knuckly brown hand clenched over hers. "Wuh-*ee*–" he insisted, swaying at the force of the word. About to topple?

Carter squeezed her hand with both of his now, his whole weight leaning on her. Gasping, Alice reached up and flattened her free hand on his sunken chest. Her bent arm tensed. Hard as she could, she pushed Carter away. All too easily, he stumbled. He lurched backwards onto his seat, bumping his tailbone. A thump: bone against plastic, no ass to cushion his fall. His head bobbed. Then he slumped.

"No–" Alice shouted, feeling hot brightness hit her back. Carter's glasses hung diagonally, still strapped onto his motionless head. "No-oh–" She spun around. Light hit her face: cleansing, blinding white. Alice met its full glare, opening her mouth to confess. Instead, she heard herself say, "Help!"

Behind her, James Carter groaned. Spinning around again, blinking through sudden blobs of light, Alice faced him. He'd sprung back up from her shove, towering over her now, his eyes darkened and stunned.

"I–I–" Carter swayed and Alice stumbled backwards one step–the lights hotter on her shirt–then rammed into the table. She fell onto concrete, bumping her padded tailbone. Her compact cracked. Her insides jarred. *Pregnant*, she felt suddenly sure JJ'd meant. She sat frozen, paralyzed by the first hidden spurt of blood. Sticks was rushing forward, boot heels clicking. Hope you are pregnant, JJ'd wanted to tell her after she'd struggled from his arms. Pregnant, anchored down.

"Wha's goin' on?" Sticks demanded. As she and the Camera and Light men gathered round, crowding the small space; as wobbly James Carter bumped against the partition, shaking its corkboard walls; as Alice's miniature flesh-pink compact spun on the floor beside her, Alice pointed up.

"Not me," she gasped straight into the light. She heard her compact stop spinning. "Him," she told them all, pointing up toward Carter, meaning he was the one who needed help. Her finger wavered. The camera man bent closer. His video's snout focused on Alice's face like the x-ray machine at the dentist's. Alice stared into the hum of the lights, feeling Carter loom tall and unsteady behind her.

"Who, Carter?" Briskly, Supervisor Sticks's long crane legs stepped over Alice's legs. Twisting around, Alice saw Sticks stop beside Carter. She saw Carter grip with his bad hand Sticks's strong but skinny arm. Steadying himself. All he'd wanted, all along? Through the bobbing blobs of light, Sticks trained her narrowed gaze at Alice on the floor. "*He's* not gonna hurt *you.*"

*   *   *

She was as good as—Mom used to begin, then (modern Mom) she'd tell Alice to finish it herself. As she was 'skinny' Alice used to say, tomboy thin back then.

In the quiet, empty Supervisor office, feeling heavy now, Alice sat on a stuck-in-one-position swivel chair and, inside her panties, on a maxi-pad thick as a diaper. A blank time sheet lay in front of her; a pen was attached to the desk with dental floss. She picked up the pen, picturing JJ still asleep. *T'work?* he'd asked her so shakily. *T'day?* And she'd thought he was concerned about her, how last night might've knocked her off balance. But maybe JJ was the one who felt shaken, scared to be left alone. She wondered now, wondering too if she and he were losing it already, their shared second language. Slowly, she marked down her shift hours: seven til noon. Her test only beginning, she sensed—and badly.

"P-Pie- I–" At this muffled cry, Alice stared up.

Outside the scratched office window glass, James Carter had been seated in a chair, a plastic bib around his neck. Vi bent beside him, balancing a plate of purple jello. Carter's wrists were fastened to his chair by long felt ties, strained now as he tried to lift both hands, intent unclear. Alice was starting to stand when Sticks shouldered open the office door and clicked inside.

"How–" Alice stayed bent in place, half in and half out of the seat. The door gave a decisive wood thump. "How come he–James Carter's– tied up like that?"

"Oh." Sticks smoothed her choppy hair. "Down 'n the caf-teria, Prez was hitting out at everyone. So it's–" She gave Alice a dismissive glance. "Not just you."

"But–but he–" Alice cleared her throat. Her voice came out small and steady, stronger than the shaky voice that had said, *Help.* "He didn't hit me or anything. He just grabbed hold of me so not to fall. Then–I panicked and *I* pushed *him* . . ."

"Oh?" Sticks raised her brows, her richly brown skin drawing the wan office light. Her no-longer-frosted lips framed her words. "Want me to tell Channel 8?"

Alice looked down, picturing again her head bowed under a coat, on TV. As she sank back into Sticks's seat, another surge of menstrual blood oozed into her pad.

"Want me to tell Helping Hands?"

Alice raised her eyes. Sticks's skeptical black eyes were radiating harsh light.

"You *do*?" Sticks asked insistently. Alice made her eyes stay locked in Sticks's. And she shook her head no, picturing JJ sunk in his helplessly deep sleep.

"I need this job," Alice managed to tell Sticks, tell herself.

"Thought so, Helpin' Ham." In one quick motion, her plum nails flashing, Sticks signed Alice's time sheet. "Now I gotta get that spineless nurse goin' for Eric's next in-jection." Sticks straightened. "His fav'rite thing, that needle." She turned on her boot heel, her back to Alice. "Now he." The strong knobs of Sticks's spine showed through her black shirt. "He got him some *thick* white boy skin."

The office door thumped shut before Alice could pull herself to her feet.

She was good as long as she was–

"What? Kept at Room Temperature?" Outside the office, her back to Carter, Alice snapped up her raincoat. Melting like vanilla ice cream now, under the rubber: her thin soft skin. Her eyes scanned the emptied workshop; everyone but Carter was in the cafeteria. Bins piled with tiny sacks stuffed with shredded dollars lined the cinderblock walls, those sacks tied with green ribbons. *Some sorta promo thing for a bank*, Sticks had been telling the camera man as Vi had led Alice to the bathroom.

No camera in sight now, Alice noticed. Before she snapped her last snap, she slipped her compact from her skirt pocket. Her face had split, one side jacked up high. Seven years? Alice clicked the lid shut on the jaggedly cracked mirror. Seven years bad luck after twenty-two of good? She slid the compact back in her pocket. So easy to seem good if your luck is too. Alice snapped her coat all the way. Then, protected, she turned toward James Carter.

He still sat tied to his chair in front of Vi. His jaw jutted out, his gaze fixed on a point beyond Alice's rubber shoulder. Shyly, she stepped closer, standing beside Vi.

"Get a move on–" Across the workshop, the cafeteria door thumped open, Sticks holding it. Eric's wheelchair squeaked in with white-clad Puffball pushing. Eric's grey-blond crewcut head bobbed, his eye-patch blurring. Maybe a real nod this time. A smile distorted his face like he knew what was coming. Sticks shut the door. As Sticks turned to Puffball, Alice caught the glint of a fresh needle.

"–han-dle this one alone?" Sticks was asking, Supervisor volume.

"Sure, he's not gonna fight it," Puffball answered faintly as she took hold of the needle. Alice looked away, down to Vi's frizzy hennaed head.

"You OK now?" Vi asked, not raising her eyes from the chopped-up jello.

"Oh yeah," Alice managed, flushing. Sticks's boot heels were clicking toward them. "'cept for having cramps, everything's fine now . . ."

Vi gave a brief unsurprised nod. "Knew you'd come out OK," she told Alice matter-of-factly, keeping her eyes on the quivering spoonful of jello.

"Thing is–" Sticks stopped behind Alice, clearly addressing Vi. "This Helpin' Ham gonna come out OK on TV too: falling down all help-less-like with big bad Carter standin' over her. She gonna look sweet as ev-er."

"Uhn-huh," Vi agreed. "Tha's th' way it is. . . ."

Flushing more deeply, Alice turned her head and saw in her office window reflection how wide and scared her eyes would seem on Channel 8. Shameful relief rose in her chest. She started to step sideways, slip away quietly. What stopped her was Carter's first direct stare. Through his straightened glasses, his wet chocolate eyes shone, wholly melted-down, brown staining his eyeballs. There was no, strictly speaking, white.

"Now *he*." Sticks clicked up beside Alice, blocking her escape path. "*Carter's* not gonna look so good on TV–" Sticks shook her head. "Anyone in th' front office see that Channel 8 mess, you *know* it'll 'fect Carter's final place-ment."

Sticks turned her back on Alice. Hands on her hips, she shouted to Puffball. "You gonna in-ject him or you gonna stand there swabbin' him all day?"

Alice's legs tensed like Eric's arm awaiting the needle. Sticks began clicking back across the workshop. Only Carter watched Alice, his steady stare unbroken as he closed his purplish brown lips around the jello. Vi eased the spoon out, settling back in her seat. Carter didn't blink. Alice started to step sideways again.

Still meeting her eyes, James Carter opened his mouth as if to speak. Alice froze. One by one, jello blobs fell from his lower lip. Purple red: startling like the stains in her underpants. Soundlessly, jello slid down his bib and hit the floor. Gleaming with saliva, smoothly slimy. See what I'm made of, Alice remembered telling JJ. And she took her side-step. Over Vi's round slack shoulder, Carter gave Alice a last look she'd carry all the way back home, his rheumy-bright eyes blank with perfect–or perfectly feigned–incomprehension. His glasses had lost their grip on his flat, broad nose, afloat again. Across the workshop, the needle no doubt sinking in, Eric let loose his throaty man's laugh.

"See you," Alice murmured. Carter jerked his chin. Yep, I see you.

Alice blinked, picturing JJ awakened at last in their empty apartment. As Eric's laughter rose, she turned on her heel, leaving behind her bubble umbrella. Her maxipad chafed her thighs, a rough comfort. Alice crossed the workshop with shaky sidewalk-square-sized steps, ready to let dirty city rain soak her face, ready to crawl under the covers with JJ–the furthest ahead she could plan–and tell him in Mother's fairy tale voice, low and soft the way grown-ups say things they only wish they still believed: *It's OK; I'm not.*

BETTY SHIFLETT

The Country Barber

AT SUPPER Father had told her sadly, around his toothpick, they could no longer trust the town barber with starched white smock and high-top shoes. He'd not get a second chance; he'd cut her ear and it bled, not heavily, but the wound cut deep into father and daughter.

Deep into the country night in Father's car they sped to find a barber who did not cut like the old one, nor ring his quarters loudly, ostentatiously checking for counterfeit, on the marble shelf by the Lucky Tiger bottles mirrored in ruby rows. Pocketing the coins, he'd click his grinning teeth, meaning he'd cut you again if he could. Out in the country a new barber would cut straight the hair that never curled, expose more severely the ears that stuck out, show more clearly the bare sheen of Deborah's neck.

Gone were the magic summer afternoons lulled by the blurring motion of the ceiling fan, when Deborah watched Father reclining under a white cloth, allowing the town barber all his whims of scissors and pomade. At the rear of the shop, over a doorway, hung a rustling curtain of green and yellow crepe paper streamers trembling with hints of the back room where Sam the bootblack counted out towels. Deborah always hoped for a break in the curtain that would reveal a glimpse of Sam.

The shimmering of tambourines, like fairy laughter, floated from Sam's back room, melting the streamers into flooding greens and yellows as the child stared passionately at them, and long, until suddenly they blazed into tumultuous life. From some place out back came

258

Sam's rich mumble broken by the squeal of trucks and rattling sting of alley gravel, a jangle of metal doors (heavy boxes smote the ground!) a flare of rough voices pursued by the crunch of stamping feet.

Once a breeze off the street lifted the streamers, as the barber pumped Father's chair up, up, up . . . and Deborah, sitting, waiting under the long row of men's hat hooks, stopped turning the pages of a *True Detective*, the same magazines Father stacked on the floor by his bed, with snub-nosed pistols in the pictures aiming up at his pillows, and bold black arrows on the page to mark the criminal's mistake, set of powdered fingerprints, dropped knife, bloodstained cushion—more disturbing, the invariable, innocent looking item: key chain, desk drawer, window, scarf. She stared at the curtain separating her from Sam, green, yellow streamers dissolving, detective magazine slithering from her lap, and caught him in the back room popping towels to straighten the hems, then folding and stacking them snowy and red-bordered on the seat of his spindle-back chair. . . . Her breath came easier. The sound of his crackling spit seemed to be his way of testing the space he entered—then a strong whiff of boot polish amazed her nose and the lean black man himself rustled in, ashy elbows first through the flowing curtain, cradling a pile of huck towels in one arm and coughing over the opposite shoulder, while with the other hand, his head smartly lowered, he ran a bit of orange comb through his brilliantined hair. The airy crepe paper streamers were still giddy with his passage when he slipped the stub of comb into his shirt pocket, tapped it down—she would guard that secret with him—the high cheekboned face smooth, the yellow-tinged eyes controlled for the shop in the front room where white business was being transacted by the barber with clicking teeth.

But never again would she let the barber swoop down grinning, his teeth long in his sallow face, and lift her, hurting, by the armpits, and dump her on the shaky red board with no back but with fancy iron curlicues wrought at either end, placed especially for children over the chasm between the arms of the barber's chair. That black leather monster was fitted out with chrome as cold as the shears at your neck.

Father crushed forward behind the wheel, sifting darkness for the new barber. Deborah smelled oil freshly sprinkled on the red clay road to settle the dust, and heard the rush of tires as they skimmed the hills in Father's grey coupe. The oil-rich air lapped at her window and made her clothes feel damp like the collar of her dress when her ear bled; and though it was cooler dipping into little valleys, the lingering soreness in her puffy earlobe throbbed with the pulsing of fireflies that glimmered here and there in the reed-grass crowning high embankments, ears being the slowest part of the body to heal, Father said.

*   *   *

They zoomed over the crest of a hill, ready for the downward drop, when a fragile moonlit shack flew up in their faces, like a moth blaring into light; yet it seemed anchored, leaning, as if blown gently in a sea of bending weeds. As they coasted downhill, diminishing distance made plain a low roof with wide eaves in an attitude of flight. Father killed the motor, drew up the brake. At sight of the shack an unruly conglomeration of excitement and old fears pumped through his stout body.

"Get out! Here's where they'll do it right." He heaved himself out of the car. So this was the place! He breathed as if he strained moonlight through his lungs. Maybe not so mean as the worst farmer's shack left to burn under a driving sun among the corn stubble and cotton bolls, but breathtakingly familiar. Like the feel of his schoolboy lunch pail made from a scoured out lard can, the wire handle swinging in his hand as he picked his uneven way over spring-plowed ground, taking a short-cut to school, cold pot liquor and greens sloshing in the pail with every stride. He stopped at a fenceline and held down the bottom strands of barbed-wire, and stooped to ease his body through. Having swung one leg clear, he was aiming his muddy boot at solid ground, when he saw the fierce, tender buttercups and immediately imagined they were defying his powerful boot. With a surge of magnanimity he spared them, setting down his boot with splendid care. He stood to his full height on the other side of the fence, drunk with spring and his aspirations. Proud with his sums done to a fare-thee-well, anticipating today's spelling bee—he would acquit himself well.

Now just last week, and all these many years later, he'd been touched again by that same heady upwelling of sentiment when, as County Superintendent, he paid his regular visit to the colored high school. Sitting with the black principal in the latter's cramped office, he mentioned, on behalf of his daughter, their recent difficulty with the white town barber. In his opinion that old piece of baggage was more tolerable for adults who could hold their own with him than for children, who, he had seen too late, were apt to be taken careless advantage of by the old goat. The black principal had understandably agreed, and promoted the expertise of a certain pair of barbers who did a little farming on the side "to make out"; they had reason to want the superintendent's business; never fear, he would put in a good word for the white school official and his little girl. Here the principal inclined his grizzled head toward the bespectacled white man, voice husky with caution: They could prudently expect to drive out there under the canopy of night. Man to man they shook on it, the two veteran schoolmen, in a refreshing conspiracy. Father congratulated himself on his gumption. What others could move about in the community as he did?

*   *   *

No gate greeted the visitors, only a walk flanked on either side by the stalks of dead flowers, and three wooden steps rising apologetically out of the dirt. The steps were spongy under Deborah's feet, the porch dark and narrow, the pale-lit screen door ripped and bellied out by those who had leaned against it with their arms folded, watching the road. From shadows by the door leaped the faded red and blue stripes of a home-made barber's pole which, having broken away from one of its rusty moorings, dangled slantwise from the remaining bracket; its dim, motionless colors seemed to cling to Father's white sleeve as he brushed past it. Deborah shrank a step backward into herself at the memory of fiery clippers biting her earlobe, and tugged at Father, trying to turn him back to the car, abandoned to fickle shadows and moonlight on the white curving drive. But Father only laughed good-bye at the distant coupe, jutted his toothpick between his teeth, and taking her by the shoulders, set her once more toward the door. Deborah felt herself dwindle under Father's urgency, his shepherd-steady hand growing moist on her shoulder. The floorboards gave unevenly. With numbed limbs she passed under the barber's pole suspended inches above her head, and arrived, safe enough with Father, at the door. Under her ribs the ugly, painted colors of the pole turned steeply with a great downward sadness.

Father knocked, got no answer, gave the door a jerk; a pointed, chesty laugh ripped loose from inside the shack. Hand in hand on the threshold, he and Deborah stopped short. Imperfectly through the screen, they made out a shadowy figure reaching around a corner to stand on end something long and glinting. He tightened his grip on Deborah's hand. He could not be sure if what he'd heard . . . or imagined, was the scarcely audible movement of a gun coming to rest. Why shouldn't they put meat on their table? He ceased his speculating when a businesslike voice cried, "Step in!"

The screen door moaned open to reveal a space harshly lit by a kerosene lamp whose insistent sucking noises compelled their attention through wave upon heavy wave of kerosene fumes. A dark hand carefully screwed a key on the lamp and lowered the white glare. Out of the incandescent haze, Deborah was surprised to see a room take shape. The lamp with stout, smoking chimney and no shade sat in the back window. Against that wall stood a table attended on either side by a kitchen chair and covered with cloudy oilcloth. On the table a red tambourine, its skin black at the center from being struck by many hands, held three quarters which shone up brightly. Over all the lamp hissed its accompaniment.

Briefly, time collapsed while only the lamp addressed them. First Deborah, haltingly, then Father, passed through the door. "They tell me at school," he said, casting about as if some expected element were missing, "that you boys give a good haircut." Crack! A long handled pushbroom, until then leaning peaceably against the door jamb, clattered from its niche and blocked their path. Its wide bristles, like a man's black mustache, nipped the toes of Father's rutted brogans, startling him.

But this harmless old pushbroom was, after all, like the silent one Mother used to clean her kitchen floors—without "raising a speck of dust!"; Mama hated stiff straw brooms that "stir up the dust", ruining good food and defacing furniture. When Mama wasn't looking, Deborah loved to swish these friendly black bristles—"filthy with germs"—curving them with that soft, tickling sensation against her palm. Why, even the town barber gave Sam a long handled pushbroom. Those sinewy black arms made it glide forward over the checkerboard floor in long, blowing strokes until the dusty clumps of hair, grayed with talc, disappeared under the curtain of green and yellow streamers that hid the mysterious back room.

That town barber hogging his cash register world up front, had porcelain and leather and mirrors to help him, clouds of glittering steam rising from the sinks. Ebony paddles of the ceiling fan worried his air, never disturbing the curtain at all. Deborah, sitting very still, detected movement on her arms and fine hairs around her face. Sickly sweet smells floated out to the sidewalk, where men in straw hats lounged against the lamppost and elegantly smoked hand-rolled cigarettes; or in the shade of awnings, magisterially propped their feet on car bumpers, spitting tobacco juice into the gutter, backslapping and deciding the fate of things. Smells of the barbershop mingled out there in the strong sunshine with gasoline and hot tar odors wafting up from the street. The town barber kept trade jumping with schemes and special rates for these men: masks of dreaming lather and steaming hot towels, then jokes and stories that he snickered in their ears while he clipped. He kept Sam to sweep his floor and shine shoes for customers. They got to climb up right by the plate glass windows and preen themselves in the wooden seats mounted high like thrones with steps going up to them. Sam's muscles, taut as banjo wires, he jackknifed low working over their shoes, popping his shine rag with the report of a gunshot. Customers stared at their newspapers, or less curiously the top of his head, or sideways through the plate glass window, regally watching the street. Later Sam whisked stray hairs from their clothes while they dug in their pockets for coins and the barber dusted their necks with talc.

Sun, striking the plate glass, rippled in the black man's marcelled hair like sunbeams playing on water. Deborah believed that every good and magic thing in this world began in the back room, under the black hand; and though no one can profitably speak of extraordinary events in a barber's shop, the prospects of these are nonetheless luminous, and in private to be marvelously entertained: their unshaped promises like radiant vapors, the dazzle of ice crystals in drifts of snow, or a young girl's secrets dissolving in air.

Fairies danced back there in the diaphanous garments of spring, and people were made well. She imagined long lines of the sick brought in on stretchers, winding down the alley in back of the barbershop; they would die there, without the black man who came out and patiently placed his hand on their foreheads. In her Sunday School pictures, it was the pastel colored Good Shepherd Jesus who performed miracles–but in her memory and certitude, it was Sam.

He made toys, too, that came alive and talked to children: tiny animals—elephants, tigers, bears, who when you took them home grew huge and filled up all your rooms. And even mechanical things which he endowed with minds and voices, his special tops and whistles and boats and small incarnated rubber figures of nursery rhymes: Mistress Mary, Quite Contrary, disconsolate in her filmy white gown with pink rose at the bosom; Jack Sprat with sailor suit and flat beribboned hat; Simple Simon in his knickers and tall prickly hat like a loaf of bread, gobbling whole stacks of the pieman's wares! Hosts of such folk peopled her waking hours, and mingled with the dreams of night.

He never spoke to her or touched her. His name was Sam the bootblack man. When Deborah saw him bustling through the curtain doing barber's chores, or snap-popping his shine rag across the toes of oblivious customers' mirror-polished shoes, the veins and muscles of his forearms floating darkly sensuous under the skin, and sun from the dust-thick window vibrating in his satiny hair—she wondered what important business they'd managed to interrupt him at now . . .

Soon she thought of Sam as Adeline's husband. Black nurse Adeline she remembered with no distinctness save the images learned by heart from the dog-eared snapshot that she rehearsed in her hands on cold windy afternoons while playing on Mother's bedroom floor, waiting out Mother's "nap-time." She had to fish the picture from a high bureau drawer: There in the small, cracked print stands fierce Adeline, remote as always in her white uniform with her kerchief standing up in the wind like a white torch lending an exotic look to that sharp-boned face which, at Mother's command, stares austerely into the sun; she's holding a fat-faced white baby on her hip and the soles of the tiny shoes kick up toward the camera. This baby Deborah can never quite reconcile with herself. She can almost remember that back yard with roses, the line of white pickets, low and drooping. Her heart turns over every time she finds the small frame garage in the background, with Father's first Chevrolet parked half inside.

The baby's fists flail energetically, her dark hair stubbornly escapes the knit toboggan hat topped with a round knob. "That's called a pom-pom," Mother, after her nap and bath, would supply pleasantly over crochet work, leaning back in the big wing chair, the hook of her shiny needle jabbing in and out. Mother's dark hair, grey in streaks, waved smoothly back from her forehead; the ecru ball of thread unwinding in her lap fed a new doily taking shape in her hands. Deborah sprawled on the living room rug in awe of Mother, but tried to recognize Adeline's inevitable white kerchief tied severely low across her forehead, hiding the brush of hair. Or did she only wear it that way in this Kodak shot for Mother, who somewhere in front of Adeline held the black box level, shading the viewfinder with her cupped hand, just so, to protect the reflected pair of images inside–black woman, white baby–from the ravenous sun? To Deborah, Adeline nicely matches Sam, high cheekbone for high cheekbone.

Deborah missed Adeline–urgently if vaguely–like she'd had an arm or a leg cut off. The "missing" never stirred in one place, identifiable to be assuaged–but surrounded her with sweet achings. They could talk and talk –"Would you like to visit Adeline?", Mother would tease, lightly amused at Father's joke: "Sweet A-do-line . . . Will you be mine?" he sang to Deborah, mimicking barbershop quartets.

Mama swore that black maids always hid her kitchen spices in slips of waxed paper which they folded into packets and slipped down their brassieres. When she thought she smelled "spices in the air!"– she ran to the kitchen and the tall cabinets to peer into her little tins of spice, weigh them in her palm, calculate her losses. This business mystified Deborah, but Daddy laughed and shrugged, "What's a little spice?" He promised to take her to Adeline's house–but they never went, and it was Adeline she longed to touch . . .

* * *

The kerosene lamp never ceased hissing as if to kill everything within reach, and patterns of shadows cast by the white glow repeated themselves on every wall. The long handled pushbroom blocked their path. Deborah turned to run, but bumped into Father. The wallet stuffed in his front pants pocket jumped leather hard against her sore earlobe, jostling the scab, so that it stung as freshly as if the town barber had just cut it.

"Scaredy-cat!" Father chided. With his familiar little push between her shoulder blades, he urged her deeper into the strange room. The circle of lamplight ended abruptly in four dusky corners now come alive with a soft rumble of voices, the scuff of respectful feet, the rustle of starched white cloth moving in and out of shadow, musical clinkings and squeaks from a dimly seen barber's chair being turned to a fine adjustment. The broom hemmed her in by the angle of its handle and bristles, and to reassure herself, as she started to step over it, she reached down to stroke the magnificent black mustache–but the long wooden handle snagged her foot. She tripped over the unfaithful broom and fell. Scrambling up, she ran straight past Father toward the door. "Whoa!" With one quick hand, he caught his skittish girl by the waist and held her at arm's length, teasing, while she, doubling over, pitted her full weight against the flat of his palm. He spun her facing back into the room.

Two towering barber chairs–broad arms, chrome fittings at head and foot rests–rose majestically out of the shadows on either side of the imitation brick fireplace that also floated into view, line upon ruled line of fake brick and black mortar printed on the cheap asbestos siding Mother said "poor-white-trash" used for fighting off the cold that whistled through their tar-paper shacks.

To Deborah's left, stooping out of the shadows, the head barber, a tall solemn black man with long straight nose and high cheekbones, ceremoniously cranked down the first chair, his white smock rustling coolly. His marcelled hair sparkled in the boom of yellow lamplight, then he turned, receding into shadow to fetch a short piece of board, ornamented with wire handles, which he carefully supported over the chair's black leather arm rests. With flicks of his whiskbroom, he readied her seat. On Deborah's right, in the second chair, the stocky black assistant, also in white smock, sat crosslegged, jauntily swinging his foot and paring his nails with a flash of jack-knife.

"I think she'll be alright," Father said, nodding briskly to the assistant. With the off-putting air of having thought of it first himself, this man snapped his knife shut and jammed it in his hip pocket. Not bothering to rise, he swiftly reached into the shadows and passed across the fireplace to the head barber an evil looking clipper whose mouth and teeth gleamed silver in the lamplight. With a snarling burst the battery-operated contraption sprang to life in the long fingers of the head barber. A wet chill spread from the base of Deborah's skull. Vibrations multiplied in her knees, as she recalled the lonesome clamor of spring lamb-shearing contests that Father, with his constant desire to instruct, made her watch. To Mother, who despised dust, and did not go to rodeos and fat-stock shows but only waved good-bye from the porch, he tossed a promise that colorful events would teach their only child many useful things.

In pale March, the transparent fronds of budding mesquite cast their greenish haze over vacant lots and roadside. Father and daughter drove outside of town through warm air perfumed by the tiny yellow blooms of algerita, past rows of shacks where "poor-white-trash" lived and Mother came to bargain for servants when she'd tired of "black help." Down the gray highway they drove to the bawling pens and manure stench of this year's Fat-Stock Show.

Loudspeakers blared over car tops glinting in the sun. Hundreds of twinkling flags cracked in the wind, silk souvenir kerchiefs shimmered, the patriotic bunting flew. Shiny ribbons of red and blue satin, stamped in gold FIRST or SECOND PRIZE, fluttered from the split-cedar railings that corralled hogs, heifers, and fatly blinking sheep. In the big arena tubas groaned and puffed "HOLD That Ti-ger! . . . HOLD That Ti-ger!," for the cowboys roping fast bolting calves, and bronc-busters "glued in the saddle" as enraged horseflesh pitched and exploded under them: "Ladies and gentlemen, all four feet off the ground!"

Every male like Daddy who showed his face downtown at rodeo time without a silk bandanna tied around his neck risked being "arrested" and tried on the spot for his sins by a judge in a ten-gallon hat and cowboy boots, and stuck in jail. The chickenwire pens occurred on street corners one per business intersection, rigged up and policed by members of the Chamber of Commerce, all ranchers, merchants, pharmacists and the like. You had to do what they said, and the price he had to pay for not sporting a flamboyant colored silk was twenty minutes in the chickenwire hoosegow enduring in good humor the calls from the street, and fifty cents for a cussed "sissy scarf" he'd have to wear until he got out of sight of the ranchers. In the month of March it was rare for the County School Superintendent to get home without two or three kerchiefs stuffed in his coat pockets. "How many times you go to jail today?" Mama jibed while he reached around behind his back to Deborah and shame-facedly made her a present of the silky kerchiefs with their florid depictions of Wild West cowboys in action—lassoes twirling, their gigantic mounts rearing on their hind legs, churning the air with powerful hooves. Why couldn't he wear one like the other men? Why did he have to be different?

Sometimes she felt proud seeing him set off from the men on the street, even when she noticed that the mighty ranchers in their hand-tooled boots didn't really tip their Stetsons to Daddy, but slouchingly brought the tips of well manicured fingers up to their roll-brims and generally kept right on going unless they had a bone to pick about the money his schools were spending; then they were interested enough. And sometimes he took her with him to his classes at the Junior College, and let her draw on the blackboard at the back with a squeaky piece of chalk while he talked to his student nurses about child psychology. She liked to turn around and watch them from behind, their shoulders and backs tensed, their heads bowed, writing down every word he said in their notebooks.

*   *   *

During the lamb-shearing contest behind the rodeo grandstand, in slats of shade from the bleachers, the crowd roaring, stomping, rattling the planks overhead, father and daughter waved their hands to part the dust smarting their eyes, gritting their teeth, as they watched the cowboys throwing lambs hard on the ground. The lambs' hopeless whirling of legs sickened Deborah who jerked backward into the crowd; yet Father always hugged her to his hip with a clamp of his hand and a judicious waggle of his toothpick, jingling change in his other pocket. He rocked back and forth on his heels to ease a certain overflow of excitement, while she trembled with the soft thrashing legs and shivering bodies. The heart-broken bleating climbed, in waves of nausea, on the din of electric shears. A lamb finished, the furiously sweating men in roll-brim Stetsons and high heels jerked their hands up clear of the victim to signal the timekeeper, and fell back, yelling "Bring another lamb!"

The shearing truck was alive with hungry machinery, whirring belts and gears and long black hoses attached to each man's shears ripping the gray wool in sheets that skimmed off the lambs and folded softly to the ground. These men left lamb after lamb bleating in the dust, nicks of blood rising through the wooly, pinkish skin, unable to rise without the slap across their quivering flanks to bring them rearing up, legs buckling, through billows of dust. . . .

*   *   *

Father delivered Deborah to the head barber's chair against the wisdom of small feet that stumbled; his attentive hand propelled her through funnels of lighted silence, hazy yet so violently real in the lamp's glare that she wanted to break off pieces and taste, like she did when the "germy" cotton candy Mama forbade her sailed by at rodeos in the hands of others. But quicker than thought could take root, the cold metal footrest bit her ankle with a sting like the bite of shears, startling Deborah and plunging her arms-first into the spongy leather cushion; it gushed with dankness as Father barked his short, embarrassed laugh. He scooped his baby onto the precarious little board and settled her there like so many potatoes in a sack.

The tall barber made solemn adjustments of the headrest that whispered its tissue secrets in her ears; lamplight glittered in his crimped hair as he stooped to work a lever that jolted the chair and Deborah up, up, up toward the murky ceiling until she stopped—eye level with the men's shoulders. The busy assistant stropped a razor against a wide, belt-like piece of leather that swooped down behind the chair. His broad strokes put ominous swishes of light into Father's voice reassuring her, "It'll only take a minute!" Deborah waited, numb with expecting the spurt and bite of shears. Her earlobe throbbed, and she wanted to pluck it off and toss it into the buzzing silence.

The squat assistant loomed closer, and lowering himself over her so as to blot out Father, began to sing, his large teeth picking up light as he purred out a tune about an old river man, his boat, and a banjo lost on the flood. How it tunnelled out of his chest! Hums lingered behind his broad nose, the words metallically burning into Deborah's face. The tall barber did hurried things with her hair as if birds were caught in it, metal objects touching her head with cold points of fear. The short man sang with his face thrust down to her level, his eyes roaming white and glaring through the darkness, his fists clamping her dovelike hands to the armrests as if, poor weak things!, she'd carelessly traded away her hands and they'd been replaced by these fists; sharp calluses cut her skin. But his hands, while tough, felt warm and greasy, too. They held the comfortable spice of the smoke-house, hams and sausage, not at all like Father's, which were softly redolent of Lucky Tiger hair tonic. Against the myriad lights of the lamp's reflections in the windows, she squeezed her eyes shut, and frowned deeply inside herself to drive away an army of mirrors that she sees behind her eyelids, flash upon flash, encircling the room.

Through storms of dread she hears tambourines shimmer the room like fairy wind, needling the sore earlobe and withering each shallow breath. Father unfolds a limp dollar bill from his wallet, drops it in the tambourine, generously extinguishing the bright quarters. His voice climbs over the drone of shears, admonishing the tall, solemn black man to take good care of his child who has been hurt once by a careless barber. That solicitous voice dying away faintly ricochets off the invading walls of mirrors just waiting behind her tight shut eyelids; a spasm of dread anticipation ripples through her body, her head turns sharply to one side against the tissued headrest; the snarl of the shears hesitates in an off-on stutter as the tall barber fails to follow accurately enough her sudden movement–her earlobe is pricked again! The heat knifing up commands her hands to rise, touch!

But her impossible hands cannot move, trapped on the armrests under the steady weight of gray-knuckled fists pressing down. The weight of mountains, oceans, years descends. A few feet in front of her, Father's dark bulk stoops, displacing the squat assistant whose usefulness, like old nurse Adeline's, is done. Watching his child's face, her clenched expression, Father characteristically tucks a hand behind his back, eager to rescue his fatherly word–"Here's where they'll do it right!" He diligently inspects her clipped neck for flaws, while Deborah suffocates under clouds of springtime dust at lamb-shearing and lulls herself in a trance of fear, watching him through slitted eyes, and wondering, as his round spectacles shine closer, if that fatherly hand will swing around and hit to bring her rearing up like a blood-nicked lamb?

She searches his now unfamiliar face so well disguised by the lamplight that saturates every sweated line of the dome-like scholar's forehead, the short nose, the cleft chin that's fun to touch. There is no recognizing Daddy in this stranger all glazed in light. These features that would be so welcome are flattened by the light; even his schoolteacher glasses are splashed with it; she could not guess that behind them hide the mild hazel eyes and the Daddy she begs at bed-time, "Tell me one more story about when you were a little boy and lived on a farm!" His hunched shoulders and protruding belly show pink through the drenched white shirt, the wing odor of his nervous sweat envelopes her.

She has dropped full within herself, listening to bell-like throbs counting out the pain that climbs higher between father and daughter then sinks within her in receding waves like tiers of Lucky Tiger bottles crashing slowly along the mirrors in ruby sprays of glass and red liquid. She dreams of early morning rain cooling her parched neck and overheated ears. In the kerosene glare which masks the most delicate detail of contour and color, Father has not noticed anything amiss. He steps back.

The lamp sucks, gloating. The assistant looks down and resumes his stropping as the head barber, his every movement made awkward, shoves a rag bandage over Deborah's ear, avoiding Father's face, and wipes with stiff fingers at the stubborn drop of blood crawling down her neck. The school teacher sees the rough bandage and flinches with chagrin. "What the devil!" Ramming forward he examines his child's neck inch by inch. With his handkerchief, he rubs his eyes up under his glasses and looks again. Deborah, tranced by the aftermath of pain, dreams of hands holding her down powerfully. Not unlike the consuming mystery of Adeline, a blanket of terror comes over her, smoky with hams and sausage, firm as steel-black mountains.

* * *

"Hunh!" Father bent closer. A single patch of fresh blood danced up from his daughter's white collar like a bad joke stored up for him by that infernal lamp which alternately blinded–then revealed. Just like the spluttering coal-oil lamps of his dirt-poor youth that taunted him until his tired eyes refused to decipher another mark on the page, or coil of the rope or tangle of harness or teeth of the harrow that was his to mend. You'll never get off the farm! the lamp hissed. Then capriciously the grainy glare lifted–and you saw your mistakes, and what a fool you'd been made of! The spot of red on his daughter's linen spoke for itself. He dreaded Marie's arch sarcasm. What?, the crochet hook paused before its plunge, Take her child to a black barber when a white one wouldn't do?

The black man's sly fumbling and servitude was too much like his own posturing in the suddenly not distant past, matching too finely all the scratching for a living, the scraping for esteem he'd put himself through to get up outta the corn crib, rake the hay out of his hair, and earn a professional dollar. All that confounded preachment he'd spread around town and before the school board of grasping ranchers who cared for little besides the price of beef, wool, mohair, and who'd strike oil next–anything to keep their families in fancy homes and Cadillacs. They wore ignorance like a badge, acting dumber around him than they'd a right to. Scrimping on school money, es-

pecially when it came to colored or Mexicans learning the least thing—
yet they thought any education for their daughters this side of Stephens
College, Missouri, not worth the having. And the townspeople idol-
ized them: "Poor rancher" has to wait to get his money, they said. My
foot! Ever see a rancher deny his family a red cent? That one smear
of blood on his child's white collar brought it all tumbling down across
the years to this.

He jerked his toothpick out, whipped it underfoot, and scooped
the child up. Her head lolled against his shirt-breast as if her neck had
lost its strength, but even as he had taken her up, he saw the barber's
long hand releasing the wadded bandage, transferring it into the care
of his little girl's nerveless hand, the man's last effort to make things
right, the bandage in the child's grip; and now came the starched
rustling of the barber stepping back into shadow behind his chair.
Father pitted his stubborn will against the greed for revenge surging
below that liberality on which he prided himself. The barber, keeping his eyes away from them, picked up Mother's quiet kind of broom
and pushed it with trembling arms. Clumps of Deborah's hair snagged
on the splintery floor and he anxiously poked their softness into the
shadows of the fireplace. Father bore her to one side between the in-
dustrious figure with the pushbroom and the scowling partner who
had once again taken up his station in the second barber chair but
now with the shotgun retrieved from its hiding place, the double barrel broken down across his lap. A blunt shotgun shell stuck between
his teeth—the air spiked with the pungent smell of gun oil and sol-
vent—he rubbed the twin barrels with a clean rag much like the one
pressed to her ear, and the dull gleams flowed up and down with his
motion.

Father's pearl buttons mashed her cheek. As he carried her through
the door, she roused, the rectangle of light suddenly behind them,
and pressed the bandage harder so no one could snatch her earlobe.
The screen door snapped. Father's stiff-legged walk, with his belly
anger-hard, punched out rapid breaths down the path lined by dead
flower stalks, and on through clouds of fireflies.

The grey coupe steamed home through red clay hills while the barber pole churned in her stomach. Lying on Father's dusty upholstery,
she absorbed its stored rays of sun—a weak reminder of the warmth
and rightness of being wrapped in Adeline's strong arms—and felt the
chill, sour sweat rise off Father as he hunched over the wheel. Diamond

pin-points of light raced off his glasses, flared ahead into darkness. Behind the car, fireflies throbbed in gaudy streaks like comets' tails. A ripe smell of oil blew everywhere, but Deborah, slipping down within herself, down beyond the reach of one night's events, opened to the thrill of the old sweetly flowing ache for Adeline whom she had lost—and lost again—and felt not a trace of worldly anticipation.

NADJA TESICH

Intruder

I AM ON the train going from Paris to Belgrade, I got on it in Lausanne. Not now. It couldn't happen. It wouldn't be possible. Forget it. Maybe that's why am I thinking about them, that couple I met in '89, the last time I took that train when everything was still wonderful and we loved each other and Yugoslavia was all of us. The most amazing country, I told everyone, their laughter, their stories, the mad ecstasy of talks through the night and how they argue. But maybe I saw nothing, or saw it poorly, incompletely, the way children or lovers do, or worse. Did I push them over the edge, the couple I mean? It was not my intention. It was meant to be a simple ride. I always took that train which covers parts of Europe, most of Yugoslavia, to end up in Istanbul eventually.

It was after midnight, chilly when I got on in Lausanne. I saw no one in the car except the man in charge of the sleeper who showed me my place, which it turned out I didn't have to share. What good luck, better than having to put up with some woman who snores. I stretched out ready to fall asleep when he knocked and said, "Make sure to bolt the door with chains, in Italy it gets to be dangerous. Sometimes I doze off." He told strange tales of young robbers sneaking in and stealing everything while the entire train slept. They even chloroformed an American woman once and stole all her jewels. At the Yugoslav border, it's smugglers of blue jeans, levis mostly. Not dangerous, he said, but hard to catch. He asked for my passport, and I gave it to him—he said this way I wouldn't be disturbed by the fron-

274

tier guards. I bolted the door with chains and slept on, better than in any hotel for some reason, as the train rocked and sang and cities passed by. After three years I was going home.

In the morning when I woke up, we were in Yugoslavia already, somewhere near the border. It was sunny outside, a landscape of white stones, here and there a village perched on the hilltop. I heard voices outside, different ones. From now on there were only Yugoslavs left on the train, and I had to decide what to do, keep quiet or talk, and if I do, how to answer the question—who should I say I am. I am not a spy, nothing illegal, but still have to invent everything: where I come from, my temporary occupation. It's not good to say I'm a writer—even in the States—because they don't act naturally after that, but here it's even more serious—to tell the truth and say New York would lead to questions, long detailed ones: do I know so-and-so in Queens and so-and-so in Brooklyn, how much do I make, what sort of car do I drive, I must be really poor not to have one. Tiring questions, facts and figures with the end result that I don't get to know anything about *them*. I know this; I have told the truth before. So what I usually do is pretend to be someone else: an ordinary Yugoslav woman, a teacher for example. It works. Same as in the States. But it was September already, what would a provincial teacher be doing on this train: a problem, and to invent a sick relative in Paris would get me all entangled. That guy had my American passport in addition. I'd better not say anything, just relax. I picked up a book, was trying to reread *The Idiot* after many years.

I would have continued this way if it hadn't been for coffee. The man in charge of the sleeper was making it next door, the smell was strong, intoxicating. I opened the door, said, "Could I please have some, too?" And he said, "Sure, wait about five minutes." He was making it on a little burner, one at a time, cups of Turkish coffee in a brass container, asking some people if they wanted it bitter or sweet. He was inefficient, that's for sure; he could have had a larger pot, he could have made it all at once and they could add their own sugar, I thought. I suggested these improvements but he only shrugged, a who cares kind of shrug. Oriental fatalism I suppose; they never got rid of it.

He had given a cup to a stocky man in a bright green suit with wide lapels, then another to a tall gray guy. Was my turn next, where was he going with that cup? I heard the stocky one say, "Everything is better quality; even the houses last longer." I gathered he came from the States and was now bragging about his store, his car, his motor boat, but when he started convincing them how the houses made out of wood are much better and last longer than anything in Europe because they have special long-lasting wood in the States, I was outraged. Why were they listening to him; did they really believe that anything made outside Yugoslavia is better? "It's not true," I said, unaware I had switched sides. "They build wooden houses because wood is cheaper, but wooden houses don't last longer. Look at those villages up there!" We were somewhere in Slovenia.

I realized I had opened my mouth. I was standing in the hall and it was too late to stay noncommitted, the way I had originally intended. Then the guy with wide lapels said, "Oh, you live there, too?" and there it was–I was not lying about my residence. It seemed too complicated to invent something on the spot. And soon the inevitable followed, again too fast for me to think up something else. When I said, "writer," it was all over. Too late. Damn! It hadn't happened to me in years.

The man in a green suit didn't defend the wooden houses. He said nothing after that. I saw I had embarrassed him, had in fact stopped what was to be pleasant bragging about his life in Milwaukee. Now he knew I knew better. In front of me I saw not a well-to-do person but a small grocer who could come here and pretend for one summer to be someone else. I felt bad. I had destroyed it for him. It wasn't my intention. I should have stuck with *The Idiot*, never opened my mouth. Then the tall gray man said, "It's expensive isn't it, to come here all the way from New York. It would be impossible for us." I said, "My ticket is cheaper than the Paris-Belgrade plane." Everyone perked up, including the guy who should have been making my coffee. They calculated, asked for the address in Paris. They wrote this down, I gave them my pen. I was surprised the grocer didn't know about this, but maybe they don't have such charters from Milwaukee. When my coffee came, I left them, having nothing more to say. From the smell outside in the hall, they were having another round.

I dozed off again, unable to concentrate on *The Idiot*, when the tall gray man appeared suddenly inside my compartment and sat down in front of me. He was very thin, and still handsome if it weren't for the ashen color of his skin. It must be really true what they say about heavy smokers; I had never seen it before.

He offered me one of his Marlboros, wanted to know if I am

really a writer because he is one, too, then, not waiting for my answer, went on in the manner that's most natural to Yugoslavs (and quite different from anywhere else) to tell the story he had been trying to write his whole life ... well, for many years. This urgent need to tell, to communicate, is so ordinary here (again I need to explain) and it could be anyone, a very simple person, a teacher, a plumber, or this one, who is a writer. Why is their, our, need to communicate so great?

He said, "It's about a woman who took over our household when I was a boy. She'd come out of somewhere, I didn't know who she was." It was a wartime so it made no difference, maybe she was a cousin, maybe not; those years were difficult; I was completing his thoughts. He didn't know more except that her influence over him, his father, his whole family was enormous. "She just took over," he said again. I was going to ask him *how*, but forgot it because he started talking about her nails and how they were long and painted. Nobody had nails like that. This is one detail he remembered well, and her blonde hair. I looked at my nails for some reason; no, they are not painted or long. Very ordinary, chopped off. "I don't know why she came or why she left," he said; all that confusion of the war years, I thought. Suddenly his face lit up; he got very excited, started on another cigarette. "Listen to this now," he said. "Many years have passed and here I am married, with a child on a bus when I see her, right in front, next to the monument to the revolution, you know the one. I jump off the bus with my daughter, who is screeching and yelling and I see her right in front of the monument, but in the next moment, by the time I get there, she has disappeared. Gone! I had the impression she simply vanished in a huge circle of light."

"Was it really her?"

"Absolutely," he says.

"Did she see you?"

"She wouldn't recognize me–I was a kid then."

"How could she look the same?" I asked.

"I saw her. She simply vanished, disappeared in that circle of light," he repeated.

Now the door opened; a pleasant looking middle-aged woman with pink cheeks came over and introduced herself: his wife. "It's time to have lunch," she said.

I ate nothing, didn't bring anything with me except some chocolate from Lausanne. But I wasn't hungry at all, too obsessed with his story. I thought and thought about it. No, it wasn't finished; yes, it would have to be worked on. I ran up to their compartment, two doors down, and said, "Why not make it from a child's point of view—it would make more sense. Then you don't have to tell who she was and what she was doing there. People are more mysterious when we're kids, don't you think?" I was as excited now as he had been before.

"I haven't thought about it," he said.

"You mean the child's point of view?"

"Everything. What's important to me is that she disappeared in front of the monument to the revolution in a huge circle of light and I *wasn't* a kid when it happened."

"It doesn't matter. Why not make it a circle then, a fairy tale, see . . . the first time you see her you're a kid and it's in front of the monument and when she comes into your house it's already the second time you . . ."

"Wait, what would I be doing on the street that day? I wasn't there." How silly he is. "It doesn't matter," I said. "It's just a story. Your dad was taking you to a football game."

"He couldn't have been doing that during the war. It would be a different story. And there was no monument to the revolution then. It was still a monarchy, don't you remember?"

"No, I don't, I wasn't born yet," I said, "but still it makes no difference. The street was the same, right, and there was probably some sort of monument at that square." Why is he so stuck on realism? The essence is what he should be after.

"Yes there was. The Unknown Soldier, I guess."

"There you have it. So . . . you see her right there at age seven, on the same spot as when you're grown up and when she takes over your house again it's even better . . . it's more spooky, a full circle of fascination," I said, feeling very excited.

"Yes," he said.

"The only thing left is to write it." I said sounding like someone I knew. "Maybe you should do it," he said. "You probably left as a child, right?"

"Yes, but this is your story. I would feel bad. It's almost there," I said.

"It doesn't matter," he said. "You can have it."

"Of course it matters, if you've been thinking about it."

"I'll probably die like that," he said, all gloom, "in one big flash of white light, I am sure of it." Our own gloom is so big it borders on joy. You sing and break glasses in both.

"Write it before you go," I tried to joke.

"He doesn't *really* write," she said: her first words. "He just pretends."

I had thought she was asleep, but now she sat up.

"It's not true," he said, "I did tinker with all those stories before life took over."

"When was that?" she said.

"You know. I just changed my mind later, sort of gave up on it."

"That's what you say," she said.

"There's a lot of worthless scribbling around," he said.

"At least they do it. Do you want some spinach pie?" she said and cut me a slice.

We sat and ate. I didn't know if he wrote or didn't; it made no difference to me except that he wanted to. Theirs was an odd sort of marriage I decided. Still, it was best not to judge it. He was smoking cigarette after cigarette. He had two cartons next to him, red and white Marlboros bought for pennies, he said. I smoke too but this was too much. I left them, picked up my book again. Croatia already. In Zagreb we had to change cars–the sleeper stayed here. The "American" got off the train, and I got ready to move my suitcase. Briefly, I was tempted to get off then take a local to the coast–why not go to Dubrovnik and see a friend on the island of Brac? Can't do everything. Maybe on the way back, why not.

The writer appeared and and said he had found a compartment for the three of us together. There's nothing unusual about this invitation–on a half-empty train, a Yugoslav will sit next to another person–two is even better. They can't stand to be alone; they thrive on this togetherness. "Sure," I said. But from Zagreb on I was in trouble. He smoked like a madman. Pack after pack, coughing and smoking. I opened the window, sat next to it. She complained about the smoke but didn't like the draft. She worried about her back. He got up, smoked outside, came back to talk. She wanted to know if I dye my hair. I said no. She was surprised. "Most Serbs are dark", she said. "Before the Turks, they were not," he laughed. I learned he was a professor, had translated many books, famous Russians, had prefaced others, and now they were coming from London, where he had attended an international conference of Dostoyevskians. "Isn't it funny?" I said, "I had been trying to reread *The Idiot*, but liked it less and less." "He had a major impact on American authors," he said. "Maybe he did but I never saw before how melodramatic he was. Some of it reads like a soap opera," I said. "Wait a minute . . ." he started and stopped. "Where are those papers?" he said to her. He looked panicky.

"You have them," she said.

"No, not the tickets, the papers," he said. He was going through his pockets, one by one.

"He is a madman," she said. "He'll turn everything upside down." He was examining everything around him, his movements faster. "For Christ's sake try the black hand bag," she said.

"It's not there. I gave them to you," he said.

"I gave them back, after you did the same craziness in Milano, do you remember?"

"What if we lost them?" he moaned.

"Please don't go into the suitcases again," she screamed.

He couldn't help himself. I saw it. Nothing could stop him. My sympathy was huge: I understood him. Am I not like that? About a photo of a dead relative, or my thoughts on a piece of paper. But this man was bigger, he was truly possessed. "What do you need them for?" I said.

"To get paid when I get back. You need to show tickets and the bills. You must have them." He turned to her.

"You can have mine," I said.

"Yours are no good, you got on in Lausanne."

He went on and on; he had emptied one bag. Then I saw a moment of relief I know: he had found them. They were in the first bag he had examined, where she said he had put them, but they were not visible under the pile of junk, newspaper clippings, cards, my charter address I bet. She snatched the papers, put them in her own patent leather bag.

I had to laugh. They were a comedy team. What a wonderful marriage, I decided, what freedom, how nice to be able to bicker openly like this in public. No, I couldn't do it. Too Western, too bad for me. Inhibitions and such.

She was laughing, too. "You should have seen him in London," she said. "When we got lost on the subway and he had both of our passports and before that we got off at the wrong train stop in France."

"It's not my fault," he said. "Nobody told us the difference between Pas de Calais and the Port de Calais."

"... then we had to take an expensive cab to make it to the ship ... and sure enough, coming off in England we ended below, with the animals. Just us, can you imagine?"

I had to laugh again. Chaplin.

"You should have seen him in Paris, running, running, and I am running behind him, and the only thing we bought in Paris are his damned books. I didn't even get to have my hair done." Her short brown hair looked "done" to me, but women get strange about their hair.

He winked at me. "Yes," he said, "it's all true. See those suitcases up there? Just books. I hope we get a cab. I'll bet anything we get in late."

I got worried now. Nobody knew I was coming. "Is it hard?" I asked. "I don't even have a hotel room."

"We'll put you in a cab," she said.

"Wait a minute, what did I do with that copy of Trotsky's letters in French?" he asked, panic in his voice again.

"Please stop now. It's in the brown suitcase. Nobody cares about your damned book. He really gets obsessed," she said.

"I ran after one beauty for about ten years and the woman finally gave in. I have it," he said.

"So what?" she said. "It's water-damaged."

"It's too bad, there was a leak in the old house and it ruined several pages."

"Half of them are moldy," she said. "You can't breathe in our place. We only have one bedroom apartment and everywhere you turn it's books and books and his smoking and books under the bed and ..."

"I would have invited you to sleep over but it's too small," he said.

"It's just one night," I said. "I'll stay with my relatives after that. Where did you stay in Paris?" I asked.

"Near Saint Michel, too expensive for us," she said.

"The food, too?" I asked.

"Oh sure," she said. "Look at this–all this cheese which I think is rotten ..."

"That's its natural color," he said.

She had orange-colored cheese in her hands.

"... this much cheese and this bread and that pie ... well ... in Belgrade I could have prepared a really nice meal for four ... let's say a kilo or two of very good meat with vegetables–let's say sauteed potatoes and even something extra like a chocolate cake." I knew she knew how to shop and cook well by the way she said "cake." Her hands were preparing it, carefully separating egg whites.

"I know a cheap place in Paris," I said. "It's a university dorm with rooms for two—not fancy, but clean. I'll give you the address." It would make no difference to him where he stayed.

"She wouldn't like it," he said. "They put on airs where she comes from."

"Why should I care? I saw nothing either in London or Paris. I just ran and ran, chasing after his damned books," she said.

"You ought to go there by yourself," I said to her. She looked at me like I'd said something strange.

"She would be afraid to leave me alone," he said. "And she couldn't stand to leave our daughter alone and her grandchild plus my young assistant might . . ." Suddenly, as if experiencing a violent thought, he stopped, was rummaging again. "Where did I put that notebook?" he said.

"He is insane," she said and winked at me. He was. The two of us were laughing together, something like complicity between us. He was a child to her, I decided, someone to take care of.

"How old is your grandchild?" I asked.

"Two, with dark curly hair—oh, he is gorgeous. Are you married?" she said.

"It's like this . . ." I began telling her.

"I found it!" he shouted happily. "See here, I've jotted it all down." I couldn't read what he had written, but it was short, two paragraphs of it. "This is another one I've been trying to write," he said. "My grandfather had a large estate by the river with a vineyard, orchids, I remembered my summers like that—lying in the tall grass near the Danube as the white ships passed."

"And your story?"

"You see, after the war everything was confiscated," he said.

"I know," I said. "My grandfather had a mill and a farm near the river. His wasn't confiscated. After his death I gave it all away."

"To whom?" she asked, a real shock in her voice.

"Local peasants. I thought they needed it more, and what would I do with a farm anyway," I said. "It was nice, especially the water mill. I do have second thoughts about it."

"So you come from a bourgeois family then—which one do you identify with, the middle class or the intellectuals?"

"Neither," I said, not having considered the question before. For him they were in opposition, I guess. Which one are you, American or Yugoslav, they ask in New York.

"The only thing that they left him is one house in Belgrade where our daughter lives now. We used to live there before," she said. "If they manage to kick out the tenants, my grandson could have the second floor later."

"Can you imagine this? My wife worries about a two-year-old's apartment."

"I worry about ordinary things, and why not?"

"What about your story?" I asked.

"You see," he said, "I went there one day about five years ago for the first time. They had turned it into some sort of miners' vacation camp. Most of the buildings were gone, orchards ruined. There were no vineyards left and this young guy says to me, 'Who the hell are you, what do you want?' The river was the same."

"And?"

"Nothing. That's it."

"The story?"

"Yes," he said.

"I think you have the mood of the return, but you need some sort of event, you need a story," I said, realizing the next second how stupid, how American, my statement was. Yugoslav writers are capable of inventing events and stories, but they don't find it necessary. The mood *is* the story to them.

"Why don't you write it," he said. "It's yours."

"It wouldn't be fair," I said. "You should do it. Don't you want to? Let's start on it now, together."

"He'll *never* do it," she said.

I resented her, in a way I hadn't before. She had no damned right. This man had it in him to write that story, or both of them. It would be nice, an accomplishment. Is this the American in me? What am I, a cheerleader, I heard an inner voice say.

He didn't answer her. He had switched to other writers, Dostoyevsky, whom he had translated, knew by heart. He knew everybody—not just the Russians, he knew American literature but didn't like anyone alive. His favorite, Faulkner, belonged in Latin America; he would have been happier there. He was talking with passion—his students must love him, I thought.

"How can you talk so much?" she said. "Doesn't your tongue ever get tired? Talk talk talk." Leave him alone, I wanted to say.

He was smoking again. I opened the window. She said, "There's too much draft." I said, "I hope I get a cab." "I'll get you one," he said. She got up to get away from the smoke and the draft.

It was in the fraction of a moment as she left, closing the glass door behind her that he said, "She is a damned bore!" the way he might have said it to another guy, a friend. I knew it was the wrong thing to say–I experienced a pain of betrayal for her. He'll never see me again; she had cooked and put up with his smoking all those years. I wished he hadn't said it. "She is just different from you," I said. I panicked next. Did she hear it? She might have. His face betrayed the same fear as mine. We understood each other well. Through the glass door we saw her back. He got up, went to her where she stood by the window, put his arm around her. She pushed him away. Then they left somewhere.

He came alone. "She is in the other compartment. She must have heard me." He went out again. He was even more upset when he came back. "She won't talk to me," he said. "What do I do now?"

I went to her. She was lying stretched out in the dark. She did hear it, I could tell. What was I now for her, an enemy, a witness? "Please come back," I said. "He is very upset."

"I'll bet," she said.

"He really is," I said. "Some of us talk too much and . . ."

She closed her eyes, a curtain of dignity. She didn't want to talk to me either. She never came back. He didn't want to talk about Dostoyevsky or anything else. He remained silent. "Go sit with her," I said. "She doesn't want me with her," he said.

Fortunately Belgrade arrived soon, but three hours late. He began dragging their heavy suitcases. My own was easy, a small duffle bag. I was only a visitor, a writer passing through, pretending. I said, "I'll go and get in line for a cab, see you there." When they appeared five minutes later, I was still there. She was not looking at me but she wasn't silent anymore. She was shouting at him. "Damn, you aren't good at anything! Go get us a cab–go be a man!" It was hopeless for me to wait like this in the line since everybody snatched the cabs way before they stopped. They were going to help me, I remembered. But it was too late for that. Still shouting, they jumped into a cab that would take them to some northern suburb. He didn't dare turn or say goodbye. I was on my own again, homeless, at two a.m., next to a large neon sign, in front of a train station.

Now everything is gone, the country and that train that linked us. Villages in flames, streets renamed, heads chopped off–can you imagine? Gone are the monuments to the revolution. A religion is on the rise. Nothing is the same, not even me. Who's that, I wonder–it doesn't sound like anyone I know. They've gone mad that's for sure, us killing them while I repeat why, how come and blame outside interference, blue jeans, Marlboros, New World Order–if only Germany didn't start the recognitions, and America too, so fast too fast–they would have bickered and made up, if only they were smarter, if only they didn't . . . My thoughts have nowhere to go, nobody to strike at, just poison. Only the Danube looks the same, even better, clean without ships, shimmering, inviting you to jump. I hear many do, more of them daily. But I am now going off, in a typical Yugoslav style, confusing you with still another story.

LESLIE WALKER WILLIAMS

Zone Sixteen

RYAN, HOLDING the jar in one hand and his penis in the other, peed into the container. Today his urine was a deep maroon, the way he imagined a red tide, although he had never seen one. He remembered a fishing trip he'd taken to Idaho years before with his daughter Jenny. They'd come upon a vividly purple lake, like a dream lake or one a child might draw. The color was nearly phosphorescent, and everything in and around the water stood preternaturally still. It was one of the most beautiful things Ryan had ever seen, the beauty enhanced by his certainty that something had gone terribly awry. The ranger had explained that Fish and Game had been purifying the lake of all trash fish, after which they intended to stock it only with trout. However, they'd released too much of the chemical and by mistake had killed everything. Ryan and Jenny had found another lake, where they had caught mostly carp.

He capped the container and carried it through the den and kitchen to the adjoining greenhouse. The plants crowded against him. His glasses fogged in the moist heat and he cleaned them on his shirt-tail, then scrutinized the Black Mission figs, the kiwis (one male, two females) twining up a beam, and the bitter melon hooking its tentacles through the bamboo trellis. He looked for yellowing leaves, signifying a nitrogen deficiency, but every plant glowed green with health. In part they were so healthy precisely because he was not. He recalled the classic instruction of stewardesses: first place the oxygen over your own mouth, then over the mouth of the infant. Otherwise one becomes like the mother in the famine, who gives all the food to the baby and ends up killing them both.

His own children no longer had any real need of him, though they dutifully came when called to pick bushels of fruit and nuts. But when he died most of the plants would die, he was sure of it. No matter how he coddled them now, when he was gone it would be only a matter of weeks for some, months for others. The ones in the greenhouse depended on him as much as a breast-feeding baby: he had to water them daily, and twice on especially hot days, which in September, the hottest month for the central coast of California, meant every day. As usual there had been no rain since May.

The trees he and his predecessors had planted out in the orchard would survive, but many of the younger trees remained pot bound, and would suffer without regular watering. In the last few years he had found it more and more difficult to put plants in the ground. It was too wrenching when the roots of a chocolate persimmon or a Tiger-striped fig were devoured by gophers.

For more than a quarter of a century Ryan had been battling the gophers. Before the drought, some of his neighbors would flood their orchards and wait with a twenty-two for the gophers to emerge. But Ryan, largely to his relief, was a poor shot. Gopher traps were another option, yet he detested prying loose the mangled animals. Instead he used to shove bleach-soaked rags into the burrows. The resultant chlorine gas, heavier than air, sank into the tunnels just as it had into the trenches of World War I, but the gophers always managed to be elsewhere. Finally he built perches for hawks, nesting boxes for barn owls, and filled his place with cats. These animals reduced the gopher population somewhat, but road noise made the raptors nervous, and the cats would just as soon kill a jay or a lizard.

Years ago he had stopped using the obvious alternative, gopher bait, when he'd discovered it worked by causing internal bleeding: when cut anywhere gophers quickly bled to death, due to their peculair inability to coagulate. Nonetheless, despite his distaste for such barbaric methods, he always encaged the roots of those trees he did plant out in wire and broken glass. It seemed fairer to use a visible device, as though that made the animals somehow responsilbe for their own demise.

Still, most of his trees from the last few years remained in their twenty gallon containers in and around the greenhouse. The roots of the older ones had grown through the drainage holes and into the ground, so that he couldn't have moved them even if he'd wanted. His son Carl had offered to trap the gophers for him, and help him transplant the trees, but Ryan had reclined. He didn't like other people handling his plants.

As Ryan continued his daily inspection he noticed the watering can, full of rusty nails, hunkering beneath the potting table. This was his former method for providing plants with iron. Two years ago his citrus trees had begun to yellow. He had given nitrogen supplements but the yellowing had continued, proceeding from the outer edges inward, until eventually each leaf looked as if it had been backlit, for educational purposes, to reveal its innards.

Once he had researched and diagnosed the problem and devised the nail treatment, the plants had responded slowly but steadily. Shortly after that, Ryan had begun to urinate blood, which in its early, diulted stages had resembled the rusty water. He remembered when it had first occurred to him to cure his plants with himself. As he stood urinating a bright red he had thought of the Masai, tenderly slitting the throats of their cattle to drink the blood, but never taking so much that it would harm the animal. Midstream, Ryan had seized the empty plastic trashcan beneath the sink, finished urinating into it, and hurried to the greenhouse. The citruses' recovery had been remarkable, and he had preemptively treated all the plants. It was hardly a practice, however, that he could recommend to others in the Society of Rare Fruit Growers.

Ryan himself had refused all treatment. Had his wife Elizabeth still been alive he liked to think she would've understood, though he suspected that if she were there he might've agreed to the radiation and chemotherapy. They had understood their responsibility to keep each other company. As she was dying on the floor of the living room nearly three years ago he had reminded her of this obligation, but over the clamorous pain of her failing heart she had seemed unable to hear him.

The urine was still warm and Ryan rolled the jar between his palms. He glanced about him but everywhere the plants appeared vigorous and shining. They had never, in fact, looked better. Perhaps they would indeed live beyond him. He unscrewed the cap and emptied his urine into the bitter melon. By administering regular jolts of fertilizer he hoped to coax it into ignoring the shortening days.

Elizabeth would have enjoyed these months he now had to prepare for his departure, but often Ryan couldn't think of what to say to his children and grandson. *Espalier cherimoyas; prune back ninety percent of a grape's new growth; never reverse the twining direction of a vine or you will kill it.* These were the things he would pass on, but of what use were they to anyone save himself? Neither Carl nor Jenny had a garden and it seemed sadly true to Ryan that children came to avoid, if not despise, what the parents loved.

Such had not been the case with him. His parents had run a nursery and his grandfather had grown prize-winning roses. Ryan remembered the afternoons of his youth, concocting potting mixes and meandering through aisles with a long-necked watering can. The whole family had hands cracked and lined with dirt, and there was no shame in it. His father had suffered later with arthritis but Ryan had escaped such a torture.

It was from his father that Ryan had learned to prune, which to this day remained one of his favorite tasks. Pruning offered a pleasure not possible, though often anticipated, with children: the ability to control the form and direction of growth, to maximize beauty and production. The rules of pruning were essentially logical: remove dead, diseased, and disoriented branches. Ryan liked to think his behavior, in fact his very soul, had been improved by his work with plants, but on morose days he thought it didn't matter. Plants were only that, and had nothing to do with the sorrier, sadder actions of humans.

Ryan spotted a branch on the Fuji apple beginning to grow toward the middle of the tree. Pulling clippers from a sheath at his waist, he cut the stray shoot back. His father had tended to prune in the central leader design, emphasizing a strong main trunk. This method produced rugged trees which bore respectable crops and withstood fierce winds. By the time Ryan taught his own children to prune, he had become partial to the open center, or vase shape, which allowed light to reach the inside of the tree and ripen the fruit on the lower branches, and thus distributed the weight of the crop. A savage storm could wipe it out entirely, but the harvest was usually greater. Ryan's preference was not, however, strictly utilitarian. To stand beneath one of these trees in the early spring was to stand within a luminescent, overwhelmingly fragrant sphere of green. He would remain there for minutes at a time—inhaling deeply, his eyes wide—as though he'd been suddenly and recently frightened.

His father had also instructed him in rudimentary grafting, which Ryan now considered his true art. Although he had been an architect for over forty years, the delicate joining of one tree to another was his highest calling. The idea of it captivated him as much as the action: to force–or rather to compel, coerce, convince–one thing to grow into another, taking the benefits of each to create something better. Grafting operated on the principle that what tasted sweet to humans was generally weak, but that what tasted acrid could endure a great deal; thus the former became the scion, the latter the rootstock.

Ryan checked the soil moisture of a tree which bore plums, peaches, nectarines and apricots. He had compiled it years ago for Elizabeth, and although the grafting marks had steadily diminished, he knew they would never disappear entirely. Ryan encircled one of the scars with his thumb and forefinger. He could think of no equivalent to grafting in the human species. Children were, if anything, fruit, not grafts. In his younger years he might have believed love, perhaps even marriage, provided such an opportunity for union, but without bitterness he now knew this not to be true. He and Elizabeth had been during their best times capable of growing side by side, but there had never been any question of their being the same tree.

*   *   *

Ryan, after fortifying every plant with his iron-rich urine, had finally gone to a doctor. He had been diagnosed with bladder cancer, which Dr. Stihl said was greatly advanced and probably in his prostate as well. Dr. Stihl wanted to remove his bladder–or "the bladder," as he referred to it, as though it were merely some hypothetical organ, not belonging to anyone in particular–which he would reconstruct six months later from a piece of Ryan's intestine. In the meantime, however, Ryan would have an external bag instead, an indignity which he did not care to suffer. He thought of the last years of his mother's life, during which she had been constantly catheterized, although fortunately in her senility she had seemed never to fully grasp that fact. Sometimes she emptied the bag, with what he found a remarkable amount of self-possession, into the bushes outside the back door, where in previous years she had disposed of the grease from the Thanksgiving turkey pan. At other times she paced about her living room, heedlessly dragging the clear sack of urine behind her. When it snagged on a corner or sofa leg she would turn to him and inquire, "What's that, Dear?" as though she had never seen it before.

On the ultrasound screen he and Dr. Stihl had viewed his tumor, which appeared, if Ryan remembered correctly from pictures his daughter had shown him, to be approximately the size of sixteen weeks' gestation. He had recalled the time some six years before when Jenny had exhibited for her parents the ultrasound photo of what would soon be their first grandchild. The incident made Ryan vaguely uncomfortable, almost as if he were present at his daughter's pelvic exam, rather than merely viewing its results. The ultrasound image, murky and meaningless to him, caused Jenny to point excitedly at different blurs, saying here lay the head, there curled a leg. Ryan recognized nothing, but had pretended otherwise, as he knew was expected of him. Elizabeth had crowed and patted her daughter's stomach dotingly. Ryan distinctly remembered how the presence of infants, in utero or otherwise, made women into entirely different creatures.

"I asked them not to tell me what it is," Jenny had said. He had realized that Jenny was talking about the gender of the child, but it took him a minute to shake the sense that what they were really pondering was the very nature–monster, inanimate, human?–of the thing inside her.

Last week Ryan had had Jenny and Carl over for dinner and told them about his illness, and that he had declined treatment. He wanted to give them the opportunity their mother could not, of becoming accustomed to the idea of his death. In truth though he doubted that that would help much. You could attempt to acclimatize a tree–through exposing it to untraviolet rays, wind, and harsher temperatures prior to planting it out–but still there was always a shock. He thought it only fair, however, to let his children know he was dying, to give them at least the possibilty of preparedness.

Jenny had immediately set her coffee down, mid-swallow, and asked how far along the cancer was. Ryan had noticed her terminology, "how far along," and been tempted to use his own analogy of fetuses, but thought she might find it offensive. He had simply lifted his hands and held up an invisible globe, about the size of a grapefruit. His children had sat there stunned, as if, like a magician, Ryan had suddenly produced a rabbit or a dove from the empty air between his palms.

"How long have you known about this?" Jenny spoke in a cold, almost haughty tone. The stiff tilt of her head was, he recognized, his own mannerism, though it was mitigated by her soft curls.

"Since the doctor's a few weeks ago."

"I can't believe you could have something that big inside you and not know it until now," she said, pushing away from the table.

Ryan reddened and sat back in his chair.

"Jenny," Carl said.

"I just want to know what's really happening," she said impatiently to Carl. "I'm not going to sit here politely while he," she faced her father again, "while you die."

"He's not doing it on purpose," Carl said, placing his large hands flat on the table, as if to steady it.

"Thank you, Carl," Ryan said, regretting it when he saw Jenny's expression.

"How can you not even attempt a cure? Don't you care enough about us to try?" she asked.

"It's not about that," Ryan said.

"It's his decision, Jen," Carl said.

"That is crap. All our lives he's taught us to fight and achieve and keep the family together and now he's tossing in the towel, just like that. What if Mother were alive?"

"She's not," Ryan said, aggravated.

"Is that it?"

"There is no 'it.' "

"What if me or Carl were sick?"

Ryan flinched at the idea, as well as at her incorrect grammar.

"Carl or I," she amended sarcastically, with her usual ability to sense his silent rebukes. "Would you let us do what you're doing?"

"That's different. You're both young, and you have a child."

"So do you, need I remind you, two of them, not to mention a grandson. But what if Carl were peeing blood and had a tumor the size of a baseball in his gut?"

Carl winced and said, "Stop it, Jen." Carl's big-boned body appeared suddenly fragile to Ryan, as it had not since his son had outgrown him years ago.

Jenny ignored Carl and leaned toward her father. "Would you resist if he didn't want help?"

Ryan stared at her. "That wouldn't happen."

"Or Todd," Jenny persisted, although Ryan could see it pained her to speculate about her son this way. But she swallowed and persevered. 'What if Todd were sick and something could be done medically but Kevin and I refused? Wouldn't you fight us?"

Ryan looked at her for a long moment. She was right, of course, and also wrong–he would fight them in such an instance, but she and her husband would never refuse treatment for their child. But it didn't matter; that wasn't what she was getting at, anyway. "Yes," he admitted finally. "But it's not the same thing."

"He's right, Jenny," Carl whispered. Ryan had a sudden absurd wish that his son too would plead with him to fight for his life–that indeed Carl would fight with him, for him. But it had always been Jenny who fought him.

"I don't care if he's right. There is no right, he has no right. He can't do this." She removed her glasses and rubbed her temples, then snapped her head up to glare at him. "How long have you known?" she demanded, replacing her glasses.

Ryan took a deep breath. "About two years."

"Two years?" Carl repeated. "Dad, how could you?"

"I knew it," Jenny whispered, staring at Ryan as though he were very far away and she could just barely make him out. "I knew it."

*   *   *

Although Ryan was an architect, he had not built his own house. He and Elizabeth preferred old houses, and throughout his career he would never escape a sense of longing for dumbwaiters and widow's walks. He could have incorporated these things into plans, but he considered them sullied by quaintness when installed just for effect, rather than use. The houses he designed were ruthlessly modern and Californian: hot tubs on patios overlooking the Pacific, living rooms with ceilings two stories high.

Instead he had designed his greenhouse, which was attached to the southern side of their 1890s farmhouse. He had bought and dismantled an old Victorian greenhouse and reconstructed it himself into a large octagon, with a high arched ceiling. In the center lay an octagonal pool full of goldfish, lily pads, lotus flowers, and water caltrops. Ryan had introduced frogs, ostensibly for insect control, and they sang loudly and often. In the cold months he regulated the temperature so that any surplus hot air blew through the house, filling the rooms with the scent of orange blossoms or jasmine; the latter he had convinced to bloom almost year round. In the summer he opened ceiling vents during the days and closed them at dusk.

He and Elizabeth had moved here thirty years ago, when Jenny was a baby. Ideally, Ryan would have preferred one of the warmer climates available in the area. But they had fallen in love with the house and the land, bordered on one side by a creek and another by woods, and subsequently Ryan had made allowances for the fact that it was in Zone Fifteen.

According to the Sunset Western Garden Book's categorization of climates, he lived in one entitled, "North Coast Cold Winters." Ryan's particular frosty winters were due to the fact that his house was situated in a small valley, for cold air, like chlorine gas, sank. Such winters prevented him from growing (beyond his greenhouse) cherimoyas, jacarandas and tamarinds, to name but a few. Many of the subtropicals–Hass avocados, Natal plums–fruited poorly, if at all. The weather of this zone, the book said, was influenced by the ocean eighty-five per cent of the time, and by inland currents the remaining fifteen. Ryan wondered how such percentages could have been accurately arrived at by the book's authors, but still it pleased him to be so affected by the unseen Pacific. When close enough to hear and smell it, you entered Zone Seventeen. Freezes hardly ever occurred there, but the fog made it impossible to grow those plants most captivating to Ryan.

Zone Sixteen, on the other hand, had an ideal subtropical growing climate. These choice locales had warmer winters because they lay in thermal belts, along slopes from which cold air drained. Ryan was, in fact, surrounded by Zone Sixteen–they existed in the protected forests, on low ridges, and on southern and western facing hillsides. When he drove to town he could spot the pockets of Zone Sixteen by the fruiting avocados, and the nasturtiums flowering in the midst of winter.

If the renderings of the great masters were any indication, then Eden lay in Zone Sixteen. Paradise was not, despite the nudity of its inhabitants, in the tropics. Not with apples, anyway, which require a certain number of chill hours in order to set fruit. Recently horticulturists had attempted to develop hybrids which bore in tropical climes, but Ryan didn't see the appeal. Who would want a second-rate apple when you could eat instead a mango, a starfruit, a durian?

But here in Zone Fifteen the apples were superb, and he knew he would live to see them all harvested. Since he had broken the news to Jenny and Carl, Ryan had found himself wishing his dying would either speed up or slow down. He preferred to die at a time when the demise of the natural world would not so achingly symbolize his own. He suspected though that his wish resembled the actions of a suicide, who leaves the faucet running or radio on to assure himself that the world will continue beyond him.

It would be best to die soon, during the height of autumn–the big leaf maples aflame, and clusters of stubbly berries hanging high in the madrone's muscular limbs. Or maybe he could last until the early spring's onslaught of rain, when the bulbs began their determined ascent into air. But Ryan knew he would die in the winter, when the woods had filled with orange-bellied newts and the grey whales glided past the misty headlands on their way to Mexico.

Elizabeth had died in late January, a month after the worst freeze California had seen in decades. Catastrophe did not distinguish between zones. That December the citrus groves to the south glistened enchantingly with ice, entire crops and orchards destroyed. When the storm cleared he and Elizabeth had hiked to a nearby ridge. Even the puddles along the trail had frozen, whereas usually the forest insulated itself. Loma Prieta, for the first time in years, was covered with snow, while below them Monterey Bay arced impassively.

Before the freeze Ryan had spent hours watering everything deeply, due to the extraordinarily low humidity, and a dewpoint forecast for a frightening fourteen degrees: dryness and cold, he knew was the deadliest combination. Then with blankets and sheets of plastic, he'd covered young trees and subtropicals that couldn't take less than twenty-five degrees. When he'd returned to the house, scratched and shivering, Elizabeth had been exasperated. "Why don't you grow things that belong here, that can survive this?" she'd said. This was an old fight, akin to the one that began, "You spend more time with your trees than with your children." What could he reply? But she hadn't given him the chance to answer. "You act as though you believe we live in Hawaii, or you wish we did," she'd said, which was of course ridiculous. They both knew that much of his pleasure came from cultivating plants that were meant to grow elsewhere.

Despite his efforts, however, many of the plants hadn't survived. The temperature had plummeted to seventeen. But the duration of the cold was what did the most damage, and it had lasted three days. He and Elizabeth walked about the property afterwards, examining each tree and shrub. Tender grafts had died down to the rootstocks, and the blood orange, chilean guavas, passion fruit and white sapotes, and most of the younger trees, had died altogether.

Elizabeth was furious in the face of such loss, while Ryan simply felt dazed. Although it was devastating to have so many of his carefully tended plants die, at least it had not been by his hand. He comforted himself by imagining what he would plant next, what mistakes he had made over the last twenty-five years that now, with his greater experience, not to mention the time he had since retiring, he could rectify. In the next week he had ordered five times his usual amount from nurseries, and sketched numerous planting designs. He decided to redo the whole property. He planned wind breaks, understories, heat-retaining walls, arbors, trellises, and a walled garden in which they could have their morning tea.

Then Elizabeth had died. And the trees had come in, from all over the country, singly or in groups and pairs, their bare roots wrapped, somehow pathetically, in burlap. It was all he could do just to pot them. The greenhouse, already crowded with trees he should have transplanted, became even more jungly.

For a while he was incensed with Elizabeth. Not only had she removed herself, but by doing so she had also taken from him the one thing, besides his family, that he loved: his gardening. That spring he did no grafting, and his pruning was half-hearted and sloppy. The crops were poor by his standards but his children did not complain, although he knew they noticed.

Elizabeth had always planted a large, year-round vegetable garden, as well as flowers here and there. They had joked about the fact that for the most part he did the perennials, she the annuals: that he aimed to keep things alive and thriving, whereas she liked to watch them be born, year after year. He pored over horticultural books and magazines, seed and tree catalogues, diligently researching any intriguing culti-var or variety. She, on the other hand, simply planted what she wanted to eat or see bloom.

Many of the flowers that spring—because they were perennials, bi-ennials, or bulbs, or annuals which had dropped seed the previous year—blossomed of their own accord. But the tulips and foxgloves filled Ryan with melancholy rather than delight, just as the weather did: that relentless California sunshine that before had been such a blessing, but which now seemed an impossible mandate of happiness. The winter cover crops of fava beans and red clover overtook the vegetable garden, but because Elizabeth had planted them Ryan could not bring himself to turn them under. Some lettuce, squash, and brassicas had self-sown, but many were hybrids and thus did not come true to seed. For the first time in twenty years Ryan had to buy vegetables and fruit.

At the market one late summer morning two years ago he had looked morosely down into his cart. It contained last year's mushy apples (in lieu of his own early, crisp Gravensteins) and tasteless oranges that had, for no good reason, come all the way from Florida. Ryan abruptly considered moving, taking a trip, getting a flat in San Francisco, maybe even accepting Jenny's offer of her garage apartment. But what then would he do with his plants? Whenever he entered the greenhouse they crowded around him, drooping demandingly. The banana and papaya trees pushed impudently into the ceiling. A fig in the corner that he'd failed to water properly had one day in revenge dropped every single one of its hard and green and still inedible fruits. In the orchard a peach he'd neglected to prune was gradually dying, due to limbs so burdened with fruit that they'd broken off and torn the tree in two, exposing its now infected center.

He couldn't exactly just up and leave. The thought of returning months later to a hothouse full of brown stalks, where once there's been lush greens and blooms, was too much to bear. Besides, he didn't really want to go anywhere else. He wanted to be at home, gardening, with Elizabeth. The latter was of course impossible but the former was not.

When he returned from the market he went into the greenhouse and saw for the first time in months the clear and righteous indignation of the plants, who had come to him on good faith and not expected such surly treatment. From that moment on he pledged to care for them. The next month he urinated blood for the first time. He had felt oddly relieved. He thought then that he could manage to live until he would die. He felt, not without irony, that new lease on life that the anticipation of death had long been purported to bring. He decided not to go to the doctor, or tell his children, or do anything about it at all. Instead he watered his plants attentively, even transplanted a few out of their pots, and rotated those in the greenhouse which were becoming lopsided from growing towards the light. He meandered through the orchard, running his hand along the various smooth and ridged and knotted trunks. As the autumn progressed and the cold came on he fertilized, he pruned, and again, in the spring, he grafted.

* * *

To Todd's delight his grandfather drew his pruning shears from their sheath like a revolver from a holster, pointed them at Todd and made a shooting sound. Todd laughed his high, spiraling laugh and formed a gun with his fingers, which he fired repeatedly into Ryan's torso.

"You're dead, Grampa," he said, with his most wicked grimace. Ryan smiled nervously, as much at his grandson's face as at his daughter's obvious discomfort. This was only the second time he'd seen her since giving her the news.

"You're not supposed to smile. You're supposed to be scared," Todd instructed. Ryan adjusted his expression accordingly.

"Don't tell Grampa what to do," interrupted Jenny.

"You tell me what to do," Todd complained.

"I'm your mother, hush up." She looked directly at Ryan. "How are you?"

Ryan felt a twinge of annoyance. Such a question, innocent enough two weeks ago, now had the irritating weight of hidden meaning.

"The Brown Turkeys are coming in," he said, in lieu of a reply. He'd discovered that one advantage of age was that people let you— in fact almost expected you to—digress, be absent-minded, lose track of the direction of conversation. Jenny, however, wasn't fooled.

"I want to see the turkeys," Todd said.

"They're figs, honey," Jenny explained. "They're called that because they're the color of turkeys."

"Oh," Todd said, obviously disappointed.

"But we can pick them." Ryan knew this would cheer Todd. He had learned years ago that children always enjoyed gathering their own food, which most adults quickly tired of. But give Todd a basket and he could harvest happily until he'd claimed every visible fruit or nut.

"Now?" Todd asked.

Ryan looked at Jenny but she made no sign either way. She was, he saw, still upset with him. But he was determined not to be swayed by her. "Sure," he said. "I'll get you a basket."

In the pantry hung the many baskets that Elizabeth had collected over the years. Ryan selected one with a wide base, which Todd could not easily overturn.

They walked out to the orchard which spread over the western portion of Ryan's ten acres. The morning shone clear and fogless. Three hawks circled in the warm air currents above the nearby woods, before settling atop an old Doug fir.

"The soft dark brown ones are what you want," Ryan told Todd when they reached the fig, which he'd planted years ago at the top of the south-facing slope. The high white wall behind the tree reflected and thus increased the light and heat, making for sweet, prolific fruit.

"I know," Todd replied indignantly. Lately he had refused to admit any ignorance, an instinct Ryan could sympathize with, though it amused him.

"And leave the ones with ants," his mother said.

"I know that."

"There's nothing he doesn't know," Jenny said with an exasperated sigh. Todd ignored her, bending earnestly to his task. Ryan thought Jenny oughtn't to tease Todd so much, although he would never say that to her. But he didn't need to; she could always sense his disaproval, just as, now, he could hers.

Ryan remembered Jenny at Todd's age, tow-headed and stubby-legged. That was only a few years after they'd moved here, but time enough for him to prune the ancient fruit trees in the abandoned orchard, remove the dead ones, plant new ones. He recalled the August morning in 1965, harvesting pears with Jenny while Elizabeth, hugely pregnant with Carl and unable to bend over, had sat in a chair nearby, wearing a wide-brimmed hat. After a while Elizabeth had risen ponderously and reached into the laden branches to remove a bulbous, perfect pear. As she bit into it her water broke. Jenny had burst into peals of nervous laughter, believing her mother had wet her pants.

Ryan recalled, with some chagrin, that he had immediately thought that the amniotic fluid would make an excellent fertilizer. The following year, however, overcome with family and work, he'd forgotten to compare that tree to the others, and now he couldn't even be sure which pear it had been. He could still see Elizabeth clearly, though—her strange, massive body radiant in the sunlight, but her face shaded entirely by the hat as she gazed down at the darkening ground,

the first water that soil had seen for months. In her hand she continued to grip the pale yellow pear, its white flesh striated evenly by her
teeth, while her other hand rested protectively on her belly.

"Dad," said Jenny, lowering her voice slightly in deference to Todd's
talent for homing in on the crucial parts of conversations. He would
appear to be still immersed in play, but he would ask, without even
deigning to lift his head, "What's a tumor?" or "Where is Grampa's
wife?" or simply repeat words or phrases: mortgage, tremor, international terrorism.

"I'm fine, Jen," Ryan said preemptively. "Let's not talk about it
today."

"Talk about what?" Todd inquired.

"Nothing," Jenny said. "Something between me and Grampa."

"What, Grampa?"

"I'll tell you another time," Ryan said, feeling a sudden lurch of
sadness. How could he have forgotten he would need to tell Todd?
"You find all the figs yet?" he asked. Todd shook his head and got on
all fours to continue searching.

"We can't just not talk about it. Admit that much," Jenny said. "Are
you feeling any worse?"

"No." Ryan bent to the ground to salvage a perfect fig, miracu-
lously not yet invaded by insects. Pain shot through his abdomen
and it took all his concentration not to wince. He could no longer
bend straight over like that, a recent development. Beyond the constant tenderness in his belly, and the deep ache when he relieved
himself, he had experienced little pain, although the doctor repeatedly assured and indeed threatened him that soon this would
not be the case.

"You're being selfish," Jenny said to Ryan as she watched her son
squish figs between his fingers. "Think of Todd," she hissed.

Ryan saw Todd's head move almost imperceptibly in their direction. "I am thinking of Todd. Aren't I, Todd?"

Todd looked up and grinned. He had been caught eavesdropping
but no one had said anything about the smashed figs. "Yes, you're
thinking of Todd," he said gleefully.

"Me," Jenny said, correcting him automatically. Then she turned
to her father. "You're not thinking of me." She spoke plaintively, like
Todd did when he wanted something. "Or Carl."

"Will Uncle Carl take me swimming today?" Todd was briefly attentive, until he spotted a yellow jacket hovering around his gooey fingers and made a swipe at it.

"Don't swat. You'll just annoy it," Jenny said.

"But it's annoying me."

"That's because of the figs you squashed," she returned. "Go rinse your hands off."

Todd stood, his sticky hands extended before him, and ran downhill to the faucet, where Ryan knew he would spray water everywhere until told to turn it off.

"Alone at last," Ryan said wryly.

"Dad, please," Jenny pleaded.

"Of course I'm thinking of you," Ryan said. "I'm thinking of all of you. Do you think it would be better for me to draw it out?"

"Mother would be furious."

"I don't think it's up to you to decide how your mother would or wouldn't feel." Ryan was often irked by his daughter's assumption of his dead wife's opinions, as though Jenny had been appointed her mother's proxy. "There's no way for any of us to be sure how she would've reacted." Ryan too assumed he knew what Elizabeth would think, but after all he had known her for over forty years; she had been his wife. Surely a spouse saw more than just certain aspects of a person, which parents and children, no matter their age, seemed bound to do.

"Next thing you'll be telling us you've found God," Jenny said with a slight sneer.

"I should think you'd be happy for me." Ryan got a small thrill from her expression, which was, he noted, nearly more shocked than when he'd told her that he was dying. He bit into the fig and chewed meditatively for a moment. "Should I be so lucky," he added.

"Jesus," she said, grinning suddenly, "you gave me a fright."

Below them Todd squirted the slats of a fence. "We'd better go before he drains my well," Ryan said. He glanced at the basket by his feet. How to pick it up? If he squatted he could avoid aggravating his belly, but squatting might make Jenny suspicious. He set his jaw before bending carefully to retrieve the figs.

When he straightened he saw on his daughter's face her certain knowledge of his pain, and he recalled vividly the particular anguish of watching those you love suffer. How could he have overlooked the fact that he would cause that sensation in his children? Over and over again he would have to witness its mark on their faces, as clearly as if he had slapped them and left bruises. Unless, of course, they learned to conceal it. Perhaps he should not have told them of his illness. For a moment he wanted to give into Jenny's pleas for treatment, as if that temporary, torturous delay would change her expression rather than merely suspend it.

Unwillingly he remembered Elizabeth's body on the rug, how after she was still he had painstakingly straightened and smoothed out her pale limbs. While doing so he had recalled a winter evening years before when, after a day spent pruning his fruit trees, he had made urgent love to her. Sprawled beneath him she had stroked his cheek and murmured, "The horticulturist espaliers his wife." That memory, and his daughter's expression now, caused in Ryan such acute pain that he wondered if he were dying right then, until he realized that the pain resided not in its customary location in his gut, but radiated instead throughout his entire body—that indeed what he felt was love so suffused with sorrow and loss that he could not distinguish between them.

"I'll get that, Daddy," Jenny said, coming forward suddenly, reaching for the basket.

"I'm still strong enough," Ryan joked feebly, intending to be affably self-deprecating, for as a man with a slight build he'd never been particularly strong. But seeing Jenny's stricken face he knew that she had misunderstood. She thought he had admitted to already being weaker, but that he could still manage to lift a few measly pounds of figs. He'd have set her straight, except that sooner or later her mistake would be true.

With her fingers wrapped around the handle, he knew she simply wanted to help him, but that was something he'd never been much good at accepting. He tightened his grip. Her hand dropped forlornly then to her side and she moved away, leaving him feeling not just foolish but selfish, for what else remained for him to give her?

"Here," he said, abruptly extending his arm. "Thanks."

Jenny didn't move. She looked down into the basket, where the leaves, insects, soil, twigs, and both good and rotten fruit lay jumbled together.

"He hasn't hit the discriminating stage yet, has he?" Ryan asked, smiling. "It's all still fascinating." He swung the basket slightly between them. "Go on," he said softly, coaxing, the way he'd spoken to her when, as a child, she'd been frightened. "You take it."

Todd gave a sudden whoop, startling them. Jenny took the basket from her father's hand. "Mommy, Grampa, look at me," Todd shouted. Together they turned to watch him. He pointed the hose skyward, then stepped beneath the water and tilted his face up joyfully, gratefully, in a perfect imitation of a farmer, after a long dry spell, at last receiving rain.

WILLIAM ZINKUS

Mississippi Blues Country Tour

CURTIS

HE LIES restless in a damp sterile room in the Memphis Veterans Hospital on Poplar, where all he can remember is red clay and the dark odor of fallow fields. This morning finds him awash in a dream that never goes away: A child, barefoot and filthy but with gleaming white teeth, a child running alongside a drainage ditch at the edge of Highway 61. The twice-a-day bus to Jackson whooshes by, trailing dust and diesel fumes, bearing the faces of bored travelers. The child stops, watches the bus pass, waves a small hand good-bye, then cries great wailing tears. An angry dream voice can now be heard. "Get your little black ass homeward," his mother shouts, "or I'll tan you a new hide!" He runs for his life, across the road and down into the cotton furrows, which stretch toward a now setting sun. The sun becomes a muzzle flash, the furrows a stream of tracers. His world turns once, twice, a thousand times over. Rain begins to fall. The fumes return, and noise—a diesel generator churning harsh light beside the battalion aid station. Grave men dressed in blood-stained scrubs rush here and there and out of view. He can feel nothing below the belt. His chest is a heaving, searing sea of white gauze and pressure dressings. He closes his eyes.

He opens his eyes. A tray rests next to the bed. Same breakfast as yesterday, as tomorrow. Toast and grits and bacon and juice. He tunes in the morning show on WDIA, fiddling with the dial, tilting the radio

304

this way and that. The Mississippi Blues Country Tour. A gut-bucket, ass-kickin' ride down South. Sendin' one out to Curtis and all them tore-up boys on Ward B. From a cracked speaker comes a recording: Sonny Boy clears his throat, rips off a vicious lick on the big chromatic harp, and tears into "All My Love in Vain."

*   *   *

When Curtis dreams he can walk again, he stands right up at the side of his bed and strides out the door. He doesn't get far but his steps are sure and the cold tile floor feels liquid under his feet. He awakens drenched with sweat and can tell that he has shit his bed.

Once in a while someone comes to see him. An elderly aunt or a batch of far-removed cousins. They bring him chocolate or magazines or even flowers if the season's right. There's this girl cousin who Curtis has met only a few times. She's tall, has skin the color of creamed coffee and attends community college in hopes of becoming a medical transcriptionist. She talks about her classes in anatomy and introductory pharmacology while Curtis watches her deep brown eyes grow wide. He could love this woman, this distant relative, he thinks, if she could find it in herself to love him back just a little.

Late-night listening on the Blues Country Tour. A lone streetlamp burns rings in the parking lot pavement as greasy black rain pelts down, soaking the ground beyond the arc of glow. These hours pass slowly. But for the radio, Curtis would lose his mind. He floats in and out of his body accompanied by a backbeat of twelve-bar blues. The Demerol comes every four hours on wings of a starched white angel. She smiles and shoots, smiles and shoots. One hundred milligrams of patience. Next door Frank the Stump gurgles fitfully. Poor sad Lymon chases demons of his own design. Curtis can see no end to it all and he vows to get the fuck homeward one day, one day when the wind and the rain drive in off the river, cleansing his wounds and washing his blood toward the muddy, fallow fields below.

VERNICE

She listens attentively, careful to take down in her notebook anything important enough to be written on the board. Learning is a struggle–she has never read very well–but she knows what she wants and exactly how to get it. The instructor draws a precise chalk diagram of the circulatory system, identifying the major arteries in red and the veins in blue. He tells about the miles and miles of vessels in the human body, which, if straightened out, would encircle the city limits of Memphis. At first the idea seems profound, but then she wonders if there is any practical use for such information.

During a two-hour break between classes Vernice considers walking over to the VA to see Curtis. The walk from Shelby State to the hospital on Poplar is a pleasant one, especially on a warm spring afternoon such as today. Then she has second thoughts. That last time he said things that no blood kin boy should be saying to his girl cousin, even three times removed. And Momma says "Don't let him touch you, girl. He ain't got his mind no more." But Vernice feels sorry for Curtis, all laid out in bed like he is. Her sorrow has something else behind it, though, something she can't put into words. When she tries she gets all confused. Her head begins to ache and her chest feels as if her heart has been torn away and replaced by a cold pool of shame.

She spends her break daydreaming in the sun, in a little courtyard facing the street off Union where the traffic flows by in a noisy rush. Her thoughts come back to Curtis.

She knows part of his life–the angry part. His stories about the war are filled with heat and pain and bitterness. But he softens when he speaks of his friends, both dead and alive. How he learned what it meant to love and trust someone he'd known for only a few short weeks. How those friendships were the most intense of his life, what with the idea of getting lost or whacked or shipped out hanging over their heads all the time. She doesn't fault him for the drugs and drinking and crude nights on the town. As a matter of fact, some of those stories make her laugh aloud. She guesses that's how soldiers keep their sanity.

An hour has passed quickly. Vernice wonders what Curtis is doing at the moment. She wishes he had a phone. She imagines him staring out the window at the Memphis skyline and the river beyond. The phone rings and he answers. His voice cannot contain his excitement when he recognizes her. He asks her to come to see him as soon as she can. He wants to tell her something important, something they shouldn't discuss on the phone like this. It concerns . . .

SMASH! And so ends the imaginary call. Shattering glass and

blaring horns and then silence. Not twenty-five feet away two cars have collided. Did you see what happened? someone asks. She heard it, she replies, but was looking in another direction. Inward, deep down into the troublesome feelings that all too often keep her awake at night and distract her from her studies. How could she possibly be in love with a man such as Curtis, who would need to be cared for as long as he lives? What kind of life would that be for her? No, what she must feel is pity, and pity is not a strong foundation for love. Vernice gathers her books up in her arms and goes early to her next class. She vows to concentrate like never before.

RACHEL

Mrs. Tully, charge nurse on the night shift, drones on in the break-room over nothing. Mostly she just complains about shortages—of linens, of beds, of competent workers. Her morning report to the day shift is always the same. Rarely does anything happen at night. A patient might awaken thrashing, a nightmare fresh in his mind, and he might have pulled out an IV in the struggle. Or the one in 42B who was on his call light the whole shift. Drank a gallon of ice water and we had to empty his bag three times. She shakes her head in disgust.

Rachel enters the breakroom to glares and whispers. She's fifteen minutes late—the traffic coming in on Popular was murder—and she knows she'll be docked for the time. Her first task is to check the med charts and prepare for eight o'clock rounds. A new batch of interns has been assigned to the tenth floor, and new interns are nothing if punctual. They get a kick out of pushing around the nurses, too, as if a small measure of empty authority gives them the right. Rachel's starched white uniform has wilted around the collar and in the armpits. No doubt the air conditioning is down again. It feels like ninety up here. The morning is off to a wonderful start.

Her last stop on med rounds is 42B. Curtis is asleep for the moment, his topsheet thrown off to the side and touching the floor. What's the sense in waking him? His breakfast sits cold, untouched. A bedside radio, propped to an impossible tilt with a paperback novel and a folded washcloth, is tuned to the Blues. Rachel has taken upon herself the responsibility of weaning Curtis from pain meds. Sometimes she gives him only a sterile saline fix and pockets the Demerol ampule. She's built up quite a collection, enough to stop a charging bull elephant.

* * *

Rachel has pain herself. She divorced not so long ago. Her husband, so sweet and so earnest as a young man, became a brutal thug prone to drunken binges and insane laughter. She knows how it happened but she's tired of blaming the war for her troubles. She divorced him while he served eighteen months for assault at the county penal farm. He'll be out next month and by then Rachel has to leave Memphis.

But she can't until she's saved enough money. One of the orderlies in PT–a kid named Deal–says he knows The Man, and in this case The Man deals in black market pharmaceuticals. Rachel isn't sure how to ask the question. Besides, she has taken to using the Demerol for her own pain. At first it was just to help her sleep, but lately–right now–she crouches over the stool in the women's commode and pushes back her sleeve. She ties off her left arm and selects a delicate blue vein. For the first time she sees faint tracks in the crook of her arm, a scabbed-over dot from yesterday, all of which she knows she can pass off as a rash if she has to. Heat rash, in fact. With her free right hand she reaches into her pocket and pulls out a disposable insulin syringe, a number twenty-six needle, the smallest made. She peels away the sterile wrapping, cracks open another ampule of Demerol, and draws the clear liquid into her syringe. She taps it lightly to force the trapped air upward and squirts a minute stream from the needle. It's ready. Rachel cleans her skin with an alcohol wipe. The tiny sharp needle pierces the vein effortlessly. A deep breath, and she plunges home a momentary pause to her pain.

DEAL

A dozen gurneys line the basement hallway passage to the Physical Therapy Department. The gurneys remind Deal of a traffic jam out on I-240–maybe the airport exit or Winchester Road–but these stripped-down rolling carts wait with far more patience than your average commuter, he thinks.

He's supposed to head upstairs and fetch the morning appointments by nine, and it's already a quarter after. Booth, his new supervisor, will be pissed. Booth is a twenty-year man, a retired 91 Charlie, and Deal hates his guts. A lifer, back to haunt the bowels of the VA with infinite wisdom and a right way to do it all. Well, we'll see about that. Deal can think of a million ways to sabotage Booth's authority if he has to. Right now, though, the first few appointments are waiting, so Deal maneuvers two gurneys on to the back elevator, closes the doors, and punches up the tenth floor.

* * *

He arrives to confusion, flashing call lights, the crash cart rushing by and disappearing around the corner. Has someone zeroed on the B-wing? Oddly enough, it must not be a patient because the Zero Team stops just outside the women's restroom. Doctors and nurses and orderlies mill in a disorganized crowd by the door. No one seems able to take charge. Deal can get no closer than the end of the hall but his curiosity is piqued, so he asks a housekeeper watching nearby what's happening. Did someone flat line? Is it a drill?

* * *

Booth feels that Curtis should be working his upper body harder so he adds ten pounds of iron to the bar and tells him to do two more sets of ten reps. Deal watches from a glass-encased office cubicle not too far away. That Curtis is a tough one to figure. Such a big, mean-looking motherfucker but he doesn't ever say much or give the staff a hard time. Just lies in bed listening to the radio, staring out the window, and comes down to PT twice a day. Never complains to no one about nothing. Curtis will talk to Deal now and then, mostly about some buddy he lost in the war or, lately, about his Brown Sugar, the cousin from Momma's side of the family. Not too long ago, after Deal smoked a joint with him out on the tenth floor sun porch, Curtis began to cry these huge blubbering tears. Deal didn't know what to do or say.

* * *

By lunch time the whole VA knows about the nurse on ten who zeroed. The rumors say she OD'd on Demerol, which nobody wants to believe, but Deal knows the rumors are true. Deal once tried to impress her with his connections, but she ignored him after that except for a sidelong glance or two when he would pass the nurse's station and she'd be there charting or counting meds. He's sure the nurses have something going with the pain meds and sleepers and he wants to get a piece of the action. Endless supply, courtesy of good ol' Uncle Sam. This little episode upstairs, though, will no doubt hurt the program.

* * *

Toward the end of his shift Deal sneaks up to ICU for a peek at Rachel. She lies ashen in a bed, IV's drip-drip-dripping into both arms. Her EKG shows a weak but regular heartbeat. Deal is struck by her frailty, her washed-out pallor, but she looks nonetheless at peace amid the wires, tubes, and starched white linen bedclothes.

BOOTH

His favorite time of the day is dusk, when he can finally sit by himself in front of the TV with all the lights out. The children are in bed and quiet. A weather update says four-and-a-half inches of rain have fallen on Memphis in the past twenty-four hours, and Booth knows that when he goes down to look, his cellar will be ankle-deep in water.

He can see the VA building from his back yard. Most days Booth walks to work, a good mile-and-a-half hike because he has to take the long way around. A deep cement drainage ditch—usually dry, but too wide to leap—lies between the back of his property and the hospital grounds. An eight-foot tall chain link fence keeps the kids from falling in, although one time he caught Tony, his five-year-old, climbing, nearly at the top. Tony doesn't climb the fence anymore.

* * *

First comes a cool current of air on his cheek, then the faint scent of spice. He feels his wife pass behind him on the way to the kitchen. She makes no sound. She has an oriental way of moving about the house in silence, from shadow to shadow, that spooks Booth sometimes. It puts him back in the war. Dark-clothed forms imperceptible against the dense forest, a steady rain, the odor of mildew and decay. And her delicate features, her almond sloping eyes, hair black as crude oil. A village, a hooch, chaotic blurred motions, voices screaming GO! GO! DON'T BUNCH UP! He pushes that from his mind and remembers instead her tears, her small voice in broken English telling him of their child awaiting birth. And, too, the angry faces in Oakland, their angry cries: SEND THE GOOK BITCH HOME! when he steps off the transport with his arm around his bride.

Well, FUCK THEM, he says under his breath and under the din of some goddamn pretty-boy cop show on the tube.

* * *

His wife comes from a family with a genetic defect–all her brothers and sisters were born with cleft palates. No money for surgeons. No surgeons in the bush, anyhow. Sometimes they would put fresh chicken livers to the roofs of their mouths in order to talk more clearly. They even developed their own sign language–urgent, graceful motion–which Huong still uses when she becomes frustrated with English.

So she asks him in her own way if there's anything he needs before she goes to bed, tired from chasing Tony and Rosalie around the house all day. Booth says no, I'm fine, I'll be up shortly. He then hears a floorboard creak as she mounts the stairs, but soon the house settles back into a damp silence. He switches off the TV, makes sure the front door is locked, and walks slowly to the back porch. Outside he can hear the crickets and the night things rustle in the air. A slippery glaze coats the wooden porch planks where Booth stands smoking one last cigarette. The black air is thick and full of a moldy smell that reminds him of another night not so long ago. But he has to look forward, instead of to the past, and the fact is that his future is in his own hands now. Maybe he'll even go back to college and earn some kind of degree. As he wonders how much longer he can survive among insensate half-men and weeping visitors and drugged-out nurses and punk orderlies, he suddenly realizes that he must look like a fool, standing there in striped boxer shorts, staring at a building he can barely see for the darkness and the rain.

BIOGRAPHICAL NOTES

Alan Davis, Editor, is the author of *Rumors from the Lost World* (New Rivers Press), a collection of stories published in 1993. His fiction and nonfiction appear in such journals as *The Hudson Review* and *The Quarterly* and in such newspapers as *The New York Times* and *The San Francisco Chronicle.* He grew up in Louisiana and now lives with his wife and two children in Minnesota, where he chairs English and co-directs creative writing at Moorhead State University.

Michael White, Associate Editor, is the author of *A Brother's Blood,* a novel published in 1995. His stories have appeared in dozens of magazines and journals, including *Redbook* and *The Widener Review.* He lives in Massachusetts with his wife and two children and teaches at Springfield College.

ASSISTANT EDITORS

Nancy Easterlin is a writer and scholar who teaches at the University of New Orleans. Besides publishing her fiction, she is co-editor, with Barbara Riebling, of an anthology on literary theory published by Northwestern University Press, and the author of *Wordsworth and the Question of 'Romantic Religion,'* forthcoming from Bucknell University Press.

Lin Enger, under the pen name L.L. Enger, has published five novels in collaboration with his brother Leif, most recently *The Sinners' League* (Otto Penzler Books, Simon & Schuster). He is a graduate of the Iowa Writers' Workshop whose stories appear in various literary magazines.

Deb Marquart's work has received numerous prizes, among them the Dorothy Churchill Cappon Essay Award from *New Letters* and the

Guy Owen Poetry Prize from *Southern Poetry Review*. Her first book, *Everything's a Verb* (New Rivers Press), won the Minnesota Voices Project Award. She teaches creative writing at Drake University. She is completing a collection of interrelated stories about road life with a rock band entitled *Playing for the Door.*

Peter McNamara, a fiction writer, manages a bookstore in New Orleans.

Maggie Risk has received scholarships from the Bread Loaf Writers Conference, the Sewanee Writers Conference and the Ropewalk Writers Retreat. A graduate of the master's program in creative writing at the University of Denver, she has published stories in various magazines (one was a finalist for the Katherine Anne Porter Prize) and has taught writing at the University of Cincinnati. She is currently working on a novel.

AUTHORS

Julia Abbott Janeway is a Ph.D. student at the University of Denver who has been published in *Sundog: The Southeast Review.*

A. Manette Ansay won the AWP Short Fiction series prize for her collection *Read This and Tell Me What It Says*, published in 1995 by the University of Massachusetts Press. Her novel *Vinegar Hill*, published in 1994, is available from Viking.

Karin Ciholas is a professor of modern languages at Centre College in Danville, Kentucky. She has published work on Andre Gide, has had a play produced and has written an historical novel. "Polraiyuk" is part of a series of short stories called *Faces of Women.*

Christian Davis is working on a collection of stories: "The Wild Horses of Jerusalem" is the book's title story. He has won several writing awards, including the 1992 Jerome Foundation Literary Travel Grant, the 1989 Loft-McKnight Literary Award, and the 1985 Loft Creative Nonfiction Award. His fiction and nonfiction have appeared in various magazines.

Pamela Erbe lives in Chicago where she works as a medical writer. Her stories have appeared in *The Antioch Review, North American Review, Ms., Redbook*, and other magazines. She has received grants from the NEA, the Michigan Council for the ARts and the Illinois Arts Council. One of her stories is included in the 1994 edition of *New Stories from the South: The Year's Best*.

Mark R. Ganem is a journalist who has worked in New York and Italy and is a graduate of the University of New Hampshire creative writing program. His work has appeared in *Christopher Street*.

Kathleen George teaches theatre and playwriting at the University of Pittsburgh. She is the author of *Rhythm in Drama and Playwriting: The First Workshop*. Her fiction has appeared in numerous magazines, including *Mademoiselle* and *The North American Review*. One story, "Rites of Burial," was cited in the *Best American Short Stories* Distinguished List of 1991.

Lisa Gill, who lives in Albuquerque, has published poetry and fiction in various journals and has performed her work with the Taos Poetry Circus and on the Lollapalooza rock tour's third stage (spoken word shows) in Las Vegas and Denver.

Carol K. Howell is a 1985 graduate of the Iowa Writers Workshop. Her stories have appeared in *Redbook, Crazy Horse, North American Review,* and other publications. She is currently teaching writing at Syracuse University and is working on a collection of stories.

Todd Lieber teaches at Simpson College in Iowa and farms. The recipient of an NEA grant, he has published in various journals, including *Crazyhorse* and *The Yale Review*.

Josip Novakovich is the author of two books published in 1995, *Fiction Writer's Workshop* and *Apricots from Chernobyl*. He has published fiction and nonfiction in over a hundred magazines and journals, including *The New York Times Magazine, Antaeus, and The Paris Review*, and has received a Pushcart Award, an NEA Fellowship and an Ingram Merrill Award.

Lon Otto won the Iowa Short Fiction Prize in 1978 for *A Nest of Hooks* and published a second collection of stories, *Cover Me*, in 1988. He has been included in *Pushcart Prize, The Best of the Small Presses* and in *Flash Fictions* and has won the 1991–92 Loft-McKnight Award of Distinctiuon for Prose Writing. He is Professor of English at the University of St. Thomas and lives in St. Paul, Minnesota.

Ephraim Paul was a 1993 Pennsylvania Council on the Arts Fellow in Literature. He frequently reviews contemporary fiction for the *Philadelphia Inquirer* Sunday Book section. He is working on a novel.

Varsha Rao is a student at the Harvard Business School whose fiction has been published in *Accent*.

Elizabeth Searle won the 1992 Iowa Short Fiction Prize for *My Body to You*. Her stories have appeared in numerous journals and magazines, among them *Redbook* and *The Kenyon Review*. She teaches in the graduate writing program at Emerson College.

Rosa Shand won the Katherine Anne Porter Fiction Award in 1991 and a "Special Mention" in *Pushcart Prize #17*. One of her stories which won the PEN Syndicated Fiction Project was one of three such winners chosen to be read at the Library of Congress in 1993. A Yaddo fellow and a South Carolina Fellow in Fiction, she has been published in such magazines as *Witness*. Her collection, *The Uganda Bookshop*, in which "Sophie Was the King" appears, was one of two finalists in the AWP Short Fiction Series this year.

Betty Shiflett has published fiction and nonfiction in many magazines and journals, including *Life, Evergreen Review* and *Writing from Start to Finish*. *Phantom Rider*, her full length music drama, received an Artists Fellowship from the Illinois Arts Council, and her theater pieces have been produced at theaters in Chicago, the Bay Area, Ann Arbor, Baltimore, Philadelphia and New York. She teaches at Columbia College in Chicago.

Nadja Tesich, who was born in Yugoslavia, is the author of *Shadow Partisan*, a novel published in 1989. She has received an NEA Fellowship for Literature as well as a Fellowship for Fiction from the New York Foundation for the Arts.

Leslie Walker Williams was reared in Georgia and now lives in California. She has received an MFA from Warren Wilson College.

William Zinkus lives in Kalmazoo, Michigan.